c
"
t
o

[
fo
st
m

"A
but

"Ver
tran
sinc

"Virg
the s
insig   ....ng Paris of messed-
up losers and relentless operators, [
society gone mad on greed, fear and ru

D1428773

"Three addictive, intelligent volumes. Comedy, a way with words, and the collision of registers of language all combine to make Vernon irresistible"
RAPHAËLLE LEYRIS, *Le Monde*

"Reflecting our chaotic times, *Vernon Subutex* III is a powerful shocking, captivating work. Despentes completes her epic with a rare mastery. Where will she take us next?"   BRUNO CORTY, *Figaro*

"A zigzagging novel that likes to let the intrigue wander, all the better to tug it back by the hair a few pages later"
CLAIRE DEVARRIEUX, *Libération*

"A final volume even more explosive than the previous ones"
NELLY KAPRIÈLIAN, *Les Inrockuptibles*

"One of the most striking literary epics of the early 21st century"
MARIANNE PAYOT, *Express*

VIRGINIE DESPENTES is a writer and filmmaker. Her first novel, *Baise-Moi* was published in 1992 and adapted for film in 2000. Her fiction includes *Apocalypse Baby* (2010) and *Bye Bye Blondie* (2004), and the autobiographical work, *King Kong Theory* (2006). She won the Prix de Flore in 1998 for *Les Jolies Choses*, the 2010 Prix Renaudot for *Apocalypse Baby* and *Vernon Subutex I* won the Prix Anaïs Nin, and was shortlisted for the Man Booker International Prize.

FRANK WYNNE is a translator from French and Spanish. His previous translations include works by Pierre Lemaitre, Javier Cercas and Michel Houellebecq. He has been awarded the Scott Moncrieff Prize and the Premio Valle Inclán, and his translation of *Windows on the World* by Frédéric Beigbeder won the *Independent* Foreign Fiction Prize in 2005. His translation of *Vernon Subutex I* was shortlisted for the Man Booker International Prize.

Virginie Despentes

VERNON SUBUTEX 3

Translated from the French by
Frank Wynne

MACLEHOSE PRESS
QUERCUS · LONDON

First published as *Vernon Subutex 3*
by Editions Grasset & Fasquelle, Paris, in 2017
First published in Great Britain in 2020 by

MacLehose Press
An imprint of Quercus Publishing Ltd
Carmelite House
50 Victoria Embankment
London EC4Y ODZ

An Hachette UK company

INSTITUT
FRANÇAIS
ROYAUME-UNI

This book is supported by the Institut français (Royaume-Uni)
as part of the Burgess programme.

A CIP catalogue record for this book is available from the British Library.

ISBN (TPB) 978 0 85705 982 6
ISBN (Ebook) 978 0 85705 981 9

4 6 8 10 9 7 5 3

Designed and typeset in Scala by Libanus Press Ltd
Printed and bound in Great Britain by Clays Ltd, Elcograf S.p.A

Papers used by MacLehose Press are from well-managed forests and
other responsible sources.

In memoriam Sven Polhammer

Index of the Main Characters who Appeared in the Two Previous Volumes

Charles: A regular in parc des Buttes-Chaumont and the neighbouring cafés and bars, he encounters Vernon at the beginning of Volume 2, when he finds him slumped on a bench, ill and running a temperature. Charles takes care of him and the two become friends. A long time ago, he won the national lottery, but decided never to tell anyone.

Kiko: Former stock market trader, coke addict, he lives in the eighth arrondissement in Paris. Believing Vernon to be a genius turntablist, he gave him a place to stay, chucked him out, then patched things up with him.

Alex Bleach: Rock star, died of an overdose in a hotel room at the beginning of Volume 1. An old friend of Vernon's, he left behind a couple of video cassettes on which he recounts his life story, particularly his falling out with Dopalet, whom he accuses of killing Vodka Satana, with whom Alex was deeply in love.

Véro: Appears briefly in Volume 2 as Charles' partner. She has always given Subutex's group a wide berth.

Pamela Kant: Ex-porn star, geek. She was a friend of Vodka Satana. She took part in the search for Vernon in Volume 2, and ultimately became friends with him.

Marcia: Trans woman, originally from Brazil, she lives in Paris where she works as a stylist at fashion shoots. In Volume 1, she was living in Kiko's apartment. After Vernon fell hopelessly in love with her, she disappeared.

Laurent Dopalet: Fifty-something film producer, father of Antoine. In Volume 1, he hires the Hyena to track down the compromising videos left by Alex Bleach. At the end of Volume 2, he is assaulted in his home by Aïcha and Céleste, in revenge for the murder of Vodka Satana.

The Hyena: A dodgy private detective, she initially worked for Dopalet but betrayed him and joined the group that has formed around Vernon.

Olga: A homeless woman who first appears in Volume 1. She is volatile and explosive. She becomes infatuated with Vernon, who she met when he was living on the streets.

Xavier: A screenwriter who has spent twenty years failing to carve out a career, married to Marie-Ange, he has a daughter, he loves dogs, and he has joined the group that has gathered around Vernon.

Marie-Ange: Xavier's wife, with whom he has a daughter.

Sylvie: One of Alex Bleach's former lovers. In Volume 1 she offered Vernon a place to stay, had a brief affair with him, then furiously stalked him when he disappeared without explanation. She joined the group that has gathered around him at the Buttes-Chaumont. Sylvie is the mother of Lancelot, who left the family home at the start of Volume 1 to move in with his girlfriend.

Emilie: A childhood friend of Vernon, she used to play bass in a band, but has since cut all ties with the music industry. She briefly gave Vernon a place to crash, and was involved in the search for him before joining the Buttes-Chaumont group.

Laurent: Vernon first met him when he found himself living on the streets. Laurent had been homeless for many years, and taught Vernon the rudiments of living a precarious life.

Patrice: Works as a temp, lives in the suburbs, is tattooed, surly and sometimes violent. At the end of Volume 2, he falls in love with Pénélope and joins the group gathered around Vernon in the park.

Antoine: Exhibition curator, the son of Dopalet. He keeps the group informed about the machinations of his father.

Sélim: University professor, atheist, he fathered Aïcha with Vodka Satana. He never told his daughter that her mother was a hardcore porn star. She finds out early in Volume 2. He is part of the Buttes-Chaumont group.

Aïcha: Law student, practising Muslim, she discovered the truth about the death of her mother listening to Alex Bleach's tapes. She took revenge, assaulting Dopalet in his home. At the end of Volume 2, she was sent away by the Hyena to lie low in order to avoid any reprisals.

Vodka Satana: Mother of Aïcha and former partner of Sélim. Was engaged to Alex Bleach. She worked in the porn industry, was a friend of Pamela and David. Died of an overdose at the age of thirty. According to Alex Bleach's confession, she was murdered by Dopalet, who was afraid that she might go public about their relationship.

Céleste: Tattoo artist and waitress at Rosa Bonheur. Her father, a police officer, used to be a regular at Vernon's record shop. When she bumps into Vernon, she recognises him. In Volume 2, she becomes friends with Aïcha, and takes part in her revenge attack on Dopalet. She is sent into hiding by the Hyena, who is trying to protect her from Dopalet's reprisals.

Lydia Bazooka: Rock critic, and uber-fan of Alex Bleach. She briefly gave Vernon a place to stay and later joined the search for him. She is obsessed with the idea of writing an exhaustive biography of Alex Bleach.

Daniel: Close friend of Pamela Kant. Trans man. Susceptible to the charms of Céleste, who has never responded to his advances.

THE TRAIN STATION IN BORDEAUX IS BEING RENOVATED, ITS belly filled with a forest of scaffolding poles. On the platform, a boy is pacing up and down chain-smoking cigarettes, he's wearing trainers with no socks, and breaks the heels as though they were espadrilles. He shoots hostile glances through the windows of the train. He looks as though he's just waiting for someone to look at him sideways before jumping aboard the train and beating the shit out of him. The ticket inspectors have spotted him and are posted by the doors to stop him getting on at the last minute. The four notes of the S.N.C.F. jingle echo through the carriages, followed by the shrill klaxon announcing the departure. The boy is left on the platform, Vernon catches his eye and is startled by the ferocity of his hatred. As though it were directed at him personally. It goes beyond the urge to kill, the desire to annihilate – this is a fury that longs to reach back through time, across seven generations, and rip out his guts.

Vernon slides back in his seat and stretches out his legs. He had forgotten how much he loves taking the train. He feels a calm euphoria sweep over him. He watches as the flashing landscape picks up speed. There is a particular atmosphere to train journeys, a collective resignation not to be disturbed for several hours, a tranquil shift between two states. Jumbled memories come of days before Christmas, going on holidays, travelling with groups to festivals or on his own to meet up with a girlfriend in the provinces. The images flicker past, and one by one are carried away by a nostalgia he would describe as feeble. His memory is filled with eddying fragments with no particular chronology. Everything about his former life has become tarnished with an otherness, melted into a shapeless, distant chaos. He cannot put this confusion down to drugs: he has not taken any in months. It happened of its own accord. As soon as he got stoned, he started to get bored waiting for it to wear off, wondering what he could ever have found fun about this debilitating disruption. Drugs are designed to alleviate boredom, they make everything seem interesting, like a dash of Tabasco on a dish that is a little bland. But Vernon no longer fears boredom, or loneliness, or silence, or obscurity. He has changed a lot. Drugs are no longer of any use to him.

In the past few days, however, while suffering from a vicious toothache, he has been popping handfuls of an opium-based analgesic that makes him feel agreeably stoned, and the feeling of moving through cotton wool is not unpleasant. He is bathed in a muted light that envelops him, adapting to the contours of his body wherever he goes. It has been a shitty couple of days. Usually, he would wait until a toothache stopped him sleeping before he visited a dentist. But this one was the worst he had ever experienced. Whenever the decayed tooth touched the tooth below, it was a knife cutting through him, the pain lifted him bodily and threw him onto the ground. He howled uncontrollably. Olga recommended gargling with grain alcohol and, having nothing to lose, Vernon swilled vodka around his mouth, it anaesthetised the pain for a time, but then he collapsed, dead drunk. The following morning, a hangover, accompanied by a searing pain from the abscess, left him in sheer agony. He crawled into a corner like a wounded animal and curled up, delirious from the pain.

Someone phoned Kiko. Because he has more money than the others, Kiko seems the most adult of the gang. Kiko immediately said, I've got a good mate who's a dentist, I'll call him right now. The doc faxed a prescription to the nearest pharmacy, Pamela took the car and went to fetch the antibiotics and the painkillers. It was the first time that an emergency had compelled them to make contact with the outside world.

After that, Vernon swallowed everything he was given without a murmur. He was convinced that no drug could be powerful enough to alleviate his ordeal. But, half an hour later, he was too off his face to feel any pain. He saw the world from a distance. The only thing better than these painkillers, he thought, would be a morphine pump. He felt great confidence in this dentist, capable of prescribing such an effective medication. Vernon was so relieved that he could no longer feel his tooth that he crashed out for three days straight, letting the antibiotics do their work, while the painkillers carried him away into slo-mo dreams.

During this time, those around him were busy planning his trip to Paris. Vernon likes to be managed. Things progress, whether he gets involved or not. He does not need to be ill to be indolent. If you allow yourself to be carried by the current, life in a group assumes you should always be doing "something" – there's always a tyre to be changed, bags to be unloaded, vegetables to be washed, a chair to be mended. Vernon says, "I look over my playlists," and he lies down on his bed. The most amazing thing is that no-one argues the toss. On the contrary, they all like the notion that they are helping him, being kind to him, doing him a favour. So, he lay down on his side, relieved that he was no longer in pain, and, when he woke, he was told which train station they had chosen for his journey, the departure time, the name of the dentist, and the keycodes to get into Kiko's apartment, where he would be staying.

He leaves the camp for the first time in more than a year. The others – or most of them – come and go between the camp and civilian life. But Vernon has no bills to pay, no family to visit, no work to turn in . . . So he no longer sets foot in towns and cities. There is nothing to be done. When they told him he would be going to Paris to get treated, he was happy at the thought of seeing the capital. But he feels more out of touch than he expected.

Sitting opposite him is a slim woman with long straight hair coloured bourgeois-blonde. Her raincoat is cinched at the waist, she is wearing high-heeled boots. She has beautiful, magnetic-blue eyes. She must be at least sixty. The wrinkles may have been filled in, but her hands betray her age. She is wearing a solitaire diamond, perhaps an engagement ring. There is something poignant about her. Vernon gives the woman little smiles to which she responds gracefully. He wants her. Something about her skin attracts him. He feels like suggesting that they get off at the next station and find the nearest hotel.

He is no longer in the habit of seeing women who are not wild about him. At the camp, even the girls who have no intention of sleeping with him flirt and flatter. He has a particular position; he is treated like a guru. It has changed his relationship with the female sex – these days all girls are his friends. They all want him, and he is obliging by nature.

He will never know whether the blonde woman would have responded favourably to his advances. She will never grace him with that famous post-coital expression of gratitude. He will not sleep with her: he is being accompanied on the journey by Mariana. She has been his girlfriend now for several weeks, which is some-thing of a record. He has trouble settling down: he is too much in demand. He gets along well with a girl, it may last, and then another comes along, makes him doubt, throws him off balance, and he transfers his affections. Young people call it polyamory. From what he can work out, this means sleeping with whoever he likes without worrying what the last girl might think. But Mariana has stopped him in his tracks. She has set herself up as his steady girlfriend with a disconcerting artlessness for someone so shy. He doesn't protest, because she reassures him more than she suffocates him. He finds her sexy. He first desired her when he saw her imitating Axl Rose, flailing like a demon and brandishing an invisible mic. He fell half in love when she danced to Tina Turner, whose dance moves she performs with terrifying brio. He knew his days as a lothario were over when she performed a choreographed routine to Missy Elliott. She's even got moves for Madball and for Korn – there is no musical register whose codes she doesn't innately understand with a very individual magic. Between her body and the sound there is a harmony that stems from an extensive knowledge that is surprising in a woman her age. Mariana hasn't yet turned thirty. She knows AC/DC as well as she knows M.I.A. She listens to things Vernon has heard of but never really paid attention to, and she knows precisely which song to play to get him into them. They spend their time listening to music and Vernon feels as though he has gained a friend as well as a lover who seems like a mermaid when she fucks – her whole body undulates, seduces, profits and provokes. She pours into sex and into dance everything she cannot put into words.

When this trip was organised, she said that she would go with him, that they would take the bus, that it would be really cheap, but the bus from Bordeaux is a nine-hour drive and Kiko said, WTF? Are you living in the Middle Ages or what? We've got T.G.V.s in France, I'll sort out the tickets right away. Mariana is going with him; it was a no-brainer. Vernon's too out of it to travel on his own, she said, he'll end up on the wrong platform and wind up in Frankfurt with an abscess ten times worse. She loves Vernon. He can feel it. And that's alright with him. It punches a hole in his chest. He succumbs. She has put her headphones on, she's listening to Amy Winehouse and looking at stuff on the net. She doesn't like the camp rule that says she cannot go online. She says it's tired old technophobe bullshit. She abides by the rule because she has no choice. She must really care about him to put up with it, as soon as they got to Bordeaux and she was given her tablet, she lit up. Finally, she could reconnect with the world.

Over her shoulder, he looks at the succession of photos on Instagram, a baby pig, a girl lying on a sandy beach, a green milkshake, Paul Pogba shirtless, shot in half-light. Soko waking up, a drawing of a trash-punk angel holding a bomb, a fat bud of sensimillia dripping resin . . . She slips her hand into his, never taking her eyes off the screen. Vernon feels a tracery of warmth course through his arm to his shoulder and flood his chest. He can visualise the feeling, he can even say what colour it is – deep emerald green. This is not the meds. This is what he's like straight. Something inside him malfunctioned, something that never returned to normal. He has changed.

He's heard many theories of varying ludicrousness about the reason for his transformation, which a lot of people at the camp call "an awakening". Some say his serotonin levels have exploded. Why not? The theory of hormonal chaos has its defenders. After all, as Daniel says, "With all the endocrine disruptors swirling around us, go figure – in you, it's produced a global reboot." Others favour the theory of a brutal, accelerated male menopause whose effects, paradoxically, are salutary. Maybe . . . Vernon doesn't feel as though his physical strength has waned, but then he was never built like a lumberjack. Perhaps his libido has changed – but it's difficult to say: previously, he wasn't surrounded by girls fighting for his favours. Too much demand kills the demand – he's less insecure than he used to be, but that's logical: in the camp, he fucks anything that moves. At other times, people talk about the awakening of the Kundalini to explain these curious sensations, the strange visions, the trance-like states that overcome him without warning. He has been breathing too deeply, or too well, and energy has been released from the base of his spine, catapulting him into a sort of never-ending acid trip. The most inventive talk about alien abduction – the visit of some extra-terrestrial that has made its earthly home in Vernon. There is also talk of shifting frequencies – reality as a radio with some heavenly hand turning the dial.

At first, Vernon felt that the camp was attracting an awful lot of weirdos. Gradually, he came to the realisation that the world is full of people with fantastical beliefs who, on first meeting, may seem completely sane. The enigma that is Vernon gives them free licence to express their bizarre nature. This is how, between the salad and the cheese course, someone can end up telling him about their privileged connection with the vibrations of macrocrystalline quartz. The country is full of fanatics convinced that the dead walk among us, that invisible creatures gambol through the forests and that by exposing oneself to the right sound waves you can restore your magnetic field . . . Give them an opportunity to expound their theories, and you can find yourself going down some very strange paths.

People from outside the camp come every two or three months when there is a *convergence*. This is the name they have chosen – no-one remembers coming up with the term, but everyone uses it – for the night when Vernon spins the music to make the participants dance. Their lives are lived to the rhythm of these convergences – finding a place to set up, preparing the space, the event itself, packing up and moving on to another site. This came about without anyone deciding that it should happen this way. Let's just say it occurred.

Applications to attend the convergences quickly became so numerous that it requires a whole organisation to select the participants without inviting more than a hundred. Something is happening. People show up, some of them are a pain in the arse, they come to "check it out", suspicious and aggressive, as though someone is trying to sell them some bullshit philosophy, when no-one is trying to sell them anything, not even a story: it's about dancing till dawn, that's all. The extraordinary thing is what the dancers feel – with no drugs, no preparation, no special effects.

*

There is always a handful of doubters who wander around telling anyone who will listen that they don't believe, that they want to see for themselves, that they'd be pretty surprised if something happened to them on the night, because they've been there, done that, and they're too shrewd for this kind of headfuck. Vernon and the others don't try to persuade them. They have only to wait. That night, on the dance floor, they start out with arms folded, supercilious little smile, determined not to fall for it. And two hours later, they've fallen for it. The following morning, they cannot pinpoint the moment when they merged with the crowd, with its slow repetitive movement. They are generally the ones who, at dawn, are most shaken up. This is one of the things that happens on nights when there is a convergence – a general upheaval. This is what people come looking for at the camp, at the convergences. A gentle, luminous confusion that makes you want to take time and keep silent. Epidermises lose their boundaries, everybody becomes every body; it is a boundless intimacy.

And, at each convergence, Vernon feels like a worm in the centre of a powerful spotlight. He is too important. They call him the Shaman. Officially, it is just for a laugh. In practice, he feels everyone looking at him behind his back, feels expectation coil around his spine. People eye him suspiciously, wondering if he's a con artist, or stare at him adoringly, convinced that he can save them. He doesn't quite know how to go about staying cool when everything depends on him. Fortunately, his train of thought quickly goes off the rails, so it does not bother him for very long. He thinks, it's too much stress, I can't handle this, and a minute later he is contemplating a leaf on a branch and is utterly engrossed. It limits his frustration. But even so, he has discovered the fear of losing. Never in his life had he feared losing what he had: he always felt that it did not depend on him. Now, he revels in a comfort that is not material. They sleep in abandoned houses – when they can find houses – which are rarely heated, pitch camp near springs when there is no running water, wash out of doors when it is –7°C, eat out of billycans, and yet theirs is a life of luxury. They are convinced that the experience they are sharing is exceptional, an extra ball that life did not owe them, something gifted, magical. And he does not want it to stop.

In the carriage of the T.G.V. the passengers have opened their laptops on the tables. They are watching movies, catching up on work, replying to an e-mail. Others are riveted to their phones. They are all in thrall. There are no longer any bodies without accessories among those who can afford to pay for a train ticket. Admittedly, there is a man in his fifties a few seats away who is reading an old-fashioned newspaper. When he turns the page, it slightly irritates his neighbour. He is the only one whose vision is not blinkered by a screen. Even the five-year-old is not bawling and running up and down the carriage disturbing passengers, mesmerised as he is by the cartoon he is watching. Next to him, his mother is watching too, though without headphones, she does not have a second to waste on the landscape, still less on her immediate surroundings.

Vernon has got out of the habit. At the camp, all internet connection is forbidden. It began with one of the Hyena's fits of paranoia, it was she who decreed that they had to learn to live under the radar, to leave no digital trace of their movements or their conversations. She constantly gives the impression that she is priming the group to survive a third world war in which not sending e-mails would be particularly important. Initially, everyone accepted this protocol as some crazy ritual whose main purpose was to establish a set of rules allowing them to demarcate the camp as a bubble. Over the months, Vernon noticed that people's attitude changed. Snowden went through the same thing. The order came to seem less outlandish. Mistrust of technology grew, and no-one now laughed cynically when entering a network-free space.

When they disembark at Gare Montparnasse, Vernon feels engulfed by the crowds, it is a strange feeling of vertigo. He is particularly overwhelmed by the noise. As though sensing his disorientation, Mariana puts her arm through his. She is a tiny slip of a girl, but there is a comforting authority in her gesture reminiscent of an adult reassuring a child.

It is not just that he is out of the habit, the city itself has changed. Paris has become hard. Vernon is immediately aware of the pent-up aggression – people are furious, pressed up against each other, ready to come to blows. In the corridors of the métro, not a single person smiles, not a single body suggests I've got time to waste. No-one dawdles, as they do at the camp. This is a grown-up city – no-one speaks to strangers, or if they do, it is only to shout. He is bombarded by images, too many posters, too many junk messages. But it is only when they reach the platform that he identifies what it is that has been bothering him since their arrival. The smell. Paris is an olfactive cesspit – a mixture of rot of air rancid with body odours of perfumes of metallic machine smells of filth and chemicals. Vernon realises that he is holding his breath. For months, wherever they have gone, he has been breathing everything in, each new place has its own smell, making it individual and unique. Here, for the first time in a long time, he refuses to smell where he is.

At Kiko's place, Mariana looks around with the air of defiance Vernon knows so well – the expression those unused to luxury adopt when confronted with it: she looks as though she has been plunged into boiling oil. It is Vernon's turn to lay a hand on the small of her back in the hope of imparting some of his calm. Extremely rich people know what they are doing when they furnish an apartment, even if they do it instinctively: every object here screams at those unaccustomed to luxury: fuck off, you filthy prole. This is the distinction between boho décor and that of the *grand bourgeois*: the former says to all comers "make yourself at home", while the latter seeks to exclude all those who do not understand its codes. But Vernon knows this apartment, it does not intimidate him.

Kiko, too, has changed a lot. Of all the people at the camp, he is perhaps the one who has undergone the most radical revolution. Vernon has become his expensive indulgence, his weekend hobby. Kiko has jacked in his career as a trader. Like a guy in a casino who decides to leave the table when he's on a roll. Take the cash and run. In hindsight, he doesn't regret his decision – as he puts it, you'd have to be crazy to be rich and keep working.

He is not the only one in his profession who has had an epiphany. He knows other guys who, one day, warming their arses in a jacuzzi under the palm trees of their villa in Mauritius, stared at the booty of the girl who had come with them and were suddenly transfixed by a lightning bolt of lucidity: their life is shit. The only good thing about it is the conviction that everyone on the planet envies them. Whereas, what Kiko discovered in the group that so astonished him was that no-one wanted to swap places with him. Anyone else might have changed the people he hung out with – might have sought out company that was more reassuring. Kiko stayed. He changed his strategy.

In the early months, he was gripped by a sort of libertarian fever. It was as though he was decompressing. In certain people, age unleashes a reactionary energy that sometimes shoots out and destroys everything in its path. With Kiko, it was the libertarian that he allowed to emerge. One that had spent too long curled up, censored, imprisoned and made a hell of a racket as it now spread its wings. Or perhaps not the libertarian: the Christian. But in the most primary sense of that word: the person within Kiko who loved Christ – repressed for all these years – suddenly took over. The whole thing lasted about six months. He went from being embarrassingly generous to a complete pain in the arse.

He never wanted to work again, swore that he loathed money, that he was going to come and live with them, he and Olga pored over leaflets for minivans, he could already see himself living in a motorhome, following them around, he no longer felt remotely materialistic. He had a new idea every day. He would sell off his Paris apartment and buy a little abandoned village in the Jura mountains, they would all settle there and form a commune. Just because the hippies fucked it up, didn't mean other people shouldn't try. Ideas always fail until, eventually, they succeed. Kiko knows a bunch of doctors and, in the hierarchy of his world, doctors are at the top – he would persuade one of them to come and live in the village. That way, they would always have someone who could tell the difference between a heart attack and a panic attack, between a tumour and a large pimple. They wouldn't have to worry about anything. They would grow old in peace.

But, over time, his ardour cooled. He got fed up with camping, moved back to Paris, got his nose into a baggie of coke and hooked up with his old acquaintances. His Christlike passion abated. He had invested in a cannabis start-up in Los Angeles. He was not as visible around the camp. But he came back regularly. He spent whole evenings regaling them with plans for his theme park – he was waiting for France to legalise weed, which was bound to happen. He imagined it as a cross between Jurassic Park and the spa at Le Bristol, all organised around the theme of weed. His crazy fantasy became so detailed that it began to sound plausible. In his theme park, there would be jacuzzis, video projections, specially designed yoga lessons for the stoned, a little contemporary art, massage treatments, a lot of music, and muffins everywhere for when people got the munchies.

Kiko has gone back to his former life, but a defiant streak has opened up within him. He is no longer prepared to give his all. All his time, all his thoughts, all his desires, all his convictions. He is no longer willing to prove that he can always add another task to this schedule. His role in the system is no longer perfect. Compliance no longer excites him the way it did. His way of expressing himself is to go back to the camp, to people who are nothing like him. He has not gone back to square one – he has found an alternative equilibrium, an alternating identity.

He always takes up a little more space than others, he talks a lot. Silence is an important concept at the camp. Except for Kiko. But no-one complains. He is the one who solves every problem. He abuses his position only in the sense that he takes up a lot of sonic space. There is one thing about which he is sincere, one thing that does not change with the seasons: the feelings he experiences during the convergences are unlike anything he can feel on drugs. And he wants to go "there". His latest hare-brained notion is that Vernon should take his role as guru more seriously. Kiko has ambition to spare.

He invites them to sit down around the kitchen table, opens the fridge and compulsively takes out all the food he can find, as though the two of them are starving. He opens a bottle of champagne and Vernon says no, with the antibiotics it would finish me off. Mariana takes the proffered glass and drains it in one gulp. She is incandescent. Seeing him at the camp, she hadn't realised that Kiko was *this rich*. She had worked out that his life was not the same as theirs from his obsession with flashing his credit card every time there was a problem. But she was not expecting this, this opulence which is an insult to those unaccustomed to it. She squirms in her chair, shooting angry glances all around. Even the red Smeg fridge, with its good-natured curves, makes her livid.

Kiko can't sit still – he puts on an Erykah Badu C.D., too loud, asks them if they want some drugs, he's got a new dealer, hot shit, never keeps him waiting. He feels the need to fill the silences – it's impossible to tell what he's so shit-scared of that he needs to make a racket all the time. Vernon is used to his feverishness.

"Hey, you know what, that tree in the Buttes-Chaumont, the one with the huge roots where you used to sit all the time? They've ripped it out. Did you know?"

"When?"

"Beginning of February."

"How did it happen?"

"Accidentally backed into it."

"A tree that size? They didn't see it in the rear-view mirror?"

"They've been doing a lot of work in the park. That's all I heard."

The news bothers Vernon. The fact that things do not stay as they are remains the most difficult thing to accept. He thinks about the tree, tall as a building, about the hours he spent enthroned like a king against the trunk. He says:

"I'll ask Charles. He knows the park-keepers . . . It's been a long time since I've seen Charles. I'll drop round his way and see him . . ."

Kiko is no longer listening. He has launched into a solo about his favourite subject: Vernon has a gift. There are few words to describe it. And, as he sees it, the whole problem, because there is a problem, stems from the fact that Vernon refuses to assume his role.

"You can't be a leader if you don't pull your weight. O.K., I get it, it works, this shit you've got going on. And the way you have of keeping people at a distance during the convergences makes you seem interesting and mysterious. That's clever, I'll give you that. It's instinctive, it's class. You leave a space for imagination. Kind of like storytelling by leaving gaps. Until the night gets going, no-one knows what's so fucking special about Vernon Subutex. Fair enough, it adds to your charm."

But this, Kiko feels, is not enough. Vernon never does anything really attention-grabbing, like healing people with his hands, or communing with the dead so they can talk to the living as if he was some sort of cosmic answering machine. He doesn't take himself seriously enough. Kiko sees the big picture. It's in his nature. He nervously taps his fingernails on the table. He's come up with a new idea:

"You know Confucius? That story about the tree, I think we could use it . . . The Romans ripped out the tree which Confucius used to preach under. I heard it on the radio. I think this thing about the tree – what was it? An oak? I guess you don't know either – anyway, I figure it would be a good backdrop for your origin story as a prophet."

"Have you been listening to France Culture again, Kiko? Knock it off. I've told you before, it really doesn't mix well with your coke habit. I'm a D.J., not a fucking prophet."

"I'm educating myself, arsehole, I'm educating myself and here you are insulting me. They figured they'd cut down the tree Confucius used to preach under to force him to leave, they did it because he was too influential . . . O.K., right there, you've got a story. We could start out with that: the French authorities, alerted to your great power, cut down the tree you used to sit under . . ."

"Kiko, you know me, I'm prepared to swallow any old shit, but I can tell you right now that Confucius and me . . . it won't work – even if they did cut down his tree."

"So you're telling me you know Confucius?"

"No. But instinctively I can tell you there's no fit."

"Instinctively . . . that's typical of ignorance. You don't understand how it works, but you're convinced that it doesn't. I've thought about this a lot, we need to tell the story. I think we should hire a ghostwriter, a novelist. I'm working on a shortlist."

"Quit listening to France Culture. You're boring the rest of us rigid."

Whenever he has a free evening, Kiko buys two grams of coke and spends the whole night making gibbering, lunatic podcasts. He fills a notepad with bizarre scrawls that, the following morning, seem perfectly reasonable – and this isn't just the coke talking, it's the social class to which he belongs: the class that believes it can do anything, that accepts no limitations. So, he persists:

"I'm thinking about hiring a female novelist, someone talented enough to knock it into shape, but not too successful, otherwise she'll do what the fuck she likes and three months down the road she'll be busting our balls with ideas we don't want to listen to."

Mariana interrupts, she is already on her third glass of champagne and beginning to loosen up.

"Why are you thinking about a woman? Is it something to do with sensitivity?"

"Let's be honest rather than politically correct: talented guys have better things to do with their life . . . Besides, they'll cost an arm and a leg, whereas with a girl, you offer her twice the minimum wage and she'll give you three years of her life . . . That's the way it goes: you're designed to take care of others. It's been that way for two thousand years; it's not going to suddenly stop just because Simone said wake up. But let's cut the shit, I mean, it's just us here, so there's no need to wank on: Vernon is a prophet who appeals to chicks."

He's been working on it for months. He's put his back out spending nights hunched over his laptop reading biographies of prophets on Wikipedia. He knows this is a sure thing: Vernon has a gift, they just need to sort out the comms and it will go viral. Mariana drains her glass, Kiko has already fetched a second bottle, he pops the cork as she asks:

"The story of Confucius was written how many years after his death? Building a prophet's reputation takes time, doesn't it?"

"Confucius is just an example, he's like Moses, they're old-school prophets. The closer you come to our era, the more you find prophets that appeared overnight."

"You mean the way cathedrals used to take decades to build, but a shopping centre can be thrown up in three or four months?"

"Exactly."

"So, who did you have in mind, in terms of a recent prophet?"

"The one who most directly concerns us: L. Ron Hubbard."

Kiko has been rambling on about the founder of Scientology for months now. This time, the source is not France Culture but a conversation he had with the person in the next seat on a flight from Paris to L.A.

Kiko is working on the assumption that what stops Vernon from truly assuming his role as a guru is the fear that, to be a true prophet, you have to be a martyr.

This is how you bind the early disciples: you need a great injustice. Ideally, a tragic death. If there's a little visceral torture in the mix, that just adds to the effect. But, Kiko can understand why Vernon would want to skip the part where he's spat on as he lugs an eighty-kilo cross on his back and ends up being stabbed in the side, and dying, on that same cross. You only have to see the guy with toothache to realise Vernon isn't the kind to suffer with dignity. This is why Hubbard seems the perfect counterexample:

"Huge yacht, chicks in white miniskirts, barely legal, awesome food . . . and when he started out, the guy was a bit like you: check him out at thirty and he's just some fucking loser – and, all due respect, but when you were thirty you weren't up to much. The real difference between you is that the guy was motivated. That's the thing you're lacking. Positive mental attitude. Just look at sports, and never forget mental attitude accounts for eighty per cent of the performance. If you can up your game mentally, we're onto a winner: the convergences keep getting more and more amazing. Ever since the girls down in Bordeaux remixed Bleach's subsonic bass loops so they can be played as a constant wave, we've turned a corner . . . Bleach, now, *there* was a guy who'd have made a great guru. Fit as fuck, there are hundreds of stunning portraits, and – best of all – he died alone and in pain, tweak the story a bit and you could call it 'The Fall'. He's perfect. When we settle on this novelist, maybe we tell her to include him, sort of a John the Baptist to your Jesus, you get the idea . . . but keep it a bit subtle, leave people to wonder who was the true prophet?"

"More France Culture?"

"No, I listen to Radio Courtoisie sometimes . . . Thing is, dude, you've got to pull your finger out. Potential, talent, the reality of the thing – that shit accounts for, like, ten per cent of the success of a business."

"Switch off the radio, stop reading books. Go clubbing. Buy yourself a motorbike. But no intellectual pursuits, you know that's not your strong suit . . ."

Kiko is not the only one at the camp who feels that things are bubbling up, that they're about to explode, that they need to do "something big". Some say they should move to Detroit, some think they should be like a circus troupe, there are those who've visited a commune in Italy and those who've just come back from the "Zone to Defend" in Notre-Dame-des-Landes . . . Everyone has an idea. Everyone except Vernon, who wants things to carry on just as they are – chaotic, formless, without having to bust his balls.

Charles, the elderly wino, has plans to shoot a movie. The project occurred to him when a number of Pamela's former co-workers joined the group and turned his head. Bimbos with boob jobs and polished nails whom he initially found intimidating before discovering that they were more receptive to his humour and his philosophy than he might have expected. Punkettes trapped in the bodies of creatures of vice. He suggested a film project about a utopia: girls marooned on a desert island, surrounded by white rabbits and cute little puppies . . . a project that, in a single evening, they managed to transform into a zombie movie. And Charles listened, open-mouthed in admiration, as one of the girls described the scene where she'd fuck the head of a corpse with a huge purple strap-on.

But he did not come back, as expected, to hone this utopian project. When Mariana says she is going to hook up with some friends near Montmartre, and stumbles as she gets up because she's had a lot to drink, Vernon gets to his feet to hold her up. He says he is going to try to see Charles. He'll make the rounds of the neighbourhood bars, the old guy is bound to be somewhere.

VÉRO SMOOTHS THE BROWN PAPER BAG WITH THE PALM OF HER hand until she can fold it neatly and stack it with the others. Never again will she have to listen to the old man kicking up a stink, seeing her spending so much time over piles of wrapping paper while the rest of the apartment is going to shit. It drove him mad that she was capable of forgetting that there was laundry in the washing machine until it was mouldering, while paper and plastic bags were carefully arranged by size, colour and material in the large living-room dresser, after she had thrown out the china because she had too many bags. We've all got our foibles. The mahogany dresser is stuffed with wrapping materials, and organising this space brings Véro inexplicable pleasure. On one side, there is the bubble wrap, then paper bags, then small plastic bags next to the big ones and, lastly, particularly beautiful bags that she finds in the street.

They bought the dresser together one day when they were visiting a branch of Emmaüs in the suburbs, because a guy who was a regular at their bar worked there from time to time. It was a veritable expedition, going to Emmaüs, but they used to have an aperitif in the garden and afterwards they would be so tipsy that they didn't remember how they got home. It was summer. They hadn't gone on holiday. They never went anywhere. A little flash of greenery can only be good for the spirit, even if Véro is not particularly chlorophyll-inclined. The dresser cost ten euros, they bought it in a sufficiently advanced state of inebriation that they were surprised when, some days later, it was delivered. Charles has always loathed it. It's true that it takes over the whole room. And they never found any real use for it. At first, they stacked plates and letters on it. And, eventually, Véro commandeered it for her bags. It has lots of shelves and drawers, perfect for her obsession. Charles used to say that she knew exactly what she was doing the day she bought it, that she engineered the whole thing. Maybe he was right: the brain of a person with irrational goals has greater depth of field than one that functions normally, it's always several steps ahead, it anticipates everything. It's the same thing with alcohol. Even when Véro wants to stop drinking, she knows that her brain will manage to get her into situations that leave her no option, and generally this happens unbeknownst to her own free will – in other words, she does not decide to drink, she remembers she needs to call an old friend going through a hard time, and once she is round at his place, she realises that what she really came for is a dozen shots of pastis. The brain is devious: it plays tricks on your consciousness, it does things on the sly, that way you get exactly what you wanted while pretending you were thinking about something else entirely.

Now she can do whatever she wants with the dresser, she can even extend her collection to the whole living room if she feels like it . . . He's not here to kick up a stink anymore. The squabbling is over.

The old man is dead. He did it elegantly, the old bastard, he slipped away without a sound. A warning twinge, just to alert her to the fact that something important was brewing, he collapsed over the bar late one afternoon, writhed on his side for a minute, coughing up blood, until the ambulance arrived. He enjoyed a spectacular recovery for about a week, which he used to put his affairs in order, as though he knew that he was taking his last bow. A devastating relapse, outside the grocer's, a stroke, the real thing this time. Véro was with him. Just before he collapsed, they had been screaming at each other because she wanted to buy a tube of Nestlé sweetened condensed milk for her morning coffee and he was quibbling that she didn't need it, that it was a waste of money, and besides, it played havoc with her stomach. Always ready with the right word to piss her off, the old bastard. At the hospital, the nurses were heartbroken at the thought of this elderly couple being separated by death. Alcoholics, obviously, it was written on their faces, but the sort of old people who held hands and didn't let go until the last moment, because Charles was gripping her hand as he had never done before, he didn't say anything but she could tell that he was afraid, and she could think of nothing better to say than, you'll be fine, old man, you'll get through this. And from the outside, that's what they looked like: an elderly couple saying their goodbyes. And that's what they were, when all is said and done. But living in harmony had never been their thing.

After the first attack, the one that didn't kill him, the old man's family didn't rush to be at his bedside. His sister did call to ask how he was doing, but, hearing that he was back on his feet, she didn't bother to visit. Good thing too, she's an old bitch. His friends at the bar were more worried. Old Michel dropped by twice – he'd sold the bar, but before he did he and Charles were thick as thieves. And fat François – practically a childhood friend, another northerner. Ahmed, who used to work with him at the Bar des Vosges when it was still a respectable bistro, came by to check on him. He'd changed a lot. Like so many others. He doesn't drink alcohol anymore, and he didn't dare tell them much about what he was up to, but they guessed – you have to move with the times, he was going to mosque and observing Ramadan. In this neighbourhood, with a name like Ahmed you couldn't knock back a beer in peace anymore without someone coming up and lecturing you. There had been others, too, drinking companions who, having heard about his condition on the grapevine, had promised to stop by – given their age, they weren't overly optimistic, they knew a stroke is usually followed by complications. Charles hadn't hung around for long. She was lucky she had been there the day it happened. Shit. The old bastard died holding her hand. It was probably the most tender moment of their entire relationship. He's not the first she's seen kick the bucket. But it does something to you. That's all there is to it, she had thought, that's it. It's no big deal, dying. People make a fuss about it, but when it finally comes, it's just a slight release.

Jesus, they were in a hell of a hurry at the hospital to free up the bed as soon as death was pronounced. It's not compassion for those left behind that's choking them up. Even when you know that to them it's just a load of paperwork, that they see it every day, that they're overworked, that there's a crisis, that it would be criminal to take up a bed when you're officially deceased – you still feel like slamming one of them against the wall when they start bustling about because they've got no time to waste on a stiff. They didn't give her five minutes' peace. At the time, she was so shocked she didn't argue. But ever since, the images have haunted her – they pounced on the cold body like it was nothing, no more important than a clapped-out old fridge.

Nearly fifteen years she'd spent with that fucker, listening to him snore every night, and that night she wouldn't hear him rattling up the house, the least they could have done was give her a little time. It's a question of decency. Even people like them need to say their goodbyes. If only so they can believe it's true. It's over. It'll never move again, that lump of lard, never shout never pound its fist on the table never scream at her for changing the channel never piss beside the bowl never call her a stupid bitch when she says that Obama is handsome, it's over. He used to sing the "Internationale" every time he heard the word "debt", so lately you couldn't turn on the T.V. without him singing. But that's over now. That, and every-thing else.

Even if there was a lot of misery, their life together, she didn't hate it. By the time she met him, she was already too old to tell herself that this was anything other than someone to cling to. She knew that she only put up with him because she was afraid of being alone. She was past the age – long past the age – of thinking love was anything other than a crock of shit, a scam to sell you micro-waves and cars on credit.

She was constantly carping at him about something. She knew they were stupid things. Not that this stopped her spending hours in front of the sink, reciting the litany of things she couldn't stand about him. But she knew that, without him, she would get depressed. Because they had a good laugh, from time to time, all things considered. He wasn't one for melancholy, her Charles. She'd told anyone who would listen, told them until she was blue in the face, that the two of them living together wasn't just about saving on rent and heating. In their own way, they got along pretty well. He was a blowhard, a brawler. She could throw a six-pack at his head, he wasn't the type to complain.

She smooths the pink plastic bag, the plastic is so sheer you can see through it. First, she pulls on the handles so that it is the right shape, then folds it in two widthways, then in three lengthwise. She stores it with the others. Now that the shops don't give out bags for free anymore, her collection is increasing in value.

Charles loved reality T.V. The dumber the programme, the happier he was. When he stumbled on a show about compulsive hoarders, people who can't bring themselves to throw out anything that might one day be useful, people suffering from what they call Diogenes syndrome, he had a coughing fit, so eager was he to bellow, "Come here, you old bat! Come and see how we're going to end up if I let you carry on the way you're going." And for three days afterwards, he followed her around, keeping an eye on her hoarding, he called her Didine, a diminutive of Diogenes, and tried to get her to throw out the bags and other things that were potentially useful. But she's not the one with the screw loose, as they call it. It's the world around her that's off its rocker. What's with this obsession with tossing everything out? Just because everyone does it doesn't make it rational.

She listens to Barbara, "Tell me when you'll be back, tell me at least that you know," and it brings a tear to her eye. She takes advantage of the fact that he's not around to play music. The old man didn't like French songs, or poetry. At first, she assumed it was because he didn't think he was able to understand what they were saying, like some kind of hang-up. Later, she thought it was mostly to annoy her, to stop her having something beautiful in her life, to keep her face pressed into the mud and the shit and it annoyed him that she might have access to something more beautiful than the street outside their door. Eventually, she realised that there was no hang-up, and no attempt to reduce her to the mediocre: he didn't like music and poetry, he saw them as bourgeois hypocrisy. Her poems by Emily Dickinson and Alejandra Pizarnik, her Aznavour and Léo Ferré albums: shit for middle-class posers. So they can think they're God's gift. Smoke and mirrors. That's how he saw things.

For old Charles, the cold hard truth of humanity was savagery. It was simply a matter of knowing who had the right to be cruel to whom. Everything else, according to him, was poetry – a way of masking the stench of the corpse that follows man wherever he goes. As misanthropes go, he was one of the best.

She puts away the bag, carefully aligned with those below, but she doesn't have time to close the drawer before she has to run for the toilet. She throws up bile. It's a long hard battle. Booze doesn't sit with her well now. Must be the stress. All this paperwork she's had to fill in.

She opens another bottle, because it's no secret: if you get sick from drinking too much you need to drink a little more, put lead back in the plumbing. She pours herself a snifter, just enough to wet her lips. The old man is dead, she spent almost fifteen years with him, which means it's not hard to do the maths: every day for more than fifteen years she's sworn she'll give up drinking. It's not decent at her age, for God's sake, it plays havoc with her insides. All good things come to an end, usually prematurely: the bottle has always been her friend, her passion, her one true love – and even that has started to cause her problems.

All this time with Charles, she made promises she didn't keep. To stop drinking. Start studying again. Leave him, dump him, find a place of her own, make a new life for herself. Sometimes, he was drunk enough he'd get it into his head to climb on top of her and when he managed to get it up, she would kick him to leave her alone. He was old school: he thought it was normal for her to say no and for him to go ahead anyway. These days, people aren't like that. They're civilised. But in his generation, men were animals. She felt disgusted when he managed to stick it into her. Bloody hell, can't you tell I'm not enjoying it. He would laugh. I'm not doing it for your enjoyment, I'm doing it to empty my balls. Shameless. Old school.

Before him, she had a thing for younger men. Young and hand-some. Before him, she could still choose, more or less. But after Charles, she was too damaged to think she could have what she wanted. Good God, what does she look like now? Like nothing at all. She hated him for that, although none of it was his fault. She used to say that if she was happy with him, she would have taken care of her figure. She used to say that if she'd been on her own, she would have looked after herself better, would have made sure there were weeks when she didn't drink, gone to the gym, gone on a diet, things that would have been good for her. Now he's not here anymore, she'll have to find someone else to blame. Or get herself into rehab somewhere. It feels strange, even thinking about it.

She still can't believe it. She had her suspicions. But she never expected such a massive fortune. Still less that the old bastard would arrange for a civil partnership, so that she could claim it. Nor that he would leave that crazy letter in his spidery old-fashioned hand indicating his last wishes. His handwriting looks like his body – crooked, unable to walk in a straight line, every letter trembling, the feet of the Ps dangling in the void, the bars to the Ts skidding to the edge of the paper. Writing that is collapsing,

crumbling, contradictory. But elegant too, the handwriting of someone who wanted to write correctly one day. He explained everything,
calculated everything – the old fool, where did he find the lucidity
to prepare his sneaky little surprise?

She can't believe it. More than a million. Deposited in a bank
account, the total barely touched. She has trouble trying to work
out the inheritance tax, but it doesn't seem swingeing, unless her
calculations are off she'll have to pay twenty per cent of the total . . .
There'll be enough left to be going on with. She has suspected
something for a while now, but she never made the connection.
When he asked for a copy of her birth certificate to apply for a civil
partnership at the court, she assumed it was to do with the illness,
that he was terrified of being taken into hospital and her not being
allowed to visit and bring him a pack of cigarettes and a bottle. He
had insisted that the civil partnership take place as quickly as
possible and she thought, you old fool, always have to make a fuss,
don't you? It never occurred to her that he was thinking about his
succession. How could she be expected to know that the old shyster
was sitting on such a fortune? She is very surprised that he was
so determined that she should get the money. She knows he hated
his sister, maybe that's what was going through his mind: making
sure she didn't inherit. She finds everything about this business
surprising.

It wasn't really their style, as a couple, tenderness and generosity.
It has to be said that he changed, towards the end. Not when he
won the jackpot. She checked the dates. The jackpot was when
he started buying trainers. The ugliest shoes ever conceived by the
mind of man, and he bought them of his own free will. He used to

say he felt comfortable in them. She will gather up his collection of trainers and throw them out on the street. No, it was later that he changed. With his gang.

When she read his last wishes letter, she was furious: if he really cared so much about those kids, why hadn't he asked her to go find them when he had his first stroke? She was always taking the piss out of him, with his crackpot city friends living down the country. But they should have been there, during those last days. Maybe they would have come. For reasons she cannot understand, they were fond of him too. It was obvious.

The caravan of a Gypsy is burned in the days after death. So that the soul is not trapped inside, so they can be sure that it takes flight. Véro looks around her – she'd be surprised if old Charles was still clinging to his armchair like a leech. No point burning it. He probably went straight up as soon as he heaved his last breath, he never was one to hang around.

She had noticed that something about their budget had changed. It was the chicken that first got her thinking. Charles loved chicken. He brought a whole spit-roasted chicken back from the butcher's one Sunday, and he did the same the following week, and again the week after that. She asked him straight out: who did you rob that you've still got money on the twentieth of the month? He dodged the question, he protested, in the end he claimed that the butcher let him have it on account. In Paris, in this day and age . . . On account? He was taking the piss. She figured he'd had a win on the horses he hadn't told her about. It wouldn't have been the first time. Then he discovered those fucking trainers, his Nike Airs. At that point, she gave him the third degree – this wasn't normal, it had been going on for too long, this money he was plucking out of thin air and squandering. He didn't give anything away. Even dead drunk, even lying in his own piss and vomit, as he was wont to do, in the toilets of some bar where she had to go and fetch him at closing time, snoring in a pool of bodily fluids – his and other people's – curled up on his side like a puppy, cute, if you could ignore the circumstances and that ugly wino's mug. She had tried, she had knelt down beside him so she could stroke his forehead, putting on the motherly voice so she could catch him off guard and get him to talk, and at other times, having a go at him when he woke up, direct, aggressive, threatening, telling him: I know every-thing, you bastard. Still he let nothing slip. The fridge wasn't the same, strange things began to appear in it, but what was most unsettling was that there was no longer any structure to the month. Didn't matter whether it was the fifth or the thirtieth, the old man was at the bistro, propping up the bar, and he no longer flew into a rage the way he used to when an unexpected bill landed on the doormat. He grumbled, and it was paid. She could see that things weren't normal. She suspected something. Obviously. But not a fortune like this.

Why didn't you say anything? She has never wanted to talk to him as badly as she does now that he's not here anymore. Why did you spend so little? And why did you stay with me? Why didn't you go off and get yourself a younger woman, like all men your age do when they've got three euros in their pocket? It's not like there's a shortage of young dipsos in the bars, he could have had a buxom little number with that sort of cash. Véro looks at herself in the mirror and it's painful. Booze makes you bright-eyed and bushy-tailed until you turn thirty, after that it's a gentle slope until you hit fifty, and the last part of the journey is the ugliest. After the menopause, good God, she turned into a monster. Puffy, red-faced, her whole body deformed from cheap plonk, her eyes swimming in idiocy.

Problem is, booze takes time to kill you. It'll get there, that's for sure, and you know it. But it's so slow, it's horrendous. At least with cigarettes, the day you're diagnosed, a kick up the arse and that's that, you're dead and buried. Not booze. From the first time a doctor says, if you carry on you're going to die, to the day you finally snuff it – you've got ten years left, easy. And not the best ones. She's no oil painting, Véro. She wouldn't live with herself if she had the choice. She wouldn't want to wake up and see her face on the pillow. Charles was ugly too. But she had no-one else to bring to her bed. You have to be pragmatic, and she hates being alone.

Now she understands. The day he threw up blood and went to the doctor, who said, it's a minor haemorrhage, nothing serious, he just needed to eat bland food and boiled carrots. She had thought it was weird, but she watched as he cracked open a beer and said that, in moderation, alcohol wouldn't do him any harm, and she said nothing. Now, she suspects that the doctor didn't tell him it was benign. Charles knew. And he said nothing. Silence was practically a religion with the man. People call it reticence, but it's more like verbal constipation. When it came to talking shit, he could open his big gob not once but several times a day. But for the things that mattered. Nothing.

This was the point when he dragged her down to the court for the civil partnership. And it must have been around then that he went to see a lawyer. It's right there in his letter, "my lawyer", with the address and everything. She called him. She was asked to come in and sign some papers and from the deferential tone of the lawyer, she realised that he knew the file perfectly well. A pile of cash like that is not something you forget, even if you're a lawyer.

In his letter, Charles asks that she divide the money – half for her, and half for Vernon Subutex's gang. Hold your horses . . . If he was so determined to shower his new friends with cash, why didn't he adopt them? There, Véro thinks, that's what he would have done if he'd been serious about this notion of splitting the inheritance in two.

She never really liked his friends at parc des Buttes-Chaumont. It pissed her off to see him happy. Might as well admit it. Charles was never one for going all sentimental. So, when he suddenly demonstrated this crass naivety Véro had never seen in him, this sickening joy at having friends and spending time with them, it made her uncomfortable. She was jealous, for one thing. Seeing him suddenly happy about something while she had nothing to cling to made her feel alone and hopeless. And it hurt her, for him to carve out a life that she had no part in. Above all, it worried her. Anything beautiful always becomes something ugly and disgusting, it's something you learn when you get to her age, and she wondered what kind of rotten trick they would play on Charles that would destroy him. At his age, getting attached and showing it makes you vulnerable. She hated to see him lowering himself to such things.

In the past few months, he regularly caught the bus and went into the country to spend a few days with them. This from a man who hated anything to do with suitcases and travelling, anything that implied sleeping in a house other than his own.

It's been bugging her. She can't believe the old duffer was serious when he wrote this letter: did he really imagine Véro would bust a gut going to see lawyers and dealing with mountains of paperwork and, after all that, give away half the money? She's keeping the lot! Bollocks! This is the simplest thing for all concerned.

She and Charles met in a bar. Unsurprisingly. They were hardly likely to meet at the cinema, given neither of them ever went. He was funny. He was up-front. He was hideously ugly. Véro likes handsome men, she has a passion for them. She likes a man's skin when it has that smooth texture, she likes sinewy bodies, square shoulders, broad chests, bulging thigh muscles, she likes fleshy lips, long eyelashes when they don't impinge on masculinity, large, gentle yet powerful hands. She likes watching fire fighters running in a group, wearing those little shorts that show off their handsome thighs and, when they sweat, you can see their back muscles outlined beneath the fabric of their T-shirt.

Charles was ugly as sin. She had never been attracted to him. But he was persistent. It had been a long time since anyone had made such an effort to chat her up. Be realistic, she thought, it's not like you can do much better with what you've got. At least the old bastard had a silver tongue. He managed to persuade her to come back with him that night. And the following nights. She never understood what he saw in her.

By that point, Véro had already been fired from her job as a teacher. In Charles' eyes, this gave her a certain prestige: "You're a real champion, you are . . . I've never heard of a teacher being fired . . . Did you rape a whole class of kids, I can't see it happening otherwise?"

She had not become a teacher out of a sense of vocation. It was the logical result of having studied literature. She sat the exam for her teacher's diploma without a second thought because she needed to put food on the table. On her first day in class, she wore a brand-new beige raincoat bought specially for the occasion. On another woman it could have looked sophisticated and given her the air of an inscrutable *grande dame*. On Véro, it was a disaster, she looked like a sack of potatoes. She looked like a madwoman escaped from an asylum. Nothing suited her. Not the coat, not the elegant pumps that reminded her of Audrey Hepburn but that, on her, looked like hideous carpet slippers. She had faced her first day in class like a woman mounting the scaffold, convinced that the children would notice her deception, the grotesque figure she cut. She expected to be booed, showered with insults, sent home. On her second day, when the little blonde boy in the third row disrupted the class, she told him to gather up his things, go to the back of the class and stop interrupting. "Or what?" the boy said, and she coolly replied, "Or, chicken, I'll rip your eyes out with my teeth." She was sure she would not see out the week. The boy flashed her a little smile and did as he was told, to shocked, delighted laughter from the rest of the class. She had waited for him to complain when he went home and for his parents to insist that she be suspended. Nothing of the kind happened. But she had earned her place in the myth-ology of the school. She had become the fearsome Madame Breton, the French teacher with balls of steel who knew how to put trouble-makers in their place. The sort of teacher you don't mess with. Firm but fair. The times were very different from what they would become. Adults were rarely insulted. Véro became a good teacher, or at least one capable of getting her pupils interested in the subject she taught. She loved the kids' energy. Then the parents changed. By the 1990s, a generation of arseholes force-fed sugar since the cradle had grown up to be a horde of degenerates. Suddenly there appeared the figure of the lobotomised helicopter parent who comes to a parent–teacher meeting and says, if my son isn't doing his work it's *your* fault. How are you supposed to respond to that? A kid who takes home a bad grade to be told, don't worry, darling, it's your teacher's fault, is tough to motivate. She asked to be transferred to a school in an underprivileged area. She claimed it was for the bonus pay, but deep down it was because she couldn't bear to spend another second with parents called Chantal and Charles-Edouard and their shitty offspring who had to be treated like the eighth wonder of the world when actually they would never be able to grasp a concept like the simple past.

In the 1990s, there were kids in deprived neighbourhoods who still believed that "knowledge is a weapon", that the ability to use a dictionary was a bonus. You could look at them without blushing and tell them that, if they carried on with their studies, their professional life would be very different than if they dropped out after a vocational training certificate in boiler maintenance. This was a lie, their postcode meant they were doomed to a lack of job security, but they didn't realise this. Véro was experienced, she easily withstood the culture shock of the northern district of Bourges where she taught. She had a good working knowledge of the immigrant population. She was what people these days call a B.M.W. – a black man's whore. From east to west, from north to south, she knew all of Africa (in the biblical sense). Say what you like about immigration, but when it comes to women's sexual fulfilment, these men did a lot for France. This gave her a certain advantage over her colleagues:

she had some idea what was going on inside the kids' heads. And not a single parent came to see her to complain that she got the kids to read Chester Himes, Bunker or Calaferte, which was hardly classic literature. The students didn't talk about their French lessons at home, and the adults never asked what they were reading. That way no-one bothered anyone and some of the pupils came to enjoy reading. Later, she would wean them on to Rousseau, the radical for the great unwashed, and every year she managed to persuade a handful of students that libraries could be useful to them. She got along well with those who were resistant to her teaching. In those days, they were noisy, they were boisterous, they were funny. She had learned not to burst out laughing as she listened to the stream of quips and jibes. There was a sort of weird poetry in their banter.

Her problem was always the hierarchy. And the internet. She didn't need to wait for blogs or Twitter to have problems with the online world. One night, coming home from a particularly boozy dinner, she found an e-mail from the head teacher. An all-star arsehole of the kind churned out by the public sector, as obnoxious as he was incompetent. These were different times. Back then, it would never have occurred to anyone to contact a teacher after 9.00 p.m. except in the case of a fire, a dying pupil, or a nuclear threat – you were not on duty, your life was your own. E-mails marked the first change in this rule: senior management realised they could send e-mails at any hour they liked. The head had had the bright idea of sending a short, irritating message, inventing times she was late for the sole pleasure of making her blood boil. She was drunk when she read it. She wrote several pages of insults, entirely deserved and expressed with the honesty that booze inspires. She remembers the circumstances, she was sitting at her black Ikea kitchen table, in front of her apple-green computer with its rounded back, an open can of beer, then another. Not the faintest flicker of writer's block, she was making up for the years of frustration under this tinpot dictator.

The following morning, the pussy had only to press PRINT, file a police complaint alleging death threats, and notify his superiors. He never thought, she's a good teacher, we can't suspend her just like that. No. The e-mail had a greater impact than she could possibly have anticipated . . . the magic of the written word. She had been suspended, permanently. It hadn't been long coming. Charles loved this story. He scolded her for not keeping a copy of the letter that had screwed up her whole life. He was convinced that it was great art, possibly her masterpiece. It's not every day you get a chance to tell your direct superior exactly what you think of him.

Charles made her laugh with a story about going to find someone called Emilie who works on rue Campagne Première so she could drive him to see his friend Subutex. All that trouble to leave them tens of thousands of euros they'll fritter away on some preposterous pipedream, whereas Véro, she has big plans. She remembers Subutex well. It hit the old bastard like a sudden urge to piss. He'd made friends down at the park. That was how it started. She never went with him. For a start, she can't stand parks. Too much greenery. She doesn't give a toss about global warming and the problems of burying nuclear waste. Her whole life she's been told that she has to consume to support national production and now, suddenly, at the end, people are giving her a hard time because she buys stuff that's made in China . . . Make your minds up! Negative growth?

She wants nothing to do with it. She has a passion for the sales, for local Chinese bazaars, for cheap knick-knacks.

She has lots of projects. She's not short of enthusiasm. She's heard all the stories about undocumented immigrants, and she'd happily build a refuge. She can picture herself, got up like a nun, strolling around the derelict hotel she planned to buy, and since she wouldn't be able to make love to them, she could at least make food for them, find out whether they needed an aspirin or help filling out a form, she'd be indispensable. She sees them on T.V., boats full of handsome lads, men who've survived, men who've been through hell and made it this far, trying to stow away on trucks to cross borders – she'd open up a centre and she'd tell them not so fast, there, hang around a little and I'll put the lead back in your pencil. Just for the pleasure of watching. She can picture them, all those young males, bustling around her, in rooms reeking of testosterone. Those tough, muscular bodies, survivors' bodies. God almighty, she'd give her right arm to take care of them! If the country wasn't run by ignorant fucking men, this whole thing could be sorted out. But no-one cares about a woman's pleasure. She would just like to pamper them for a while. Play lady bountiful among guys who look like something. Now that he's dead, she feels a great tenderness for old Charles. Given all he's left her, it would be churlish not to.

She can see herself, Scarlett O'Hara in a roadside camp in Calais. With good healthy food, passionate cuddles and lots of radiators everywhere, she'll persuade them not to go to England. She doesn't give a damn whether they're Muslim or Christian, or from some shithole country where people talk to stones and call them auntie. What matters in a man is not the god he prays to – it's his ability to make you dream, to make you feel like a woman, to make you quiver at the thought of what might happen if the big lunk took you in his arms.

She could open a school, too. She might even name it after Charles, because it would be a beautiful gesture. A private school. She'd found a school where pupils wore grey smocks and clogs, the boys would love that. Kids love to suffer. It is in their D.N.A. The school would be free, but there would be an entrance exam. The best pupils, trained to conquer. She feels she would be capable of creating an elite, a true elite. Not that posh neighbourhood bilge where the only thing that matters is who your father is. She has no shortage of ideas. She'd make it a training camp, she'd have the kids crawling through mud every morning to the sound of the Marseillaise, you'll see, the boys would lap it up. Four hours of Latin every morning, then a study of Arabic literature, sprinkle a bit of algebra and a solid grounding in history over the top and you'll see the sort of boys who would graduate from her institution. When you see the state of the elite today, you realise you need to create a new one. Based on merit. The rich brats and the trustafarians are in for a shock when her pupils enter the job market. The country needs new blood. Just look at the elite we've got now – if it wasn't bad enough that they're corrupt to the bone, they're dumb as pot plants. They're obsessed with ripping up workers' rights, you stupid fuck, if you don't have a clue how to run your company, go ahead, hire slaves, your turnover will never take off . . . She will open a school. Boys who have walked the length of Africa and crossed the Mediterranean on a raft, she'll choose the best among them to create European capitalism. We'll see what happens, not that she has the means.

Shit, if someone had told her that Charles would one day give her a gift like this. She's also considering a rehab clinic in Switzerland. She's looked it up online, it costs an arm and a leg, but the clinic is really beautiful. She'll reread Thomas Mann, high in the mountains, she'll be a bit like a senior-citizen Heidi. And she'll leave the place perfect, her complexion immaculate, her mind rested. All set to organise all the things she needs to organise to do something beautiful and important with this money. Now she's scared of being ill. Of having drunk too much, screwed up her insides so badly that she won't have time. She needs to get help, to deal with this. But with all this money, she doesn't need to stop drinking completely. Stability will come naturally. In the meantime, she'll focus on little – what do they call them? – biodynamic wines. It's not good to stop abruptly. Besides, wine is good for what ails you.

Why do you think that *banlieues* are shit factories? It's the Debré law supporting private schools that's to blame. Back then, it wasn't secularism they used to intimidate immigrants, it was the battle against alcoholism. Politics was thrashed out in bars. And in the 1960s, no-one wanted Arabs involved in politics. People felt guilty, but it was better not to talk about it too much. So, in bars all over France it was decided that alcoholism was patriotic. But not for the Arabs. No social life. No card games, no jokes propping up the bar, no space for you when you got out of the factory. And this is the result. It worked, it has to be said. As alcoholics go, they're not alcoholic.

In the advanced school for integrating those who have escaped destitution that she's planning to open, wine will be served in the school canteen every night. She doesn't believe that it's such a good thing, abstinence. This is one point where religion can be criticised.

You don't build a nation with men who are teetotal. No war, no big business. You need wine, you need beer, you need aperitifs in order to weave the social fabric. How can a man prove that he's a man if he can't demonstrate that he can hold his booze? This is why those kids end up planting bombs. Men need booze. It's always been that way in a country that suffers from harsh winters. You live in France, you drink. It rains too much to get through the days without a little snifter in the evening.

As it happens, she is just about to open a second bottle when the doorbell rings. She has no intention of answering. She never picks up the phone either. She doesn't need people bothering her with condolences. She tiptoes as far as the spyhole to have a gander, careful not to make any noise. Her movements are approximate. She's had a lot to drink. She trips on her own feet and bangs against the door as she's leaning forward for a peep. The guy on the other side hears her. She recognises him instantly. She knew he was bound to show up. She's convinced that he knows what's going on. The vulture. Charles probably told them. Subutex has found out that the old man is dead and has come to claim his pound of flesh. She shouts, go away, I'm tired, and he says, "I've been calling Charles for hours, and I can't find him in any of the bars, I'm starting to get worried. Is he sick?" He's quite a handsome man. It's mostly about the eyes. And his long legs. There's something of Johnny Hallyday about him in those boots that make him look a little sleazy. If he made a move, she wouldn't go sleep in the bath, as they say.

She mutters for him to wait two minutes, and, without hurrying, she slips on her dark red cardigan and a pair of Crocs she wears even in winter, with socks – this isn't a fashion show, does he really think she's going to put on her glad rags for him?

Even if he were in a fit state to say something, Vernon would not know how to respond. Blinded by the dazzling glare, his mouth wide open, he emits a strange sound from his throat. Hands gripping the arms of the dentist's chair, he is hoping that the antibiotics have done their job and this guy will be able to pull out this fucking tooth. He doesn't ever want to hear about it again. Hopefully, it will come out in one piece and not shatter into little splinters. He dreads the sound of the implements drilling into his mouth as though he were a stubborn shelf a workman is trying to repair. There's a little of everything in Vernon's mouth, crowns, bridges, implants of porcelain and of various exotic alloys . . . If you add up all the money he's spent, there's the equivalent of a Porsche stuck into his gums. The dentist frowns as he continues his examination.

"It's like a building site in here . . . You're lucky I'm good at my job, a less-experienced colleague would have tachycardia just surveying the lay of the land . . . We'll fix you up pronto – Kiko has explained your situation. But I'm warning you, if you don't get this sorted, you'll be hopping off the walls again pretty soon. There's damage everywhere."

*

With the money old Charles left them, he could suggest to the others in the group who need dental work – he's not the only one with a mouthful of rotten teeth – that they make a group trip to Hungary and get treated. They should hire a camp dentist, with a mobile surgery, that way they wouldn't have to worry. A dentist and maybe a decent physio, that would be useful – they're constantly putting their backs out lugging heavy loads around.

The previous night, he had rung the doorbell and kept ringing, assuming Charles was too drunk to hear, or that he had a bad cold, something to explain why he was taking so long to answer . . . He couldn't understand why he had disappeared. Without a word. A guy who had been with them from the very beginning and had never missed a single convergence. It had occurred to Vernon that Charles might have problems with his health. He had not imagined the worst. Charles was the doyen of the group and it could hardly be said that he kept himself in shape by eating green vegetables and steamed fish. He was a sedentary, alcoholic smoker who loved meat in rich sauces and Haribo sweets . . . There is an urban legend that true alcoholics are never drunk. The ones Vernon knows get themselves into apocalyptic states. Charles was like that. A day that didn't end with him falling flat on his face was a day wasted. He didn't drink to stay standing.

Véro is more resilient, though the difference is marginal: when she came to the door, she was bumping into the furniture and he had to make an effort to work out what she was saying, but, once decoded, her words made sense. She was not happy to see him. He wasn't surprised. She had never liked Vernon. During the few nights he spent sleeping at Charles' place, she'd say – without troubling to close the door so that he didn't hear – that his pretentious clowning bored her rigid and that she hoped he'd soon skedaddle because having to look at his ugly mug was ruining the view. Charles would call her a mad bitch and try to give her a kick to shut her up, miss his target, stumble, try to steady himself on the dresser, and end up sprawled on the floor. She was laughing. They were the sort of couple who could have been on any number of reality T.V. shows and been successful, because their relationship was a non-stop vaudeville act.

Vernon had still been standing on the doorstep when Véro said: "You're hardly likely to run into Charles: he's dead. You lot didn't even come to his funeral, miserable little shits, after all the things he did for you . . ."

With a smooth, practised kick, the dentist rolls his chair backwards, spins around and studies the X-ray for a long moment, elegant and sophisticated. Vernon has noticed that chairs dentists use seem more comfortable than ordinary chairs. Now that he's got the means, he thinks, he should ask for the name of the furniture shop so he can get one just like it. For the sheer pleasure of gliding around the room with a little flick of his heel. He can already picture himself, the turntablist in his fancy chair, spinning around the room, arms in the air, happy and aerodynamic.

"The amoxicillin has done its job. We'll take another quick X-ray just to check, but I'm pretty sure we can get it out."

The guy is wearing a pair of Pumas. Blue. Brand new. He's got the look of a fighter about him. Virile, comfortable in his skin. Reassuring. Or completely sociopathic, you can never tell with people you don't know. He might be the type who hunts ancestral giraffes in Africa. A bloodthirsty maniac. He's definitely a biker. Vernon can't imagine him taking the métro, or driving around for years looking for a place to park. There is too much Indiana Jones in him for that.

The dentist wedges a little piece of white plastic between his jaws, pushes it a little too hard. It's amazing how enormous things seem when you're expected to put them in your mouth. He must remember to raise the subject with Pamela. When girls give blow-jobs, do they feel like they're sucking off the Empire State Building?

The dentist and his assistant step out of the room for a second, while the optical arm takes the X-ray. The dentist reappears, jabs at the computer screen, gesturing at the inflamed root like a weather-man trying to banish a low-pressure system.

Vernon avoids looking at the implements he uses. Objects that have absolutely no business being in his mouth. He closes his eyes when he sees the fat anaesthetic syringe looming. He tries to think about something else. It's not exactly complicated. His mind is already elsewhere.

He must have pulled a peculiar face when Véro announced that Charles was dead, because she instantly softened. She took a step back and ushered him inside. She was listening to Christophe, cranked up to eleven, "Les Paradis Perdus" echoed through the house and Vernon found it strange because Charles was the only person he knew who didn't like music. At the camp, he was the only one who wore noise-cancelling headphones at the conver-gences. At first, he was happy with earplugs. Then Sylvie talked to him about noise-cancelling technology and everyone was shocked to see him rock up wearing a pair of eye-wateringly expensive Bose headphones that he loved, though they made him look like a Teletubby when he tottered around the camp with them perched on his head. Today, Vernon has a better sense of where Charles came up with the money to fund his caprices.

Véro poured him a glass of white wine. This was hardly the time to refuse a drink and explain that he was taking antibiotics. She wouldn't even have made the connection between the two pieces of information. Without thinking, he took a small sip, and even Vernon, who knows nothing about such things, was instantly aware: this was an exceptional wine. He glanced at the label, a Chablis, and noticed that she had several more bottles stocked next to the sink. No expense spared.

The widow was on the defensive. Even allowing for her grief, her cantankerous nature and her animosity towards him, she was over-doing it. Vernon suspected she was a little jealous. He and Charles adored each other. A great friendship invariably entails an affinity, an intimacy, an alchemy as inexplicable as physical desire. They liked to sit next to each other and comment on what they saw. Together, they were never bored. The pain Vernon felt at Charles' death was too overwhelming for him to worry about Véro's bad mood.

She didn't throw him out. She got muddled up in reproaches Vernon didn't understand, she kept saying that they had taken advantage of Charles, the bastards, and that they needn't think that the money would keep flowing, she was sure that they had already had much more out of him than was decent, and she touched on the terrible problems of abuse of the elderly. She worked herself up into a rage as she tugged at the yellow oilcloth covering the table. Vernon allowed her to rant, increasingly concerned about her mental health. It was true that Charles had bought them a lot of beer, and he had made them laugh when he showed up one day with a huge crate of tinned sardines because he thought there was nothing better for their health. And Vernon had already said to him that he shouldn't keep spending so much money, that they had everything they needed. But it was a long way from that to accusing them of taking advantage of an old man's kindness.

Charles had been a pillar of the group. If they had been a motor-cycle club, he would probably have been the president. He had a surly affection for the group that did them good. He liked to take the piss out of people, without a whit of tact but with a shrewd sense of observation. He had a knack for coming up with the perfect remark at the perfect time, the little jibe that cuts the ground from under your feet and makes you realise that you're on a slippery slope. There was no-one more grumpy, more mistrustful, more critical than Charles. But he was joyous. And happy to be a part of their adventure. He loved to see them, skipping about, dancing in the darkness, and his enthusiasm validated their collective adventure. Charles laughed a lot, he warded off fear with a highly contagious laugh.

It felt strange to be sitting in this living room with this disagreeable old lady. Vernon had drained his glass. He felt drunk. Was it the booze rushing to his head, or his brain playing one of its dirty tricks – he would never know. A series of brief hallucinations came to trouble his stream of consciousness. He saw Véro at different ages. Or at least he imagined her so well that he could see her clearly – thirty years younger, a naive girl. An unprepossessing figure, certainly not pretty, but with a charm laced with intelligence. For a few seconds, she was metamorphosing before his eyes. Véro's manner was changing too. As she drained the bottle, she mellowed. She even started coming on to him. And he could see her – a prisoner of that ruined face, of that damaged, dolorous body – as she still was inside. She had the gestures of a diva, the wit of an intellectual – flashes of a very different period of her life appeared in this gloomy kitchen.

Vernon drew her out. Had the old man had time to be afraid? Had he asked to see them? Had he died at home in his own bed? Charles had always refused to bring Véro to the camp. But their relationship was much more solid than he claimed. That was his way, he oversimplified: Véro was an old cow who had moved into his place and outstayed her welcome, that was that. It was as though Charles had consciously decided to avoid all nuance. To protect himself from something. He snuffed it out. With booze, with his refusal of words, with crass jokes. He switched himself off as much as possible, like switching off the lights in every room. In Charles' mind, intelligence was a plaything for the rich. A disgusting con trick that served only to mask their fetid stench. This was not subconscious: he could expound eloquent theories on the subject. No need to ponce about using pretentious phrases and sweeping gestures: human beings were morons. You really had to be two clowns short of a circus to worship a god that could create such a shower of shits. Liars thieves poseurs and predators. That's what they were, the whole lot of them. If you got him onto the subject, there was no shutting him up. He hated people who wanted to be decent, wanted to be pure. He hated smart-arses.

And yet, sometimes Charles would get caught up in a discussion and forget that he was an old soak. At such times, they felt as though they were seeing his huge carcass unfurl – and the old bastard would reveal a surprising knowledge of politics, an unexpectedly analytical mind, and a tenderness, wounded but very much alive, for what the future might hold for humanity.

Listening to Véro that night, Vernon realised that they were better suited than the old man claimed. She was whiny and manipulative like a lot of alcoholics late in their career. But she had the same ability to briefly lift the curtain, offering a glimpse of that same intelligence, marked by flashes that illuminated vast swathes of reality before the curtain fell again, as though hurting what was luminous within her was a matter of survival.

Vernon was drunk. A little belatedly, he started to cry. Unaffectedly. Tears coursed down his cheeks as he stared at the sink spewing dirty plates and glasses. He would never again sit next to the old man, listening as he lampooned everything and everyone in the camp.

Not having said goodbye weighed heavily on him. He couldn't understand why Charles had not let them know. But he suspected that the old man had not wanted them to see him terrified. Because Vernon was sure that he had been afraid. He thought about the hideous Bermuda shorts Charles used to wear on sunny days, proudly flaunting his pale, hairy, bandy legs, and it brought a lump to his throat to realise that this would no longer be a part of his reality. Aloud he said, "Shit, the ridiculous fucking shoes he used to wear. You had to wonder where he dug them up. He always swore they were genuine designer kicks. Like a little kid. We didn't believe him. Those things cost a small fortune." Charles loved it when people mocked his appalling taste in shoes. He squirmed with pleasure when people teased him about them.

Véro gave a curious smile. "Don't pretend you don't know. Why else would you be here? You're never going to convince me that you genuinely cared about that old deadbeat. You're too young, you've got your whole life ahead of you. You've got better things to do than come looking for Charles because he disappeared. You knew all along."

This was far from being the first thing she'd said that Vernon did not understand, so he simply nodded and waited for her to continue. She heaved an exasperated sigh. "Don't kid a kidder. He didn't leave you much. I don't know what-all he promised you, but he was having you on. He'd frittered away most of it by himself. After the government takes its cut, I'll have enough to pay for a headstone and that'll be that." She emptied her glass in a single gulp, never taking her eyes off Vernon. She was testing him, but he didn't know what it was about. He laid his hand on hers to soothe the rage he could feel welling inside her. She clutched his hand and collapsed into a heap. "He asked me to give you half. Half! Can you imagine? Sharing doesn't come easy. You have to feel sorry for rich people. Human beings don't like sharing: it's in our blood. I never understood that as clearly as I do today. We're not built for it. But the truth is, deep down I'm scared that if I don't respect his wishes, I'll be haunted by remorse to the end of my days . . . like something out of Dostoevsky. I wasn't born rich. I don't have the effrontery of the moneyed classes. I wasn't going to say anything to you, but I'm scared . . ."

Vernon was beginning to realise that she was talking about some kind of inheritance. It was difficult to imagine Charles having saved any money, so he assumed it was a few hundred euros and, had Véro let him get a word in edgeways, would have immediately reassured her, "Keep the money, don't even think about it." But now she was in full flow, it was impossible to Vernon to interrupt.

Kiko was right, in his madness. Vernon should devise a ritual, a gesture, a ceremony. Something to warn others that, in his presence, they run the risk of losing their head, of saying things they planned to keep secret. He is used to it. It is a slight, almost imperceptible uncoupling followed by a torrent of words. He has this effect on certain people. He opens them up.

She poured her heart out about everything. The lottery. The old man's last wishes. It sounded to Vernon as though she was losing her marbles, but it fitted. It was like a child's toy, when you try to put a square peg into a square hole, it fits. The trainers. The crates of beer Charles would leave behind at the camp. The vintage wine. The Bose headphones. The fact that he never said, I can't come visit next month, I won't have the money. Never mentioning his rent. His bills. Vernon remembered a series of minor incidents that made it clear the old man had considerable savings for a working-class stiff. And the endless conversations he had with the porn stars about that famous B-movie he wanted to make. He pictures the old man, sitting surrounded by the girls, solemn as a pope, as they told him how much such a shoot would cost. But while Charles loved pulling people's legs, he wasn't the kind to convince girls that he could help them just so they'd be nice to him. He was serious.

Exhausted from talking, Véro sat, her chin jutting, a cigarette dangling from her parted lips. She added: "I'm shocked that he didn't go to the lawyer and leave the lot to the Society for the Protection of Animals. Just to fuck me off. He'd changed a lot, the old bastard. That was your influence. He was kinder. It was a sort of courage. Please, take me to visit this camp of yours so I can understand why he changed."

While waiting for the anaesthetic to take effect, the dentist engages Vernon in conversation.

"Kiko's told me a lot about you. He says you're a shaman of the turntable, that David Guetta had better watch his back . . . I'm not really into music and that kind of thing . . . I remembered your name because my sister was a junkie for a couple of years, that was twenty years ago, but even today she still takes Subutex. She can't get off it. Apart from that, she's fine . . . If you think of it, remember to thank Kiko for sending you to me: you're a textbook case! There's not much of the original tooth structure left . . . but it's hanging in there . . . given your age and the state of your gums, by rights you should be wearing full dentures but . . . it's hanging in there. Just goes to show what you can do with a bit of composite and a drill . . ."

Vernon tries to get his head around the fact that, with what Charles has left them, they could go to the dentist every day, have every tooth in their heads replaced with gold if they wanted . . . He can't understand why the old man never said anything. It makes him sad. He would have loved to clap old Charles on the back and say, so are you really planning this zombie Z-movie of theirs? Shit. The old soak had been serious when he sat there taking notes, the length of the shooting schedule, the cost of the fake blood, et cetera, and Vernon never took the trouble to talk to him seriously. Then again, the old man never wanted anyone to talk to him seriously.

*

Vernon said nothing about the inheritance to Mariana, who was in bed, glued to her smartphone as though making up for lost time when he got back from Véro's place. She had just downloaded a dozen new apps recommended by her girlfriends and was studying a map of the planes currently flying above their head in the Paris sky. She was checking where the planes were headed, what time they took off. She found it exciting that she could track such things.

Vernon said, Charles is dead, then lay down. Mariana never really knew the old man. She hadn't been at the camp long enough. And in her eyes, he was just a dirty old man everyone was infatuated with. But she snuggled close to him and laid the palm of her hand on his solar plexus without saying a word. And he felt the connection – she soothes his pain.

He didn't talk to Kiko about the money, that morning, as they were having coffee. They shared a man-hug. Kiko used to have interminable conversations with Charles – the trader explaining why, according to him, the struggle of the working class would never succeed now: "It's all over, that era when people cared about abolishing slavery and the Front Populaire. These days, no-one wants to get rid of poverty. If we needed labour, we were forced to negotiate with you, the workers. We had no choice. But now, with automation, we don't give a shit about the working classes. We'll kill you. I'm not talking about opening fire on protests and demonstrations, we've always done that. No, we'll exterminate you en masse. You serve no purpose. That's where you're behind the times. You're still reasoning like you did when Papa Marx was alive – when the proletariat was essential so that people like me could make a profit. Maybe, as science improves, we'll breed a small number of sturdy proles, so we can transfuse your blood, transplant your organs, graft sections of your skin, get you to carry our children so that our wives don't have to do the work . . . but, frankly, given the future of bioprinting organs and hi-tech incubators, we won't need you. We'll eliminate you. It's common sense. You cause far too much trouble for the little you actually contribute. That's why it's inevitable: the poorer classes will be wiped off the map." These arguments seemed completely logical to old Charles, who gave as good as he got, delighted to have finally found someone sincere and clear-sighted with whom to argue. "Are you suggesting we should take the initiative and wheel out the old guillotine?" Kiko shook his head. "If you could, you'd have done it long ago. But you respect alpha males. Just look at the way the poor worship Putin. I'm not saying it's in your D.N.A., but it's been handed down for generations. It's like a culture coding, you'll never manage to emancipate yourselves in time. We've taught you to love the boss man."

They could carry on like this for hours at a time. Kiko immediately asked whether anyone had thought to pay for Charles' funeral and Vernon became evasive. He said nothing about the inheritance. The idea of so much money scares him. It is too big a change. He thinks about the camp as he left it, about the life they have been leading these past few months and he wishes he could enfold time. It's too early for such a massive upheaval.

The sound, fucking hell, he'd completely forgotten the sound of a root canal being wrenched from the gum – he cannot feel anything except the dentist's huge paws tugging at the tooth. But he can hear. Everything. The repulsive squelch of the gum being probed. The tooth does not come out in one piece. This is something he has experienced before, in other chairs, in other dental surgeries . . . God, the number of dentists he's visited in his time . . . No-one in his family has healthy teeth. And, in his case, a lifetime of excess hasn't helped. He takes a deep breath, but, given the situation, it's difficult to relax.

He could decide not to say anything to anyone. Decide not to go back and see Véro again. Or leave the cash sitting in a bank account, like Charles did, use it only for small purchases, so it's there in case of an emergency. That's what a real leader would do. But, as Kiko says, Vernon hasn't got what it takes to be a leader.

At the camp, they are kept informed about what is going on in the outside world via the stories told them by visitors. They know what is happening in Greece, for example. What Vernon finds surprising is not the brutal way in which Europe is pushing the country to the brink of ruin, but the silence of the elected representatives. Why is it that, as soon as they come to power, people stop telling the truth? Why don't they sit down in front of a microphone and say, simply: "This is how it happened. This is how I championed an idea I thought was right and just and this is how I was persuaded to lead my country to the slaughter"? There has to be a reason. Did some-one rape your wife before your eyes while you were forced to listen to your four-year-old son being tortured? Tell us, what's happening? It must be because they feel too humiliated. They're ashamed to say what was done to them. How they were compelled. How badly they were crushed. People in power never tell the truth. Never. He should take a leaf out of their book. Go back to the camp and say nothing about what happened. People in power never tell the truth because it allows them to make decisions on the quiet. They hold private discussions above the heads of the people. They do their own thing. But Vernon is not a man of power. He doesn't feel able to lie to those around him. It would leave a bad taste in his mouth – even he would stop believing that their adventure is worthwhile.

The dentist straightens up, pushes away the lamp and turns it off. "All done. You're a free man." He hands Vernon a little paper cup filled with pink liquid to rinse his mouth. Vernon sits up, his head is spinning. He cannot bring himself to run his tongue over the neatly stitched gum.

THE TAXI IS WAITING OUTSIDE THE DOOR. SEEING DOPALET struggle to cross the road, the driver gets out to open the car door for him. It's amazing how much the G7 taxi service has improved since it got a kick up the arse from Uber. It just goes to show that the stick is still the best strategy for bringing about change.

The producer gingerly settles himself on the back seat with the prudence of a major burns victim. He sits with his body tilted forward. If his back should inadvertently touch the back of the seat, he would howl in pain. Each session is more painful than the last. He finds it difficult to believe that some people undergo this needle torture of their own volition. If he had the choice, he would never submit himself to such agony.

He gave up on the idea of coming by scooter – after three hours' tattooing, he is too nauseous to drive. His torso is trussed up in cling film, he looks like a rotisserie chicken. The skin is burned. Beneath the cling film, he can feel the sticky blood mingled with ink macerating his flayed body. It has got worse and worse, and it is far from over. This time, at least he remembered to take a muscle relaxant, a couple of painkillers and a Lexomil. The tattooist smeared his back with anaesthetic cream. But to no avail. The moment he hears the needle whirr, his body tenses and he clenches his teeth. He's shelling out two hundred euros an hour for this butchery. In cash. When he thinks how he hounded his children to stay in school – when they could just as easily have earned a living by buying a colouring book and a tattoo machine . . . Two hundred euros an hour – that's more than a shrink. And the tattooist claims he's giving him a discount because it's a large piece . . . He's got Dopalet by the balls. And he knows it. Every forty-five minutes, he takes a break to smoke a cigarette and check his text messages. And why not? The breaks are not deducted from the hourly rate . . . Dopalet does not protest. He has to get this thing on his back sorted. And this tattoo parlour has the advantage of being open early in the evening when he is the only client. He has no desire to accidentally bump into god-knows-who and have to explain what he is doing there. Once a fortnight, the film producer summons a taxi and, with iron in his soul, he heads to the northern zone of Paris. To an area he never visits, near Crimée. A neighbourhood of staggering ugliness dotted with drab businesses, murky bars and dubious shops.

The tattooist is a fan of techno. Preferably hardcore – a thought-crushing jackhammer. A deranged drum machine accompanied by two notes on a synthesiser, on a loop, for hours at a time. Dopalet politely asked if he could listen to music that suited him – he had brought the soundtrack to "Tous les matins du monde", he loves Marin Marais. But the tattooist insisted that it made him "emo". This was the word he used. Marin Marais made him "emo". How are you supposed to respond to that? Dopalet packs away his euphonious utopias and he endures the moron's hideous cacophony without protest.

It was his son, Antoine, who discovered this paragon of the tattooist's art. Told Dopalet he was a virtuoso. Praised his talent and his discretion. The guy is Polish. He has the face of a serial killer.

Come to think of it, the guy probably can't even read French. This makes it less likely that he'll go around telling stories about the guy who showed up at his place with RAPIST tattooed in huge letters on his back. That said, from the look of him, he probably wouldn't see it as an insult. Maybe he thought Dopalet had been banged up for a long stretch and was forcibly tattooed by another inmate. When he first saw the scale of the catastrophe, the guy simply shook his head and gave Dopalet a knowing look. Having taken endless measurements, the shrewd bastard suggested they start with a few laser sessions to remove as much as possible before covering it over. Beneath that moronic exterior, the guy has a Machiavellian business sense: he invested in a laser tattoo-removal machine and set it up in his shop. He has a finger in every pie and charges a fortune for the removal sessions. The machine apparently costs an arm and a leg . . . In terms of pain, tattoo removal is like being skinned alive, a real picnic. The Pole swore that, by doing it this way, none of the original tattoo would be visible. It has to be said that things are beginning to take shape. The tattooist has copied the design chosen by Dopalet from the Hokusai exhibition catalogue: a Samurai fighting a huge dragon. The two are entwined, locked in furious battle. The drawing is not by Hokusai, but it was included in the exhibition at the Grand Palais. The tattooist had recommended a bold statement piece and Dopalet immediately thought of this illustration, which had struck him as he was trudging through the crowds drawn by the works of the Japanese master. This is his life – a merciless battle struggle against super-powerful enemies. The time has come for him to slay his demons. To stop being afraid. But when he chose this illustration, he did not realise that every detail, every tiny scale of the beast, every faint shadow on

the warrior's armour, would be inscribed onto his skin with agonising pain. And the worst is yet to come: the whole thing has to be
coloured. Sometimes he whimpers and the tattooist tenses, as
though his concentration has been disturbed. So Dopalet conjures
pleasurable images, he pictures his torturer being plunged into
boiling oil, very slowly, starting with the toes and ending with his
neck. It helps. But it is not enough.

Antoine says that the Pole is an artist acclaimed at international
conventions. He was always like that, even as a child. He has a
knack for saying things that make you want to slap him. "Interna-
tionally acclaimed", my arse. Dopalet had had no intention of telling
his son what had happened that night at his apartment. They are
not close enough for him to confide such a thing. The producer
would rather lick his wounds in private. He knows his son thinks
he is indestructible, still feels a childlike hero worship for his
father – something that can make him aggressive at times. With
Antoine, you're always worried that he'll get up on his high horse
and start spouting moralistic claptrap. Antoine loves to hold forth
like an intellectual, problem is that in their family they have no
intellectual grasp of abstract ideas, so he ends up babbling inanely
and making himself look ridiculous. Antoine would have been
quite capable of launching into a defence of the two airheads who
assaulted Dopalet in his home, arguing that they weren't sent on
tropical holidays when they were young or they were given short
rations of chips at the school canteen. Antoine frequently gives the
impression that he is still trapped in the socialist daydreams of
the '80s – a decade he's too young to remember. But what Dopalet
really feared was that the boy might insinuate that his father had
done something to warrant such a punishment. Antoine is not

clannish. He is incapable of siding with his father for the simple reason that they are flesh and blood. He's an ungrateful brat. Children, Christ, who'd have them? You pay for the best schools, you let them use your contacts, you buy them a little apartment, and they talk to you like you molested them throughout their childhood . . .

But, for once, Antoine behaved like a dutiful son. He sensed that his father was vulnerable, and, rather than taking advantage of the fact to berate him, he turned the incident into a moment of comforting intimacy. He came by regularly to see him, he was concerned and attentive. So Dopalet opened up to him. And his son was not callous. On the contrary, he showed great empathy. So much so that his father agreed to unbutton his shirt and show him the unspeakable wound. No-one had seen his back since the incident, no-one except his wife on those first nights when she disinfected it. He sleeps in his T-shirt. He puts on a dressing gown as soon as he steps out of the shower. He no longer takes off his shirt. No more going to hotel saunas, or the swimming pool at Hotel Costes, no more jetting off to the Canary Islands in February . . . These days, if he has a one-night stand, he fucks with his shirt on. But he confided in his son, he allowed himself to be vulnerable. And it had been the right decision. Antoine had said, omigod, Papa, that's terrible. Not a single indelicate question. He treated his father as a victim, someone who should not be expected to explain the assault perpetrated on him. It was a touching moment. And it was his son who had come up with this brilliant idea – you have to get it covered up. It was obvious. But the idea had not occurred to Dopalet. The assault had left him so shaken up. For the first time, the son had been able to support his father. Even if Dopalet has to go through hell every fortnight, even if he curses this fucking tattooist, he is conscious that he is no longer passive, no longer a victim. And, in a few weeks, he will have recovered his dignity. He will have earned it. The hard way.

After the trauma, Dopalet was devastated. The home invasion, being held hostage, the acts of torture . . . He wasn't the same man. He couldn't sleep. He had to move out of the apartment. He no longer felt safe at home. It was months before he managed to sleep through the night. The slightest sound made him jump. He suffers from terrible tinnitus, as though a swarm of demented cicadas were following him everywhere, which means he can no longer tolerate silence. His whole temperament has changed. He has lost his gung-ho enthusiasm. He finds it difficult to concentrate. He can't read anymore. At the office, he has had to recruit someone to read the film scripts he needs to be familiar with.

He has uncontrollable bursts of rage. The panic attacks he had learned to keep in check have become unmanageable. Something in him was broken that night. He knows that if someone were to study the map of his brain, they would discover whole neuronal areas have been devastated, as though he had suffered a brutal head injury. He has been to see specialists. He tells them that his home was burgled while he was there alone. He doesn't say that it was an act of revenge, the two girls broke into his apartment intending to kill him, that they believed he was guilty and had come in search of justice. He said, I thought I was going to die I was tied up I couldn't do anything I think my brain exploded. The therapists take him seriously. Any good shrink knows that a burglary is a profound emotional trauma. There is no specific word to describe the symptoms, so they use the term that most closely describes this barbarous act – a violation. The total obliteration of his faith in the safety of his private world. His body has been profaned.

He feels fierce flashes of empathy for women who, barely six months ago, he simply found disgusting – those who have been disfigured, who have suffered female genital mutilation, who have had acid thrown in their faces for refusing to marry. And he also recognises himself in those men unjustly accused of sexual harassment when they are guilty of nothing more than freely expressing their desires. He is nostalgic for an era when men and women knew how to give each other pleasure. People think that radical feminists hate men, but what they truly despise are the women who know how to live with men. Dopalet loves women, madly, passionately. He loves to look at their legs on the street, he loves the way their feet arch when they wear high heels, he loves their soft voices and their ability to act like sluts while preening like duchesses. He loves the fact they prize seduction over all things. He respects the mystery of their pleasure, and the more troubling mystery that is the gift of life. He loves women, and he has known many. But he can no longer bear the puritanism imposed by feminists. These days he says as much, loud and clear. He is tired of keeping a low profile, of avoiding clashes and conflicts. Of putting up with the tyranny of feminazis who, because they're incapable of loving or being loved by men, are trying to eradicate all the wantonness that made this country so appealing. He is no longer going to hold his tongue for fear of upsetting some snowflake. He is determined to trade blow for blow. In every sphere.

The effects of the assault have not all been negative: he is fed up with being polite. He is sick and tired of being submissive. Tired of saying nothing and tolerating the intolerable. Gone is the magnanimity that he has practised for years, the striving to be politically correct, not to offend their sensibilities. He no longer has the strength for political correctness. If he had been stricter, clearer and less indulgent with himself, he would never have taken it into his head to have any dealings with Vodka Satana that might be construed as a friendship. He would happily have screwed her in the context of a fuck-party – why not? – but would never have stooped to having a conversation with the mad bitch. That was where it had all started. With the idiotic notion that it was possible to have relationships with people from inferior social classes. The poor invariably resent the rich for succeeding where they have failed. There you have it. It's all about jealousy. One good thing came out of the assault: he's done with bleeding-heart socialism. Not that he doesn't still think of himself as left wing, but he has had it with Care Bear communism. From now on, there are no filters. He is consumed with rage, the rage of a victim, a pungent flavour he has not experienced before. He is no longer the same man. Circumstances have decided for him.

His assault, the *Charlie Hebdo* massacre, the pervading dread, the financial crisis brutally impacting feature-length movies – trauma follows hard on trauma leaving Dopalet no time to catch his breath. He spends months sweating blood over projects only to have to abandon them. They're solid projects, he still has the instinct. But unless you're pitching a comedy about a middle-class family taking in an undocumented African immigrant, there's no money out there. He doesn't know what to go for anymore, he's no longer in sync with those who make the decisions – the distributors and the financiers on the terrestrial networks are like demented rabbits zigzagging in headlights, it's impossible to predict how they will react. His colleagues are as disconcerted as he is – no-one knows what people want to see at the cinema, and there's a zero-tolerance policy: one flop and heads roll. In such conditions, it's difficult to suggest to his partners that they should be taking risks . . . Never in his career has he been so badly treated. By people who have never experienced the same frustrations and humiliations. Not that he hasn't had his share of bitter disappointments, excruciating times at the Cannes festival, and a few dismal opening weekends – he didn't come down with the last shower. But he has never experienced this level of violence. The ground is collapsing under their feet, and people don't have time to waste on being tactful. He is at a complete loss – on every level.

He is surprised by his own reactions. He is nurturing a vast, obscure grudge against the world. He harbours vile thoughts. He knows this. He feels a mounting resentment towards the people who trigger these thoughts. He is obsessed with the Jews. This is recent. For the first time in his life, his consciousness has let loose a terrifying hostility that, until now, has been held in check by a total taboo.

But, in this respect, too, he is sick and tired of being politically correct. Are we really going to spend the whole century apologising for crimes we didn't commit? And he talks to young people and it's obvious that they're not going to let themselves be pushed around anymore: it's all over, the code of silence, the taboo, the nervousness. On the radio, on the T.V., in the newspapers, at dinner parties, Jewish intellectuals are calling for war. He remembers an interview with Céline he watched years ago at his lawyer's house. This was long before the internet, such curiosities were preserved on V.H.S.

tapes. Céline was saying, "You wait and see, the Jews will trigger the next world war, you'll see." And Dopalet had been a little embarrassed that his host had shown him the tape. At the time, he felt nothing in particular when he heard these words, which seemed to him to belong to a different age, a madness – a historical dead end. But the words of the author marked him. He often thinks about them. They have taken on a different colour. The Jewish people are belligerent. Authoritarian.

He belonged to a generation that believed in "never again" – a generation raised on World War II films that you stumbled out of thinking, how could people have fallen for all that? Later, his opinion changed. Not that he dreams of anything murderous. He is not insane. He'd just like to be able to talk, in his own country, about how difficult it is to be a film producer, for example, if you're a goy. That's all. They witter on all day long, they talk about France as though the country belonged to them, by right, and that Christians like him are tolerated only on condition that they bow and scrape.

His hatred spews out whenever he listens to Zemmour. And sooner or later, everyone is forced to listen to Zemmour: if he's not on the biggest radio station in France, he's writing op-ed pieces in the popular press, or he has been invited to speak somewhere. Since the assault, it has become an incontrovertible fact: Dopalet no longer wants to be a laid-back guy. He feels a loathsome hatred welling inside him and he is astonished by its power. Repressed emotion, probably . . . What he finds most unsettling is the pleasure he feels when the hatred courses through him. He feels connected to primitive energy that has been denied him for decades, an energy that is French, patriotic, powerful and rich. He is aware of the monstrousness of his thoughts. He is fifty years old, all his life he has been told not to think such things. But when, for the first time in his life, as he was listening to Zemmour on the radio in a chauffeur-driven car, he said aloud, "Why can't he shut his fucking mouth, the dumb kike, and go back where he came from!", it was like losing his virginity. And the smile on the face of the driver – the guy wasn't even an Arab – after he'd got over his surprise, made Dopalet happy. Finally, he had manned up.

He doesn't like the Arabs any more than he does the Jews, when he takes a taxi all the way up avenue de Flandre and into Stalingrad, he has no desire to get out and have a coffee, what with the halal butchers, the mosque and the bookshop specialising in djellabas and prayer rugs . . . But he doesn't give a toss about the Arabs. He only ever sees them when he goes to his tattoo sessions, and then he has other things on his mind. The Jewish lobby, on the other hand, now that is his business, and he's more than paid his dues. And they make no bones about wielding their power.

He has never taken much of an interest in politics. Cinema isn't right wing or left wing. He doesn't read the front pages of the newspapers – he goes straight to the back pages, looks for the culture section, that's the only part that interests him. Well, he says "the culture section", but actually he only reads the articles about movies and television. He misses newspapers. On Saturday afternoons, he used to go to WH Smith to buy *Vanity Fair* and *Rolling Stone*, or *Entertainment Weekly*, and spend his Sundays leafing through them. He would look at the photos. Reading English was too much effort for him, it was mostly to get a sense of what people were talking about. The tablet is a different thing. The tablet never sleeps. Reading newspapers and magazines was relaxing. Once they were printed, they didn't change. You could set down a magazine, open it again two months later, nothing had changed. And the idea of reading an article two months after it was published didn't seem bizarre. The online world is a war. He turns on his tablet and he is dragged into battle – every time he reads an article on his iPad, he ends up taking a tranquilliser.

This is another positive aspect of post-traumatic stress: he spends less and less time at work. He spends hours doing fuck-all. And it is in this sort of depressive couldn't-give-a-flying-fuck space that brilliant ideas come. Ideas are drawn to shit, to boredom, to whole days spent sprawled on a sofa. And it's been a long time since he gave himself that kind of space.

He spent the days after the assault prostrate, shutters down, licking his wounds. His wife, Amélie, was very attentive. They bonded in adversity. She didn't ask any questions. This is what he loved about her. She knew her place. There was a little of Anne Sinclair about his wife – she rolled with the punches and kept her head held high. On the other hand, it is highly likely that Amélie suspects that, at the root of the assault, was a peccadillo on his part. If she had asked the question, Dopalet would have sworn the contrary: that was the least that he owed her. He'd go to the gallows denying he'd ever cheated on her. But the most wonderful thing about that proud, jealous woman was that she did not ask a single question.

Amélie had spent her days slaving over the stove, telling the cleaning woman not to go into his study, she had fed him, mopped his brow, got him back on his feet. In the oven she roasted thick côtes de boeuf that she bought from Desnoyer and salted at the last minute, she knew how to cook them perfectly. In a way, the assault had excited her. She pursed her lips, painted them a vivid red, pulled her hair into a chignon and adopted a ramrod straight posture. A mixture of Charlize Theron's determination to do battle in "Mad Max", Uma Thurman's thirst for vengeance in "Kill Bill" and Sabine Azéma in "The Officers' Ward" for aesthetic reasons – physically Amélie looks a lot like Sabine, it's something about the pixie face – but chiefly for her devotion. In fact, there are times when he would prefer it if she did less. The support she gave him was precious, but the way she talked about "their" revenge was a little terrifying. Obviously, he planned to even the score. To get revenge for the offence. But the revenge was his. Amélie was the daughter of a military man. When it comes to reprisals, she thinks big. Too big for him. He had described little Aïcha, with her hijab. Without mentioning how intimately he had known her mother, in very different circumstances. Amélie had flown into a rage that lacked moderation – to slake her thirst for justice, she demanded nothing less than the head of every Muslim in Paris, by which she meant the greater Paris area, extending as far as Tours, Lille and Metz, let's say; a Paris equal to the size of her fury. And when she said "the head of", she was being literal, she wanted the severed, bleeding head proudly displayed, held by the hair – the kind you see in paintings in the Louvre or the films of Mel Gibson. Nothing symbolic. Initially, he had appreciated this radical empathy. But very quickly he saw it as a reproach: a way of telling him that he lacked manly determination. It didn't bother her that, for self-evident reasons of discretion, he had not wanted to report the assault to the cops. But, to her, the idea that he was not stalking the streets of Paris with a sabre was unendurable.

Dopalet, for his part, simply wants to get his hands on the two mad bitches and give them a rough time. Something like what they put him through. A little session about which he could say: they won't forget that in a hurry. An eye for an eye. A tooth for a tooth. When all is said and done, it's *his* assault, he has every right to do as he pleases. He'll get his own back in his own way. After all, it's a pretty personal thing, revenge.

At first, he thought he would easily be able to track them down. He has heard great things about henchmen from the East and a couple of photos of the girls' faces, ideally disfigured or maimed, would have been enough for him to feel that they were quits. But he hasn't been able to find the girls. He hired the finest private detectives. They drew a blank. For a fee that seems exorbitant given the information obtained, Dopalet has been able to leaf through a file of their scholastic achievements, their former addresses, friends, acquaintances, their previous online postings and extensive documentation on their respective families. But he's not interested in family trees, for fuck's sake. Amélie begged to differ: she argued that if they hit the families, the girls would be devastated. Dopalet is pragmatic. He wants to hit hard. But he wants to hit the right target. He wants the girls. And even if he has sufficient spiritual enlightenment to one day forgive them, he needs to be sure that they won't go around telling anyone what they think they know about him. Not that he's afraid of a police investigation. The incident is outside the statute of limitations. He is afraid of rumours. In getting them, he'll get what he's spent months searching for: Bleach's confession. Once he's tracked down the girls, everything will be done and dusted.

*

The taxi drops him off outside his building. A few weeks ago, he moved into a place in the thirteenth arrondissement. It's the first time he has lived in a new build. A magnificent apartment, quite small, but well laid out, with a view of the Seine and the Grande Bibliothèque. He has to drive all the way across Paris to get to his office in the eighth arrondissement. He wanted to settle in a neighbourhood that holds no memories for him. He needs to rebuild, to look to the future. No memories of how things were, before. Amélie has kept the large apartment on boulevard Saint-Michel. He never had the time to grow attached to the place – they were still unpacking boxes when they separated. She couldn't take it anymore. He understood why she felt the need to distance herself from him. These days, an all-engulfing rage destroys everything he touches. One day, Amélie said, "I need to take a break." The words are familiar, usually he is the one who says them. There is no such thing as a "break". Once things are broken, there is no way back.

THROUGH THE WINDOW OF THE CAR, VERNON WATCHES AS they flash past, the prefab buildings with their garish logos, the car parks, the billboards planted between high-voltage pylons. A mournful procession, the architecture of desolation, an assemblage of thankless materials, a landscape with nothing to please the eye. Everywhere they have settled, they have driven through similar zones. On the outskirts of Saint-Brieuc or Perpignan, the same superstores, Go Sport, Boulanger, Auchan, Decathlon, Jardiland, Darty, the same companies selling organic food, the same vast outlet stores selling shoes at factory prices and D.I.Y. materials. They come to a roundabout in the middle of which an improbable sculpture sits enthroned like an insult to common sense: giant mushrooms holding hands and dancing a farandole.

Vernon feels a sudden wave of tenderness for this bleak topography just as Jésus declares, "When something's this ugly, it has to be saying something." Mariana quips: "Yeah: fuck you and the horse you rode in on," and everyone laughs. Véro is sitting in the front seat. On her lap, an enormous plastic bag – brand-new, apple-green, pimped out with multicoloured flowers – starkly contrasts with her general appearance. When she showed up at the car, she announced that she suffered from motion sickness and couldn't sit in the back. But Vernon could see that she had almost fallen over backwards when she saw the ripped body of Jésus, their driver. What she wants is to sit next to him and lech over him, with feverish sidelong glances. During their train journey, Vernon notices that she has a tendency to stare into space, her mouth hanging open, which makes her seem more disturbing than moronic, especially since she moves her lips without making a sound, as though talking to herself.

In that tone of a capable woman she adopts when she talks about serious matters, she declares: "France is the worst offender in Europe when it comes to destroying peri-urban areas, it's cancer, that's what it is. It used to be beautiful, this country. But developers didn't give a damn whether shopping centres worked or not, as far as they're concerned it's just numbers on a balance sheet . . . It's ridiculous. We're being governed by idiots." It is something that comes over her from time to time, she starts talking like a passionate local authority official. Immediately afterwards, she slips back into silence, mouth open as though to catch flies, engrossed in her thoughts.

Vernon is trying to understand how the developers can make these crumbling aircraft hangers look good on a balance sheet . . . How do you make something so ugly look good? He promptly dismisses the question. He thinks about Charles. Now there was someone who could launch into virulent tirades on the subject of technocrats destroying everything that worked in the country in order to make a quick buck. The old man's rages were spectacular. He would launch into logorrhoeic diatribes punctuated by obsolete insults. There are people who ruin the mood when they get angry, drowning out every other voice and leaving those around them in stunned silence. Charles' outbursts were completely the opposite. They loosened tongues, they made people want to launch into the fray.

*

Vernon looks at Mariana's profile. Eyes closed, she is singing "Satellite of Love" in a soft voice. A half-smile plays on her lips. When he looks at her, his resistance gives way. It is an almost painful tenderness, haunted by the presentiment that it will not last. That she is just passing through. Every moment must be savoured for what it is – a grace before ruin.

She hadn't wanted to leave Paris. Hadn't wanted to leave behind her girlfriends, the bars where she likes to hang. And she worries, about money – she pays her rent by subletting on Airbnb, one of her friends looks after the keys in exchange for a cut of the rental. But Mariana needs to find work. She cannot imagine living the way they do, from what people leave behind between convergences.

Vernon said, stay, if you like, you can come and meet up with us later, but she wants to be with him. She would be worried to think of him on his own. It's not jealousy. It's not very likely that Vernon will have a mad, passionate affair with Véro. Not because Véro is ugly, but because she's a complete pain in the arse. She's constantly bellyaching. At the train station, she was disappointed to discover they weren't travelling first class, and, as soon as Mariana went off to look for some free seats, she grumbled, "All the money the old bastard left you, it's a crying shame that you're so tight-fisted," and Vernon took it as a joke as he struggled with her suitcases, because Véro has a bad back and can't lift heavy objects. Véro is constantly bitching. Next, it was the price of beer in the buffet car. Outrageous. Not that it stopped her buying one, and a croque monsieur that stank out the whole carriage. She hasn't touched a cent of the inheritance, not yet, but she spends money like it's burning a hole in her pocket. She says she's afraid she'll kick the bucket before she has time to blow it all.

Vernon tried to persuade Véro to wait until the next convergence to see what the camp was like. She insisted, and he agreed. Jésus has not said a word since they set off, but Vernon can read the disapproval on his face. Jésus is used to being stared at. He is so staggeringly beautiful that it almost makes people uneasy. Even so, he must be surprised at the way Véro is eyeing him with that slightly scandalised air. Slightly worried, even.

Between convergences, there are only four or five people living at the camp, the others come and go, and while it's not forbidden to bring in outsiders, it happens so rarely that it has become a sort of unspoken rule. Jésus is Pamela's boyfriend, he's one of the regulars. They are often off travelling, since they are the ones who scout for locations for the next camp. Jésus showed up at one of the convergences. Pamela immediately took him under her wing. Before becoming her full-time assistant, he was a surfer. He is accustomed to the nomadic life. He is a good ten years younger than Pamela and hails from Kenya. Vernon checked it out – his beauty has nothing to do with where he was born, it is utterly exceptional. In the same way that he finds it's somewhat exceptional for someone to be African and a surfer – not that he knows anything about it. When he is not acting as the camp chauffeur, Jésus spends his days on a bike. Everything he does becomes interesting because of the perfect body that goes with it. Pamela doesn't have a driving licence – she's a true-blue Parisian. It is Jésus who drives the battered old bottle-green Polo. And even that he does with style. At the camp, it's not just the girls who gaze hungrily at him – he has an animal beauty of the kind you never get used to. Aside from him, and, more recently, Mariana, the other permanent residents are founding members: the Hyena, Olga, Pamela and Vernon. There are rarely six. Then there are the veterans – Kiko, Sylvie, Emilie, Xavier, Patrice and Antoine – who visit regularly. And the sound engineers, two girls who came from Bordeaux to the very first convergence and have joined the group to work on Alex Bleach's tapes. Before they showed up, Vernon had come up with a hack that allowed him to mix some of the audio fragments into certain songs. The girls know all about binaural beats and have considerably improved the process. Their work is incredibly precise. Vernon has always loved watching sound engineers at work, the way they obsess over details that are incomprehensible to mere mortals. They show up without warning between concert dates. In hindsight, it's strange to think that, for months, the group was completely focused on the tape of Bleach's confession, whereas his real legacy was his work on these strange sound waves, which are neither melodic nor even made up of identifiable sounds, but produce an effect on the listener. Now, they all believe, Lydia Bazooka has transcribed Alex Bleach's statements. She's got it into her head to write a book about him, one that no publisher seems to want. She's been working on it for months. No-one around her can understand why it's taking so long.

Vernon has found his groove here in this communal life. There are few arguments. At first, sure, it could take two hours of negotiations to decide whether they were going to eat rice with tomato sauce or tuna and corn. Since then, they've progressed – they've learned to be still. In a community, silence is a priceless commodity. But when Vernon imagines a ten-way discussion on how to use a sum that amounts to almost five hundred thousand euros

. . . he's not sure that everyone will easily come to an agreement.

He withstood the knowing look Véro gave him when he asked her not to mention it to anyone. The sardonic little smile that seemed to say – yeah, yeah, you hippies are all the same, you're all cold and laid back about money when there's no food on the table, but when it comes to divvying up a fortune, it's like getting a bail-out from the I.M.F. Vernon has no interest in knowing what she thinks about them in general, and about him in particular.

The car turns off the main road. Jésus says he has a photographic memory, at the very least he has a G.P.S. in his brain – every time they set up a new camp, he knows how to get back there from any given location with no need for signposts. He drives through villages and fields. Véro says, "Oh, look, cows. It's been years since I saw a cow. I haven't been out of Paris since . . . fuck, I've no idea how long. I don't like cows. They remind me of when I was a kid and used to go on holidays to my aunt's farm. We had a little stick we used to lead them out to the pasture every morning and bring them in again every night. I was scared of them. I've always hated cows. They've got beautiful eyes, I know . . . but I can't abide them." Then she suddenly whips around and, as though the two were logically connected in her mind, she scowls and says to Vernon: "You don't wander around buck-naked in this commune of yours, do you? Because let me tell you right now, I'm keeping my clothes on!" Vernon snaps back: "You should know that at our place people do whatever they want," and from the faint smile she gives him he's willing to bet that she was hoping that young Jésus would strip off as soon as they arrived at the camp. But she says seriously, "No, because when I was young, I went to a commune once. No-one warned me. And when I got there, everyone was nude. I didn't eat a thing the whole week I was there, I can tell you. Imagine – you're sat around a table for twelve with tits and balls hanging out everywhere, so when someone passes you the salad, it kind of puts you off your food a bit." Then she falls silent. The car thrums to the first bars of Johnny Cash's version of "Personal Jesus". Mariana, who knows it by heart, leans forwards and croons into the driver's ear. They get along well, they spend a lot of time together. Vernon considered being jealous – but the boy is too beautiful. He can't see himself telling his girlfriend, "If the opportunity arises, I forbid you from sleeping with him." He is not particularly broad-minded, and he's never had fantasies about swinging, but this guy is fucking hot. Even the lesbian separatists want to sleep with Jésus. He is the only person at the camp who has a more devoted gang of groupies than Vernon. The guys want to sleep with Jésus. He and Pamela make for an unsettling couple, to say the least.

There is something of the goddess about her since she has been with him. Unless it is the camp that agrees with her. She quickly got her bearings in this new life they have fashioned for themselves, which consists of finding a site to pitch camp, staying there a few weeks while preparing a convergence, then cleaning up everything and moving on. Vernon plays the diva – he allows himself to be moved from place to place. Pamela is a gifted administrator. She takes on an improbable list of responsibilities and dispatches them with disconcerting ease. When the convergences begin, she is in her element, she is transformed into a stationmaster: she directs the throng of people, telling them where to pitch their tents, recites the list of things that are allowed and those that are frowned on, checks they have no mobile phones, hands out schedules, reassures the timorous, calms the panicked and sets the more resourceful to work. When the time comes to strike camp, it's the same story: who does what, who leaves with whom, in which car . . .

Vernon gets out of the car and stretches. The dogs scamper around them, barking. Véro freezes, petrified – "You never told me you lived in a kennel. I hate mutts!" – and Mariana laughs as she opens the boot. "You're a real godsend, you are, you don't like cows, you don't like dogs . . ."

Olga and Victor have taken in seven dogs. Each one saved from certain death, according to the rescuers. Olga tends to them and feeds them. But although she has an innate authority over humans, when it comes to training dogs, she is hopeless. So they do whatever they like. Luckily, they're good-tempered animals. Sometimes, Xavier will say, "Since I'm here for a couple of days, I'll make the most of the time to train the dogs," and he can be heard giving orders in a splendid stentorian tone, truly his master's voice, which, as a sound, is superb, but has not the least effect on the pack. When she first saw them, Mariana said, "Fucking hell, even your dogs are activists, they fight for the right to do as they please against the oppressive human regime," and this notion delighted Olga, who let them run wilder still. She gives an order and the dogs look at her, astonished, not necessarily restive or rebellious, just surprised at the change of tone in her voice. Set a stopwatch and within thirty seconds she will have given in, dropped to the ground and be rolling around with the dogs, burbling, "Who's got lovely eyes then, huh? How did you all get to be so cute, so cute?" When she genuinely needs something, she takes out a biscuit – anyone would think that her pockets are routinely restocked with dog biscuits –

and simply leads the animal to the desired goal. And everyone has grown accustomed to living with the dogs, to tossing a ball seven hundred times a day for the arthritic pit bull, seeing the Westie scamper over at the clink of cutlery, rubbing the schnauzer's tummy, taking the chihuahua onto their lap otherwise he'll yap tirelessly because he doesn't like being on the ground or reassuring the elegant white greyhound brought here from Spain by a gang of punkettes who know that Olga loves dogs.

Olga has had several different phases with the group – during the first months she threw herself into building work with a passion that was astonishing, and a little worrying when she was heard getting up in the middle of the night to saw timber. She was drinking less, she had become an enthusiastic woodcutter, with plump cheeks that made her look so young she was barely recognisable. She continued to put on weight. Although she worked constantly, tirelessly, she regularly holed up in the storeroom digging into the stock of crisps. And a lot of convergents remember to leave her some crisps.

Then, though there was no radical change, all this joy and optimism began to wear her out. She started yelling that she wanted better-quality crisps, and more beer. And fights. That she was sick and tired of all this living in harmony. That she was bored. She put down her hammer, her nails and her tools and was never again seen trying to build anything. "It does my head in, this redemption shit, I think it makes people dumber." But she has never thought of leaving the camp. And no-one wants her to leave. Olga fulfils a crucial role: without her, who would throw out the hangers-on? While she may lack authority with dogs, with humans she never misses an opportunity to win respect.

The end of every convergence is like the end of a house party: there are always two or three people who don't want to go home, and you don't know what to do with them, because you need to clear the place up and go to bed. Olga has an innate talent for getting them to leave. She doesn't raise her voice. She doesn't use her fists. Once she has decided that it's time for them to pack their bags, she always succeeds in her goal. She is a one-woman crowd control unit. She is so unpredictable that she invariably destabilises the audience, especially as she expounds her theories with an implacable seriousness. She can outflank Xavier in his right-wing extremism, or explain to the young female anarchists who complain that dancing is not the answer that they're right, that all pregnant women should have ultrasounds to detect and abort male embryos. Fewer men, fewer wars. To her, it seems blindingly obvious. She'd like to know why no society has ever tried it. As long as women agree to carry male babies, humanity will be trapped in a disgusting quagmire. Olga is convinced that this is the solution.

Needless to say, people quickly stop arguing with her. She manages to get inside their heads, almost by force. She also lays into those who show up expecting extraterrestrials, she is categorical: no alien intelligence will ever attempt to contact people. Human language is too rudimentary. They'll communicate with dolphins, with dogs, with eagles. But not with humans. Who'd want to deal with such a species? Olga's political fictions are always so extreme, so absurd that they defy common sense. This makes her the only person capable of managing Pamela. Left to her own devices, the poisonous brunette would spend all day wearing a toga and burning sage – she has a problematic relationship with hippy customs that she has rechristened "pagan rites". Olga channels her energy.

She demands so much attention that dancing beneath the full moon has to be postponed. So, although she now refuses to build stools at every opportunity, doesn't look after the dogs, takes no part in any other chore, she still earns her place at the camp. Without her, they would already be overrun by a horde of undesirables.

Olga comes over and calms the dogs. Véro scowls – "Can you lock them up somewhere? I was bitten on the face by a spaniel a few years ago, I've got a complete phobia about dogs" – and the giant sighs, already exasperated. "By a spaniel? It couldn't happen to anyone but you." Vernon clarifies the situation: "This is Véro, Charles' other half." "His wife. We were married." Olga instantly pounces on the past tense, "So you're separated?" and Véro retorts, "He's dead."

The giant is drained of every atom of strength. All that remains is her carcass and that fixed stare. Her shoulders have slumped. Vernon hunkers down and strokes the dogs one by one. He knows that Olga is going to cry. She's easily moved to tears. When it happens, it's heartbreaking. It's always strange to see a brute crumple. Véro moves away a little, disconcerted by the dogs and the sudden display of emotion she finds disagreeable. Olga grabs Vernon's arm and asks him what happened. He tells her. But he does not mention the money. He decides it would be better to wait until dinner, when everyone will be gathered around the table.

The old man worshipped Olga. He always showed up with a bottle of pastis, to make the "electric coffee" she loves. He used to say that he got the recipe from a rock dandy he used to hang out with in the '90s at Café La Fontaine near Bastille. This heady brew would put them into an unspeakable state and they would throw up all over the camp with the glorious energy of confirmed alcoholics.

Sélim runs across the courtyard towards them, pretending to be an aeroplane. It is a curious sight, a middle-aged man running with his arms outstretched, knees slightly bent, in what is probably supposed to be an impression of a footballer who's just scored a goal, and when he reaches them, he runs on the spot, wildly kicking his legs backwards in a version of the skank that looks clumsy and potentially dangerous.

Usually, Sélim is rather solemn. In recent months, his daughter Aïcha has gone into hiding, no-one knows where, no-one really knows for how long, and although he regularly hears from her and knows that she is fine, he is eaten up with worry. But, as it happens, he spoke to her on the phone just last night. This he tells them as he loops-the-loop around the trio; better still, she seemed in good form.

Sélim rarely talks about Aïcha. It is the Hyena who is taking care of hiding the girl. And, when it comes to secrecy, no-one can accuse the Hyena of doing things by half. She has imposed a strict veto on all online communication, including the idea of setting up a blog and communicating via the comments section.

According to her, only choirboys, noobs, virgins and morons imagine that it's possible to exchange messages without being tracked. Sélim proposes using the darknet and gets a tirade: "And how are you going to explain why you've got Tor on your computer when the police raid the place? Jesus, you only have to use Linux for them to think you're hiding something . . . Leave the girl in peace. She's fine. Stop worrying."

Vernon was surprised that the Hyena decided to live with them. It was her idea to completely cut herself off from the online world. To give up her phone, her mobile – anything that could be traced. No-one realised how important it would turn out to be.

When the school holidays roll around, Sélim shows up at the camp, dragging a twenty-kilo suitcase stuffed with books, photocopies and magazines. He sets himself up in a corner he calls his study and after that no-one hears a word out of him, but he's happy to be there. He has the disturbing ability to sink into his work the way other people sink into the bottom of a bottle. But today he is euphoric. So he is doing this weird dance and focusing so hard on not falling over that he doesn't immediately realise that Olga is crying her eyes out while Véro is sulking because the dogs are still there. So, Vernon blurts out, "Charles is dead." Then he introduces Véro, and gets the distinct impression she has the hots for Sélim. He is beginning to realise that this woman is as randy as a cat.

All of Sélim's joy has slipped away. He feels sheepish for playing the fool. To each new person they encounter who asks if things went well in Paris, Vernon repeats: "Charles died a few days ago, this is Véro, you know, his other half." Vernon announces the news to Antoine who's listening to Tupac, sitting in a car that recently broke down but whose radio still works. He tells Sylvie as she is hanging out the washing – every time she comes to the camp, she feels the need to do motherly things, when she's not cooking, she's cleaning something or other . . . It's best not to get too close to her, otherwise she will collar you and set you to work. She has a knotted red bandana in her hair, she is wearing no make-up. When she hears the news, she throws her head back, the gesture is histrionic, exaggerated. But sincere. The old man worshipped her. She is the first to put her arms around Véro and say, I'm so sorry. Then he has to give the news to Xavier: "Fuck. Not Charles, no! God, we'll miss him . . . He wasn't even all that old . . ." It is this kind of remark, Vernon thinks, that reminds you that you're not as young as you were.

By the time they get to the farmyard, Pamela has already heard the news. She stands for a moment, motionless, but when Sylvie comes back from the store – the building where they pile up all the things the convergents give them when they leave – cradling a couple of bottles of fine wine, she gets up and wanders off. Vernon follows. Behind him, he hears others uncorking bottles and drinking to the health of old Charles.

Pamela is sitting cross-legged on the mattress in her room. She is listening to "The Hanging Garden" by The Cure and eating thick white prawn crackers. Her chin is covered in crumbs and Vernon instinctively wipes them away. She is not crying. "What about the tooth?" she asks. "Are you fixed?" He sits down next to her and recounts the visit to Paris, the tree uprooted in parc des Buttes-Chaumont, Kiko and his champagne, the people in the city he found most depressing. Then, in a neutral tone, she says, "So, the widow wanted to meet us?" Vernon turns his head towards her, moving only his neck, and hears a few vertebrae crack, as though he has started to rust. "Charles was a millionaire. He won the lottery. He left us half his cash. Well, assuming the widow is prepared to part with it. I'm not really sure what I think about the situation." Pamela carries on chewing, not taking her eyes off him.

"The lottery? And he never told us?"

"I don't think he ever told anyone. A million, maybe two, I'm not sure."

"And that's why you've brought the widow back here? You were afraid that otherwise she'd do a runner with the cash?"

"No. She was the one who insisted on coming."

"But it's in his will that he wants to leave us half the money?"

"He left a letter. Just a letter."

"That bitch. She'll never give us our share. You were right not to let her out of your sight."

Pamela leans towards Vernon, slides her hand along his neck and strokes the nape with her fingertips, a gentle pressure, then she kisses him on the temple and he has time to notice her scent, she smells a little like grilled almonds, she whispers into his ear: "Charles wouldn't like to see you with that face. Have you told the others?" "I'm heading there now." "Are you sad?" "He was a friend."

He does not say what he is thinking. He is thinking that no-one is solid. Nothing. No group. That it is the hardest thing to learn. That we are tenants of a situation, not landlords.

ON DEPARTURE DAYS, STÉPHANIE IS ALWAYS STRESSED. She knows that everything will be fine, that there's no reason to worry. But she is plagued by an invisible force that makes the most absurd ideas seem entirely plausible. She no longer wants to go on holiday, she was wrong to agree to this plan of going away with friends, she finds the prospect of leaving her apartment overwhelming, she's not ready, she has to pack the cases, print the tickets, her whole life seems to her to be a huge catastrophe, she has to make a superhuman effort to get a grip on herself and remember that no, suicide is not the only solution. You don't kill yourself just because you've planned to spend a few days in Barcelona. Even if it does mean catching a plane and remembering not to forget the kid's passport, you don't top yourself because of a weekend away.

In the kitchen, laundry is spinning. The frozen beans are simmering while a brief alarm, five shrill notes, reminds her it is time to take them off the stove. It is hot, and not a breath of wind comes through the open windows, she is stifling. The list of things she has to do before she leaves grows longer and, despite her rational sense, she is consumed by panic.

If it weren't for Lucas, she would cancel. She'd send a text message: "Got a vicious dose of diarrhoea can't be away from the toilet sorry". Anyone would understand that with a serious dose of the shits you can't go anywhere. She would feel so relieved to be able to weasel out. The tickets were ridiculously cheap, she doesn't care about wasting them. But it's a really big deal to Lucas. Disappointing her son is not the worst thing – it's hardly likely to be his last disappointment in life, he might as well get used to them early on – but she's worried that his father might make trouble. And when it comes to reprisals, Max is capable of the worst.

As she was buying the tickets, the voice of reason warned her – careful, you're always doing this, you launch yourself into things that are easy for other people but difficult for you – but she didn't listen. Stéphanie is bipolar. She made the diagnosis herself using the internet. During a manic phase, she is incapable of looking out for the person she will be in her other phase: a woman consumed with fear.

There were four girls in a small two-room apartment – ceiling roses, a small fireplace in the living room, polished parquet floor and a balcony blooming with geraniums overlooking the slate roof-tops. They had chugged white wine, dug out the karaoke machine and they were singing "Papa Don't Preach", one of their girls' night classics. Stéphanie had grabbed the mic for "Bitch Better Have My Money", she loves karaoke. Then the neighbour had buzzed the intercom to ask them to dial it down. He claimed he had knocked at the door but they hadn't heard. The evening was fucked.

Pénélope had just had surgery after doctors discovered her fallopian tubes were full of polyps. She had gone in for a routine examination, she and her fiancé Patrice wanted to start trying for a baby. She had three little holes in her belly where they had inserted the endoscopes. Grey sweatpants, purple cashmere top, she pinned up her hair, slipped on a coat and, despite the distance and the fact that she didn't have a red cent, she caught a taxi to go and meet up with them, she couldn't stay cooped up in her place a minute longer. Ever since they had met at the Bussang convergence, these evenings had become a ritual for the four.

The girls met up every Wednesday night. Pénélope, having had her operation three days earlier, drank several beers, each time announcing, "This one's the last." She was anxious. She needed to talk. She was afraid that she wouldn't be able to get pregnant. "Patrice better have commando sperm, because getting as far as the eggs is an obstacle course, my tubes are a bloody maze."

Stéphanie found it difficult to work out exactly what the doctors had said to her, since Pénélope changed her story several times during the evening. Marie-Ange and Sylvie reassured her – given her age and all the modern technology they have these days, there was bound to be a way to help the little spermatozoids to reach their target. Stéphanie was honest: "And if you can't get pregnant, well, you need to remember that you don't have to be a mummy to be happy in life . . . it's not all fun and games, let me tell you."

Stéphanie loves her son. He is full of the joys of life, he has lots of friends, he tries his best at school. He's a filthy little pig, but aside from that he's a good kid, she's lucky. Even so, if she had her time over again, she wouldn't have a child. When you weigh up what it's cost her against what it's brought her it's simple. As a single woman, paying the bills every month was tough – add a kid to the equation and it's a disaster. Ever since he hit his teens, she's been a robot that says no. No to a tablet, no to a smartphone, no to tickets to see Maître Gims, no to the official Barça shirt . . . He treats her like a money tree. She sees friends who don't have children living amazing lives. Long lie-ins, going out whenever you feel like it, if you want to spend all day lying on the sofa in your socks, munching Haribo Strawberry Softies and binge-watching "Gilmore Girls", it's nobody's business but yours . . . When you've got a kid, you spend your days peeling vegetables only for him to tell you that he hates them, tidying up after him, making sure he does his homework, going to see his teachers, washing and ironing his clothes, taking him to football practice . . . Lucas is fourteen. He can empty the fridge in a day. He's constantly hungry. What can you do? He is growing so fast that it costs her a fortune in shoes. She can't complain when they're too tight, even though they're still wearable. The kid is growing in every direction. Since he hit puberty, she can't tell what he'll look like when he shows up for breakfast. One day, it's his nose that grows – bam – he used to have a cherubic little face and suddenly he's Quasimodo, another day, it's acne . . . What are you supposed to do? You survey the disaster, the suppurating pustules, you break open the piggybank and take him to the dermatologist and when she prescribes creams that are more expensive than La Prairie anti-ageing serum, you fork out. Then you have the orthodontist telling you your kid's teeth are growing crooked and he needs braces. The things cost a bloody fortune, but all the kids have them. You can hardly leave him with his teeth in that state just because you need to replace the old washing machine that stalls at the spin cycle. Then he needs glasses. You haggle over the frames, but in the end, you can't let your kid be ridiculed by the whole class for wearing cheap, nasty glasses, so you fork out . . . Meanwhile, you haven't had a new pair of shoes since 1997. But anyway, you call up the bank and ask for a loan. Doesn't matter whether you've got the means or not, the bill is the same. Recently, it's his voice that has been changing. When he phones her, she doesn't recognise him. When he talks she has to stop herself from giggling. Jesus – they don't call it the awkward age for nothing.

She works at a rehab centre where people are remanded by the courts. When someone is caught with drugs and the judge orders mandatory rehab, they wind up in her office. She sees all sorts, from the posh boy who's been caught snorting a line to a cocksure dealer who managed to get his charges knocked down to simple possession. But no, she can never spend an extra two hours at the office if there's an emergency, and no, she doesn't have time to have dinner with the therapeutic team, and no, she can't apply for an administrative role that would mean she had to travel, or work overtime. No-one has ever thought of her when it comes to promotion. Single mother, everyone knows what that means. Unless you live next door to your parents and you can dump your kid on them all the time. Which is not the case with her. From the day she became a mother, it was settled – no promotion. When she talks about this, there's always some mother insisting, not at all, it's just a question of getting yourself organised. This is bullshit. Stéphanie is super-organised. But a kid is a good twenty hours' extra work a week, work you can't wriggle out of. And she can't imagine being so organised she has no time to sleep.

When she said all this, Marie-Ange looked daggers at her. Like, motherhood is sacred, it is the core of a woman's happiness. Easy for her to say, she's got a guy at home. Xavier doesn't work. And, on the subject of guys . . . good luck falling in love when you've got a kid in tow. You fuck during school hours, so if the guy's got a job – you don't get laid. Besides, Lucas doesn't like the guys she sleeps with. And she can hardly claim it's because he's possessive. He'd really like her to find someone. It's just that he's more clear-sighted – she's constantly dragging home losers. When there's a conflict of interest between your son and the guy you've got the hots for – it's not your son that gets kicked into touch. The girls were outraged to hear her talk like this. But she tells it like it is, that's all. O.K., sure, you're never on your own again. But that's the problem: you're never on your own again. Marie-Ange and Sylvie glower at her, saying, you're not fit to be a mother, you should be ashamed. She doesn't give a damn. She's used to it. She drove the last nail home. She said to Pénélope, "Are you happy with your boyfriend? Yeah? Well, just remember that everything you love about your life with him ends the minute you have a kid. Having a family is the death of a relationship." At this point, she stopped, because Marie-Ange looked as if she could strangle her. Most women have trouble being honest about these things. Motherhood is like F.G.M. – women feel obliged to make sure everyone else does it.

She stopped there, having delivered the crucial points of her message. Having created a tense atmosphere, she backpedalled – she made her friends laugh. She started telling them about Lucas' recent fixation with jerking off. The girls were shocked but howling with laughter. It's true. For the past year, she's had to change Lucas' sheets every day. She buys boxes of Kleenex Man-Size and leaves them everywhere, otherwise he'll wipe himself off on whatever comes to hand. Poor kid must be exhausted. She never goes into his room without knocking. Sometimes she teases him when he spends ten minutes in the toilet after some torrid scene in a movie.

She goes through his phone to check that he's not getting threatening text messages from the other kids at school – she's afraid of him being bullied. It's her worst nightmare. Lucas is a sweet boy, he's incapable of defending himself, physically or verbally. She's terrified that one day some moron at school will film him naked doing something dumb and he'll end up being a laughing stock. This is how she knows he looks at porn, his search history is an encyclopaedia of XXX. His father says she shouldn't go rooting around in his things, that she's invading his privacy. That she doesn't know what it's like, being a teenage boy.

Only when he's singing can she be sure he's not jackin' the beanstalk – he can't manage both at the same time. Lucas sings out of tune. And there must be – what? – four billion songs in the world . . . But Lucas, he sings the Marseillaise, he does little segues, a sort of Addams family "buh-buh-buh-BUM", then he launches into Maître Gims.

She managed to ease the tension with stories of her son's wanking feats. Marie-Ange had tears in her eyes from laughing so hard. "But what's with him singing the Marseillaise?" she asked. "It's because of the January 7 attacks. He's become patriotic. After the *Charlie Hebdo* massacre, he came home all proud of himself and told me he'd observed a minute's silence without clowning around. I said, I should hope so, don't think I'm going to congratulate you for that. Though it has to be said that the kids at his school . . . you should see them, they're terrifying. Even back when he was in primary school, I'll always remember this, he was playing in his room with a couple of classmates and suddenly I hear him yelling, 'Better watch out, I'm dangerous as Mohamed Merah' like he was saying he was the Pope, or Batman. I burst into his room and snapped, 'What did you just say?' and my kid smiles up at me, pleased with himself, and says, 'I'm dangerous as Mohamed Merah.' He'd learned it at school. He didn't expect me to take it badly. I read him the riot act and, let me tell you, by the time I finished he knew there was a problem. And the other two, they were just like my son – one look at them and you knew they hadn't heard something like this at home." Since that day, every time she sees Latifa Ibn Ziaten on T.V. she fetches Lucas and sits him down in front of the screen. And then she asks him: "You think he's powerful, the moron who murdered that woman's son?" All that to end up here: her son singing the Marseillaise as he brushes his teeth. It almost makes her appreciate Maître Gims. But at least when he's singing he's not wanking.

By this point of the story, Marie-Ange did not have the heart to laugh, she asked, "So are there a lot of rough kids at his school? Have you never thought of putting him into a private school?" And Stéphanie shook her head. "Where I come from, we go to secular schools. It's not like I've got the money to pay for a school, but even if I was stinking rich, I wouldn't send my son to a private school. And if you think that sending your daughter to Notre-Dame-de-what-the-fuck means she'll turn out less of a fucktard than my son, you're kidding yourself . . . She'll come home reciting passages from *Mein Kampf*, and you won't be very happy either. The only solution is not to have kids, the times we're living in are completely screwed-up. We keep coming back to the same situation."

Marie-Ange was not prepared to let her have the last word. "I don't agree, I think that's precisely why it's important that people like us have kids – because we educate them differently, and the world we live in needs well brought-up kids." Stéphanie did not respond. Marie-Ange's boyfriend is a bit fascist around the edges and, the way Stéphanie sees it, there's no shortage of guys like that these days, rather the reverse. She had said what she needed to say to Pénélope – you never know, she might even listen. You're looking at twenty years without parole. And that's it, that's the real difference between men and women.

It was Max who wanted a child. It was his idea. She had the child. But him, he's a father when he can spare the time. A little less than every other weekend, as it turns out. The same goes for child support: he pays it when he can. And all his friends slap him on the back, "Respect, bro, you're really looking out for your kid." He takes Lucas to a boxing match once a month, to a concert, or to Disneyland because he's got a friend who works there on and off and lets them in for free . . . and if you ask Max how he's dealing with fatherhood, he'll tell you: "I'm nailing it." But if a woman treated her children the way Max treats his son, she'd have the perfect parenting police on her tail, non-stop. And they've got spies everywhere.

Pénélope changed the subject. "I'm fed up, it's supposed to rain again tomorrow, I'm sick and tired of this weather," and Marie-Ange said, "I really fancy a weekend in Barcelona." Sylvie said, "You know if you book in advance, the flights cost less than thirty euros?" and Stéphanie piped up, "I've wanted to go there for years. Max's sister lives there and she has a daughter Lucas' age, she's forever suggesting that he come, so she can take him on a tour of the Barça stadium, but I'm worried about putting him on a plane on his own, Lucas isn't the brightest crayon in the box, he'd probably end up in Bamako, the moron . . ."

And that was how she had ended up in this nightmare situation.

The girls looked up the price of tickets, opened their diaries to find a weekend that suited everyone. And Stéphanie went along with it . . . in spite of the little voice of reason.

They were still in a warm bubble, an extension of the atmosphere at the convergence. Stéphanie had shown up there by accident. She had had dinner with Olivier, a guy she had met twenty years earlier in Angers, when she was still a student and never missed a gig by Les Thugs, Casbah Club, or Cut the Navel String . . . Olivier used to hang out with the guys from the indie label Black & Noir, and he had been a little in love with her. It had been a late-night friendship, a flirtation that had never come to anything, one that should have faded and died with time. But when she moved to Paris, they bumped into each other at La Cantada. At the time, Olivier was working for Radical Production, he got along well with Max, whom Stéphanie had just met. Olivier had become a happy, contented father, but unlike most of her former suitors who cut her dead the day they stopped dreaming of a future with her, Olivier had remained friendly. Ever since, they've regularly met for dinner, without any blurred lines – something Stéphanie finds faintly disappointing. One night, Olivier spent the whole evening talking about Subutex's convergences and Stéphanie listened, though she found it a little boring. She thought maybe he was having a mid-life crisis, a bizarre kind of time travel that involved going to raves in muddy fields and necking handfuls of Molly. It's such a waste, she thought, if you're going to lose the plot, you'd be better off cheating on your wife with me . . . Olivier was invited to the next convergence. He was happy as a sandboy. He explained that the selection process was very rigorous, because the organisers didn't want to end up with four hundred arseholes. "It would ruin the magic." This was the era of V.I.P.s and velvet ropes, of people who knew people and appreciated things precisely because others are excluded. Then, suddenly, he said, "I'm driving down tonight, why don't you come with me? I'm allowed to bring one guest. You've got a licence – aren't you from some godforsaken village in the country? We can share the driving. What do you say?" And it was so unexpected that Stéphanie did not have time to panic. From the ambience of a grown-up dinner, they slipped straight into youthful pandemonium, Stéphanie just had time to swing by her place and grab a couple of T-shirts and some clean underwear while Olivier skinned up a mild spliff "for the road", between them they felt a wanton bubbling excitement, the sort of rash complicity that prompts such adventures.

She felt intoxicated by this freedom, this recklessness that for years had characterised her life and which she had completely forgotten. If he had let her sleep on the idea, she would have changed her mind – the notion of driving through the night to go dancing in a field would have seemed grotesque. But he swept her along. She had left her mobile phone at home, as he had requested. For the first hour, this panicked her – if something happened to Lucas, no-one would be able to contact her, etc. But Olivier calmed her, he reminded her that people had lived for most of their lives without smartphones, besides, this was how things were at the convergences – no-one takes selfies, no-one goes online. It's important. She almost snapped, "Well, excuse me for thinking my son is important," but Olivier simply shrugged. "I've got kids too. We're talking twenty-four hours when they can't get in touch. We grew up without our parents calling us every hour, remember?

And we didn't exactly suffer." She said nothing. He had annoyed her. But when he put on the Bee Gees she relented and started singing in the car. It's difficult to sulk convincingly when you're listening to "Stayin' Alive".

They had driven all night. They listened to Curtis Mayfield. Olivier had stopped at a petrol station and bought dark chocolate. Dozens of bars of dark chocolate. He had explained that all participants left something behind "for the commune", it could be whatever you liked. He said, chocolate is good, it's full of magnesium and it's easy to store. Then they pulled over and slept for a while in the car and she was a little disappointed that he didn't slip his arm around her shoulder, that they didn't abandon the idea of the convergence to go and discuss geopolitics in a hotel room, but she was too exhausted to truly focus on her frustration.

They had arrived in the city in the late morning with the sun beating down. Olivier's face was drawn from exhaustion, it made him look older, Stéphanie decided it suited him. He had left the car in a car park and they had walked to the square outside the train station.

They had to wait for the "shuttles", in this case, three beat-up little cars ferrying people back and forth. Needless to say, it was a long wait, since there were a lot of people. They had sat on the ground and gorged themselves on croissants. Stéphanie wondered how long it had been since she had last sat on the ground doing nothing. It was strange. There was already something in the air. A childlike joy. The convergents acknowledged each other, smiled at each other. Stéphanie had been to a few raves back in the '90s. She had good memories. She loved M.D.M.A. She doesn't take it anymore. The comedown leaves her with a vicious headache. As with most new drugs, it had taken a while before people realised the dangerous side effects. Molly can make you depressed. The reverse of how you feel coming up on it. A nasty boomerang.

When they arrived at the place where the convergence was being held, she hadn't been surprised at the sea of tents being pitched, the calm good humour of people glad to be there. It was a familiar atmosphere. It takes a little while to read a crowd, at first all you notice is the multitude. Gradually, her eyes took in the details. The crowd was largely white – though not as disproportionately so as at a techno night or an indie gig. In terms of age, it was pretty mixed. There were a lot of people her age, but there were young people too, there were even older folk who couldn't strut about and needed someone to support their elbow and help them sit down. There were slightly more women than men, which immediately made Stéphanie stress out – if this was a girlie thing, she couldn't imagine it being anything extraordinary. If something's truly brilliant, guys show up – Q.E.D.

Thankfully, there were a number of fine specimens of manhood to make up for it. They ranged from the sensational – there was one young black guy in particular, with piercing eyes and abs that looked like they had been precision-moulded, who made such an impression she figured she was in the right place at the right time.

Stéphanie recognised an ageing rock critic she hadn't seen in years and they said hello. He was walking through the grass in his oilskin boots and his tailored three-quarter-length coat, bald but elegant. He talked to her about chemtrails, pointing to the white streak in the sky, and she was surprised that a guy like this would buy into that kind of conspiracy theory. She said: "Do you really think the government would poison us just for the hell of it, and do it in broad daylight, without even trying to conceal it, when it would be a whole lot easier to put something in the water supply?" and the journalist said, "Yeah, that's what's so intense, they don't even feel they need to hide it anymore. After all, what could we do?"

She carried on walking while Olivier napped under an oak. In the distance, she saw a couple of forty-something punks, one guy had orange liberty spikes, the other had a red mohawk that was black at the roots, both pretty craggy. Khaki jackets, beat-up sneakers, old tattoos with fading ink. Seeing them, she thought, there they are, typical gutter punks. As she drew alongside, they shared a long, languorous kiss. Maybe not so typical, then.

There was no stand selling drinks. There was nothing for sale, no booze, no kebabs, no T-shirts. That, and the absence of her mobile, which she instinctively rummaged for in her pocket at regular intervals, seemed a little worrying. How were you supposed to kill time if you couldn't drink, couldn't buy food, and couldn't check your timeline? People were taking the rules so seriously she began to wonder whether she hadn't stumbled into a sect. Not a single selfie, not a single surreptitious text message . . . It took some time for her to put her finger on what she found most troubling in the pre-rave atmosphere: the gentleness. And with gentleness comes an innocence: to be gentle is to assume that everything is going to be fine. Strangers were smiling at each other. People who didn't know each other were chatting, as though they had been transported back to childhood and were at a holiday camp. There was something old-fashioned about the collective atmosphere that was reminiscent of '70s music festivals.

She had recognised Patrice, whom she had known back when

she was with Max but had not seen since. He'd always been fuckable. Highly fuckable, in fact. And he hadn't changed much. He introduced her to his girlfriend, Pénélope, and Stéphanie sized her up: too pretty, too young, too comfortable in her own skin. No way would she be able to steal the guy from under *her* nose. Since Plan A was a non-starter, she befriended Pénélope, who was also fairly new to all this. Together they headed off in search of the little girls' room – a row of compost toilets at the far end of the camp, unsurprising, given the location. Pretty well kitted out, as it happened, you didn't retch the minute you stepped inside. Everyone was so responsible that no-one splashed their piss all over the sand. All this consideration was starting to get on her tits.

Pénélope said that this was her first convergence, although she had visited the camp a month earlier. "When there's just seven or eight people the atmosphere isn't the same, obviously . . ." "I don't get it – what the hell do they do? Play cards? Breed sheep? What's their thing?"

Pénélope could not say with any certainty.

"They're just unemployed, I suppose . . . They talk, they cook meals, they fix up some old banger . . . It's Patrice's trip, really. He's known them for ages. He says the convergences are magical. He persuaded me to come, he said that it's like levitation. That you have to experience it in person." Stéphanie was beginning to think that this was going to be like one of those movies everyone tells you is genius and when you see it you're disappointed because of all the hype you've been fed . . .

*

Marie-Ange and Sylvie were lying on a purple sarong embroidered with Indian elephants, in the shade of a yellow parasol. Pénélope had introduced them to Stéphanie, who sat down with them, since she didn't know anyone else at the camp. Further off, people were joining groups to take part in workshops – she hadn't bothered to find out what kind, she wasn't interested. Discussion groups, thanks but no thanks. Group hypnosis, not her kind of thing. Olivier was nowhere to be seen, otherwise she would have given him an earful: what the fuck is this place? Sylvie had not wanted to take part in anything either. Stéphanie spent the afternoon listening to people talk about life at the camp. Sylvie could talk at you for four hours straight without thinking to ask what you did for a living. And, in fact, this was how it had begun, their strange indolent complicity – that afternoon, lying on the grass with three girls she had just met. There was something childlike about the atmosphere between them – more bloody gentleness – a way of seeing each other, of joking.

As night drew in, no-one turned on a light. The girls sat chatting in the darkness. It was not dark enough to trip or bump into things, but you had to be attentive to capture an expression, a change of tone, a gesture.

Gradually, the crowd began to gather in the hulking former printworks where the ritual or ceremony was to take place. The vast room was plunged into semi-darkness. Stéphanie had found herself alone. Since it was impossible to see exactly what everyone else was doing, being on one's own was not embarrassing in the way it usually was – she didn't have to worry about what other people might think, about Olivier seeing her from a distance and thinking, poor thing, she's hopeless in social situations, about some stranger judging her: "It's because she's not pretty enough, no-one's interested, she's a wallflower." She had only to huddle close to the wall, wrapped up in a blanket, and she disappeared. She had thought about the Thiéfaine lyric, "solitude is not a shameful disease", and, in that moment, her whole plan for the evening was to close her eyes and doze off – catch up on a few hours' sleep before heading back the next day. She no more believed in the magic of this gathering than she did in the chemtrails explained to her by the rock critic who she now spotted in the distance, whirling round, like some dazed, ageing dervish. From the loudspeakers placed at random along the walls came a soft, bizarroid techno drone, sound waves that occasionally prickled the base of her spine, her throat or her solar plexus . . . A mic was passed from hand to hand, people had come prepared with short texts, poems or political manifestos. She paid no heed to the words. She did not resent Olivier for bringing her here, because the trip had done her good, she felt as though she had been away for days. But she couldn't understand why he would drive all night to listen to adolescent poetry over a backwash of boats creaking or the earth crumbling. She had probably fallen asleep. She recognised the first bars of "Roadhouse Blues". After that, she remembers nothing until she was suddenly wide awake. The voice of Grace Jones was echoing around the building. The centre of the room was filled with people – the silhouettes had converged and were moving, some slowly, others still entwined, or tracing circles around each other. And then she saw – not with the clarity of a hallucination brought on by acid or shrooms, but even so she *saw*, and could not claim it was a dream since the illusion lasted long enough for her to be entirely aware of it – light waves surrounding the bodies and she could perceive ribbons of energy, writhing and moving between people. She is a rational person. Unless on drugs, she did not expect to see coloured streamers connecting people.

She doesn't like it when people read her cards, she doesn't believe in the supernatural, she has no truck with spells and curses. But here, in the darkness, she could see things that did not exist. And the most unsettling thing is that she did not deliberate, did not decide to get up – she simply found herself on her feet, hands in the air, an idiot smile plastered to her face. She was dancing. And although she was not touching anyone, not brushing up against another body, she recognised the feel – she was orgasming. It had nothing to do with sex and yet this was the most incredible fuck she'd ever had in her life.

The sun came up and she was still dancing. She had gently emerged from the trance at the same time as the other convergents. She had tracked down Olivier, smiled at him, and two hundred kilometres down the road, as they were hurtling back to Paris because she had to work early the next morning, she became aware that the smile had not left her lips. For several days, she found herself enveloped by this mild, very distinct state of euphoria. And when Pénélope had suggested that they meet up for a drink with the girls at Sylvie's place, she had immediately accepted.

The washing machine beeps to indicate the cycle is finished. Stéphanie sets down her newspaper and automatically gets to her feet, obedient to the house. To her time-consuming need to be regulated. She piles the wet laundry into a basket and takes it into the bedroom to hang it next to the window. She is also anxious because this will be the first time she has gone on holiday with Lucas' father, Max, since their separation.

When she arrived back from the convergence, she was still spaced out when Max brought Lucas home. Her eagle-eyed ex had said, "You've met someone . . . over the weekend, you met someone . . ." She related her strange adventure with Olivier. Max listened, pulling ridiculous faces and saying, "What's with this New Age bullshit, honey, honestly, don't you think it's time you did something with your life?" He rarely missed an opportunity to let her know he thought her work was mediocre, that she should make a new life for herself, have another child – because, for women, the clock is always ticking – take herself in hand, etc. Max has a knack for demolishing her morale, which also gives him the opportunity to console her – he is adept at both.

Two weeks later, he came back to pick up Lucas and she mentioned the weekend in Barcelona. "Guess who I'm going with. You remember Xavier? I'm going with him – well, with his girl-friend. The other girl is going out with Patrice – you remember Patrice – though he's not coming because he has to work." And against all odds, Max said: "I'd love to go with you. I think it would be good for Lucas to see us together sometimes. We've been separated for long enough that I don't think he'd get his hopes up . . . I think he'd realise that his parents are close enough to want to spend a little time together. Don't you think it would be good for him? To see that adults can have other relations besides the nuclear family?"

She had not wanted him to come. The idea was absurd. Agonising. But Max is someone who takes no notice when a person says no. Every time she reads an online profile of the narcissistic pervert, she thinks of the man who fathered her son. A man who always ends up getting what he wants.

Narcissistic pervert . . . The phrase completely describes his behaviour and yet says little about him. Max was brilliant. He was funny, sophisticated, original, intelligent and caustic. He would take any subject and interpret it according to his highly individual intellectual perspective, he would shed a new and pertinent light on it. He saw the world from above, or at an angle – he was never quite where you expected him to be. Stéphanie owes a lot to him. Being with him changed her. Max was both demanding and generous. When they first met, he believed in her, supported her, pushed her, encouraged her. Then he got bored. She had disappointed him. He remained affectionate. But distant. As he might with someone he found profoundly tedious, whose best efforts were no longer good enough. She had simply not been good enough. A thought that she found devastating.

It is not that love is blind. You can see what's happening. You know you're being conned. You correctly analyse the situation. And still you stay. That's what's so bewildering. Stéphanie couldn't tell herself, I woke up one morning and I realised that he was gaslighting me so I decided to leave him. The evidence was already there. She had not been oblivious to the six hundred and fifty clues that indicated the guy was toxic. But love is not a cost–benefit analysis – you don't say to yourself: I'm getting out because this situation isn't good for me. Being Max's wife was more important than being happy. Because he was amazing. You don't stay with a "narcissistic pervert" because he blows hot and cold or because he undermines you. You stay because he is more brilliant than any man you've ever met before, than any man you will ever meet after. You stay because you realise that you're lucky to be granted access to such intelligence, such power. You stay because you know that, after this man, you will always be a little bored. Stéphanie lost a lot, being with Max. He cheated on her, humiliated her, lied to her, got her to believe that she was mediocre . . . and even so, it was worth it.

Lucas did not jump up and down at the idea that his father was coming with them to Barcelona, in fact he found the thought of having both his parents with him a little dreary. So, Max made promises – the Dragon Khan rollercoaster at PortAventura, tickets to a football match . . . promises he would not keep. That was his thing. When he says, "We'll have an amazing weekend," he's sincere. He's persuasive. Later he reneges and, because he feels guilty for reneging on his promises, he becomes aggressive. He looks for reasons to justify his behaviour. But Lucas is too young to mistrust his own father. He was taken in.

As she hangs out the laundry, she turns on the radio. They are talking about the migrant ship that sank off the coast of Libya on April 19. Eight hundred dead, they say. Twenty-eight survivors. They mention Syria Eritrea Somalia Libya. A cartography of terror. At the centre where she works, they sometimes deal with refugees. They get caught with crack. The voices of the experts who talk about this shipwreck never quaver. You get used to things. Not long ago, she had a boy of about twenty in her office. He had learned to speak French at the detention centre where he was held when he arrived. He told her about how his parents were massacred. About the money for the crossing. She was distraught. She found it discomfiting that he had learned to speak French so easily. What he is interested in is his papers. Not rehab. There is nothing she can do for him. You get used to things, of course. But even then, you can still remember a time when people pretended that human life had some value.

Stéphanie has been dosing the plant on the tiny balcony with heavy shots of fertiliser this year. The thing has grown into a shrub, it has produced bursts of flowers. Of a pink that is much paler than last year.

CAN SOMEONE EXPLAIN TO HIM WHY CLOTHING MANUFAC-
turers sew on labels so that they itch around the waist? You'd almost
think they do research to find the fabric that will chafe most. And
even if you carefully and meticulously cut the fucking thing off
with a pair of nail scissors, it still itches. Xavier would like to track
down the bastard who gets a kick out of designing these things,
break both his legs and see whether he still finds it funny to ruin
the lives of the people who buy his clothes.

He had been forced to buy an emergency T-shirt because he
hadn't packed enough clothes. He had never imagined Barcelona
would be so hot in spring. He had assumed light sweater, jacket,
jeans, not sweltering heatwave. He found himself wandering a
pedestrian precinct in the city centre at 10.00 a.m. He didn't feel
disoriented: the shop signs are the same as the ones on his street.
Doesn't matter where you go, it's always the same shit. Except that
here, you need a pedestrian permit to be able to wander around
without walking slap-bang into a tourist. They travel in herds, you
have to wait ten minutes to cross the street. There are Germans,
Chinese, Russians . . . all pug-ugly. Maybe governments make a
selection of their most unprepossessing citizens before dropping
them on Barcelona. Unsurprisingly, the French are the worst.
Noisier, more arrogant and more aggressive than tourists from
anywhere else. He's not planning to come back anytime soon. He
feels sorry that he belongs to this horde of parasites.

Xavier is waiting on the pavement with his dog while Marie-Ange and their daughter are buying a few things in a minimart run by Pakistanis. He studies the people inside, standing motionless in front of shelves of butter and cream. They are all painstakingly reading. Give them the complete works of Tolstoy and you couldn't get them to sit still, but when it comes to buying a litre of milk, you've got their complete attention. It's probably also because it's cooler next to the chill cabinets. Fucking stupid idea to come to a city like this in spring. The heat is crippling. Xavier loathes sunshine. He got more than he bargained for.

It was Marie-Ange who had come up with the idea of having lunch in the apartment Pénélope and Sylvie are renting. Everyone was sitting out on terraces, under huge parasols, in a lovely, quiet little plaza. Xavier had already checked out the menu and decided on the fried fish he was going to order when the ladies suddenly decided they wanted a healthy meal. They're terrified of putting on weight. It's true the Spanish seem to like their oil. But all they need to do is go for a thirty-minute jog every morning, they wouldn't put on an ounce. Instead, there had to be a forty-five minute debate to decide who was going to buy what to make lunch – and now here he is, standing outside the minimart, waiting for it to be over.

She can spend three hours buying broccoli and a dozen eggs. He knows his wife. She reads the labels of every product. She's capable of learning the language just to annoy the sales assistant. Meanwhile, he's dying of heatstroke and the dog has her tongue hanging out. Xavier keeps bending down to touch the tarmac to make sure it's not burning her paws. There are a lot of dogs in the city. He wonders how they survive the heat. His has been wandering like a lost soul searching for a patch of shade.

He loathes the heat because it makes everyone sluggish. But it also poses serious fashion problems: ridiculous hats, hideous sunglasses, short shorts, repulsive footwear. A smorgasbord of grotesquery, a cut-up of the worst that humanity can produce. He is surrounded by a sea of morons, drunken teenagers, fat women in sarongs, kids hamming it up for their parents' photos, lard-arses gorging on multicoloured ice creams . . . And the most preposterous, the most commonplace: tourists on wheels. They rent bicycles, scooters, rollerblades, skateboards, anything as long as it moves, and they glide around with smug smiles almost running over everything and everyone in sight . . .

Recently, his wife has been complaining that Xavier hates everything. What does she expect? Have you seen the shit we're surrounded by? And you want me to clap and cheer? He is not about to sit down and look at passers-by and think, they're clean, that's good, or, they're not going around killing people, that's great. Casting a benevolent eye over the world is fun: level zero.

He hates the yachts lined up in the harbour on the far side of the avenue. He abhors them, despises them with a fury that is delectable. When he was young, common people would walk along the marinas and stop to gaze at rich people's yachts. They were symbols of travel, of the exotic, of true luxury. These days the poor don't stop and stare anymore. Wealth is something they experience like a slap in the face as they pass – they take the beating, like an uppercut. Why would anyone drool over these things? Metric tonnes of shit, all looking like oversized plastic toys. The only advantage to these things is that everyone knows how expensive they are. The way Xavier sees it, anyone shelling out money for a yacht should have to undergo a psychiatric evaluation. The glories of the one per cent. A line of utterly identical yachts. All that differs is the size. It's the size that allows them to say to their neighbour, "Look, I've got more money than you." There's only one flag that flies on these yachts. The flag of tax evaders who stash their money in offshore accounts, who cook the books, who aren't subject to the same laws as everyone else. The flag of the one per cent and their inner circle. The owners may have been born in different countries, they may be Chinese or Arabs or Russians, but they all sail under the same flag. The language of banking is a metalanguage. It has taken the place of universal Newspeak. Compared to this, the divine right of kings was a botch job, a ham-fisted system that allowed anyone to slip through the net. The language of banking is something else. No-one can escape it.

Where are the fucking terrorists when you need them? Why couldn't they come here and blow them all up – one after another, like a roll of firecrackers. If anyone needed conclusive proof of the imbecility, the rank uselessness of those warriors of the apocalypse, this is it: they're capable of spreading terror, but they're utterly fucking useless when it comes to attacking the people who are really screwing up the world. If they came here and blew everything to smithereens, Xavier wouldn't be the only one to think: yeah, well, maybe they've got a point . . . Even guys like him would be forced to admit that they have a goal, a purpose, a plan.

In front of the yachts, four black guys are sitting on a low wall with huge Lidl bags between their legs. They're not talking. They're waiting for the police to move on so that they can spread out their blankets and sell their junk. Fake Nikes, fake Chanel handbags. Poor bastards don't exactly look like they're happy. No-one can tell him they wouldn't have been better off staying in their own country.

How much does a guy selling fake Adidas make? How much can he afford to send home to the family every month? Go figure ... Last night Marie-Ange got a foot massage from a Chinese woman worn out from hunkering on the sand all day long. He had asked himself the same question – how much does she get to send home at the end of the month?

What the limousine liberals don't understand is, just because he thinks "these migrants would be better off back where they came from" doesn't mean he's incapable of realising that their lives are shit, that they're victimised in ways that are inhuman and shouldn't be encouraged. Ferrying that misfortune to countries that are already at bursting point is absurd. It might not be a pleasant thought, but it stands to reason.

The left-wingers are the scourge of the convergences. They rock up, scowling like a bunch of middle managers unhappy with the efforts of the cashiers. They're offended by the idea that a guy like him can suggest that Christians and Muslims might have trouble living side by side. What about them, do they mingle? The reality is right there in front of their eyes in its glorious reciprocity: everyone hates everyone else's guts. Cultures don't come together in a harmonious melting pot with mixed-race babies scampering about and gurgling. Anyone with eyes in their head can see it doesn't work out like that. But no, they don't want to hear about it. They've been stuck in the same Benetton billboard ideology since the 1980s and they won't budge an inch. But, if you actually listen to them – not that you have much choice, they never fucking shut up – you quickly realise that it's just a question of labels. In general, they have only one idea in their heads: shifting the parameters that define their enemies. Those they don't want to talk to, those they refuse to respect, those they consider dangerous, guilty. Those they refuse to listen to. They want war just as much as everyone else. But they don't want to continually go around killing the same people. It's a difference of scale, but it still works out well for the arms manufacturers. The yacht owners don't have to worry. Everyone wants to buy their weapons. The left wing refuses to admit that Christians and Muslims can't live together for long without killing each other. That said, deep down, there is a fundamental agreement: exclude the impure, the unclean, prevent them from expressing themselves. Create a category of massacrables. The frontiers might shift, but the attitude of the border guards remains the same. You: get out. I don't want that sort of thing in my country. The only variable is who gets put into the camps. Who is torturable, exterminable. Who deserves to be excluded. Some people don't want to live with bosses, for others, it's Cameroonians, there are those who can't bear macho chauvinists, others who can't abide Gypsies, there are those who hunt down the anti-Semites in their own ranks and others who hunt down queers posing as married men . . . but we all wash whiter. We're all on the side of right. All we really care about is legitimising violence. It must be in a noble cause. Because we're happy to have blood on our hands as long as we have a clear conscience. That's the only difference between the sociopath and the political militant – the sociopath doesn't give a shit about being on the side of the just. He kills without the foreplay, without wasting time turning his victim into a monster. Militants, on the other hand, do it by the book: first the propaganda, and only afterwards the massacre.

But in the end, what everyone wants is to be among their own. To only have to rub shoulders with people like themselves. No interlopers. And the best way to cement any group will always be the common enemy. Xavier is not an idiot. All the great fortunes in France have modelled their speech on his, and it's not because they've been seized by a sudden burst of genuine patriotism. It's because it is in their interests for the little people to think of themselves as true-blood Frenchmen, victims of the great mosque rather than poor workers expropriated by the one per cent. He doesn't believe in the "great replacement". It's no accident that it's a queer conspiracy theory. Men who live with straight women know that. White people realise that they have to reproduce. Just look at Marie-Ange, she wants another one. This isn't for the personal satisfaction, they're perfectly happy as they are. It's because women know. There will be a war and if we haven't churned out enough little soldiers to fight it, it will be lost before it begins. So they breed, they breed, they breed . . .

The problem isn't the birth rate. The problem is the Church of France. If Christianity could heal itself, the darkies would have converted long ago and they'd be observing Lent instead of Ramadan. The sharp decline of missionary zeal is a much bigger problem than people attending mosque. Xavier is no fool. He understands things. Fifty years ago, the Church should have built cathedrals in the middle of every deprived *banlieue*. And sent out their best preachers. It wouldn't matter if they cuddled a few choirboys as long as they understood their mission. To help those most in need. To occupy the territory. Instead of which . . . the dumb fucking Christians congregated in rich neighbourhoods so they could celebrate the mass in Latin. How else can you explain why there are no French scouts in Seine-Saint-Denis? The only people who set foot inside the Basilica of Saint-Denis are tourists.

Even Africans change their religion. It's not exactly rocket science.

Listening to Sélim describe what it's like to see his daughter getting up at six in the morning to perform her ablutions before putting on her hijab to pray – this from a girl who was listening to Avril Lavigne and Miley Cyrus three months before she got sucked into Islam . . . it breaks Xavier's heart. It could happen to his daughter. He's been hearing a lot of stories like this. Girls without a care in the world who come home from school one day madly in love with Ahmed or Karim or whatever, and – bam. No more Haribo sweets – apparently they contain pork fat – no McDonalds – the cooking oil is contaminated – no vinaigrette – because there's alcohol in vinegar – no more lip gloss – because a good girl doesn't wear make-up. Sélim's daughter got to the point where she had to ask the imam if she could still eat sushi. Because of the rice vinegar. Luckily for her, the imam said yes, Japanese food is halal. If something like that happened to his daughter . . . But what can you do? Xavier often talks to Sélim and, though he often says he'd lock his daughter away, it's hardly a solution. When he listens to Sélim, he's reminded of his brother – he says, look, it could be worse, she could be hooked on heroin. Five daily prayers or five daily fixes – religion is not as harmful. The dealers are the same. You can bet that the kids of the guys who sold smack back in the '80s are Islamic fundamentalists now.

As a result, when he's with his daughter, he is more attentive than he used to be when it comes to the subject of religion. When he's in Paris for the weekend, they always go to Sunday mass. He's enrolled her in catechism class. You can't expect your kids to believe in nothing but the sanctity of Samsung.

*

At the camp, he talks to lots of people who are different from him. It makes a change. But he can't bring himself to stop hating the little ghetto thugs when he runs into them. Those guys don't like him. And he doesn't like them either. Where's the problem? Hatred is invigorating. You only need to go on Twitter to realise that everyone's at it. Trolling, insulting, fighting, it's good for the soul. It realigns your chakras, as the hippies in the camp would say . . . because the camp doesn't just attract left-wing loonies, you also get druids of every shape and size. It's astounding, the number of fuckwits the place attracts. There's something for everyone. Militant fatties, commie dykes, surly anarchists, university punks, political whores, macho transsexuals, people who are convinced there's another level of reality and there are doors that lead to it, etc.

Stopping racism, that's something he's against. They claim it stems from fear of the other, of the unknown . . . What dipshit came up with that brilliant idea? Someone who went to a posh university, probably . . . someone who had no idea what they were talking about, in any case. Hatred is a form of contact. You can only cordially despise people you rub shoulders with. Has there ever been an anti-Peruvian movement in France? Never. Because there aren't enough of them. No-one gives a shit about Peruvians, no-one knows any. Where are the Parisians who feel a knot in their stomach when they see a South American? Now, Muslims, on the other hand . . . The only fly in the ointment is that everyone gets involved. White people want the right to humiliate Arabs. It's something they've always done. It's amazing to think that these days it's the other way round. That they can show up anywhere and terrorise us. Not a comforting thought, when you're white. Firstly, because you're not used to it. And secondly, because once that happens how can you feel superior? If you allow yourself to be walked all over by people you've kept under your thumb for centuries, you can hardly be surprised that society is in crisis.

The people at the camp don't understand this. The minute he says, I'm racist, everyone looks at him like he's a retard. He's no fool: it's obvious that Sélim is more cultured and more articulate than most people who vote for Le Pen. But he's the exception, the one that proves the rule. The root of the problem is that my worth as a white guy is your worthlessness as a raghead. My high life makes you lowlife. My whiteness is something I take pleasure in only when you're drowning in your thousands and no-one gives a shit. It's nothing personal. That's why every racist has a close friend who's African. They're not dumb. They know that, taken on a case-by-case basis, there are always exceptions.

People tell him, it's stupid to be racist, it'll only bring you trouble, the whole thing is a nightmare. Maybe, but in the meantime, he finds it entertaining. While he's waiting for his wife outside the minimart, he finds it relaxing to see that the group of kids a hundred metres away are not Spaniards from the south, but Arabs from France who've come for the weekend. And to all the good souls out there, I'm sorry, but you can spot them a mile away. They always have to be causing trouble. And it does him good to cordially despise them. It keeps him occupied. Obviously, he's too old to get excited at the prospect of a war. No matter how macho and determined he feels, it's not what he dreamed of for his daughter. He imagined her studying abroad, then, when the time came for her to start a family, moving back to live near him. Things are not going to go as he expected. On that, at least, everyone agrees.

Sometimes he wonders if maybe he doesn't believe, at least in part. If Marie-Ange asks, "What's so interesting about this whole camp thing?" he laughs and says some people play golf, why shouldn't he spend the occasional weekend dancing with his buddies? He's always played the guy who's been there, done that, burned the T-shirt. He doesn't want to be caught nurturing naive pipedreams. So, he plays it cool. The people at the camp are his friends. He finds it relaxing, getting out of the city, getting a bit of fresh air . . . But, deep inside, a small thought has burrowed its way. There is something magical about the convergences, something that pervades their communal life. It is a very particular group of individuals who have nothing in common and yet instinctively manage to speak as one. In a dark corner of his mind, a space he doesn't talk about to anyone, Xavier feels that it's not impossible that one day he will say to his daughter: we created new possibilities. New openings. They are viable. We created a place where you can live differently.

On a bench, he sees a tramp lying on his side, asleep, surrounded by the crowd of tourists. The guy must be about his age. Xavier thinks about Laurent. The tramp at Buttes-Chaumont, one of the permanent residents at the camp in the very beginning, when some of them decided to terminate their leases, give up their former lives. For Laurent, the decision was not difficult, he didn't have an apartment. He integrated well, like Olga, the other dropout. Laurent would shuttle back and forth to the Zone to Defend in Notre-Dame-des-Landes, he became politicised. It was not a pretty sight. A lot of people complain that Xavier is tactless, but when it came to being subtle, Laurent was positively crass . . . He was racist too, though closeted. He was the sort of poor bastard who would lie about everything just so people would leave him in peace. But he was there, and he worked like a black whenever he came to the camp, he looked after the dogs and he liked to cook. He put too much onion into everything, but he was part of the landscape. He was the one who first mentioned the "tiny house movement". Xavier was none too happy about Laurent spending time at the Z.T.D. because they're all crust-punks with dogs in strings, and Laurent was easily influenced . . . every time he came back from the Zone, you had to spend three hours talking him down to set him straight again. Then, one day, he disappeared. It was Emilie who found him, completely by accident. Under the elevated métro on place Stalingrad, lying on a heating vent. Completely shitfaced. When she tried to talk to him, he called her every name under the sun. He didn't want to go back to the camp. He hated the lot of them. No-one ever found out what happened on that last trip. But redemption proved to be too much for him. After that, Olga lost the plot. She stayed at the camp. But, as though in solidarity, she stopped getting better. Xavier gets along well with Olga. Because of the dogs. They don't agree on anything, but it doesn't matter because when it comes to feeding the pack, you don't give a shit whether you're politically aligned or not. That's the point when you realise that what people think isn't really important. What's important is knowing whether the two of you can work together without wanting to smash each other's face in. And he and Olga, they get along. Since the day Laurent lay in the street, shrieking that he wanted nothing more to do with those punk-ass pansies at the camp, Olga has changed. It's something Xavier can understand. It's something they have in common: a certain reticence to being team players.

And they're right, both of them, to be on their guard . . . He has avoided thinking about it since his last visit to the camp, and yet he can feel an uncomfortable knot in his chest. Something is not quite right. Vernon came back from the dentist with that loathsome widow in tow. The news quickly spread – Charles is dead – and, each in their own way, they came to terms with this absence. Vernon said, "We need to talk," and everyone gathered around the table. There was something fishy going on. Otherwise why say "We need to talk"? That's what people say when they're about to break up with someone. Then came the announcement about the inheritance. Well, the possible, promised, inheritance. Because there's still no cash on the table.

Vernon should have been the one to inherit. It's only logical, he's the leader. Even if he's not cut out to be a leader. Or maybe *because* he's not cut out for it, because this group of fucked-up losers couldn't deal with a real leader. They needed this kind of weird guy at the helm, that way they could all carry on with their personal bullshit without feeling constrained. They cohabit as best they can, and, all in all, it's worked pretty well up to now.

After the announcement, there was a free-for-all of fucked-up fantasies. Olga wanted to buy camper vans so they could be like real gypsies. Sylvie talked about finding a farmhouse to renovate with fields around it that they could cultivate. Just like a baroness, Xavier thought, they always want to be driving around on tractors. Patrice could already see himself taking a year's sabbatical, he said, if we plan things properly, we could go round the world, all of us, we take a year, and we hold convergences up in the Andes . . . The notion of not seeing his kids for a year didn't seem to bother him unduly. Vernon thought that Charles would have wanted them to produce the zombie movie he was always talking about with the crazy airheads he was so fond of. He had looked to Xavier, probably assuming he'd be in favour of this film idea, since it would be an opportunity to write a screenplay. But no. Naked zombies eating everyone in sight? Soz. He's not twenty anymore. And he's not about to start working with a bunch of former porn stars and prostitutes. He has trouble enough with monogamy as it is. Daniel, who had just arrived, couldn't understand why they were arguing: they should put all the money into sound equipment. Because that's what they do, they make music. The Hyena was the last to speak, she waited until she was asked for her opinion and then announced, "We should follow the old bastard's example: put it in a bank account and get on with our lives. There's bound to come a time when we really need it. But right now . . . we're fine as we are. I don't see the point of changing anything." Patrice immediately sided with her. There was a hesitation. She said, "No-one knows where we are. There aren't many people who know what we do. That's important. If we start dealing in cash, we'll be back to square one, and we all know what happens when you've got money: it's never enough. Give it a couple of months and all we'll be talking about is how to get more." Pamela was rubbing her temples, it was obvious she found the whole thing stressful. "Yeah, but this thing about not having social security, it's not a religion . . . we're allowed to evolve. It wouldn't do anyone any harm." At this point, Olga, who was still thinking about her camper vans, said, "The one thing we do know is that we've got enough problems managing this place as it is with every fuckwit in a hundred-mile radius telling us what we should do and how and in what order, so if word gets round that we're sitting on hundreds of thousands of euros, it'll become impossible.

I propose we blow the lot, in less than a week. We open an account, we hold the widow hostage until she coughs up our shares. And 5, 4, 3, 2, 1 . . . we blow the lot. At least we'll have a laugh." Olga had managed to tame the widow, and they made a disturbing couple. They had started discussing setting up a refugee centre that would also be a kennel. Xavier couldn't help but blurt out, are you fucking insane? The Syrians will eat your dogs before you can blink. It'll be war. She had hesitated for a second, unsure whether he was serious, then she burst out laughing – "The worst thing is you're right! These guys, they've been through hell, so it's going to be diffi-cult to explain to them that they have to be nice to the little doggies."

It was pandemonium. Everyone was in their own little bubble, working their own crazy idea. No-one was getting angry, because no-one was listening to what anyone else was saying. It didn't feel like the mood of the camp. It felt like any random group of individuals who had nothing in common.

Marie-Ange emerges from the minimart carrying two huge plastic bags. His daughter is sucking on a bright-red lollipop. She eats too much sugar. He doesn't say anything. He hands his daughter the dog lead and takes the two bags. It's nearly two o'clock. They're not going to be eating any time soon. Jesus, he fucking hates weekends away with friends! But he makes an effort. He fakes it. He figures it will all be over soon.

Marie-Ange is accommodating with him. She looks after their daughter when he goes down to the camp. She likes to tease him, mocking his tent and his plans to go to a rave, but it's not hurtful. It's all in fun. She claims she doesn't understand what the hell he's doing with those crackpots, but she can see it's good for him.

She says you know there are people who pay a hundred euros a session every week to feel good about themselves . . . O.K., so you need your bus fare, but we can live with that . . . It matters to him that she's able to accept something that she doesn't understand. God, it's fucking depressing how *nice* they are to each other! Niceness has replaced love. What remains is this respect, this wish for the other to feel happy. A tenderness. It's not as ugly as hatred. But it's not as intense, either. They are both in mourning for the time when they really loved each other, when they believed.

Xavier is faithful. This is no mean feat. He has uncontrollable urges. Elsewhere. During the convergences, he listens to young guys talking about polyamorous relationships. He cocks his ear. Kids of divorced parents who don't want to repeat their parents' mistakes. So they are trying to find a way to reconcile desire with a long-term relationship. It's a typical left-wing idea: it only works on paper.

Xavier is faithful, but he hasn't touched his wife in more than a year. He is faithful to their agreement – faithful to their shared apartment, the affectionate gestures every morning, the after-dinner conversations. He is faithful to the family structure of parents supporting their daughter. He knows that it cannot last. And that terrifies him.

Vernon is racking up conquests and Xavier wonders whether he would enjoy that. He never stops, the dirty bastard. The haughty athlete, the Italian princess who looked like a catwalk model, the fragile little blonde who was so sweet she was irritating but pretty as a picture, the androgynous skinhead with the bee-stung lips and pale eyes who never smiled, the Venezuelan stacked like Miss World who could spend all night talking about Chavez if you let her . . . One after another they came and went with no drama. The latest has lasted a little longer. The girls are surprised that she's not the prettiest. But the guys all know what Vernon sees in her: she's chill. Xavier himself would be happy to have a girl like that by his side. Shit.

They go back to the apartment on the harbour that Pénélope and Sylvie rented on Airbnb. The women commandeer the kitchen. They summarily take the little girl with them and it occurs to Xavier that maybe he would prefer it that his daughter not feel constantly obliged to make food when she grows up.

He cracks open a beer and, gazing out at the street, he waits for it to be over. They chatter and peel and giggle and one of them puts on an album by Marianne Faithfull and they sing out of tune as they make something vegetarian that's going to take two hours before it's edible. He watches the tourists in the street wander around with their road maps. Stéphanie and Max, her ex, show up, raving about the weather and the palm trees. They've just come from the beach, trailing fucking sand everywhere. They arrive laden with bottles and packets of crisps, which does something to alleviate Xavier's distress – he knows that if he tells Marie-Ange he's just popping down to get some beers, she'll give him that mournful look she has when he drinks too much and she's afraid he'll embarrass her in front of her friends. He's delighted to see they brought the right crisps, the ridged-cut ones he prefers. He senses Max trying to catch his attention. Ever since they rocked up, he's been trying to buddy up to Xavier. Bingo: he leaves Stéphanie to scurry into the kitchen and sits down next to him. Even though it's obvious Xavier is in no mood to chat. He's only interested in eating.

For this to be over. Not that Max could give a flying fuck, he tells Xavier about the problems he's having with the guy subletting to them, with whom he's been in an e-mail war all day. "So, yesterday, when we go out, I leave the window open a crack, just to air the place – the apartment is really humid – and when I get back, what do I find? A note telling me not to do it again – fucking gibberish Google translate, to boot – I mean if the guy doesn't speak French, why write in French? When I talk to him, I speak Spanish. Well, last night, when I found the message, I went and told him exactly what I thought, and not in Spanish, in French, and I swear he understood every word and I bet today he leaves the window open. The cunt is charging us a hundred and fifty euros a night for two rooms, and I'm not allowed to open a window?"

Xavier doesn't understand why Max came with his ex-wife. It's a subject that fascinates Marie-Ange. At night, she loves to debrief him on the state of other people's relationships. Xavier gets the impression that this is her way of talking about their own problems, in a roundabout way. Last night, she went on for hours. "You think he's trying to get back with her? They didn't even take Lucas with them today to do something as a family . . . That's weird, isn't it? I don't think Stéphanie is interested. Or maybe she's playing hard to get . . . who knows?" Xavier wanted to sleep, but for the third time he had to tell her everything he knew about Max. He doesn't know the guy personally. But in the rock industry, everyone knows Max's reputation. He was Alex Bleach's manager. The legendary first manager, like Malcolm McLaren, Kim Fowley or Marsu . . . the one who turned a two-bit singer into a rock star. He was also a legendary crook. A colourful character Xavier has always avoided like the plague. He was surprised to discover Stéphanie had never told the girls that her ex, the guy who fathered her son, had had his fifteen minutes of fame. Though it does date back to the early '90s, it has to be said . . . Stéphanie isn't the sharpest knife in the drawer, she always has to be the centre of attention, she's loud, he finds her exhausting.

Xavier has no desire to hang out with Max. Last night, Max buttonholed him about the convergences, making no secret of the fact that he'd like to be invited, and Xavier had to kick the subject into touch. He's not the kind of character you want to bring back to the camp. A shady, lying, swaggering, devious manager . . . no thanks. Xavier acts like he's on the spectrum, sipping his beer and staring out the window. He is watching a group of girls, they seem young, they're elbowing each other and laughing too loudly. Some of them are wearing short shorts and high heels, they've got legs that go on forever, narrow hips and big breasts. They look like characters in manga porn, too much leg, tiny arse, huge tits. They're all strutting around with their phones, the way people used to strut around with cigarettes – Xavier is convinced that if one of them takes a picture, they'll each have their little pose: duck face pout, cheeks sucked in, fingers making a V sign. Max is looking at them too.

"So, it's the girls down there that have got you in the mood? They remind me of majorettes. Do you remember majorettes? I've never said this to anyone, but – did you ever wonder why sex shops sell handcuffs and nurse's uniforms, but not majorette costumes?"

MATHILDE HAS BEEN BOMBARDING HIM WITH TEXT MESSAGES. She is furious that he has gone on holiday with the mother of his child without suggesting she tag along. She is too young to understand. Max has tried to explain things to her calmly and gently. But she refuses to listen. He likes the fact that she's jealous. That she ruins her make-up crying like a spoilt little girl who can't have everything she wants. She bitches that she hasn't had a holiday, that she's always wanted to visit Barcelona, tells him the weather in Paris is grey and adds crying-face emojis. And when she realises he is not going to give in, text her back and say, O.K., darling, I'll buy the ticket, come join me, she shifts into overdrive, screaming that she knows he's still sleeping with that old cow, that he prefers his ex to her, that he's a fucking pervert, and a variety of bullshit accusations she makes up over the course of the weekend. He's put his mobile on silent. It won't do her any harm to torture herself a little. That's how people grow attached. A few days alone in her studio apartment, worrying that he's cheating on her, reading her cards and phoning her girlfriends will bind her to him more securely than all the gifts he could give her. He knows she's going to spend all night sending horrible messages, making a fool of herself. And this will break something between them. He will lose a little of the respect he has for her. It's a pity. He really had to spend this weekend in Barcelona. He can't go into details, but he had to come. If she can't understand that a man of his age needs some autonomy, well, too bad for her.

Mathilde is pretty as a picture. Her legs are a little too short, her nose a little too big, he's already suggested surgery, she's afraid it will hurt. She has lots of ambition. But she lacks the essential: grit. She's been too spoiled. She thinks it's possible to be a success without getting hurt. He's very fond of her. But he also needs a bit of air. She lives in a tiny studio tucked behind place Pereire, in a dreary neighbourhood, miles from anything. So, she spends all her time round at his place. It was different in the beginning. She was more independent. He had to work to get her. It follows the same arc as all his affairs: he struggles to get the girl he wants and when she gives in he's embarrassed for her.

He was happier when she had that little job at the C.S.A. – she watched T.V. shows and ticked boxes on broadcasting authority forms to indicate whether the cast included enough Arabs and women. She did that for a while and then they said thanks, that she'd been on a fixed-term contract for too long and the only way they could keep her would be to make her permanent. When she told him that they had made her redundant and she was going to take up singing full time, it broke Max's heart. He knew that, from this point, things were going to get ugly. He is twenty years her senior. He knows the music business. She's with him to further her career. She's convinced herself that she's in love because she doesn't want to admit the truth to herself – a pretty thing like that sleeping with a man his age, it's always about self-interest. It's his contacts she's interested in. He'd like to be able to help her. But she doesn't have the talent.

He still finds her just as attractive. Except that she smothers him. She is completely transparent. She thinks that if there was a problem, he'd talk to her about it. It infuriates him that he enjoys it, her puppy love. Her faith in him. She is completely untainted, and her huge eyes gaze at him adoringly. He's got bad breath. She pretends not to notice. Her smile is worthy of an Oscar. She says: "You're handsome." He knows that he's ugly. He is touched that she makes the effort to lie. How could he believe her? Looking like he does. Bloated, old, decrepit. But he swells with gratitude. She turns to him with her big green eyes, a very particular green. Which have such a profound effect on him. He'd love to have the nerve to ask if he can tie her up, put a ball-gag in her mouth and trample her on the shitty carpet in the living room. He knows that she would say no. She's not very talented when it comes to sex. She has trouble letting herself go. And it's not because she's too cerebral. He longs to see carpet burns on her knees from being fucked too hard. He has rarely come across a girl who rations sex so much. That's something else he's tired of. It's humiliating to have to beg all the time. In her, everything is repressed.

Max would love to delude himself, to think that, in her, he has got something, that he could make a great singer of her. She has a sweet voice. The way she moves is cute. Her songs are fine, but not incredible. She's very much of her time. She doesn't know how to start a song. She can't write lyrics but she doesn't want to ask anyone else to write them because she wants the publishing royalties. On her computer, she picks out tunes that aren't terrible. But she doesn't have what it takes. She doesn't have the talent or the mindset of a great artist. She thinks all you have to do is a quick booty pop, pout your lips like you're sucking cock and hey, presto, you're Beyoncé.

Max has known better days. Alex was an amazing performer back when Max managed him. During gigs, he would go down into the crowd and whoop with joy between songs. He would let out long, deranged howls and it wasn't about hype, it was completely sincere: he was crazy about the guy. If you've got an ear for it, talent is easily recognised, it's obvious. He feels nostalgic for that period of his life.

Even when Mathilde tries to play the slut, she lacks the depravity. She's not even lewd. Just docile. She checks out hot moves on YouTube and mimics them. And she's headstrong. Clueless and headstrong. Max tries to convince her to do cover versions. She might make something of Lio's "Bébé vampire". Everyone's forgotten that amazing first song. Maybe one of the best French singles ever. Mathilde wants him to help her, but refuses to take his advice.

Audiences have changed. God, what a fucking blast it was back in the day! Kids who were supercharged, savage, uninhibited. They'd come away from a gig completely drained. Because it takes two to put on a gig. Alex Bleach was great because he had a great audience. He had a following to die for. Max had a hand in it too, he took care of the fans. Kids who were political but not parochial, always listening to whatever was exciting, always on the lookout for a new album that would blow them away. You should have seen them after a gig, gangs of them hanging around the backstage door waiting for a wave from Alex.

With Mathilde, it's more difficult . . . her following is mostly young girls, fifteen tops, naively cynical, difficult to read for a man his age. A volatile, demanding audience, proud of what they don't know. For an artist, breaking out of the YouTube tsunami is no mean feat. Oh, he's invested a couple of hundred euros buying "likes" and followers to boost the little video she made. It's done manually in Bangladesh, apparently. Talk about a McJob. But it's not enough for an artist to take off. That would be too easy. He managed to get a couple of articles to highlight Mathilde's online success – he still has a few press contacts – but he couldn't generate a buzz. It's no secret: if you want to be a success, you've got to have something to sell . . .

The alchemy between him and Alex is something he's never found again. They held all the cards, and together they were a phenomenon. They were epic. Jesus fuck, they made a killing! And winged it when they had to. Max had the patter, the brilliant ideas, the vision and a real rapport with producers, journalists, tour managers . . . and Alex had the beauty, the voice, the lyrics, the swagger. An insolence that wasn't fake – the kid was dangerous. He was determined to succeed, he'd have lopped off his right hand with a chainsaw if it meant filling Bercy stadium. But betraying your roots is never easy, and he hated himself for his success. That tension made everything he did interesting. Seven years they spent riding the wave together – every door opened for them. And then Max, who'd given 110 per cent, hit a bad patch. He made a few minor slip-ups. But managers are forgiven nothing. The artist can get away with whatever he likes. But a manager makes one little mistake, and they're calling for his head on a platter.

Max committed a few minor budgetary indiscretions . . . Not that he's looking for an excuse. He owns his mistakes. He managed to get hold of Alex's banking details and made a few insignificant transfers to his own account without telling anyone. Bupkis. Alex blew it out of all proportion. In his paranoid state, he forgot a few details that mitigated in his manager's favour. Like the fact that Max was underpaying himself and basically starving to death, that he simply couldn't live on the pittance he was drawing from their partnership. Not in Paris. Not with the lifestyle he was obliged to lead. In contracts he had drawn up, Max had made the mistake of not making sure that he got a decent percentage. He was making peanuts. There he was, sweating blood. Anyone else would have done a lot worse than siphoning a few hundred thousand euros from his protégé's account.

He never, never signed anything that might taint the singer's image, even when it might have been favourable to him. He always put the kid's career first. And in fact, from the day Alex gave him the axe – he was fucked. Oh, he kept going for a while, managed to put out a couple of records that did well – but the gravy train was running on empty. All that fury because of a couple of bank transfers . . . Not even to him – to other people! He had been looking for an excuse to get rid of his manager so he could sell his soul to a big tour promoter. On the advice of his record label. The cretin didn't realise that the reason they all wanted rid of Max was that he was doing too good a job, and was stopping them from growing fat off his protégé. They all had a vested interest in getting shot of him. He was tough, loyal and demanding. He was a visionary. But Alex had fallen for their scheme.

A manager is the architect of a work he is never allowed to sign. In the fashioning of Alex Bleach, the songs and the singer were merely a component – simple raw material. Artists understand this. And it makes them furious. Obviously, without good raw material, there's nothing the manager can do. But without his expertise, his synchronising of all the elements and his ability to create a story, to bend fate to his will – nothing happens. What he did for Alex Bleach was absolutely extraordinary. But these days he appears in biographies only as a minor con artist. As though he was just some anonymous nobody who was fortunate to ride on the coattails of his friend, the artist. And he never tried to get in touch with him again. He skulked away like a whipped dog. He never phoned to say he was sorry.

Mathilde shows no interest in the story. She should realise that it's important to understand other people's career trajectories so she can better understand her own and not fall into the same traps. But as far as she is concerned, Alex is just some tacky, forgotten singer. He doesn't interest her.

Max never takes anything when he's with her. That's another reason why he needs to take a breather every now and again. Willpower is all very well for a couple of minutes . . . When they're in Paris, he patiently waits until she has a meeting somewhere, gives her a little wave from the balcony to make sure she gets into the taxi. By the time she slams the door, he's already contacting his dealer, Vince, and he's preparing the rock pipe and the baking soda while he waits. One little pipe, just for tonight, so he can chill. It's partly her fault that he smokes whenever he gets the chance – she doesn't realise that she is smothering him. She doesn't have keys to his place. If she happens to get back early, he rushes out onto the landing and sends the lift to the twentieth floor before answering the entry phone. That way he knows she'll have to wait at least five minutes before the lift arrives at the ground floor – giving him a little time to hide his gear. She's a naive little girl. She's not suspicious when she sees him crawling on all fours looking for a nugget he might have dropped. It's a crack smoker's tic. He knows that he hasn't dropped a rock behind the furniture. But he can't help himself. So, Mathilde goes to bed, convinced he's looking for his glasses.

He doesn't want to smoke in front of her. Crack is what heroin used to be in the '80s – the ultimate taboo drug. He's always loved grown-up highs. But Mathilde wouldn't understand. Or she would want to try, and he's not a sleazebag, he doesn't want to get her into this shit.

He had a long war of attrition with her over Ecstasy. When he met her, she was taking it all the time. Every time she went out, she "needed her vitamin X". She was ruining her health. And when she's off her tits, she goes around kissing everyone. This was how he met her. She was all over him before she even knew his name. So he encouraged her to stop. To cut a long story short, he gets ripped when she's not there. It balances him out. It's his one little pleasure. Deep down, he doesn't even really like it anymore. But as soon as she turns her back, he reaches for his pipe. That's almost the definition of a hard drug: all you can think about is taking it, and when you do you realise that wasn't what you wanted. You're constantly looking for the feeling you got that first time, a memory of that epiphany. That never comes back. So you start over.

He gets on well with his dealer. They've known each other a long time. Vince has got to be a police informant. He rides around Paris on a bike with a rucksack full of every pharmaceutical high imaginable. He's been doing it for years. And he never sweats it. Every year, he takes a couple of months off – he does the music festivals, the ski season. Recently, he's got it into his head that he's going to stop dealing and retrain. Talks about upcycling himself. Says he's careful about his personal use, that he's been putting money aside. But he still takes more than he sells. Vince's latest big idea is setting up a contactless payment system. He's developing it with some guy, probably a client, who first came up with the idea. Like an Apple Watch, but something slimmer, more stylish that can be charged off your mobile phone. Vince is convinced that he could sell the watch and the app at festivals. You pick up your bracelet and you've no need to carry cash. Max listens, squirming in pain. Some guys really have no head for business. What the fuck would people want with a bracelet that looks like a tatty third-rate Apple Watch when they can just buy an Apple Watch? Of all the things you could improve about a festival, why focus on something that isn't a problem in the first place? Either you don't have a credit card in which case, sure, you could use a contactless bracelet to pay, but if you haven't got a credit card, that means you haven't got any cash so you can't afford the bracelet. And even if he could prove that his dumb idea might work – how would he convince a major festival organiser to manufacture thousands of disposable bracelets? It makes no sense. Typical crackhead logic: neurons whizz around crashing into each other without managing to come up with a coherent idea. Max makes no comment. He's not about to waste his spit trying to reason with a junkie who won't remember a word of the conversation by morning. Getting ripped is like waterproofing your brain. Memories just roll off. Nothing interrupts your train of thought. That's why Burroughs' theory was spot on: junkies remain the age they were when they first started using. So, every time Vince brings up his idea for a contactless payment bracelet, Max just trots out one of his festival memories. He did them all, back when he managed Bleach – Les Vieilles Charrues, Les Transmusicales, Eurokéennes . .

*

The last time they saw each other, Vince told him about some skanky happenings. Somewhere in the back end of the Vosges, a kind of free party, a shuttle drops you off a thirty-minute walk from the site. Vince had been invited by a friend and had gone along to sell. He'd been told it wasn't a good place to deal but he had a rucksack full of whizz and P.M.A., he didn't believe in the concept of a rave with no drugs. He said, "There's no such thing as a gathering with no drugs. Except maybe a World Youth Day rally and even then . . . I'm pretty sure if you had the right gear, you could make a killing at a boy scout jamboree . . . But once I was there, you can't imagine – I was billy no-mates . . . no-one wanted to buy anything. I offered it left and right . . . they weren't aggressive or anything, they just weren't interested. Their mantra was: 'We get a better buzz without taking anything.' I'd never heard shit like it. It wasn't rammed, but there were maybe two hundred people . . . Given that I'd had to walk to get there, I wasn't about to head back in the middle of the night. I figured I'd just crash there. They started playing these weird sounds, they were quite nice really. And people started lying down all over the place, like this was a yoga class. It reminded me of nursery school, when we had to take a nap. Did you do that? Do you remember? I hated napping when I was a kid. I hated sleeping generally. So, anyway, I lie down – what else can I do? And they start in on the poetry. I tell you, it gave me a fucking panic attack. . . I felt like popping a Red Mitsubishi but I figured what with the atmosphere and stuff I'd probably have a bad trip . . . I waited for it to pass, listening to the wash of synth waves and the dopey poetry . . . people around me started dancing, all floppy, not sexy or anything. It was shady. Except that, like, an hour later, I couldn't tell you how much time had actually passed because I had a sort of blackout . . . I don't remember getting up, I don't remember deciding to join them . . . but when I come round, I'm dancing. Like I've never danced in my life. My toes were dancing, my hair was dancing, my fucking nostrils were dancing . . . Connected. That's the only word I can think of. Not spaced-out like when you're on shrooms, but that kind of trip . . . I could see light streaming from my palms and intertwining with the light of other dancers. I asked them about it the next day and they reckon it's a kind of mass hypnosis. You feel like you're completely straight, except that you can hear the sound of blood reaching the heart of a girl thirty metres away. Swear down.

"The sun comes up and I'm still dancing, I hadn't stopped, except now and then to take a piss, and even then . . . and everyone was in the same state. Even when the music stopped, I was still inside their heads, under their skin, in their belly, and in every note, in every instrument, I could hear the silences that create the notes . . . It was wild. They've hit on something. And the next morning: fucking Woodstock, man. Lots of kissing, hugging, a crowd of teddy bears, that's what we were like. The D.J. was better than decent, he'd come up with completely unexpected tunes, but they worked – but if I think back to the setlist it was, like, a decent set, but nothing that could explain the state we ended up in . . . Subutex, he's called, have you heard of him? The folk at the camp worship the guy. Good feels. Good-looking, like if you spliced Bruno Mars with Keith Richards. Never saw anything fucking like it. Just as well, you'll say, otherwise I'd be out of business. Can you imagine? Getting lit up with no need for pharma? Worse: you get completely ripped and the best thing is the comedown . . . that's not just competition, that's a whole new freaking concept . . . I'd love to go again, but you've got to get yourself invited and the guy who brought me last time has disappeared. Sound that's a drug, can you fucking believe it? That's what we're talking about, man. We're gonna live it. People mixing sounds that modify the prefrontal cortex. Unless maybe they're pumping gas or something into the air. But if it was gas, there'd be a comedown. I swear, in the future, people are going to be selling U.S.B. flash drives pre-loaded with a mix. And the speakers to go with them."

Max lets him burble on. As long as Vince hung around, they were smoking his rocks . . . Max didn't believe the story about this rave where no-one takes anything. There was a simple explanation: Vince was so drug-fucked that he had a flashback from something. But he had given a little start when he heard Vince mention the name Subutex. He remembered the record dealer. Alex loved to surround himself with losers. Vernon was one of his friends. The sort of guy who hits you up for an Access All Areas pass when he hasn't got the swank to raise the level backstage . . . Max particularly remembers Vernon because of a pretty lesbian, slightly shop-soiled, just his type, who rocked up a couple of years ago because she was combing Paris trying to find Subutex . . . Strange that he remembers her name. She called herself the Hyena. God, he would have liked to give her one . . . he's always had a thing for lesbians. He's already had two girls in bed prepared to feel each other up for his viewing pleasure. But never two genuine lesbians. With strap-ons, fisting and all that sleazy shit. It's a dream he often strokes to. He has thought about the Hyena since. Imagined scenarios where they would go to a party, choose some little lipstick lesbian, the Hyena would seduce her, bring her back to him, in his fantasies, the Hyena is his dog, she fetches for him. Right in front of him, she'd get the girl hot and horny, fuck her while he lay back and enjoyed the show, then he'd give a sign, just one, commanding her to present him with the girl's arse, or her mouth. There were variations of this scenario, but it all came down to the same thing: it was epic.

Max would have moved on to something else but for the fact that, a few weeks later, Stéphanie told him the same thing. One Sunday when he was dropping Lucas off at her place, he came up to the apartment so she could sample the Japanese whisky someone had just given him – and that he didn't want to drink with Mathilde, who drinks too much for someone who can't hold their liquor. Stéphanie had the glow of a woman who's spent the whole weekend doing the horizontal mambo. With Stéphanie, you've got to be wary – she's capable of setting up house with an ex-con with a dozen rapes on his rap sheet and not seeing why it might be dangerous.

It took some time for them to work things out after the breakup. They both made an effort, for the sake of the kid, and eventually things sorted themselves out. Stéphanie has a lot of problems, she's unstable, she's ungrateful, she spends all day playing the martyr, she's a rattlebag of tics and neuroses . . . but she's the mother of his child. He refuses to write her off. The hardest thing, when you split up with someone, is seeing the other person unable to be happy. She'd like them to get back together. That's never going to happen. It's too late. He feels sorry. For her. Often, when he brings Lucas home, he'll come upstairs and chat with her. She is so lonely.

That night, he had to worm the information out of her – "What have you been up to that you're so radiant on a Sunday night?" When she started telling him about this amazing night she spent dancing in the middle of a field, he pricked up his ears. O.K., she's certified batshit crazy. But she doesn't do drugs. And here she was giving him the same spiel as Vince: the numinous convergence, the darkness, the feeling of entering into the body of the group, and so on. He was careful not to mention that his dealer had already talked to him about these raves. Tell Stéphanie you're interested in something and she'll make sure you don't get near it. She is still in love with Max. Unsurprisingly, she's never met another guy of his stature. She's still a little bitter. He doesn't completely trust her.

So, when she mentioned this weekend in Barcelona, when she asked if he remembered Xavier – fuck no, he doesn't remember all the nobodies who went to the same gigs he did back in the '90s – and, listening to her, he realised that this Xavier was part of the group that organised these weird raves . . . he jumped at the chance. Instinctively. He said: "Barcelona? Why don't I come with you? It would be good to hang out together for a bit, wouldn't it?"

Xavier is not the friendly type. He's been giving Max the cold shoulder all weekend. He eats like a pig, hunched over his plate, with his stubby fingers. He has the face of your typical inbred French peasant. Nose like a potato, thin hair, teeth like tombstones. The sort of physique Max finds physically repellent.

Max tried various approaches, attempted to soften him up. He patiently exhumed various topics of conversation that might appeal to this fat fractious fuck. And after a couple of cans of beer, he hit on it: Xavier let slip that he'd spent a long time working on a biopic of Drieu la Rochelle, but now he was thinking of ditching it for a biopic on Bernanos. And Max said, "I love *Diary of a Country Priest*."

Not only had he never read it, but he had no idea what it might be about – he only knows about Bernanos because of Pialet and the scandal he caused at Cannes: "You don't like me, and let me tell you, I don't like you either." But it was at this point that the miserable fuck started to soften. He was so desperate to talk about his projects that all you had to do was listen for him to think he'd made a new friend.

That night, Max dragged him to a vast nightclub on the outskirts of the city where a D.J. called Black Madonna whipped the crowd into a frenzy. "A boys' night out." Xavier was shitfaced so he tagged along, relieved to get away from the giggling girls. They wandered around the heaving club for a while, then Max scored a wrap of speed and they headed for the toilets – a little line can create a bond. Xavier never stopped prattling. They found themselves on the rooftop, smoking a cigarette. "It's just like being in New York," declared the ignoramus who had probably never set foot in New York. They talked about Bob Dylan, whom they both hated. But every time Max tried to talk about the convergences, the fuckwit dodged the subject.

Then, the miracle happened. It was still pitch dark, not even a sliver of moon. They were on the rooftop bathed in an orange glow. And Max was starting to give up hope. Then he saw Xavier's expression change as he stared at a group of girls holding forth just behind them. Cute little chicks, tattooed, sassy, boisterous. One of them was staring at Max. Max fished out his phone. He assumed Xavier wanted to hook up with her and was trying to give him some space. Much good it did him.

Pretending to listen to his voicemails, he slipped behind them. He could hear what they were saying. It made no sense to him, but he did not miss a word. Xavier was obviously too drunk to worry that someone might be eavesdropping. The girl's name was Céleste. She wasn't supposed to be in Barcelona. She obviously knew the famous group, and Subutex's name was mentioned. It seemed very important to Xavier that he had run into her here. And Max's instincts rarely failed him: it was very important that he was also here, at that moment.

A SCURRYING ANT ZIGZAGS ACROSS A BLANK PAGE OF HER notebook. Pamela is having trouble concentrating. She gazes at the leaves quavering in the light. She found this wooden table abandoned by the side of the house a few days ago. A little rickety, but still solid, covered with dense, vivid green moss. Jésus helped her carry it a few hundred metres downhill to the edge of the forest. Pamela went down with her notebooks tucked under one arm and some cold bitter coffee in a black mug with the "Star Wars" logo emblazoned in silver. Facing her, serried ranks of identical trees as far as the eye can see. She has to look up to find the light. She has watched too many horror movies. She knows what happens to girls who find themselves alone in such isolated places. She flinches at the slightest noise whose source she cannot determine.

She increasingly feels the need to stay on the sidelines. To keep out of the quarrels and the possible consequences. The group seems to her like a mane of hair that has to be brushed every morning to untangle the knots that have formed during the night by simple contact and friction. She spends most of her time listening to people, preventing minor squabbles from escalating. It's something she is good at. It is what she liked most about the camp, until now: she has found her niche; she knows what she has to do. Everyone talks about magic, the magic of the convergences, of nights spent dancing, the magical harmony of the group. But behind that magic there is this gruelling, practical effort. Scullery jobs, rolled-up sleeves, elbow grease. Woman's work. Invisible and essential. Never rewarded. Much as Pamela mistrusts feminists, over time their ideas have found their way inside her head. All ideas find their way inside her head. This was something she enjoyed, at first. But now she is tired of this, too. Her thoughts are full of noises. Like being deep in the forest: noises whose source she cannot determine.

In the distance, she hears the two girls from Bordeaux who have arrived earlier than they usually do, as though they sense something. Two poor little rich girls of staggering stupidity, full of themselves and without a flicker of self-doubt. One of them recently said, "I think I've just OD'd on sugar, I'm, like, bare depressed, you know?" She'd eaten about half a croissant. They're obsessed with their weight. They talk about nothing but food. Carbs, fats. Organics. Gluten. They refuse to eat at the common table. When they see Pamela eat a piece of white bread, they make faces like she was flicking the bean right there at the table. How do you go about creating such dumb airheads? How do you go about instilling that class superiority complex? Pamela has no idea, her own mother was a crazy bitch, incapable of hanging on to the same apartment for a year. Pamela never saw her work. When she was young, it seemed to her that getting into porn was a reasonable way of being more integrated than her mother. It only lasted for a while. It had been a relief when she cleared out her apartment, handed back the keys and dropped out of circulation. Paying the bills every month is beyond her abilities. She can't understand how other people manage.

*

This year has passed without her really noticing. She slipped into the rhythm. Scouting out a new campsite, preparing the convergence, welcoming people, clearing up, packing up, starting over. She is listening to Tuxedomoon. "Bombay Tension" on a red Discman. She is too young to remember portable C.D. players like this. But someone left it behind – a battered old Discman. She listens to The Nomads, The Saints, And Also the Trees. Groups she had never heard of and is gradually getting used to. She got along well with the shy, nervous boy who left behind his C.D. collection. He wore a black Teddy jacket and brand-new black Converse high-tops. He spent two hours talking to her about London in the 1980s when he was working in a restaurant in King's Cross. He was anxious about not being able to drink at the camp. He was looking for some beer, and Pamela found a couple of cans to reassure him. New arrivals are often panicked at not being able to drink. They quickly adapt. The convergences transform people.

The death of Charles has changed everything. His legacy has changed everything. That amount of money. A sudden switch. A loop-the-loop. The inverse movement to that produced by convergences: a destabilisation, but not towards something better. Certainly not towards greater harmony. And that was only the beginning.

Pamela's imagination got carried away before she even had time to realise what was happening. The improvements they could make, the logistics, the comfort, the time saved . . . And when the Hyena brought up the idea of not touching the money, she dug her heels in.

For weeks, she had been completely exhausted. Jésus was saying, "Get some rest, stop being a good little soldier." Daniel was saying, "I'll give you my keys, go spend a couple of weeks in Paris – I can crash with Elodie. You need a change of air." Vernon was saying, "You and Jésus take the car, go to the seaside. You're the one with all the contacts, you must know someone in Brittany who can put you up for ten days . . . We'll get by." Sylvie didn't say anything, but every time she showed up at the camp, she went looking for oranges to make Pamela some juice. Everyone, in fact, has been telling her she needs to take it easy. But Pamela hasn't been listening. She can't see how anything would keep running if she stopped dealing with it.

She is changing. She used to love managing the storeroom, for example. Whenever they pitch camp, they set up a little shack where convergents can leave whatever they want. It's part of the trip. This is how the permanent residents have food to eat. And more new socks and T-shirts than they could ever wear. You can find just about everything at the depot. An eiderdown, a rose quartz as big as a fist, Himalayan salt, batteries, a box of paracetamol, tins of food, a bottle of mezcal, candles, chocolate, a pair of scissors, a fountain pen, a harmonica, a tiny statue of the Virgin of Guadalupe . . . Pamela sorts through things, boxes them up, makes an inventory. She takes a childlike pleasure in managing these cardboard boxes. When Laurent still came to the camp, they used to do the inventory together, as though they had V.I.P. access to Ali Baba's cave. He would roll up his sleeves, crack open a bottle of wine, tuck a pencil behind his ear and jot down everything Pamela was putting into the boxes. He never really attended the convergences – dancing in the dark wasn't his thing. But he seemed happy around them. He talked too loudly, he drank too much, he played pranks on the girls that weren't always funny. But he never made Pamela feel uncomfortable when they were alone in the stores together, and it was a very cramped space. This boorish guy who was perfectly capable of groping the arse of some girl he didn't know never stepped out of line when he was with her. She misses him. She was upset when he left. The piles of tinned sardines made them laugh like drains. They speculated as to which idiot kept rocking up to the camp with crates of tinned sardines. They never found out. Laurent isn't around to help her with the storeroom now. She doesn't find it fun anymore. She could ask someone else to look after it. Anyone – it's hardly brain surgery. Olga would happily do it. Her obsession is dealing with the crisps and the peanuts. Someone told her peanuts belong to the haricot family and are really good for your health. On nights before a convergence, she stations herself outside the door of the stores and, to everyone who comes to drop something off, she whispers, "Next time, think about bringing peanuts. The nutritional value is off the charts!"

When Vernon announced how much Charles wanted to leave them, Pamela wanted to go to the supermarket. She would never have guessed that this would be the first thing to flash into her mind: a full shopping trolley. Not filled with strange, random things – but with things that she had chosen and paid for. She realised that, ever since she quit the porn business, she had never walked into a shop and just let herself go wild. Suddenly, she misses it. She wanted to spend time in the city, to watch television, to put on a beautiful dress. To buy a second vehicle, so there would be no need to go looking for cars to transport the participants before every convergence or argue over who is taking the stuff from the stores and everything else when they break camp. Not having to rack her brains to work out how to transport the duvets, the cushions and everyone's bags. A little van that could also be used to shuttle people to and from the train station. Cut down the list of things to be done. Cut short the arguments. Frankly, buying a second vehicle is the least they should do. And a new sound system, one that meant they didn't have to rely on the girls from Bordeaux anymore. They do a good job at mixing, but the camp could get along without them.

When the Hyena said, "Let's not touch the money," Pamela felt as though she had just been slapped. In front of everyone. She should have realised that her reactions were no longer in keeping with events. She knows that no-one was trying to humiliate her. No-one opposed her. And yet she felt threatened, and betrayed. She knew that what she was thinking was rubbish. But this did not stop her throat tightening, her heart hammering and her eyes welling with tears – though she could not have said whether what she felt was rage, sadness or fear. Vernon did not come to her defence. No-one said the words that she had expected: "Pamela is the person who works hardest here to make sure things run smoothly. She should be the one to make the decision." The issue of the importance of individual voices in the group had never been raised. The most heated arguments were usually about the day's menu. It was manageable. The most voluble person carried the day: if they wanted potatoes, they would eat potatoes. When Pamela and Jésus went scouting for locations – going to visit campsites that had been suggested to them – no-one ever questioned their decision. Discussions took place in darkness. You are more aware of the person next to you in the dark. She could make out Vernon – slightly withdrawn. Usually, he was a weightless presence, capable of moving easily from one person to another, as though gifted with sensitive antennae. The evening when the inheritance was announced was in the past. In the end, she had cleared her throat and muttered, "All this is a lot to take in, I'm gonna crash, good night," but no-one was taken in. Nor did she feel as she normally did. She was seeing red.

She went and found Jésus, who was with Mariana, smoking some weed she had brought back from Paris. They were listening to "Jardin d'Hiver", singing along with Luz Casal. Véro was sitting next to them, legs apart, elbows on knees, manspreading. Pamela was sure she saw a malicious smile play on Véro's lips as she watched her approaching. As though she knew. And she was happy about it. And for the first time in a very long time, Pamela wondered what her role was. She did not feel like slipping an arm around her boyfriend's waist – he was doing his own thing, hanging out with Vernon's girl. She had nothing to say to them. Without a word, she went to bed. An invisible millstone tied around her neck.

The following day, Pamela got up feeling rested. Then, over breakfast, she listened as Xavier went into raptures about an idea he had just come up with: grants to ageing rockers – the people who worked for the cause, who had spent their lives on tour, making records, giving interviews, the ones who have a fanbase but never hit the jackpot, now pushing sixty, finding it difficult to make ends meet, and still touring. Xavier was full of his idea. He planned to draw up a list of ageing musicians who had never really made it, so he could distribute the cash. A sudden, powerful urge to smash Xavier's jaw made Pamela realise that she was feeling no better.

The Hyena came and sat next to her. She said: "You left a bit abruptly last night . . . What I said last night, it wasn't a dig at you, Pamela, you know? All I was trying to say was – right now, we're fine as we are. This thing is fragile. We need to protect what we've created." But Lydia cut into the conversation. She had been smoking. It was eleven o'clock in the morning. She was completely stoned, her voice slurred, her eyes vacant. Blitzed. "We're, we're like too fucking *poetic* . . . let the rain come down. Why don't we all treat ourselves to a couple of weeks in a palace and blow the lot and toast the old bastard?" "Because we've got a brain," Pamela retorted and got up from the table. Lydia didn't take it badly, she giggled. "Charles would agree with me, don't you think?"

Vernon was defending his idea of making the movie Charles was always talking about with the porn "stars". Girls who had shot three video clips and proclaimed themselves porn stars on Facebook. A zombie movie. No-one had ever taken the idea serious. The only funny thing about it was that it gave the girls an opportunity to do their zombie shtick. To suggest a bunch of porn stars pull faces, make horrible noises and contort themselves is to open Pandora's box: everyone inside is a gifted bullshit artist.

Pamela was prepared to negotiate: a second vehicle, then, sure, fine, use the rest of the money to shoot the film. Let's assume that Charles really cared about the project. Xavier pumped the brakes: "You've no idea of the work involved, we'll end up wasting all our energy on it. And you don't seem to realise what it would cost – we'll get, what? Four hundred grand, max? You'll never shoot a feature film on that budget."

And from the incandescent rage she felt with every new comment, Pamela knew she was starting to lose the plot. She was not usually like this. Otherwise, why come and live here? She was being visited by old demons she had not seen for a long time. Vernon, who was washing his coffee cup in the sink, nodded to her and said:

"Don't stress out over this inheritance thing. Let it go. We don't know whether we'll even get a cent."

"Has Véro said something?"

"No, but she's thinking about it. I can understand: a last wishes letter isn't legally binding, technically the money's all hers."

And Véro had packed her bags. That same night. Without a word of explanation. She had spent the afternoon with Jésus and Olga getting hammered on Zubrowka. Seeing her staggering, laughing, having to be propped up by her drinking buddies every time she went for a piss so she didn't knock down the tents, Pamela had thought that Vernon was wrong, that Véro was acclimatising. She'd even thought, I hope she doesn't decide to live with us full time, because she was troubled by Véro's presence. There was a maliciousness to her sadness. But she was a cheerful drunk, grabbing anyone who came within reach and covering them with slobbery kisses and protestations of love. She overdid everything. She had to be the centre of attention. Even her happiness was aggressive.

At dinnertime, she was nowhere to be found. At first, everyone assumed she had passed out somewhere and was sleeping off the booze. But Xavier had searched the whole camp – her bag and her suitcase were gone. She had to have left on foot. Or she had hung on to her mobile phone and called a cab.

They talked about the incident amongst themselves. It was as though, like Pamela, they all felt ashamed of the thoughts that had been going through their minds of late. It was like a collective hangover. Everyone had slept badly that night. They needed time before they could admit that they had got carried away for nothing.

*

The two girls from Bordeaux were there for two days before they started shit-stirring. They made the most of the fact that Olga and the Hyena were not at the camp, having taken one of the dogs to a vet in town. Pamela knows that, if they'd been there, the atmosphere would have been different. She hates herself. She was the weak link.

The girls were sitting on the terrace, preparing salad, when Pamela showed up to make herself a coffee. The girls exchanged a knowing look and said:

"Hey, d'you think it's possible Vernon cut a deal with Véro so she would split and he could pocket the cash for himself? Everyone's wondering, but no-one has the guts to ask you."

"Who exactly is 'everyone'?"

"We don't want to snitch. I mean, we don't believe a word of it. Why would Vernon do something like that?"

Pamela should have ignored them. But she had sat down at the table, picked up a knife and helped them out. The worst thing was that, in that moment, she felt she needed to reassure them.

"How did you dream up a scenario like that? It doesn't sound like the Vernon I know . . ."

"That amount of money can change a man."

"Then why did he stay? If you'd just trousered four hundred grand, would you hang around, camping with the friends you'd just screwed over?"

The girls had shrugged, feigned indifference, as though this was just idle conversation.

"I don't know . . . The time it takes to get the money into an account in his name, he gets to avoid any arguments. And because he didn't do a runner, no-one's going to suspect him . . . Just saying. I'm only repeating what's being said around the camp . . ."

*

Pamela knows exactly why the girls from Bordeaux are accusing Vernon. In the months they have been studying, mixing and reworking Alex Bleach's sounds, they've come to the conclusion that they are the secret of the convergences. That Vernon is just a third-rate D.J., some boring old guy exploiting a gullible group. They're convinced that anyone could do what he does. That it's a waste to hinge the convergences on some slacker they think is too weak. Not manly enough. Too passive.

The girls have gone on the offensive in the hope of splintering the group. They want to use Bleach's tapes for other club nights. They've already tried to get around Kiko. Persuade him to dump this gang of morons and their fuckwit guru and shift into top gear. They made a mistake when choosing their first target. The former stockmarket trader is fanatical about Vernon. But they refused to accept defeat. They want to exploit the idea of the convergences. They want the mythic happening without having to deal with the dipshit D.J.

Pamela knew all this. She carried on preparing the salad, a smile still plastered to her face, convinced that the girls' machinations were having no effect on her. She was wrong. Since then the idea has been going round and round inside her head. What if. What if. What if Vernon did cut a deal with Véro?

There is no way to distinguish between a run-of-the-mill day and one in which everything changes dramatically. In hindsight, Pamela reviews the hours that preceded the incident. Vainly, she tries to pinpoint some detail that might make it possible to better under-stand what happened. But what is most striking is that everything seemed completely normal. Except that the poisonous suspicion was now coursing through her.

She was the one who summoned Vernon. He was not expecting it. He was sitting with his headphones and his little bag of batteries, his charger and his collection of obsolete iPods – people love to leave him old iPods preloaded with their favourite tunes. He was busy jotting down the songs he found interesting. Lying on her stomach, Mariana was engrossed in a novel by Zadie Smith. Pamela had come to fetch him. "We're making tea, we have a few things to talk about, do you want to join us?"

Supposedly, she just wanted to clear up the situation. People invent virtuous motives for themselves and wear them like masks – so they don't have to face the sordid reasons driving them. Jésus had warned her: "You can't let people go around wondering whether this is true or not. You have to talk to Vernon, in private, he'll explain why this is all bullshit." But Pamela hadn't listened. "No, he has to respond to the rumour in front of everyone, otherwise people will carry on talking behind his back for weeks."

Though she would not realise it until after she had provoked this awkward confrontation, what she actually wanted, deep down, was revenge. In the discussions about the inheritance, Vernon hadn't supported her. She wanted to hurt him. Everyone gets a turn.

Vernon didn't suspect anything. He listened to the question, realised that they had been talking about it for a while. He did not reply immediately. He is slow. None of them can tell whether it's because he's an idiot, or because he is too wise to charge in. He was hurt. Seeing his expression change, Pamela was ashamed that she had put him in this situation. She barely recognised him; in all the months they had spent living together she had never seen him troubled. In a preternaturally calm voice he said, "You've brought me here, in front of everyone, to say I didn't do some shady deal with Véro behind your backs? Are you for real?" then, without answering the question, without looking at anyone, he got to his feet and walked away.

Silence is one of the good qualities of the camp. The silence of people who feel no need to talk when they're together. But the silence that followed was new. Even the girls from Bordeaux did not dare break it. Everyone knew something had just happened, something ugly. Most of all Pamela, who considered following Vernon to his crash pad to explain herself, but didn't. You can't engineer this kind of clusterfuck and instantly claim that you regret it.

She has cut herself off from the others. In the distance, she hears forced laughter – it's like those couples who kiss in public to prove their relationship is solid. She hears someone call her name, recognises Lydia's voice. From her tone, it's clear that there is something wrong. Every action has its consequences. She knows, she has known since her eyes met Vernon's during that grim lesson in humiliation that he would not be able to pretend that nothing had happened.

VERNON TRAVELS ON SOMEONE ELSE'S PASSPORT. HE LONG since lost his own papers and is hardly likely to apply for a new one, as he has none of the necessary documentation. These days, when he catches a flight, his name is Nicholas Nil. The guy came to one of the convergences, he said, I love the way you layer your sounds, and two minutes later, since they were talking about techno raves in the desert and Vernon was saying, that must really be something but I can't leave the country so I'll never get to find out what they're like, Nicholas suggested lending him his passport. The guy is super-intense, and although Vernon declined the offer, thinking it was too much, the following morning the passport was there and the guy was gone. He'd left a note explaining that the passport had nearly expired and that he'd get a new one when he needed it, and, in the meantime, "Enjoy." It is not the first time that Vernon has been stunned by the insane generosity of strangers the morning after a convergence.

They don't look remotely alike. Nicholas is heavyset, he's cross-eyed and he's five years younger than Vernon. But he has pale eyes, he's Caucasian and, when the passport photo was taken, he had a beard so people only see the eyes and don't notice the squint. It could easily be Vernon, if he'd been on a tapeworm diet in between times. The first time he handed it over at passport control, he was trembling, but the officer didn't even raise an eyebrow.

At the airport, Vernon trails behind Mariana. He loves the way she moves, the way she holds herself erect, her every sense heightened. Her eyes are scanners, her sense of direction is uncanny, she doesn't even have to slow her pace to check their flight on the monitors. She barely slept last night, by rights she should be complaining, trudging along, barely able to remember her own name. But she is gambolling from check-in desk to escalator, perfectly confident, happy to be here. She loves travelling, loves being on planes, discovering new cities, talking to strangers. She has been given her mobile phone back, and Vernon is stunned at her dexterity using apps – within minutes, Mariana can find the best restaurant in any neighbourhood in the world, a parking spot in Berlin or an apartment where they can spend the night. She even has an app that tells her the best seats on the plane. She can tell you where the international space station is at any given moment. Not that these things are always useful, but they distract Vernon who, seeing her reunited with her phone, finally understands how much she suffers when she has to give it up at the camp.

In the interminable queue for security, they find themselves behind a guy with a horseshoe moustache like José Bové. Vernon elbows Mariana, "Do you think a moustache would suit me?" and she screws up her nose. "I hate kissing guys who have moustaches." "Have there been many?" "One, that was enough, it's itchy." Vernon is feeling a little delicate, he drank too much last night. He was bored. He only refilled his glass three or four times in the course of the evening, but he can't hold his liquor anymore, either that or he is coming down with something. He woke up feeling lousy. As every morning, it took a few seconds before he remembered he was no longer with the others. His mind resists – wants to believe that it is a bad dream. That everything will go back to normal. A hotel room. Spacious. Dark red blackout drapes. He has no choice but to accept that this is real. He has left. On a whim, on an impulse that he'd like to believe was intuitive. He had imagined they would try to stop him, that they wouldn't let him leave. It somehow didn't feel real. He didn't feel anything; he wasn't expecting to do what he did. Pamela called him, asked him if he had lied. He had felt the group open up beneath his feet. It's crazy just how fragile trust can be. These people with whom he has shared so much – it took just a single remark for him to sense that it was over. That his place was no longer with them.

He went back to his bunk. He said nothing to Mariana. He felt ashamed at what had happened. Ashamed of them. He listened to some Syl Johnson and tried to think. Then he laid a hand on Mariana's shoulder, "I want to get out of here," and it was only as he said the words that he realised that this was what he wanted. She turned towards him, pulling a funny face: "What's happened?" and Vernon realised he was finding it difficult to articulate his thoughts. A friction, a confusion. There have been other moments of crisis in the two years he has lived with this random, ramshackle family. But he couldn't explain the incident that had just occurred.

It wasn't a matter of principle. It wasn't a question of exhaustion. He lied to Mariana, pretended to be offhand, "I don't know, must have been our trip to Paris. If I split, are you coming with me?" And she knelt up on the bed, laughing: "Wherever you go, I go . . . but where are you going?" Elsewhere. He was leaving. It was a moment of madness. He didn't want to have to explain himself to others, or to wait until things settled down. He felt that the time had come to pack his bags and get some fresh air. Simple as. In that moment, at least, it seemed straightforward.

His belly aches. As he collects a grey plastic tray, he allows a group of vindictive Russians to go in front of him because he is having trouble taking off his jacket. Mariana sighs. She hates it when people queue-jump – it's a matter of principle. He smiles at her.

The previous night, they had hung out at some blonde girl's place until three in the morning. She looked like an American in one of those '80s soap operas: retroussé nose, diaphanous skin, soft voice – not quite a grown-up. After Vernon's set, she had invited everyone back to her place for an after-party. She was saying, "I'd like to leave France, there's no future for young people here, but I can't leave on account of my children." She worked on a check-out desk, she said her back ached from humping crates of bottled water. And the customers are increasingly aggressive and she was sick and tired of getting it in the neck. She had produced a bottle of incredibly good rum that scalded the throat and warmed the body. Her apartment was almost barren. What there was, was brand new. She had just split up with her partner, who wasn't the father of her kids. Seeing them in a photo in the hallway, Vernon realised that the girl couldn't possibly be under thirty, which was what he had assumed – her kids were obviously at secondary school. She had spent the whole night coming on to him. There was something intoxicating about her that he found attractive. He allowed himself to be seduced. Mariana was chatting to some boys in the kitchen. She's not the jealous type. As she puts it, "I'm the best, but I'm not the only one," and Vernon assumes that this means she has no intention of being faithful.

He had had a skinful and was staggering by the time they started walking back to the hotel through Montpellier, which was deserted at that hour. He could hear the heels of her boots hammering the pavement.

This morning, he had woken up alone. Mariana had gone out for a walk. It's something she always does. She likes to be alone in the morning. As does Vernon. They agree on so many things without even having to discuss them. It was 10.30 a.m. and he was hungry – he hadn't eaten the night before. He rushed to check what time breakfast was served, his head was all over the place, simply finding the card with the times printed on it seemed complicated – 10.00 a.m. weekdays; he thought I'll call down, ask them to bring it up, maybe there's still time, but it took him a long time to find the number for reception, and the phone wasn't plugged in, he never did find the socket. Fuck it. Too late. He threw open the curtains, the room overlooked the hotel courtyard, nothing spectacular. He took a shower. When he went to put on his socks, he felt a wave of nausea as he realised that they smelled of a dying animal and hoped that the stink would not trouble his travel companion. He has little in the way of spare clothes. At the camp, he did his laundry whenever necessary. Being on tour, things are more complicated. If this can be called being on tour.

They left. Mariana only realised that the departure was permanent when they boarded the bus to take them back to Paris. The heating was on full-blast, the driver was saying that the thermostat was broken and there was nothing he could do about it. Mariana took matters in hand. She cancelled the Dutch couple who were supposed to be renting her apartment for a week and they went back to her place. Vernon settled himself in front of the television, with his iPad on his lap and sat there for three days without saying a word, engrossed in the articles he was reading and the garbage he was watching. In the meantime, Mariana worked frantically and managed to get a series of bookings for D.J. sets that were fairly close together so that he didn't have to worry about not having his own place. According to her, getting the bookings was easy, everyone has heard of Vernon Subutex. There was something almost worrying about Mariana's frenzied hustling, until Vernon realised that she knew exactly what she was doing. She knows a lot more people than he had expected.

He is constantly telling himself that it was a good idea to leave the camp and head off on an adventure. He tells himself that it's not good to get stuck in a rut. That comfort is the enemy of inspiration. He remembers Olga coming back from the vet and stopping, dumbfounded, when she saw him with his bag packed, ready to leave. "But . . . you're coming back for the next convergence?" and Vernon had shrugged: "You can take my place. Everyone knows I'm replaceable. Good luck."

This was how it ended. He did not take the time to say goodbye to everyone. Jésus dropped them off at the bus station. He cried. Not Vernon. He didn't want to cry. He had to get away. He is still wondering why. Something was broken. Or maybe he has finally lost the plot. Because ever since he left, there hasn't been a day when he has felt fine. Mariana went with him, though she did not understand. When she said, "Why didn't you just tell them you were going away for a few days?", he said, "I needed to get out of my comfort zone," and, hearing his own words, he wondered what was happening to him.

Since then, he has been going with the flow. Mariana has proved to be a brilliant manager. With a talent he had never suspected, she keeps their lives organised. When they have a couple of free days somewhere, she rents an apartment and they wander the streets of unfamiliar cities, gorging on pizza and T.V. box sets. They don't fuck very often. He doesn't care about sex. His head is filled with so many disparate memories that the present reality feels like Catch-Up T.V. All things pass, he thinks, and in the end it's not very important.

In the train stations and the airports, he travels with his ghosts. He can throw away photographs, dispose of things, cast off old clothes – still his former lives are entwined with the present, and he can hear his roots shriek, refusing to be sacrificed. They throb, connected, ripped from the fields of consciousness. His past is becoming an encumbrance. If he assesses the situation point by point, his life is fine. He's getting good fees for the sets he plays. The promoters offer a warm welcome. He is getting to see the world. Mariana takes care of him and he loves his life with her. But he is bleeding dead stories, cradling beloved bodies against his belly, he is inconsolable. He suddenly feels incomplete.

In retrospect, he realises that his decision was taken before Charles' death and Véro's betrayal. He thinks about this inevitability – it had to be done – without knowing whence it came. The absence is so heartrending that it is a black hole in the centre of his consciousness, an abyss in which everything is engulfed. He finds it difficult to believe that from now on he will live life without that flame. But he had to do it. Just before tedium set in. When he wants to turn the knife in the wound, he listens to Miossec – "I'm leaving you long before I must, I'm leaving before I betray your trust" – and yet his body does not bleed out. Besides, since he left, there are a lot of songs he can no longer listen to without feeling he is being split in two. He is filled with regrets, but he will not go back.

Last night, at the pretty blonde's place, some roadie was saying, "I can't get onto the tour bus anymore." For months he hasn't put in the hours. He can't do it anymore. He has too many questions. As he sipped his rum, the guy said, "I've got a daughter. I want to see her. I can't bring myself to pack a bag and leave. I can't spend my whole day in the truck anymore. At ten o'clock in the morning, the sliding doors close and I feel like I'm in a prison. I used to get a kick out of stealing things from service stations. Now I don't even want to stop at one to take a piss. Unloading the gear from the truck, setting up for the soundcheck, collapsing backstage. I can't bear to look at an Ibis hotel. This was the life I dreamed of, a life I loved, I treasured. Then one day I couldn't do it anymore. I want to be at home with my daughter." And Vernon felt like putting his arms around him. He spends all day playing the guy who's laid-back, cool, sorted. But he finds the intensity of his emotions is unsettling. And for some reason that he cannot understand, he feels incapable of getting in touch with the people from the camp and asking, "Where are you?" He read somewhere that people release a specific oxytocin when they're with members of their group. He knows this is true: he is in withdrawal.

He finds the harsh light of the airport aggressive. The queue is moving slowly. Behind him, hands reach out to pick up plastic trays. Certain people are not accustomed to moving in such situations. Others slip through the crowds, whipping off their shoes and belts with one hand, clutching their boarding pass between their teeth. The questions are absurd – do you have any shampoo or toothpaste? – and the answers come in deadly earnest – no, of course not, no – in an almost indignant tone, "Do I look like the sort of passenger who has a bottle of aftershave?", while the neophytes and those women who somehow believe that this time their bag won't be scanned start feverishly rummaging through their bags for the bottle of body lotion they will have to throw away when they could buy the same product a few metres away, just past security, before they get on the plane. The absurdity of the situation is so flagrant that no-one is shocked. This is a manège. The word that pops into Vernon's head is "performative", it is one he has heard several times at the camp and pinpoints the speaker as belonging to a particular social class. Performative. Here, taking off his heavy black leather belt, then leaning against the conveyor belt to take off his old red boots, he feels as though he is being stripped of his armour – as though he is being subjected to a special ritual. Performative. He is forced to move forward in his stockinged feet with the rest of the passengers, all of whom are subjected to the same humiliation. The security officer points to a bag and asks its owner to follow him and witness its complete evisceration. On the little screens, the suitcases look like exposed bodies, filled with strange black and orange organs. Security is secondary in all this. Everyone knows that it cannot be guaranteed. What matters is discipline. That people learn to obey any rule without complaint.

*

Vernon sits on the floor to pull on his boots, there are no free seats around. The waiting areas are full. A number of flights have been delayed, passengers who should have taken off hours ago cram in as best they can. A sudden burst of sunlight illuminates that space. Outside the windows, a huge jet is turning around, looking for its gate. Mariana takes some chocolate out of her bag, complaining that this terminal has no smoking area.

They have a busy schedule over the coming weeks. They are flying to Liverpool, where Vernon will do a set on the roof of a derelict superstore. He has advance playlists for a dozen sessions. He made so many of them at the camp. Removed from his context, he is not a sensation. Nor does he empty the dance floor. The kids, unaware of his micro-legend, wonder what this unknown old fart is doing, and pop tabs of Ecstasy while they wait for some real techno.

On the plane, in spite of the best efforts of SeatGuru, Vernon is uncomfortable. His legs are too long, his knees dig into the seat in front. There is a crying baby. Vernon recognises the guy with the handsome moustache sitting a few seats away. He is doing the sudoku at the back of the in-flight magazine. His hands are hirsute. Mariana is experimenting with recent Snapchat filters; she shows him a photo of herself with cat's ears.

Vernon thinks about Pamela. He has imaginary conversations with her that last whole days. Sometimes Mariana catches him in the act, she comes out of the shower and finds him talking to himself. He explains what happened to Pamela, without ever actually getting in touch with her. How could someone so clever, so shrewd have imagined that he would con his friends so he could get his hands on the old man's legacy? A part of him still believes that this is just a parenthesis. That everything will go back to normal.

That they will manage to find a way to erase this incident and go back to the life they had before.

The day it happened, a storm had broken at three in the morning, he had sat watching apocalyptic lightning bolts cleaving the sky – never suspecting that they might herald something. Unable to get back to sleep, he had listened to the Velvets' first album – and later he thought that maybe this, too, was the harbinger of the looming catastrophe. When Lou Reed is cast as the messenger of fate, you can be sure that the news is not good.

The energy was muted. Pamela was not coping well. She can't bear to be betrayed, and she had felt betrayed when Véro left. Pamela cannot bear to be abandoned. And she had felt abandoned when Vernon had not made a big deal of it. Day after day, he tries to make sense of it. Each of them has reacted in their own way. Instinctively. Intelligence is a useful tool for justifying a decision made, after the fact. We use it to makes our lies plausible.

We pretend, to see things clearly, to be coherent. But the truth is that we act without thinking. That's all.

"ARE YOU SURE YOU WOULDN'T BE BETTER OFF WEARING trainers?"

Emilie is buckling the straps of her high-heels. Her hand hovers in mid-air and she stares at Sylvie in surprise. It's patently obvious that the shoes suit her. It takes a few seconds for her to understand the comment. She puffs out her cheeks and says:

"If I need to run, I'll take them off."

She stands up, looks around for her watch, then changes her mind.

"O.K., go call the lift, I'll be there in a minute. You've got me completely freaked out now. I'll change into a pair of Nikes."

"I haven't worn heels since the thirteenth. Excluding holidays, when I wear flip-flops, I've never worn flats this much in my whole life. I'm terrified my back won't be able to adjust, it's not used to flat shoes . . . but I open my wardrobe, look at my heels, remember the Bataclan, and put on trainers. Those bastards. I never thought that I'd be so quick to give up the one thing that's essential to my look."

"Fuck, I'd never even thought about it before now, and I love these shoes, they give me a booty just like J-Lo's."

Sylvie manages to stop herself saying, "Sounds like wishful thinking." Emilie has a big booty, that's a given, but even in six-inch heels no-one would mistake her for Jennifer Lopez.

Someone who smelled of sweat and greasy hair obviously took

the lift just before them. They wrinkle their faces in disgust as they close the gate and squeeze into the tiny compartment. Emilie holds her nose; Sylvie carries on talking.

"Obviously, it's unlikely that less than three weeks after the attack at the Bataclan anyone's going to target Bercy . . ."

"It's not called Bercy anymore, did you know that?"

"Who goes round changing the name of a place everyone knows? A fucktard."

"We're going to be searched, like, ten times before we get into the arena. Can you imagine – terrorists killing Madonna?"

Outside, it is bitterly cold, typical pre-Christmas Paris weather, so they stuff their hands in their pockets and head for the métro. This is all they talk about. For the past three weeks, it is all anyone talks about. In a way, this suits Sylvie: if it weren't for the terrorist attacks, Emilie would ramble on endlessly about her love life. Three months ago, she met someone. The guy's a total suit, the sort of boring arsehole no-one would hook up with unless they'd gone for years without a decent shafting, but Emilie is in love. And it's starting to get ridiculous. She's capable of telling the same story ten times over. There are people like that, when you hang out with them, you feel like you're training to be a Samaritan . . .

Sylvie catches her reflection in a shop window. This is the first time in her life she has gone to a gig wearing trainers. When she was really young, she liked wearing Converse Low Tops without socks, showing a bit of ankle – like Jane Birkin. But it's been donkey's years since she gave up the Lolita look. In profile, she finds herself depressing. It looks as though her legs have got shorter. She can do anything in heels – run down a grassy hill, brave an icy pavement, skip through gravel or prance down the stairs – she is possessed by the spirit of Tina Turner. It's just a question of habit. Her legs are accustomed to high heels, her ankle never quivers, her eyes can spot the slightest obstacle at ten metres: metal gratings, cobblestones, slippery floors. She's not afraid of anything or anyone. Except those fundamentalist fuckers. They've won. She needs to feel that she can run in order to have the courage to venture out. Because, in the end, this is no joke: like everyone in Paris, she is still terrified three weeks later. That said, her white Fila Disruptors are sublime.

Emilie has launched into her stories again. She met some guy at the camp who was looking for a bassist. Emilie was up for it. She almost cried during the first rehearsal, she says, because she felt so happy to be back in that whole atmosphere. But the night before a gig as a support act at Petit Bain, her boyfriend said, I can't come, I've got a dinner that night, and when she insisted, he sweetly said, "At your age, it's ludicrous. I don't want to see you and think you look ridiculous." The first few times Emilie talked about her new boyfriend, Sylvie tried to tell her – tactfully – precisely what she thought: the guy's an arsehole. It's a no-brainer. You've landed yourself a bona fide scumbag. It's not surprising, there are a lot of them out there. But Emilie has waited fifteen years to land a decent guy – decent, well, everything is relative, let's just say a guy who's into her – so she refuses to listen. Give it a couple of weeks and she'll invent some reason to drop out of the band, that way there won't be any more unpleasant conversations.

When they reach the platform of the métro, Sylvie takes out her mobile phone and interrupts Emilie. "Let's take a selfie!" She cranks the Facetune Filter up to ten and holds the phone up so she can get them both into the shot. She knows her best angle, cheeks sucked in, pouty lips. She notices a girl giving them a withering look that says, makes you sick, two wrinkly old cougars posing for a photo . . . Just wait till you're my age, kid, you'll see what filters are for.

When Max left the voicemail offering her two tickets to Madonna, various thoughts crossed Sylvie's mind: surprise that he should think about her, joy at the opportunity to go out and to be able to give Emilie something cool for her birthday, given that she's flat broke and any gift would pose a problem, excitement at the prospect of seeing Madonna and at remembering the last time she saw her, wistfulness at realising how much everything about her life has changed since then and how bitterly she misses everything about her former life . . . And it seems that what little she has left is doomed to disappear. The camp was the last thing she could cling to. Now that, too, has collapsed. But in the surge of joy she felt on the day Max left the message, never for a second did she imagine that going into the city would be an act of resistance . . .

On the night of November 13, she had turned on the T.V. She was absentmindedly zapping while waiting for "Ce soir (ou jamais!)" to come on so she could see who the guests were. Olga, who by force of circumstance had become her flatmate, had gone out that night. Sylvie did not immediately realise what was happening. At first, people assumed it was a gangland shooting. And although she knew the place, the name of the restaurant didn't ring a bell. At first. She had idly turned on France Info. From that moment, she would remember every second of how she spent the night. Because of the loneliness. Though actually, she had received numerous text messages. People were asking each other – where are you, are you O.K.? Xavier messaged first, then Patrice, then Olga, who had had to borrow a phone and was stuck in a bar on the other side of place de la République, then Daniel, who knew a guy who was trapped on the roof of the Bataclan, then Sélim, one of whose pupils was actually working as a waitress at Le Petit Cambodge. And Sylvie, who was sitting with her phone in her lap, sending text messages, the laptop open on her Facebook timeline, the T.V. turned on and the radio to hand, had started sobbing. She suddenly realised that tomorrow morning there would be no coach trip back to the camp to debrief with the others. Fat tears had rolled down her cheeks, and with them came a feeling of tenderness.

She had waited for her son, Lancelot, to reply to her messages with a sense of mounting panic that the mantra "there's no reason he would be among the victims" did nothing to allay.

She did not know it, but he was spending the weekend in Normandy. He was at the cinema and it took a while before he texted back to reassure her. Now it was his turn to worry. He texted, don't go outside, no-one knows what's going on, and ended with, I love you. The words warmed her heart, and she began to sob harder. She wept tenaciously – about everything at once. About Lancelot sending her an affectionate message given that, lately, he has been angry with her all the time. She knows what's wrong – ever since she moved out, he can't bear to see her in this shabby two-room apartment. Alone, penniless, growing old. It's too difficult. He finds it easier to be angry. They upset each other. She can tell that he is sad. Nothing is going the way he had hoped. Not with his studies, or his girlfriend, or his friends. Every time she sees him – so, not very often – she tells him everything is going to be fine, that it's just a phase. But she is not convinced. She can perceive the man he is growing into. And she is not sure that this man is destined for a happy life. She finds it devastating, this realisation that her child is not very good at being happy. And so she cries harder as she rereads the affectionate messages from her son.

In a tearful frenzy, she had sent messages of love to everyone she had met at the camp whose phone numbers she had. Every one of them. And the more she sobbed, the more she loved them. Every fucking one of them. She learned how many victims there were when she woke up. She had no tears left. The WhatsApp group chat carried on until daybreak. Olga was still stuck in the bar. The police had cordoned off the whole area. She said there were boys crying, young men, and that she was trying to cheer them up. And for the first time that night, Sylvie had smiled. She could easily imagine the young men Olga was attempting to console and the thought distracted her. For the unwary, the giant's train of thought can be genuinely unsettling – a sort of semantic earthquake.

Sylvie had been one of the few people to go out the following morning. It felt like mid-August without the sunshine. A city forsaken. Crushed. The grief was palpable, it clung to every wall. But at everyone you met, you could smile. It was so poignant that she hadn't stayed outdoors for long – she had to go home to cry. Usually, when she's out in the street and so depressed that she feels tears begin to well, she finds a church. It is the one place in the city where you can go in, sit down and weep. It's also the one place where a single woman can linger without some creepy guy deciding to strike up a conversation. But that Saturday morning, Sylvie did not have the courage to go and weep in a church.

When she got home, she found Olga wearing a bright pink dressing gown that made her look like Barbapapa. She had just taken a shower. She had not slept a wink all night. But she was full of energy. She was waving her arms and screaming down the phone at Xavier: "Are you fucking dumb or what? People weren't even out of the Bataclan and there you were, already on Facebook writing #stopIslam? I couldn't ring you at the time because I didn't want to freak out the people in the bar I was stuck in, but I was gobsmacked that you're this far gone. Have you no heart, or just no fucking brain cells? #stopIslam? What the fuck do you mean by that, dipshit? Stop Islam from what, you ignorant twat? What the hell is going on inside your head when you write shit like that? We should kill all refugees? Haven't we had enough death as it is? Or maybe you haven't had enough, dickwad? Hasn't there been enough grief, enough anguish without you adding a sprinkle of your fuckwit frustrations? For God's sake, Xavier, go buy yourself a brain, they're pretty useful, ask anyone . . ." And then, against all expectations, having bombarded him with insults and without giving him a second to reply, she had ended the conversation with: "O.K., right, see you tonight, yeah, later," and as she hung up, she had asked, "What do you say all of us meet up here at your place tonight? Just this once . . . We need to meet up, don't you think?" Sylvie had opened her eyes wide. "What do you mean, all of us? The apartment is too small, Olga. Who else did you tell to drop round?" She had invited everyone. The whole camp. And now she was staring at Sylvie in genuine surprise – she saw no relationship between the size of the space and the impossibility of seating twenty-odd people. "They're not coming for a comfortable sit-down. They're coming so we can all be together . . . because there's too much misery. Don't add to it. Are you annoyed that I invited them to come round without clearing it with you first? I'm completely screwed up, I've had the night from hell, I might as well be a first responder with all the people I helped and supported. France isn't ready for war, believe me . . ."

At the time, Sylvie had been annoyed. But, in the end, it was a good idea. Olga was right – they needed to stick together.

Sylvie had never thrown a party at her place. Out of embarrassment. Because it was a dreary, low-ceilinged little apartment with no features. Because it contained the only three pieces of furniture that fitted. Because it was an ugly, charmless street and the lobby of the building smelled of boiled cabbage – of poor people's food. Because the dealer on the sixth floor blocked the doorway and junkies pissed in the lift shaft. She had allowed Olga in, so she could squat on the sofa. She knew Olga wouldn't notice any of these things. She's used to it. In her eyes, this squalid filth was normal.

Sylvie had made crêpes and the circumstances were so serious that she even had some of the Nutella Xavier had brought. God, it had been ages since anything containing so much fat had passed her lips. Besides, ever since her menopause started, it's been straightforward, she stopped eating properly. Strangely, she doesn't feel weak. Her girlfriends tell her that, after she hits fifty, a woman only needs five or six hundred calories a day to feel good. She doesn't know whether it's true. Even on an anorexic diet, she doesn't lose an ounce. She can't afford to put on weight. She doesn't have the money to buy herself a new wardrobe.

At around eight o'clock, Pamela had said, shall we switch off the lights? And they had found themselves, not exactly as they used to be, but with something of their old complicity. The moon in the window was a waxing crescent, a slender scar against the darkness. Patrice had asked, "Has anyone heard from Vernon?" when everyone was thinking about him but not daring to mention his name. But he had disappeared. It was the best evening she had spent since the camp had been dissolved.

She still hangs out with the same people she used to – but she no longer invites them back to hers. She lies. She says she's moved because, without Lancelot, she finds the house depressing. That it's too big, that it's pointless, that she needed a change of scene, that she loves her new neighbourhood. She says she's found a beautiful little two-room apartment just outside the Marais. She lives in Parmentier. She tells her girlfriends, I'll have you round soon, but I'm not finished decorating. In her friends' eyes, there is no cachet to social disgrace. Any more than it had in hers, before. But she does not have as much fun as she used to when she meets up with old friends.

The conversations haven't changed. It is her ear that has shifted. Comments she would previously not have noticed, she finds unsettling. There is always someone around the table to tell stories about the local yokel in the village where he has his country house, the one who lives on handouts rather than looking for work. The scrounger, the layabout, the benefit cheat – all of her rich friends seem to know at least one. He is an archetype. He twiddles his thumbs and rakes in fifteen hundred euros a month. He is a spendthrift. Two years ago, Sylvie had her own tame pauper, her cleaner's husband who had spent years lying around at home and knew every trick for getting money from the state. But now that she no longer has a cleaner, now that she has been personally forced to jump through all the bureaucratic hoops to get the allowances and the benefits to which she is entitled, she has never managed to rake in the mythical monthly fortune so talked about at the dinner parties of the rich. She is not a spendthrift, since every bill that lands on the mat is a blow to the solar plexus. She doesn't dare bang her fist on the table and scream, will you for God's sake stop spouting such rubbish, you go try and wheedle money from the state, go and fist the poor, shiftless people you're always talking about . . . Why don't you see how easy it is to make ends meet on less than a thousand euros a month? But she says nothing. She who was always so quick to open her big mouth has discovered shame. It is also because she knows these people: reality does not affect them. All that matters are the stories they tell each other over a bottle of fine wine. She was once one of them. A member of that left-wing faction. The left that is suspicious of the poor. That cares about them, granted, but knows them too well to be duped. Too nice for their own good. And can see no other way than to whip them into shape. Because that is what they're like, the poor, they're ungrateful dogs. They bite the hand that so lovingly strokes them. They are badly trained. And the rich are to blame. They've been too generous.

For a long time, Sylvie, too, had cherished the belief that someone like her could never fall so far as to be dependent on state welfare. It was not malicious, she did not even think of it as patronising. She simply believed that she was too smart, too resourceful. Genuinely not realising that this implied that others could make a bit more effort. As though, ultimately, the elegant apartment, the weekly groceries from Le Bon Marché, the taxi rides and her son's private school were attributable to some innate personal quality.

When she lost everything, a great weight had descended over

her former life – little was spared. She pounded the streets, she knocked on doors, sent letters, made proposals – she was happy to work as an usher, a translator, an assistant, a salesgirl, a temp, a freelance journalist, a toilet attendant . . . but she might just as well have saved her energy and stayed in bed scratching her arse and staring at the ceiling, because she could get no job of any kind. Not part-time, not off-the-books, not even minding children. Nothing. She began to see her friends at the camp in a different light. They had not changed. She began to notice the way she had passed judgement on them. A judgement so deeply rooted that she was unaware of it. Until her social disgrace, she had thought that Vernon, Lydia, Xavier, Patrice and the others were adorable but . . . well . . . fundamentally, a little feckless. They lacked drive. They didn't go about things the right way. Oh, she didn't hold it against them, but a part of her genuinely assumed that if her life was easier, it was because she deserved it. She would sometimes say, "I know I'm privileged . . ." but, deep down, she did not think this was quite accurate. To complete the thought, she would have had to add ". . . and if worst came to worst and I had to, I'm the sort of person who would know exactly how to hang on to those privileges." She identified with luxury. With ease. Life took it upon itself to show up her flawed thinking.

Her personal journey had mirrored that of the country: within a year, her world had completely collapsed. It had begun when Lancelot left. Her ex-husband had bluntly informed her that, from that day forward, he would not give her another cent. Legally, it made sense. But she had not been expecting it. She had always assumed that he would take care of her for as long as she needed. As though some tacit arrangement, some overarching covenant meant that he would not be so graceless as to ever leave her in the lurch. She had raised his son. She had made a good job of it. She had been his first wife. She would always be. He didn't see things the same way. He talked about the financial crisis, income taxes, hard times. Not another cent, and this from one day to the next. Sylvie had gone to explain the situation to her mother. She thought perhaps she could get an advance on her inheritance. Just a little, enough to get by, while also avoiding death duties. Until she found a more permanent solution. She had expected to walk away with twenty or thirty thousand euros, which she would have used sparingly. But, against all expectations, her mother had waffled, said she would see what she could do and more or less showed her the door. A few days later, she was hospitalised. In hindsight, Sylvie was horrified to realise that the stroke that had felled her mother was related to her request. There was nothing she could do. She could hate herself, but there was nothing she could do. Within a few short days, she lost her mother.

Since hearing of her death, Sylvie has woken up every night to sheets sodden with sweat. Paradoxically, it is almost pleasant. She feels as though she is purging her fears. It is not exactly practical – sometimes she has to get up in the middle of the night to change the sheets. She has had to deal with everything. It's unbelievable how much paperwork a death entails. Her father is almost ninety, he is in no fit state to close accounts. Her brother was hardly likely to help, he lives in Australia and made only a flying visit to attend the funeral. Sylvie had installed herself at the little desk in the living room where she had seen her mother sit when dealing with the accounts, as she often did, since she managed the family fortunes with great seriousness. Or that, at least, was what everyone in the family had always thought. At first, Sylvie could make neither head nor tail of it all. So many bank accounts seemed like a pointless waste of ink. Amused and a little bewildered, strangely touched by her mother's scatty accounting system, she had assumed the first revolving credit was an anomaly. When she found the second, she wondered what could possibly have got into her mother. But the more papers she dug out, the more folders she opened, the more she delved into her mother's affairs, the more the vast edifice was revealed in all its terrifying prodigality: an outlandish series of financial arrangements, a complex network of loans taken to repay other loans, to pay off other loans. She had spent several days deciphering the spidery scrawl, horrified at the extent of the cataclysm. Her mother, a woman whose seriousness bordered on steeliness, a *grande bourgeoise* who could always trace the line between what was correct and what was deplorable, had actually been a brilliant fraudster. And her father, drunk on Fernet-Branca and tranquillisers knew nothing about it. Sylvie looked around the opulent apartment, remembered what a happy couple her parents had made in this regal splendour. She pored over the accounts. The debts ran to hundreds of thousands of euros. All to keep up the facade. There were many other family secrets that had never gone beyond these four walls that Sylvie knew – how her father could be handy with his fists when he had had too much to drink – other people might have called it domestic violence, in their house they said, "He's a forceful personality." Her mother was hit by cupboard doors, her eyes were blackened by unruly branches, she fell down the stairs. But that was alright. The edifice remained solid. It was only as she plunged into the intricate maze of debt so patiently fashioned by her mother that Sylvie realised: it had been nothing but a facade. All this so as not to have to sell the Porsche Cayenne, or give up membership to the Sporting Club that her father had not set foot in in years. It was too complicated. She had called her brother for help, he had said, I can't come home right now, sell everything. He was disappointed. Like her, he had been expecting a handsome inheritance. Sylvie had taken her courage in both hands and broken the news to her father, who called her a liar and a lunatic. Only to phone her a few weeks later when the first summons arrived from the bailiffs. She had come back to sell the car and the furniture, and file for bankruptcy.

Her father looked at her as though she were a gutter rat. He was convinced that she had stolen the money. Yet he had to have known. Sylvie could not see how he could have been oblivious to the fact that, for decades, money kept going out when there was no money coming in. This is an equation simple enough for even the rich to understand. He had had no choice but to move to the south, to live with his sister in Avignon. She had never heard from him again.

Sylvie and Emilie reach the gates of Bercy arena. There are very few people given that there is a concert tonight. An uncannily beautiful bouncer is explaining to new arrivals that he cannot allow a crowd to gather on the corner since it would be an easy target for a drive-by shooting – and he points to the spot, conjuring the image of a car slowing and the ensuing carnage – so everyone has to go through the park behind the stadium. Without even exchanging a glance, Sylvie and Emilie stand facing the bouncer and listen as he gives the explanation several times. Eventually, he notices them and they are forced to follow the others.

"Jesus Christ, where did they get that guy – he's sex on legs!"

"Isn't there something else we could ask, some other information we need?"

"Unfortunately not."

"I'm telling you right now, if Madonna sees him, he's getting an All Access pass."

A few metres ahead, guys in fluorescent yellow jackets are waving torches and shouting directions, trying to direct the crowd. They are already hoarse. Paris is very different. People have put aside their superciliousness. They are meekly following orders. It is a long walk. No-one complains. If they were told to circumnavigate the entire arrondissement on their hands and knees, not a single Parisian would protest.

Sylvie and Emilie walk around the park behind Bercy and take their places in the queue. Everyone is probably thinking the same thing. Is that ditch deep enough to hide in? If a sniper were to appear on the balcony overlooking the crowd, how long would it take to overpower him?

Sylvie gets a text from Max, he has arrived, he's looking for them. She is dreading the thought of seeing him again. When he offered the tickets, she wondered whether he might be trying to pick her up. Not that she has any desire to sleep with him. But she would be upset to think that he might be thinking about it and then, seeing her, decide, yeah, maybe not, she hasn't aged well. For her part, there's no risk of being disappointed: Max was never an oil painting. As a general rule, ugly people age well. And ugly as he was, Max was always a ladies' man. He had flirted with Sylvie back when she was with Alex. And she had given in. He was the sort of lover you feel ashamed of when you're young, because he's not remotely sexy. But he was persuasive. He had never said anything uncalled-for, so she had not worried about him – in fact, she had never even considered him fuckable. They had been going up the steps in front of the Elysée-Montmartre, it was taking ages because everyone recognised Max and everyone had something they wanted to tell him, and as he dropped her off backstage, he had whispered into her ear, "I know I shouldn't even be thinking this, but fuck I love your smell. I really want to screw you." Sylvie had found the comment disgusting, and completely out of place. And incredibly arousing. That he should dare. In that loutish, offhand tone, that deep, self-confident voice. And that night, during the second half of the gig, she gave him a blowjob in the toilets while he held her by the hair and told her to suck him good. More than twenty years later, even the thought of it is terrifying. It had been a one-off, they had never talked about it. But he had always paid her special attention. And when Alex had left her, he was one of the few people in her circle who had worried about her. Max had never again found an artist who had the scale and ambition of Alex. In the music business, he lives from hand to mouth. Sylvie heard that he sometimes manages young singers from T.V. talent shows. They lost touch. Then Max had reappeared in the most unexpected way imaginable, during a weekend in Barcelona, with Xavier and Pénélope . . . As it turns out, Stéphanie, one of Max's exes, had been to one of the convergences and she and Sylvie had become friends . . . so Max got in touch with her, and they agreed to meet up for a drink sometime. And then this gig, and Max offering her a couple of spare tickets . . .

She recognises him from a distance. From the strange way he has always walked – as though about to fall flat on his face. But mostly from the garish colours. He always did have shitty taste. He's wearing a shiny purple jacket with a silver collar. Truly hideous. Max always wanted to be a dandy. But he has no fashion sense. He wears clothes two sizes too small that make him look obese. They say hello, Sylvie introduces Emilie – they talk for a couple of minutes about the extraordinary coincidence that brought them back together. The queue slowly trudges forward in the biting cold. And then, within five minutes, they're back to talking about the terrorist attacks. Terror has slipped inside their bodies like a puppeteer's hand. Except that Max shows no sign that he is afraid. On the contrary, he seems to find the situation auspicious, exciting. He is a hustler, a con artist – the sort of guy who can turn the most chaotic situation to his advantage. And Sylvie knows enough about his career to know he is not faking it. Max never mellowed, he never joined the bourgeoisie. He's still the same aggressive working-class punk – someone who's not fazed by violence because it's his preferred element. In this turbulent atmosphere, he is like a fish in water. He lights a cigarette and, laughing, turns to Emilie who has just asked whether he has known Sylvie long. "I'm not going to give you the precise date, it would make us both sound old . . . but she was already venomous back then." Then, turning to Sylvie, he adds, "You've hardly changed at all, just enough not to be even more terrifying than you used to be," and he slips his arm through hers, as though escorting her to a ball. She smiles at him, trying not to make it obvious that she is enjoying his flirtation. The compliments he whispers into her ear have the same effect as slipping into a sweet-scented jacuzzi – massaging and relaxing her. It's been a long time since anyone flirted with her like this. She presses herself against him gratefully.

Max talks to her about Alex. He says that at terrible moments like this, he misses not being able to talk to him. Sylvie sees Emilie wrinkle her nose when she explains that, during the convergences, they use the tapes recorded by Alex. But Max slides a hand down her back, a casual, elegant gesture. She craves his attention. And she talks and talks until she feels a little dizzy. She is aware that she is telling him things he doesn't need to know. She wants to talk about what it was like at the camp. Because it is the only thing in her life that is not pathetic. The words come in a torrent, and she makes him laugh, piques his interest.

Men kneeling with their hands tied behind their backs have their throats cut, one by one. In all seriousness, Dopalet wonders: is it better to die by having your throat slit by a cannibal or to have your entrails devoured by a horde of zombies? He has set his laptop on the kitchen counter while he defrosts Cantonese fried rice in the microwave. Without taking his eyes off the screen, he opens a bottle of Coke Zero and pours it into a glass of crushed ice. It's one of the typical questions raised by "The Walking Dead": decapitated or disembowelled? You really have to be a hardcore masochist to watch such horrors – the whole show is a series of unbearably tense moments set against a bloodbath of slaughter and evisceration, peppered with pathetic metaphysical dialogue written by some geek who's probably spent his whole life holed up in his bedroom feeding on doughnuts and comics. But Dopalet is fascinated by "The Walking Dead". He is watching it for the second time. Every time he thinks, that's it, I'm used to it, I'm not terrified anymore, some atrocity comes and he is once again a frightened child, teeth clenched, delighted and appalled.

He did not go into the office today. He did not go in yesterday either. He calls his assistant. He says he has lumbago, the doctor has said to rest up and not to move for a couple of days. The simplest things are becoming complicated. Only at home does he feel alright, he finds it more and more difficult to go out. He needs to get help. He doesn't know who to turn to. All of his therapists have let him down, he doesn't want to call them. He is literally consumed with terror at the very thought of opening his e-mail. When he manages to force himself to do so, he forwards every message to his colleagues – he tells himself he needs to learn to delegate. But he simply cannot bring himself to answer them himself. He deletes all his voicemails without listening to them. Just swipe left on his phone and everything is gone.

Lately, when he went into the office, he would fake it. As he pushed open the main door, he would automatically plaster a smile on his face. No-one could guess how he felt. He let nothing show. He would chat to a few people for five minutes, then go into his office with orders not to be disturbed. He would spend hours on YouTube watching old videos of McEnroe, wearing a headset so no-one would realise that, on the other side of the door, the C.E.O. is at the end of his rope, he is at a complete loss. This is the least that he owes his team: the illusion that someone is at the helm. In the late afternoon, he would emerge, make up a meeting to justify leaving early. He knows what is happening. He knows that things are not right. But he can hardly choose a psychiatrist online. And he doesn't want to phone a friend to ask for a contact. He doesn't have any friends. All the people he knows would be only too happy to know he is foundering.

A zombie devours the intestines of his victims, whose screams fill the kitchen, mingling with the hideous groans of the walkers. The intestines spill out, slick and bloody across the ground. The story of his life. A momentary lapse of concentration and the enemy is on top of you – ripping your skin with his teeth, eating you alive, feeding on your pain. The millions of people who watch this series identify with the situation – you can never rest, never stop. Danger lurks everywhere. That is the reality. There is no safe haven, only brief periods of calm. The outside world is a nightmare. You cannot weaken or they will surround you, flay you alive, feast on your guts. The T.V. show may have been written by some halfwit American, but its message is universal: kill before you are killed. If your hand trembles, if you hesitate, you're dead. There is no place here for finer feeling. You're either the butcher or the cattle. There's no room for nuance. To survive is to be prepared to kill.

For as long as he doesn't leave his apartment, Dopalet doesn't feel too bad. He's not bored. Morning coffee, he puts on an episode, lounges around in sweats. He keeps peripheral thoughts – unpleasant thoughts – at bay, by concentrating on the heroes' journeys. He knows that his assistant didn't believe him when he said he could barely move. She wanted to set up Skype meetings, wanted to e-mail him files. He refused to give in. He stood his ground. The attitude of people in the office is beginning to change. Dopalet is aware that they are talking about him behind his back, saying that he is behaving oddly. Thankfully, the Christmas break is coming up soon. At least he'll get ten fucking minutes' peace.

His daughter won't be with him this year. She is going to visit her mother. He will make the best of it, get some rest, rebuild his strength. In a few days, things will be fine. Tomorrow, he will go for a run. Every day – or almost every day – he works out on his exercise bike while watching an episode. It's by working on his body that he'll get back on his feet. His mind will follow. He really should call his personal trainer. He cancelled his sessions a few months back.

He would love to produce a series. He enjoys the company. You set out with a group of characters, a rhythm. It's like a tap. It keeps running. No-one lets you down. No-one asks you to think. People look after each other. No-one ever abandons you.

Things were so different when he was young. Kids like him went to a cinema club. They would emerge from screenings of Kurosawa, Pasolini, Wenders and listen to each other talk for hours. Dopalet would pretend to understand. He has never been an intellectual. He read "Cahiers du Cinéma" every month without understanding a word. He would memorise phrases, expressions, learn the names by heart so that he could keep up with conversations. Kids today don't bother with all that shit. When they're fed up kicking arse in some massive multiplayer game, they watch violent T.V. shows. These days, no-one pretends to be an intellectual. It's old hat. They're right. What was it for, all that brain juice?

Dopalet wishes someone would bring him a good idea for a T.V. series. But the French are morons. From time to time, a good pitch comes in, he meets with the screenwriters, they come to his office and do a whole number, they win him over, he says, O.K., let's work up a shooting script. And six months later he finds himself with a third-rate cop show ripped off from "Julie Lescaut". Regardless of the premise of the show, that's how it always ends up: Julie Lescaut with her battered AK-47 lurking against a dark background. That's French television. Dopalet dreams of fighting tooth and nail to produce a first-rate project. If he got his wish, everything would change. He'd make an effort. He'd forget the fears, the attacks, the disappointments, the betrayals. He would move mountains. If he got his wish. If someone brought him a half-decent proposal.

The cinema as he has always known it is dead. People like him are on borrowed time. At least he knows that. It's exactly like "The Walking Dead": the world is divided into two groups. Those who realise that this is war, and those who cling to their former lives. A lot of people in the business persist in believing that everything will carry on as usual. But the whole thing is fucked. He can't raise the money to fund his projects. And he's not the kind of producer who takes unnecessary risks – he's not interested in arthouse films, low-budget projects or ambitious movies that don't sell tickets. He has no interest in producing the next Palme d'Or. He thinks box office. He thinks dream cast, comedy, family entertainment. But it's not enough.

Why would the public bother to trek to the cinema to see a French movie? They stay at home. They can get everything they need online. He's the same. He torrents like everyone else. What choice does he have? He's not going to wait six months to watch the next episode of some T.V. show just because syndication contracts take time to nail down! Anything that's not on an official site, he watches for free on a streaming site. Netflix, because Antoine has given him his login. A site that stops you streaming T.V. shows via a video projector . . . The difference between him and other people is that he doesn't delude himself that things are going to be fine. They're not going to be fine. They're going to go from bad to worse.

He starts a new episode. Sometimes he makes lists. What do the walking dead in the series represent? Refugees? Aids victims? The unemployed? The poor? Memories? The dead who have not been forgotten? The victims of historic genocides? Or he makes a list of all the shelters used in the series. Prison, farmhouse, motorway, military research centre, hospital, supermarket, slaughterhouse.

The lists are pointless. But Dopalet knows that this is how it works. By intently studying a successful project, by picking it apart. That's how he knows that, the day someone offers him a good project, he'll be ready. He'll be on top of his game. Maybe "The Walking Dead" is just a fucking allegory about the Jews being led out of Egypt by Moses. He needs to make a list of the enemies faced by the survivors. Because obviously, in the series, the real threat is not from the walking dead. The most brutal enemies are the other groups of survivors. Zombies are fine: they're slow, they've got nothing upstairs. He would love to have these conversations with someone. He has never been so alone.

There's rarely been a leader as dumb as the guy who leads the survivors in the series. That's a really clever idea. It makes it contemporary. There are about twenty of them, they've all got skills, intelligence, physical strength. And what do they do? They pick the dumbest fucker to lead them. It's really well observed. It's like the French political system. Look at all the available options and choose the most inappropriate.

At times, he doesn't know whether he identifies with the humans or the zombies. He too is little more than a shambling, monstrous form clacking his jaws and moaning from a hunger that can never be sated.

Laurie is not coming round to sleep at his tonight. It's been three days. He needs to clarify things with her. But when he has dumped her, he will have no-one, Laurie has signed up for night classes at the Beaux-Arts. She's in the habit of having a drink in the ninth arrondissement – the hippest area these days. She hangs out with some girls she's made friends with there. As to what she's actually doing, go figure. Maybe she's seeing someone else. Laurie is a liar. About big things as well as small. When he first met her, he imagined that he had only to reassure her for her to be more reliable. It's insane, the lies people tell themselves when they don't want to admit that the person they fancy is a slimeball. They go through all sorts of contortions, convincing themselves they can fix things. It never works. Someone who behaves like a shit is someone who has already had lots of opportunities to change and has no intention of doing so. Laurie is a dirty little bitch who manipulates him. He read her diary. A few days ago. "I don't know why I spend so much time being nice to people who deserve nothing more than a good slap. I don't know why I worry so much about what that fat fuck thinks about me." Outside, the rain fell relentlessly, like a grey sheet hung in front of his window. He was standing in the doorway. He was devastated. He would never have expected such savagery from her. Pages and pages of sheer loathing, all devoted to him. Schmuck, dirty old man, grandad, fuckwit, needle-dick, arsewipe . . . Laurie is so pretty on the outside. An adorable little pixie – she has a sexy, husky voice and loves to be cuddled. Dopalet had been afraid of hurting her. He didn't dare tell her that he often thought about his wife. He was afraid that she would get too attached.

That particular night, he had been on good form. He was thinking, I feel a lot better in this new apartment, this new area. He had been full of good intentions – he had been thinking about Laurie and telling himself that he should give the relationship a chance. That he was lucky to have stumbled on such a gentle woman.

Laurie had forgotten her sports bag, the one she takes when she does Krav Maga and aquabiking. The zip had been open. He had not been prying. That's not his style. But he had seen the blue Clairefontaine notebook sticking out. He found the fact that she had an exercise book strangely moving. He had flicked through it. He realised that he had never seen her handwriting. These days, it's possible to spend months on end with someone without knowing whether their handwriting is round, slanted, illegible or spidery . . . He had been surprised by Laurie's writing. It looks like that of an older, more mature woman. Desultorily, he had read a few lines. He hadn't known that she kept a diary. He assumed she used the notebook to jot down ideas for diets, song titles, the address of a hairdresser or the name of a masseuse. "He never asks my opinion, he fucks me even when I don't feel like it and I stare at the ceiling and don't move and it doesn't even bother that filthy pig, he climbs on top of me though I'm lying there like a corpse but he jerks off in my pussy he doesn't care that I don't like it. That'll teach me to sleep with dirty old men." He had not immediately realised that this torrent of excrement was devoted entirely to him. He initially assumed that she had copied out the text from something written by someone else. Maybe she was preparing an audition. A role. Some piece of gritty realism. The words could not come from her. Her delicate little mouth, her slender fingers, her splendid buttocks. Little Laurie, so feminine, so smiling, whose fundamental quality was gentleness. She had nothing in common with these words. He had put down the exercise book, a little disgusted. After a few minutes he had gone back to the sports bag, taken out the notebook, and settled himself on the sofa to read it seriously. It was a chronicle of day-to-day hatred, together with a list of the gifts he had given her. The worst thing, she said, was having sex with him. Alright, granted she had never shown a passionate enthusiasm for the act. But women in general are like that, except the ones who have a problem, obviously. It's a natural dissymmetry – something to do with hormones, easy to understand. Men want sex and women want love. It had already occurred to him that Laurie might be frigid. He had never imagined that she despised him because he liked sleeping with her. He had read the words she had written about him. Outside, the downpour had stopped and the living room was ablaze with ironic late-afternoon sun. He had carefully put the exercise book back where he had found it and listened to Gould playing the Brahms intermezzi. He wished he could wash out his insides.

He has said nothing to Laurie. He has spaced out their dates. Soon, he will ask her to delete his address and phone number. He won't mention the notebook. A flickering joy in him has guttered out. He hadn't realised how happy she made him until now. What a waste.

He thought that she liked his tattoo. In the notebook, she mocks him "and that tacky yakuza tattoo on his back, the muppet". He doesn't care. He likes his new back. It means something. Several times a day, he goes into the bathroom and, using a double mirror, contemplates the finished artwork. It's sublime. Now that he knows he will never have to see the guy again, he feels a sort of gratitude to the tattooist. Magnificent work. In the last two sessions, as he worked on the shadows and the details, Dopalet had seen the image on his back suddenly appear, become three-dimensional. Exist. He loves the image that adorns his skin. It is a powerful shield. Any guy capable of enduring what he has had to endure to gain a second skin can't be a complete loser. When he gazes at his back in the mirror, he thinks he will get through this. Get back on his feet. He has forgotten the original inscription. It has been covered over, buried. He is getting used to the idea that this powerful, unsettling body is his. He wants to start going to the swimming pool again. To shrug off the water wings and start doing lengths again.

He is once more as round as a balloon. Worse than before he dieted. His fondness for Michel and Augustin desserts has been his undoing. He wolfs down a bucket of chocolate mousse every night while he watches his T.V. shows. Plus a variety of other shit that he munches on during the day. Everyone has a defence mechanism. He has placed a layer of fat between himself and the world.

He feels like taking a break between episodes. But he doesn't want to turn on the radio, or B.F.M. Business. Rolling news channels are factories that churn out fear. Since the terrorist attacks in November, he has not had the strength to watch them. He is stunned. He often thinks of an article he read about dogs. "Learnt Helplessness". You lock dogs in a cage and you slam them against the floor. Pretty soon, the dogs stop trying to get out to ward off the shock. Or to bite. They just lie on the ground and take it.

Like the rest of his compatriots, he had still not got over the *Charlie Hebdo* massacre. How could he possibly process the Bataclan? So, he no longer listens to the news. He does not want to hear about Syria. Or the Congo. Or Palestine. He has reached peak saturation for atrocities.

On the day of the *Charlie Hebdo* attack, he had been in a bakery buying a galette des rois when he heard two men talking and the taller of them saying, "There've been shots fired at *Charlie Hebdo*." The guy looked like a hipster. Instinctively, Dopalet had taken out his phone. He was thinking about the mentally disturbed man who had fired shots in the offices of *Libération*. But this was not the same. He didn't often buy *Charlie Hebdo*. The annual "caricature issue", by way of support, like everyone else. He had spent the afternoon on Facebook. He had watched as, one by one, his friends' Facebook icons turned black. Like a landscape growing dark. He had called the office to tell the staff they could go home. He had been on the January 11 march. Although an ochlophobe, he felt no fear in this vast, slow-moving crowd. He had already been emotionally devastated by his own recent assault. He had never quite got back on his feet. He never wanted to watch the video of the bouncers being slaughtered that was circulating on the internet. Nor will he ever watch the videos of those who survived the Bataclan.

But this time, he is done with being complacent. You're either the butcher or the cattle. Whether Arabs or Jews, these people have to learn to shut up. People like him are in shock. It's temporary. The country will pull itself together. Defend itself.

On the night of the Bataclan, he had been with Laurie. This was before he knew who he was dealing with. She had been terrified. He had assumed the protective male role. He missed Amélie. He didn't dare call her. He hadn't told her that he had met someone else. He doesn't want to hurt her. He felt that telling her he was with a girl ten years her junior would be hurtful. Not that he blames Amélie for anything. Her behaviour has been exemplary. After his assault, she was so supportive. She put up with his insomnia, his migraines, his weight gain. He would explode with rage over trivial things. He would scream because the internet connection was down. He would seethe and fume because his flight had been delayed. He could no longer control himself. He reminded himself of the nervous cases of the nineteenth century who were advised

to stay in bed and avoid all activity. This would have suited him –
having nothing to do, no irritations to deal with. But he had a
company, a staff that depended on him. Amélie had put up with
everything. Later he had been unfair to her. She had warned him.
She had told him, I'm constantly on edge, wondering what's going
to set off your next outburst, I'm exhausted. His ugly mood infected
all around him. He knew that he needed to calm down. But he
would call her a bitch when she came home late from a dinner with
her girlfriends while he had been brooding at home. He would
make rude comments about her English accent when they enter-
tained American friends. She would spend Saturday at a sauna
leaving him at home, pacing the floor, waiting, and cursing her for
spending her weekends on such frivolities when she had the whole
week in which to sweat. He would dwell on these slights. Sharpen
his knives. And when she was least expecting it, he would let rip
with a diatribe of insults. One night she told him she needed time
out. On the night before an important premiere. Even though she
knew that he was in the shit at work, that he needed her to back
him up. He had said, are you fucking kidding me? Who has time
outs? Who? But she had simply said, I can't do this anymore, I need
to find myself again, to protect myself from you, I can't put up with
it anymore, your problems, your demands, your mood swings. I've
asked my father for the keys to the house in Biarritz, I'm leaving
tomorrow morning. He had raged and pleaded and wept all night.
She had left with their daughter.

Since the assault, everything has been crumbling. At work, in
his private life, in the country as a whole, and beyond the borders
. . . a succession of terrifying news stories. The whole world is
falling apart. He no longer listens to the news on the radio or on

television. He no longer listens to his voicemails. He takes a square of dark chocolate with sea salt and a handful of almonds, settles himself on the sofa and presses PLAY on a new episode. The battery on his laptop is dead. He sighs, then gets up and goes into the kitchen to look for the charger. In passing, he glances at his mobile phone. He opens his e-mail. In an act of sheer bravura, he reads the most recent message. The characters in "The Walking Dead" would laugh if they knew that a guy like him, holed up in an apartment with running water and a freezer full of food, panics at the thought of opening an e-mail.

He doesn't know the sender – probably some smart-arse who's about to tell him he's written the finest screenplay of the century. Someone who doesn't include a subject line – that in itself is infuriating.

"Bleach. Subutex. Céleste, et cetera . . . We haven't met yet, but I think I have something to say that may interest you."

Shit! Every time he thinks he is getting back on his feet, life punches him in the face and he falls down again. The first e-mail he has opened in weeks, and it has to be this?

Feverishly, he Googles the name of the sender, Maxime Chapio. He has to sit down to organise his thoughts. On the second page of Google results, he finds a blue hyperlink to – a former manager of Bleach. He'll break the little fucker's face for him. What is this? Some kind of revenge? A threat? Dopalet feels rage roiling in his blood. In his hands, in his legs. In his churning stomach. The terrorism has gone on long enough, in all its forms. The time has come to stand up to it. Although for days he has not had the strength to write a single e-mail, he immediately pings back a reply to this one. "What do you want from me?" They'll see what he's made of.

He's sick and tired of letting himself be walked all over. People think he's down, that he's on the ropes, that they have done for him. They think he is finished. A sudden madness wells in him. He is going to get this guy. How dare he? How dare he send this kind of message? Instantly, he receives a reply: "Why don't we meet up and talk about it?"

He arranges to meet in the bar of the Georges-V. It is a place he rarely goes. The last time was to meet Sophie Marceau, which was five, maybe six years ago . . . It is a long time since Sophie went out of her way to have a drink with him. He's no longer the sort of producer she might find interesting. It will come back. He showered, shaved and dug out the old Armani jeans he had stuffed in the back of the wardrobe, convinced that he would never again be fat enough to wear them. Before slipping on his Dior Homme shirt, he stood in three-quarter profile and glanced at his tattoo. The fuckwit who sent him that e-mail had better watch his step. He doesn't realise he's messing with a guy with a tattoo. A modern-day yakuza. Dopalet will eat him alive.

He is glad that he went out. The moment he steps into the bar, he realises he made the right decision. Everything is muted, the rosy glow of the lights, the carpets, the wood panelling. That particular bustle of Parisian palaces. Everything is arranged to reassure him, to make him feel comfortable. It is working. It's good for him to get a little fresh air. He has succeeded. He dressed himself, he went out. Now that he is calm, it occurs to him that the guy he is meeting does not necessarily wish him ill.

His appointment arrives ten minutes late. Who the hell is this guy? He is wearing a jacket tailored in purple velvet. Dopalet would never dare wear such a thing. He has often envied those people who fashion a look. He finds them ridiculous, but he envies them nonetheless. They create characters for themselves. It's an artistic thing. He could never do it; he has responsibilities. The guy is tall, with a jutting chin, he doesn't take off his dark glasses. In the bar of the Georges-V. He's got some nerve. Dopalet waves him over. Difficult to guess his age. He could be a jaundiced thirty-something or a well-preserved fifty. He is clearly not accustomed to opulence, but he acts casually. If he is impressed, he does not let it show. His handshake is firm, his wiry body and his smile remind Dopalet of Willem Dafoe.

Having spent days holed up watching "The Walking Dead", Dopalet weighs up the man with the eye of a man setting off to war. If a zombie were to walk into the bar, Max looks like the type to plunge a razorblade into his throat. In a zombie attack, he would be a good partner.

The waiter comes over to their table before they have time to get to the heart of the matter. The guy orders a whisky. Either he has no idea how much things cost here, or he is assuming that Dopalet will be picking up the tab. The producer folds his arms in a gesture of defiance, but smiles, to show that he wants to see the other man's hand.

"I was a little thrown by your e-mail. What a mystery!"

"Oh, I like to think that we immediately understood one another. Otherwise, it was pointless either of us coming here."

Max twists a huge scorpion-shaped ring around his middle finger. Dopalet finds the gesture irritating, though he could not say why. He is afraid that the man has been sent by those two little bitches. It seems obvious that he has underestimated them. This has sometimes been a weakness with him. He had assumed that, in hiring the finest professionals, he would quickly track them down. He was wrong. They are still on the run, and he has had time to have a Japanese print tattooed on his back. Dopalet waits for the man to explain himself. Max leans towards him, his tone shifting as he makes a confession:

"It has taken a staggering number of coincidences for me to trace this back to you. At this stage in the contest, I'd go so far as to say that we were bound to meet. Our paths have crossed many times. I eventually realised that, in one way or another, Alex Bleach was always at the centre of this."

"You were one of his managers, if Google is anything to go by."

"I was his manager. His first manager."

"Good, good. And how does that concern me?"

"Bleach's confession. Subutex. Céleste. Aïcha. The Hyena. We have a lot of things in common."

He counts them off on his fingers as one might calmly set down the cards in a royal flush. Dopalet feels his heart begin to race. He needs to hide his excitement, keep control of the conversation. He cannot reveal his amazement. He sips his whisky, forces himself to move slowly. He says:

"A charming list. But what has the Hyena got to do with anything?"

"You hired her to track down Bleach. She came to see me, back when she was working for you. I remember her well. A very beautiful woman. I was surprised to find out that she's one of Subutex's gang these days."

The rush of adrenaline is so intense it is almost painful. Dopalet feels as though he is emerging from a coma – from a fog that has lasted for months. His body is exultant. He is finally facing the right person.

"Do you know where they are?"

"Would I be right in assuming that you're looking for them?"

"That depends."

He's bluffing. He's sure it's obvious. He can't hide his excitement. He is probably about as convincing playing the blasé guy as he would be if Scarlett Johansson offered him a handjob and he said, hang on, *chérie*, let me just check my schedule. Already, he sees his interlocutor in a completely different light. He'd like to be the kind of guy who can wear purple, a pair of Ray Bans and ghetto jewellery. Max sits up, baring his teeth as he smiles. Makes a sweeping gesture with his hand.

"I would imagine that someone like you, a man with your firepower, already has all the information he needs about that gang of crackpots. Do stop me if I'm being presumptuous . . ."

"It never hurts to be audacious . . . You tell me what you know and I'll tell you if it interests me."

"As I already said: a number of highly improbable coincidences has led me to you . . . As it happens, I know several of the people who hang around with Subutex . . . who I also know, as it goes."

"Small world . . ."

"And I've taken an interest in their stories, for reasons of my own . . . I like to think that I might be able to track down Céleste, for example. I certainly know where to look for her."

"O.K. You've got my undivided attention."

Céleste. She was the one who had wielded the needle. She was the one who had branded him. Not one of Dopalet's private detectives has been able to locate her. This guy is serious. He knows things. The producer gestures to the waiter, drawing a circle in the air to signal for the same again. Two whiskies. They have much to talk about. It is his turn to lean close to his interlocutor, to lower his voice to a whisper, forcing the man to move closer, as he says:

"Would you like to start from the beginning?"

And Max wraps both arms around the back of his chair. The smug fucker flashes a winning smile and answers pat:

"I'm waiting on a payment that has been held up; financially, I'm in a very sticky situation. I don't suppose you could speed things along?"

"Shall we wait until our glasses have been refilled? I get the impression that we have much to toast, you and I."

"To our fortuitous encounter."

"To us."

VERNON WAKES UP IN A PURE WHITE, HIGH-CEILINGED ROOM; the wooden floorboards are in terrible condition. It takes some effort for him to remember which city he is in. There are some mornings when he has time to make coffee before he resolves this question. It is the biting cold that puts him on the right track. The tip of his nose is frozen. Belfast. He's been freezing his balls off since he got here. On the floor, next to the bed, a book in French that he found in the living room the night before and picked up, thinking he might read it, only to plunge into sleep as into an abyss. *The Long Goodbye*, in the Gallimard "Série Noire" edition. It is too cold for him to get out of bed, he grabs his mobile phone and pulls the blankets over his head. Max has sent him a message on Facebook. He doesn't open it. An uncomfortable feeling washes over him: last night, he had been gobsmacked to see Max rock up in a club in Northern Ireland – a very different context from their former meetings. But after the surprise and the trite platitudes – fuck me, what are you doing here it must be what fifteen years it's wild running into you here God it was so sad about Alex – Vernon had felt an uncomfortable sense of foreboding, one that floods back now as he collects his thoughts.

He opens the Facebook app he has been using since he left the camp. It's not a personal profile, it's one to which everyone at the camp has the password, allowing them to share a timeline – a profile from which no-one posts. At the top of the page is the one-liner "Lemmy out of here!" next to an ace of spades icon. At first, he doesn't get it, but six photos later the penny drops. Lemmy from Motörhead is dead. Seventy years old, from cancer. He tries to read an obit on one of the news sites, but a bunch of advertising pop-ups make it impossible. He puts down his phone and rolls onto his side. He thinks about the last Motörhead gig he saw, November 2013 at Le Zénith. The whole arena filled with guys his age. Guys who looked like they work in the service sector who were transformed into headbangers by the opening chords of "Ace of Spades". When he thinks about Lemmy, he pictures that photo of him in denim micro-shorts, puffing on a cigarette, looking wasted. Lemmy never took himself seriously. He never invented a public persona – he never needed to. He had the attitude, he had the sound. Motörhead were like the Ramones or AC/DC, not so much a rock band as a load-bearing wall. Love 'em or hate 'em, the house you live in was built out of that sound. Vernon has listened to Motörhead in vans, howling along at the top of his lungs with his mates. On headphones, walking down the street, chest puffed out, happy, filled with that distinctive happy-warlike energy. He'd stick on "No Sleep 'til Hammersmith" when he was opening up the shop to get his head in order, and from the first notes he would know it was going to be a good day. He got through more than one break-up listening to the old bastard's shrapnel voice. That jagged, re-assuring sound, a vital bellow that came from the pit of his stomach. This was music as therapy, music that slaps you on the back and says, "You're gonna be O.K."

Vernon thinks about the people from the camp. He doesn't write to them. He hasn't replied to any of their messages. The more he waits, the more complicated it will be for him to reappear. He knows the score. Even on the night of November 13, he didn't get in touch. He was in Wolverhampton, where he had played a set the night before. He had feverishly scrambled to open Facebook to check everyone's status. Lydia sent him a message. Sylvie sent him a message. Sélim sent him a message. Vernon felt too churned up to feign nonchalance and send them a few thoughtful words.

The life he lives these days is not unpleasant. He is adapting. Lots of hours spent doing fuck-all, and the rest of the time he's on the move, and it suits him, this somewhat empty rhythm. He daydreams, he contemplates, he listens to music. It's like social death, with two hours every night when he shows up and spins some discs.

Vernon picks up his phone again. On social media, a young woman is protesting: "Everyone's posting tribute photos to Lemmy – can I just remind you this is a guy who collected Nazi memorabilia." The objection is so irrelevant that even the trolls don't bother to flame her. Lemmy was a moron. It was part of the act. He wasn't a saint. Motörhead made music for guys who were thick as shit and proud of it, for guys who never raised their hand in class, who didn't want gold stars, it was a rallying cry for retards, misfits and incompetents. It was music that proclaimed, I'm happy to be a cretin. Lemmy was not made for swots and prudes. But these days, nobody wants to deal with specific cultural codes, everything that appears on the internet has to be instantly comprehensible and completely without nuance. Seen in that light, Lemmy is just a pathetic sex maniac who collected military memorabilia.

*

Vernon hears voices on the other side of the door, the other residents are awake and having breakfast. They number three D.J.s and a handful of musos – Vernon doesn't know precisely how many of them are staying in this huge apartment. Mariana did not come with him for these dates. In Liverpool, she ran into a particularly ugly guy – scraggy beard, deep-set beady eyes, thin lips and the face of a mouth-breather. Wherever they go, Mariana runs into people that she knows – otherwise she would never have been able to get Vernon so many gigs. As they travel together, Vernon realises that she has spent a lot of her life at raves. When he first met her, she told him she did piecemeal work here and there. She had seemed like the sort of vanilla thirty-something spewed out by the financial crisis – people who don't seem to have even started their career although they've been in the job market for a decade. But Mariana's little jobs paid the bills, she was involved in techno in the same way Vernon was involved in rock. It was hardly surprising that she showed up at a convergence: she'd already travelled all around Europe to dance in the most extraordinary places. Anyway, she runs into this guy and Vernon can see, from a distance, flirting. He realises that there's something between them, something that doesn't make him happy. It upsets him. It makes him sad. But he no longer feels the familiar paroxysms of jealousy. He is not overwhelmed. This surprises him. He anticipates, he waits, but there it is: the wave of jealousy doesn't come. That night, as they are walking back to the hotel, he hears himself say, "Is there something between the two of you?", Mariana says no, Vernon presses her and she admits, "It's ancient history. I never expected to see him again. He was disappointed to see me with someone else." Vernon had waited until the following morning to be sure of how he felt, yet still it does not come, that irrational flare of jealousy. Maybe because the guy is so ugly. He cannot imagine that Mariana will not come and join him, as arranged, two days from now at the end of his British tour. They haven't talked about it; they both know what she is doing. Vernon plumbs and probes his feelings and, to his surprise, nothing. Dead calm. If she were to definitively dump him, it might be different. If only because she is a brilliant manager, and because without her he would be completely lost.

He has a pragmatic explanation for this strange serenity: a lot of girls want to spend the night with him, and he's not a big fan of monogamy himself. This makes it easier to be magnanimous. Having left the camp, he is no longer the hero of some YOLO night, but even so there's always some girl he likes who's thirsty for him.

Last night, he was spinning a set in a club, it was pretty basic. Then this fierce Asian girl shows up. It was like a movie: when he saw her checking him out, he had looked over his shoulder to make sure it was him she was looking at. And there had been no-one behind him. She had huge, almond eyes and a body that made him feel so freaky he had to try not to stare. And he knew – although since he left the camp, he has lost a lot of his intuition, with her, he knew: Korn. It wasn't obvious. When you see a girl like that – savage as a panther, bearing of a queen – you don't immediately think: Korn. Actually, as a rule, you rarely think about Korn. But that was it. He had her sussed. And she danced, my God she danced. He was enthralled. And convinced that she'd be waiting for him after the set.

And there she was, standing at the bar. Except Max stuck to him like glue so he couldn't go and see her up close. Eventually she got bored. Vernon had been glad to see Max. They threw their arms around each other and Vernon happily agreed to have a beer with him. He never imagined he'd be stuck with him all night . . . As soon as he thinks about that part of the evening, he feels something ugly gaping in his solar plexus. Vernon doesn't mix Bleach's sound-waves into his set anymore. He's stopped. When people are ripped, it doesn't work. Drugs seem to create some kind of static interference that cancels out the effect. If you imagine a corridor two metres wide, the drug is like an elephant standing in the middle – every inch of space is already filled, and Bleach's soundwaves have no effect. Besides, the strange gift he has for making people dance as they've never danced before needs the group to work properly. Without the others, without their passion, he's just some guy with a lot of tunes loaded onto U.S.B. drives, a guy who knows a good segue. And yet, they were only onto their second beer when Max started quizzing him about Bleach's sounds. He knew too much shit for this to have been a simple coincidence.

Max had never been a decent human being. Vernon had been surprised the guy remembered him so well. Back when he managed Alex, he didn't waste his time hanging out with someone as unlikely to be useful to him as the local record dealer. At best, Vernon was tolerated backstage, and then only because Alex insisted. And he rarely saw Max in the record shop. He was the sort of guy who always knows what he should be listening to, what it is acceptable to be listening to. But his musical tastes had little room for honesty.

A lot of people liked Max because he had a talent for bigging himself up, and he managed to convince them that he, not the singer, was the true artist. Max talked a lot, and he had a silver tongue. A Trotskyite education. A Lambertist. Vernon had never known what it meant. The one thing he knows about Trotskyites is that they have a thing for radical feminists, with whom they indulge in passionate sexual relationships that leave Vernon perplexed. Max was no exception to this rule: the moment he spotted a feminist, he had to fuck her. Not that there were many in the music business. But the guy had radar – he could pinpoint a lone feminist in a heaving Bercy arena. Besides this, he was capable of pontificating about every conceivable market practice and selling it to you as a militant, revolutionary act, and hence no more refutable than Christian dogma. Max fed on Alex's brain, turned him inside out, wound him up: he didn't have Bleach's best interests at heart, and often encouraged him in his disastrous choices. Max was always the first to champion serious substance abuse as a revolutionary act by the abuser. In this, it must be admitted, he was sincere: he himself was a premium junkie.

People were too scared of the manager to contradict him. He liked to humiliate. He wielded arguments the way he might wield an axe, and had a thirst for blood. He would never say to someone, I don't like your ugly mug. No, he would dismiss them as a traitor to the cause, a sell-out, a conniving *petit bourgeois*, none of which ever stopped him making a packet off the singer. Max lived in style. He frittered money away without thinking. He had not been born into wealth. He did not have the virtuous frugality of the well-heeled.

Even back in the day, he wore preposterous outfits. Vernon particularly remembers a pair of pinstriped stretch jeans . . . Last night, seeing him appear in a lurid purple jacket, Vernon had smiled. But by the third beer, he did not know how to get rid of him. Vernon shot pleading glances at the girl waiting for him, but could not manage to interrupt Max, whose ceaseless chatter was making his head spin. Seeing the girl wander off, he admitted defeat and followed Max to a nearby bar. Vernon had no desire to drink. He has a delicate stomach, probably something to do with his age. Every time Max "went for a piss", he emptied his glass into the sink on the other side of the bar, beneath the placid, not particularly surprised gaze of the barman.

Max had treated him like the meek little record dealer he had been twenty years earlier. The manager had lost something of his presence. No point deluding yourself – you don't spend a lifetime pickling your brain in booze and Class A drugs without frying a few neurons. He babbled on, he sermonised, he offered flashes of wit. He did not notice that Vernon was aware that he was steering every subject back to one thing: the convergences. Max had got it into his head that he could be Vernon's manager. Or, more precisely, that he could organise convergences, but not in the arse end of nowhere with a couple of candles and a megaphone, no, on a grand scale. With refreshment stalls, merchandising deals and sponsorships.

Max talked about Pamela, Daniel, Sylvie and Xavier as though they were old friends. He talked about Alex's tapes, about mass hypnosis, about the girls from Bordeaux. He knew too much. Vernon played the role of the unsuspecting idiot. He allowed himself to be gripped by the shoulders, it was such a pity, here he was wasting his talent doing third-rate club nights when he should be back presiding over convergences, with his gang of friends, he wasn't going to let them down, not really. Max had big plans for them. He had the contacts, the ideas, the vision. He had moved on to whisky.

He had ended the night sprawled on the bonnet of a car outside the bar, trying to bring a cigarette to his lips while Vernon listened to his perorations, forcing himself to grin and bear it. Max was no longer even looking at Vernon, he was mumbling incoherently, it was almost impossible to understand his jabbering. Then he said ". . . and we could even make a movie about your life, I've got this buddy, Dopalet, he's a film producer, the guy's under serious pressure, we can get him to buy the rights to whatever the fuck we like, you stick with me, dude, you'll see, I'll get you into the big time, black tie, all that shit . . ." At times of danger, playing the fool has always been Vernon's go-to strategy. So he carried on smiling naively, giving no sign that the producer's name had triggered a wave of panic.

"I'm gonna organise the biggest fucking convergence you've ever fucking seen, I've heard so much about them and I'm pissed I never got to experience one . . . Alex had, like, moments of genius, between your potential and his talent, we're gonna start a revolution, swear, we're gonna knock the world off its axis . . ."

It was no trivial matter. Something had happened the previous night. Max knows too much about them. He wasn't in Northern Ireland by chance, trying to sign some local band. He had come specifically to see him. Vernon pads into the living room. Last night, when he came back to the apartment, it was dark so he hadn't noticed the big windows overlooking a park. The room is bathed in light, he is struck by the beauty of the scene: young people sitting around a huge table, dappled with sunlight, a sense of peace that feels almost ceremonial. Their movements are graceful, they speak without raising their voices. O.K., so maybe the garish American Apparel V-neck T-shirts are a bit much, but all the same. It is a mesmerising scene. On the other hand, it's unlikely that Vernon will get to reminisce about Lemmy with anyone at this table. It's not that kind of place. These kids probably know Marshall as a brand of headphones.

Bags of pastries and a few baguettes are set on the table already scattered with crumbs and spattered with jam. Vernon looks around for the coffee pot. It's full. He can't find a clean mug. There's no hot water, and simply rinsing a stray glass he finds in the sink leaves his fingers frozen. Someone opens the windows and, within a minute, the room is filled with cold, as though it were a tangible substance. Vernon takes a seat, sets his phone on the table in front of him and avoids looking at the others. There's a queue for the bathroom, in his approximate English he asks whether there is any hot water and the guy he asks smiles and says, "I hope so." He's not much younger than Vernon, and he seems likeable enough. He's one of the gang wearing V-neck T-shirts. His is a violent green. Vernon's English is incomprehensible, his accent is atrocious, and he insists on using sentences that are too complex for his level of fluency. Otherwise, he might try to have a conversation with the young guy whose face is half-hidden by a floppy fringe and who could be a guitarist in a pop band. He has big, childlike eyes, high cheekbones and a slightly astonished air. At the far end of the table, a girl whose temples are shaved and tattooed is reading tarot cards for another girl. They are talking in low voices. Vernon sniffs the milk carton on the table and pours some into his coffee. He needs to warn the Hyena. Max mentioned Dopalet. Something is very wrong. He turns to the guy who seems friendly and says, "My phone is out of credit and I have to send a text message may I borrow yours?" The kid understands what he wants and slides his phone across the table. "No problem. By the way, loved your set last night. I was high as a kite and you made me travel real far," and Vernon, who hasn't the faintest idea what has just been said, gives him a smile. He looks through his contacts for the Hyena's emergency number, which is listed under "Potato". He had laughed like a drain when he first entered this code name. He laughed a lot more when he was living at the camp. He doesn't call from his own phone, because he knows that she would have a conniption. She's completely paranoid. So paranoid, in fact, that he'd be very surprised if she wasn't interested to hear about Max's visit.

AÏCHA'S CHEEKS ARE STREAKED WITH TEARS AS SHE PRAYS, and she is disgusted by her tendency towards self-pity. It was so pleasant to surrender herself, she wallowed in sin and she enjoyed it – now, as she weeps, she cannot be sure whether it is because she has strayed from the true path. She wants to punish herself. She never realised it was possible to hate oneself so much. She can't pretend that she wasn't warned. Between a man and a woman, there is always Shaitan.

Dawn fills the room with greyish light. On the far side of the wall, in the kitchen, Faïza is bustling about. Aïcha can hear little Yanis – who always gets up before everyone else because his school is furthest away and he has to catch an early bus – making bird calls. He imitates them brilliantly – no-one knows where he gets it from. Crouched on his chair, he chirps and rolls his head. If asked what he is doing, he says he is talking to the birds chirruping in the trees along the avenue. He speaks in German, even if the question is in French. He is her favourite of the three boys. Yanis is six and she does not feel embarrassed when she misuses the words he teaches her. On the contrary, whenever she tries to say anything complicated, it makes him laugh. It has become a private game: every time she says something unintelligible, he says, "Bist du verrückt?" The rules require her to reply, "Aber ich kenne dich, du bist ein

Kartoffel!" and scoop him up into the air as he howls with laughter.

She needs to make the most of this moment of peace because soon Abid and Jafa will come downstairs and it will be impossible to listen to birdsong . . . Abid, the bigger of the two, is grumpy when he wakes up, he sobs until he is red in the face and, if his whims are not met, he stiffens and wails even louder. Jafa is more cheerful, he is eight and still has to suck a dummy to get to sleep. Brown curls long eyelashes small sleepy head – he looks like an angel. But he quickly emerges and is transformed into a demon: cycling around the kitchen, bounding on the sofa, swinging off the light fittings . . .

Aïcha enjoys the children's company. At first, when she found out there were three boys, she was afraid that she might not know how to look after them. She speaks to them in French, they answer in German, which she struggles to understand. The first time she saw Jafa dangling from a bungee cord he had hooked onto the wardrobe while Abid was shitting himself and stamping his feet and Yanis was throwing his Playmobil figures around the room making noises like a tail-gunner, she thought, I'm going back to France, I'd rather be stabbed to death get run over by a car or be thrown in jail for no reason, I'd still be better off at home than with this pack of Gremlins. She hadn't known which way to turn. Those first few days, she simply did her best to ensure no-one died. And then one day, Yanis – whom Aïcha suspected of making the most of the fact that she spoke no German to insult her in order to make his brother laugh – had said, "Shut up, bitch," and she had given him a slap. She was ashamed of what she had done. Her own father had never raised a hand to her. She couldn't understand what had got into her. To her great surprise, when the parents came home that evening, Yanis had not rushed into their arms to tell tales, in fact none of the three boys had said anything. The incident was never mentioned again, but from that day Yanis had kept his nose clean. Aïcha no longer loses her cool. Though there is no shortage of opportunities.

Aïcha immerses herself in the games, their mealtimes, the baths, their childlike babble. They wear her out and leave her little time to brood. In time, she managed to tame them. They squirm but allow themselves to be kissed, she calls them my little brioche buns, they wrap their tiny arms around her neck and, at their touch, she feels restored. She recognises these instinctive, affectionate gestures: they are the same gestures her father used to make. Which she had forgotten. She considers how much she was cared for, encouraged and educated. Recently, all she has thought about the education she received is that it was too lax. Now, she realises it was nothing less than a feat, to raise a girl without ever raising a hand to her. More than indulgent, her father had been present. She had been loved. She had been treated with consideration. Her talents had been encouraged, her efforts applauded.

Usually, by this hour, Aïcha has already slipped out of her room and turned on the coffee maker. In this, too, she is imitating what her father used to do for her. She knows how pleasant it is to be welcomed by the aroma of hot coffee. Faïza appreciates the gesture. But today, she cannot bring herself to go through this farce. She needs to leave. Her decision is made. Even though she is scared. She is revolted by her concerns for her own comfort. She despises her hypocritical remorse. She knows that it is not fear of the unknown that is keeping her here. It is sin.

Aïcha ended up here not long after the incident with Dopalet.

She had been driven to Lyon during the night. She had asked no questions. The Hyena had told her to lie low, that she was in danger. She had said that, with a little luck, the producer would not go to the police, since he wouldn't want to have to explain the reasons for the assault on him. But he would try to find some other way to get his revenge. Aïcha said she was prepared to stand trial for what she had done, but the Hyena had said, "Are you kidding me? All Dopalet needs is a half-decent lawyer for you to be charged with terrorism – you study law, do you realise what that would mean?" And this had been before the terrorist attacks . . .

Aïcha had balked: she was worried that, if she ran away, the producer might take it out on her father, but the Hyena had re-assured her. "Dopalet's not like that, he's more primal. He's not going to go after your family, you're the one he wants to punish, believe me, I know him . . ." This was serious. She was going to miss a year of her studies. While it seemed to her logical that she should have to pay for what she had done, she realised that there had been no excuse for forcing Céleste to go on the run. Here, too, the Hyena had been reassuring – don't worry, she said, the time will fly by, you'll see each other again. It's just a little break. A couple of months, max . . . She would spend the time working as an au pair for a couple in Germany. She had promised to do nothing under her real name. No driving licence, no gym membership, no paid employment, no applications for grants or university courses. And, especially, no social media and no mobile phone. She disappeared, leaving her passport with her father.

At the bus station in Lyon, she had paid for her ticket to Berlin in cash. She had removed her hijab for the journey so as not to attract attention. It was a long bus ride. She was not afraid of what might await her. She had been met by a young man. He was like a secret agent from a movie, not because of the way he looked, but because of the way he managed to reel off a vast amount of information while pretending to be casual. He was about thirty and, although he kept a safe distance from her, she had noted the regret in his voice when he talked about the capital and she assumed that he, too, was in hiding and would have preferred to be at home. Since then, she has met a lot of immigrants working in Germany and this changed her mind – they all wished they could have stayed in their home countries. No-one moves to Frankfurt for the balmy weather, the striking architecture or an easy life. Especially not foreigners. The city is ugly and Germans are boring. No-one wants to live among them. But everyone has to eat.

The young man had hailed a taxi and taken her to the train station – she was heading to Frankfurt. There, she would be an au pair with a family who thought they were hiring an unemployed French girl determined to learn German so she could find work.

At Frankfurt station, she was met by the mother of the family. To her relief, they were Muslim. Aïcha could say her daily prayers without looking as though she was planning a coup d'état. It would be a change from life at home. In Paris, her father sometimes wept when he saw her performing her ablutions. She looked at the little hand of Fatima that hung from the rear-view mirror swinging to and fro, and it was a joyous gesture – like a sign of welcome. On the back seat, there was a Kiki doll – a stuffed animal that sucks its thumb. The car was a disaster area, and though Faïza blamed it on the children, the fact is that she's completely disorganised. She trails clutter and mess in her wake – she's a cyclone, if the house is spick and span, it takes less than ten minutes for her to turn it upside down, Aïcha cannot help but wonder how she physically manages to take out and scatter so many things in such a short space of time – if you watch her, you never see her opening drawers and furiously strewing the contents everywhere. She has a gift for chaos.

From the first, Faïza welcomed her. She is garrulous, cheerful and a little eccentric – but in all things she is decent and pious. She doesn't flaunt her religion constantly to prove that she has read the Qur'an more attentively than her neighbour or that she is the most devout, the most respectable woman in the neighbourhood. She doesn't make a fuss. But she never does anything that might be considered haram. She never parades her religion, she is a believer, not an exhibitionist.

Faïza has no time for hypocrisy: she envies her neighbours, she is materialistic, she doesn't like other people's children, and she makes no attempt to hide the fact. She doesn't pretend to be other than who she is. She is not a gossip, even if she sometimes harbours evil thoughts. She is modest, does not draw attention to herself, and would not dare to speak to a man in anything other than a serious tone – everything about her is flawless, considered, gently and discreetly feminine.

In the car, that first day, she asked no embarrassing questions. She is an old friend of the Hyena and owes her a favour. She genuinely believes that Aïcha has come to look for work in Germany and needs a job to tide her over until she has mastered the language. Faïza does not ask many questions because she is not particularly curious. She spends too much time talking about herself to be inquisitive. She needs help at home, since she has three young children and cannot give up her work at the hospital where she is a nursing aide because her husband has just lost his job at Amazon and the household now relies entirely on her salary. She did not tell Aïcha all this to justify having her work full time in exchange for room and board – that does not seem unfair. It's quid pro quo.

As she set her bag down in the middle of the living room, Aïcha had been shocked: it was bright, colourful, full of amusing objects, but mostly it was a complete pigsty. It wasn't dirty – just a complete shambles. There was a towel hanging over the back of a kitchen chair, a toy truck on the living-room table, a pile of D.V.D.s in the hall, three newspapers on top of the fridge . . . Aïcha had thought about the childhood home her father had kept so neat and tidy, and it was at that precise moment that she realised that she would never go back there. And that she would always miss it.

For the first few days, the Hyena called her on the landline every morning, as though even from afar she was familiar with Aïcha's timetable and knew that she would be alone. She never gave her name and never addressed Aïcha by her first name, she would simply say, I just wanted to let you know that everything's fine here, that everyone is well – and the word "everyone" was a comfort, meaning that her father was well and that Céleste was managing to fend for herself. Aïcha felt terribly homesick. She would often use the family computer to listen to France Inter or France Culture – the sound of home, the radio stations her father listened to in his apartment.

But after the terrorist attacks, it had gradually become impossible to listen to these programmes without hearing discussions about Islam. The French intelligentsia were leafing through the Qur'an and getting it to say what suited them. They were doing their utmost to force the words of the Prophet to justify the blood-bath devastating the country. As though the terrorists had just invented politically motivated murder and had done so at the behest of Allah. As though the ignorant men who had perpetrated these crimes had not been primarily inspired by Hollywood movies and video games . . . Let them seek out the roots of violence where it grows, not in her prayers. None of the murderers was a practising Muslim. Not one. Not that this seemed to puzzle the pundits on the radio stations her father listened to. They frantically consulted the Qur'an as though it required only a Western eye to unearth the truth. To get it to spew out its violence. They never thought to examine their own propaganda. It was not hard to see that since 9/11 the killers invariably chose to speak the language of the West: graphic, spectacular violence. The aesthetics of slaughter are decided in Hollywood.

She wondered what her father thought about all this. Was he duped? Was he demoralised? She had to manage in silence. She was confident. Dopalet would forget. Rich people have their whims, he would move on to something else. She would go back to her father. She would go back to her studies, maybe go to university in England. This thought kept her going. As the days passed, she got her bearings in the household. Faïza did not treat her like a servant, but rather like a younger cousin helping out in exchange for her upkeep. She was relieved that Aïcha was there and was effusive in her gratitude. If she brought back cakes, there was always one for "la petite". As was only right, Aïcha kept her distance from Walid, the father of the boys. Islam forbids fraternising. She could not be alone in the presence of a non-mahram. They both knew this, and did not need to talk about it. She refrained from going into a room if she knew that he was alone in there. He did likewise.

Aïcha did not eat with the couple, she had her dinner earlier, with the children. But sometimes, over the weekend, she would have coffee and dessert with them. Faïza is obsessed with food – she can talk about it for hours, she is capable of making a thirty-minute detour to buy a cake she loves. Walid is as taciturn as his wife is voluble, but he enjoys talking about France. They would sometimes exchange a few words. Mostly, they met when she was playing with the children in the park opposite the house and he came to take Yanis cycling, or to play football with Jafa. Walid did not say anything, but he made it clear that he understood how difficult it was to look after three boys under ten. She respected Walid, he was devout and reserved. Though not an educated man, he had a mathematical intelligence – logical and agile. She liked his common sense, his natural authority and his stillness. She did not worry about him. She was too focused on her own thoughts and the three boys monopolised her attention.

With Faïza, on the other hand, a friendship blossomed. The nurse had to spend all day speaking German, a language she hated and spoke badly. In the evening, she was happy to be able to sit with Aïcha and chat. More often than not, Walid would go out. He would go to the shisha bar to meet up with French Muslim friends, immigrants like himself, and would come home late. Meanwhile, the two women would binge on T.V. box sets. After two episodes, Faïza would turn to Aïcha – shall we watch another one? I can sleep in the next life. And Aïcha would giggle and settle back on the sofa. After the third episode, if the cliffhanger was particularly tantalising, they would sometimes look at each other and burst out laughing. "We can't just leave it at that, shall we watch one more?" It was often Walid who sent them off to bed when he got home: "Are you gone in the head the two of you? Do you realise you've been watching this rubbish for four hours?" and they would laugh at their own foolishness and clear the coffee table of the pyramids of gold wrappers from the Ferrero Rochers they devoured by the kilo, and the empty cups from the herbal teas they made between episodes. All in all, it was a nice life. Just monotonous enough and lonely enough for Aïcha to feel exiled, yet cosy enough for her not to get depressed. One evening, Walid joined them. But there were too many scenes of fornication in "Game of Thrones" for Aïcha to watch it with a man in the room. She had got up to leave but Faïza had said, "It's alright, we're watching "Sherlock" tonight – stay."

And Aïcha had enjoyed the sense of family. Having never lived with two parents, she felt as though she was being granted access to a privileged haven. She did not think to worry about the special pleasure she felt during such evenings. In hindsight, she knows that she was guilty of inexcusable carelessness. But in the moment, she had not seen the looming evil. She had committed the sin of pride. She had thought herself above common laws.

During the day, Walid looked for a job, went to see friends and spent the afternoons in his workshop – a small room he had set up next to the children's bedroom where he fixed things given to him by other expatriates. Usually faulty mobile phones or computers. But sometimes he repaired other things – a vacuum cleaner, a PlayStation, a food processor. He had even updated the firmware on a drone. He did these little jobs cash in hand. He would often pick up his tool bag and go and take a look at a fridge or a washing machine; before setting off, he would look up the machine online, and when he got there, he would sort it out. He was talented. And generous with his time. He would spend hours on the internet looking for the right tutorial, the correct installation manual, the software that he needed. Faïza said that Amazon had made Walid redundant, he had gone through a bad patch. He had been a team leader. He would have liked to get a job at a similar level, but was only offered work as a packer at a derisory salary. He earned more doing repair work here and there. When he was in a good mood, he filled the house with a luminous joy, he played with his sons and joked with his wife. At other times, he scowled and could curdle the atmosphere without uttering a word. He couldn't help it – it was as though his mood seeped out into the room. Aïcha paid little heed – it had nothing to do with her.

It was easy to mind her own business: she scarcely had a minute to herself. She woke up in the morning reaching for her socks and collapsed every evening after dinner with an armful of dirty laundry, during the day she didn't even have time to stop for a coffee. At most, she allowed herself a ten-minute detour when she went to shop for groceries in the morning, and would walk along the banks of the Main. She has always loved walking. During these rambles she did not speak to anyone.

Every day, she listened to a little German, telling herself that, since she was here, she might as well learn the language, after all Germany was a rich country and it might prove useful. When she was alone in the house, sweeping the floors or folding clothes, she would listen to language lessons on YouTube, softly repeating the phrases she wanted to remember. In the street, she found a German copy of *The Little Prince*, as though the book had been waiting for her. As she read it, she realised that she could remember certain passages in French word for word, because, when she was little, her father liked to play her a record of Gérard Philippe reading it. She experienced her first linguistic epiphany in the corner shop when she managed to explain that she was looking for milk that was easy to digest and the young Turk running the shop had immediately understood her and she had understood his answer. These were the first words she had spoken in this alien language, aside from her babbling with Yanis.

And then evil showed its face. Shaitan is patient. He advances his pawns in a leisurely fashion. When she tries to go back in time, to find the first speck of sin slipping into her thoughts, she dates the beginning of the fall to the day she went for a walk . . .

Aïcha knew that strolling along the banks of the Main by herself was not strictly correct, otherwise she would not have carefully avoided mentioning it to her host family. She granted herself this narrow window of freedom because, she reasoned, she never left the house and she needed to get some fresh air.

That particular day it was very mild, the weather was pleasant although the sky, as always, was grey. The banks of the river were densely wooded. She was placidly daydreaming when she came nose to nose with Walid walking in the opposite direction. Seeing her, he had slowed and spoken to her, not angry but surprised, "Where are you headed?" and she had felt her cheeks burn with shame. She had not lied, "I just felt like taking a walk," and Walid had sighed, doing nothing to conceal his annoyance. "I'd rather you didn't wander the streets. People might see you, they might think all kinds of things, and everyone knows you work for us." She had not had time to reply before a clap of thunder boomed and an almighty storm broke over them. Seeing Aïcha walk away, Walid had called her back with a loud click of his tongue. He was in one of his foul moods. "Take cover," he had barked, "you can't walk home in this downpour." Her head bowed, she went and stood next to him under a jetty. "What do you want me to say? What choice do we have?" Aïcha's heart sank. Walid did not say another word but stood, chain-smoking. Then he had jolted, literally, as though an electric shock had shunted him onto a different complete track, because when he did speak again, after some minutes of silence, his tone was amused. "Seriously, what the hell are you doing walking around on your own like that? Have you nothing better to do? I'm surprised at you, Aïcha. I didn't expect you to be a hypocrite. This is not a nice part of town, there are drug dealers, junkies, flashers, didn't you notice that it was a disreputable area?" Aïcha had apologised. No, she hadn't noticed that it was a dangerous area. The rain had begun to ease off. Walid had flicked his cigarette away, saying that it was best to say nothing to Faïza, she wouldn't understand. "But I don't want to see you hanging around here again. Is that clear?" Then, as he glanced at her to make sure she understood, he saw that she was on the brink of tears and he softened his tone. "You're not going to cry on me, are you? I'm just saying don't hang around the tourist areas, find somewhere else to take your walks . . . Take the kids with you, they need to get out more. I'm not angry with you . . . It's not like I caught you in a bar whoring around with men, I'm just saying that you don't seem to realise what kind of area this is, that's normal, you don't know the city . . ." He had walked several metres with her. Aïcha was uncomfortable, but did not feel that she was in a position to remind him that it was not proper for them to be walking side by side. Eventually, he nodded to a path. "I'll go this way. You know how to find your way back, don't you? You're so different from the other girls I know, you're obviously not a city girl. I never really know how to talk to you . . . But I didn't mean to be cruel . . ." She avoided looking directly at his face, but she could see his hands – the bone of the wrist, the long slender fingers, and, finding this unsettling, she stared out at the water. He had laughed. "I never know what's going on in that head of yours. Go on, hurry back."

He had taken the path on the left that led uphill, and after a few steps he had turned around and given a little wave signalling her to hurry up. Seeing him from a distance, it occurred to her for the first time that he was attractive. And Aïcha, who had never been rash, never been flighty, had greeted this notion as though it were familiar. As though it were something with which she could play without risk of getting burned. But now, when she thinks back to when it all began, it was in that moment. His hands as he told her that she was different from other girls. His breath as he stood next to her. His height. His scent, which she could smell. And his silhouette, on the hill, waving to her.

She had not made the connection between this embarrassing encounter and the strange light-heartedness that washed over her and Walid. Suddenly, she was bathed in light. It was warm, a gentle breeze caressed the nape of her neck. She could still pretend that she was simply in a good mood. And we give less thought to what puts us in a good mood than to what annoys us. She paid little attention to the extraordinary pleasure she felt the following day when she heard Walid moving around upstairs. She did not immediately notice her ability to capture his every movement, out of the corner of her eye, as she pretended to go about her chores, the thrill of hearing his voice, the quiver when she recognised him standing at the gate of the park . . . This intoxication at his very presence seemed natural to her: she worked for him, she cared for his children, she tidied his home, it was hardly strange, she thought, that she enjoyed his company.

She was convinced that she was trustworthy. This was what led her to fall: head first, without even a flicker of doubt. It was a powerful urge, firm yet gentle. The lure of joy and of light. An ecstasy. She could find no other word to describe it.

Then everything happens at once. One evening, in the park, Walid comes to collect Jafa. He spends a little longer than usual gathering up the boy's things and he gazes at Aïcha, who pensively picks up Yanis. Then a huge smile breaks over his face and she notices the whiteness of his teeth even as she pretends to look elsewhere. He says, "You're good for us, you know that." It was not his words that should have alerted her, but the joy she felt when she heard them.

Another day, early afternoon. A sweltering heat, but a sky that is leaden, overcast, lower than usual, making it difficult to breathe. Aïcha was cleaning the living-room windows and had decided that, this time, they would be spotless – she had watched a number of YouTube tutorials because each time she cleaned the windows, she left streaks. The weather was so muggy that she had taken off her blouse and was working in her T-shirt, she was concentrating on her task, wondering whether this trick of using newspaper was the best solution. The living room windows look out onto a broad avenue, the dust gets in from the traffic, but the building is not overlooked so she did not think to cover her bare arms. She was fighting the urge to slump into a chair with a tall glass of cold water, and listen to a TED talk on the family computer which she had turned up so that she could hear it while she stood on the stool, polishing the glass.

Walid always rang the doorbell before coming in, to give her time to vacate the communal rooms. But that day, she had not noticed him coming in when she heard his voice behind her: "I'm no window cleaner, but your technique is . . . how can I put it? It looks to me like you're getting them dirtier." He was laughing. Knocked off balance by the surprise she had teetered, he had taken a step forward, arms outstretched, laughing as she flailed wildly to stop herself from falling. They had not touched. But that step forward, those eyes meeting hers, briefly, that casual complicity. As he left the room, Aïcha was still giggling. Like a ninny. She had had time to notice his mouth. And if she thought about it, the image triggered a thunderclap in her chest. The contour of his lips, the roundness, the deep red, the apparent softness. This time she knew that something was not right. But she had simply dismissed the image from her mind. She had thrown away the newspaper and washed the windows as she usually did, with soapy water, before wiping them with a cloth.

All these fleeting memories whose importance she had refused to acknowledge at the time . . . But the feelings she allowed to stir could not be tamed.

Walid is always relaxed around her. Another day, she is in the kitchen. He knocks, and without waiting for her to answer, he comes in and makes himself some coffee. She is washing the breakfast dishes. She feels a man's eyes on her. Self-conscious, she instinctively adjusts the veil around her face, and from the tone of his voice she knows that he is smiling. "Yeah, yeah, you're pretty, stop tugging at your veil, don't worry, you're beautiful exactly as you are." She turns to him, surprised and offended, but he is completely calm. He behaved as though he didn't see the harm. As though he didn't realise that it is wrong for a man to seek pleasure in looking at a woman other than his wife. She should have protested, but she went back to doing the dishes, waiting for him to leave the kitchen.

Walid is almost forty. He lived in France at a time when Muslims had little respect for their religion. A time when they had been stripped of everything – their history, their culture, their god. They were not good enough to be French, but nor should they behave like Arabs. They were expected to be invisible. It was in this no-man's-land that Walid grew up. He has three sisters – Aïcha knows this from Faïza. He probably didn't see anything wrong in coming into the kitchen while she was there alone. This, at least, is what Aïcha chose to tell herself.

And, a few days later, in the little windowless room where she does the ironing, at precisely eleven o'clock – she had just glanced at the old clock-radio on the white plastic shelf where the cleaning products are kept – Walid had wandered in with a cup of coffee, as though getting into the habit of seeking her out to chat for a couple of minutes whenever he takes a break. He had pushed aside the pile of crumpled shirts and sat, facing her, on the little red stool. The spoon tinkled against the glass coffee cup. He had sat in silence for a moment, and then said, "I can't seem to work today, I can't concentrate." If she had been watching this scene, she would have known the correct attitude to adopt. Without hesitation. She should have immediately left the room, making it clear that she was uncomfortable with the lack of respect shown her by Walid. But she had not reacted as she should have. She thought taking him to task might be hurtful. And perhaps misplaced – he could have burst out laughing and said, who do you take yourself for? Improper. Surely you don't think I'm flirting with you? Don't worry, I don't even think of you as a woman!

She had stammered, "Some days it's harder than others," and Walid had smiled. "I like watching you iron. I find it relaxing. It reminds me of my mother, she was always ironing something. I'd be doing my homework and I'd hear that sound, you know, *tssss*," and he had made a little whistling noise while Aïcha stared down at the duvet cover, at the pattern of blue flowers she had been ironing now for ten minutes. "What about you, did your mother spend her time ironing?" he had asked and Aïcha had felt as though she had to keep her composure and answer: "No, it reminds me of my father. He used to iron his shirts, they were perfect – you should have seen them, better than when they came back from the dry cleaners," and Walid had said, "Strange home you grew up in. What was your mother doing, hanging out in bars?" And Aïcha, realising that she had said too much and eager to put an end to the conversation, explained, "My mother died when I was little." Walid had apologised for prying and left it at that. Tears welled in her eyes at the image of her father setting up the ironing board with a deft movement, one he had mastered by dint of habit. And it was of her father that she had thought that day, with a particular intensity.

It was a tender, pleasant sorrow – she indulged the feeling. She thought about the sadness of being separated from her family and friends only to avoid facing what was happening. It is possible to prepare oneself to do something irreparable while manoeuvring one's conscious mind so that it does not know what it is doing. Nothing in her routine of devout thoughts was troubled or concerned. Nothing could have derailed her train of thought: if she had been asked about her mood, she would have honestly replied, I'm thinking about my poor papa. Looking back, this is what she finds most devastating: the skill with which she manipulated her conscience so that she did not see what was coming. Because, from that day, though always hoping that it would not happen, she began to wait for Walid to appear with his coffee and exchange a few words with her.

He did not return until some days later. She was topping and tailing a punnet of runner beans she was intending to use in a salad. He told her about a recent incident when an arsonist had torched a refugee centre and a crowd of Germans had gathered round and sung for joy. Walid's features had hardened as he talked about the incident and Aïcha had thought that this was not the moment to say that he should not come and sit in the kitchen when she was there alone. A dozen times, she had the opportunity to do what was right and proper. A dozen times, she made the wrong choice.

She enjoyed listening to him talk. Not that he was particularly brilliant. In fact, compared to the conversational skills of students she usually spent time with, his reasoning was somewhat crude. It was not what he said that pleased her, it was his tone. That kindly reassurance. And the smile that hovered over everything he said.

That day, before he headed back to his workshop, in a curious tone that was both tense and tender, he had said, "I like your gestures, the way you do things," and this time she had defended herself. "What you just said is not appropriate." She was shaken by the sense of danger that he had so calmly sparked in the kitchen. He had emptied his cup into the sink and apologised. "You're right. I don't know why I said such a thing – I'm sorry. I'll get back to work." And in that moment, a voice inside her head hammered out the words you're imagining things it's not what you think it's impossible everything is fine. While everything around her was crumbling, it was still drowned out by her bad faith.

But Walid had retraced his steps and, perhaps encouraged by her silence, which in his eyes equated to consent, he had said, "Stop lying, Aïcha. You know you put me off my work. I'm on the other side of the wall and all I can think about is you." She had stood there, dumbfounded, knife in one hand, a decapitated runner bean in the other.

She had heard the front door slam. She had assumed he was giving her time to pack up her things and leave. After what he had just said, she had no choice. Instead, she had run into her room and buried her head in her pillow, just like in one of the old-fashioned movies she had seen too often. Those hours spent crying over her fate were so much time gained. Faïza had come home with the boys and Aïcha had taken them to the swimming pool. She had hidden her red eyes, her mechanical gestures, once again she had made the wrong decision, convincing herself that she had to look after the boys, that she could not simply disappear. That evening, she had not watched T.V. with Faïza. She had sworn to herself that she would go the next day. Once she had left, she would find a way to let the Hyena know. She was lying to herself. And the following day, she managed to convince herself that he would never speak to her again, because he too realised that he had gone too far and was filled with remorse.

But where men are concerned, "to desire" is conjugated in the imperative. Seeing that she had decided to stay under his roof, he justifiably persuaded himself that she was tempting him. He disappeared for a whole day, then another, finding ways to keep himself occupied elsewhere. And still Aïcha did not leave.

On the third day, while she was folding the laundry in the little room where she did the ironing, she had heard him climbing the stairs. She was terrified. She prepared stern words, knowing that she was in the wrong, that she should have packed her bags. She instantly recognised the smell. He stank of alcohol. In his eyes, there was a troubling gleam, a sadness she had never seen before. Without a word, she had tried to leave the room; he had grabbed her arm. She had tried to break free, but he was stronger than she expected, he effortlessly managed to immobilise her and he said: "It's so wonderful, this thing happening to us, it can't possibly be a sin," he had turned her to face him and stared into her eyes. She was overcome by a strange feeling, one that was doubtless familiar to him, a feeling that violently coursed through her. It starts in the knees, but it radiates to the back, to the hollows of the elbows, to the throat – he had brought his forehead close to hers and all her strength drained away. It was too late for her to flee. Standing there, her body pressed against his, she could no longer do anything. She had never experienced this desire. Not a sound passed her lips. She had surrendered herself.

He had placed his hands on her hips, she had felt his eyelashes brushing against her skin. Her conscience seemed like a little figure cast adrift, waving its arms and calling from a great distance, so far away, so far away, and drifting still, until it was no more than a speck, until she could not hear it anymore. As though a cardboard facade had slowly fallen away to reveal the reality. The cardboard facade was her dignity, her respectability, her seriousness, her composure. The reality was that what she felt for him was beyond anything she had ever imagined. There was not a millimetre of her skin that did not long for his touch.

For long minutes they had stood, motionless, face to face, he had wrapped his arms around her back, he had nuzzled her neck. "I don't know what you do to me Aïcha I've never felt like this you drive me mad I dream about you I wake up and I think about you I look for you everywhere I've never felt like this it's impossible to resist we want it too much."

With a superhuman effort, she had broken free of his embrace, she had said, it's impossible, Walid, and she had run away. She knew that the transgressing sin she had committed was as serious as fornication. So she had launched into her private melodrama, "I have lost my virtue, this time I have to leave, but before I do I have to get in touch with the Hyena, what can I do in the meantime, I'll pack my bags, but what am I going to say to Faïza?", and she told herself that if she heard his footsteps, she would jump out the window – she would rather die than sink deeper into sin. She had known pleasure with a man who was not her husband. Technically, she had just lost her virginity – and in the worst possible circum- stances. Then she had gone back to looking after the children as though nothing had happened. She felt empty, sullied, ruined. But she had done everything she needed to do. And that evening, Faïza had said, Walid went to visit a Chibani, he was bewitched, I'm sure our neighbours put the evil eye on us, he has spat out the poison now and feels much better. I'm so relieved.

For several days, Walid had not so much as looked at her. Aïcha felt relieved. She could not expunge the sin. But things were returning to normal. He had sought help, from outside, he was cured. Everything was clear: it had been a moment of madness, the work of the devil. Aïcha, obviously, was responsible for her own actions. She prayed with the fervour of a sinner. The moment she heard his footsteps, she took off, bustling the children into another room. She was too ashamed to face him anymore, too ashamed of herself.

And then, one day, Faïza had taken the boys to the circus. Aïcha had gone out to do some shopping. Suddenly, at the corner of the street, he had appeared. Seeing him, she could tell that he was angry, she thought, he was waiting for me, and she had turned on her heel. Walid had grabbed her. "I don't want you to talk to me," she had said, staring at the ground and he had said nothing. His elbow had brushed hers. She had turned her head. He was smiling. And once again, she felt that madness in every pore of her skin. The voice of reason was far away – it no longer reached her conscious mind. Standing on the corner, he had kissed her. In the street. Full on the lips.

It was her first kiss. She wasn't that kind of girl. She had always been hard on women who did not know how to control their sensual urges. And now, at the first opportunity, she had given in, with a feverishness of which she thought herself incapable. She did not recognise this body – impetuous, possessed. He had taken her by the hand and they had got into his car. She could feel the shame. But its power was much weaker than the desire impelling her. To fornicate in a car in a blind alley was the most degrading thing imaginable. But she was not thinking about that. Though it was her first time, it had not been painful. Because she desired him so much, perhaps. She had not been troubled by the steering wheel, or the possible witnesses, or the cramped conditions.

Then they had gone back to the home of his wife and his children. She had performed the same actions she did every day.

That night, she had taken off her shirt, she opened the windows on the freezing darkness and she had stood, motionless, staring into the night, her skin smarting from the cold, praying that she would be dead by morning. She was aware of everything. Her cowardice. Her lies. In a whisper, she pleaded with Allah to take her life, to deliver her.

All she got for her pains was a fever that had kept her in bed for a whole day. Then she had gone back to work. She was waiting. He was an order. A fist had opened up inside her and now clasped another hand – a fearsome grip that nothing could break. She waited for him to look at her. For him to summon her. She wanted him again. She truly was her mother's daughter. These things are handed down. Vice, deceit, wantonness. One night, coming home from the park, she had seen herself in the hall mirror while rummaging in the youngest boy's bag for his toy tractor: how changed she looked. Usually, Aïcha did not look at herself. She was neither vain nor conceited, she took no interest in her appearance. But looking at herself in the mirror that day, she had been shocked to see a stranger. She was thinner, there was a cunning to her eyes, something paradoxically proud and brazen in her expression. She had blushed at her own thought – you're becoming beautiful. The voice of the devil whispering into her ear.

At night, she wept, she pleaded, she tossed and turned, she rolled her eyes, and when she woke in the morning she made firm resolutions that she kept until he appeared and made the slightest move in her direction, to which she responded with the same docility.

Walid was gentle with her. They did not discuss what was going on between them. They would have liked to be able to put some order into their actions. But as soon as the children were absent, Walid would take her down to his car and it would begin again. The windows would mist over and the more they did it, the more she enjoyed doing it. She found that she knew manoeuvres, unimaginable caresses that came to her from she knew not where. She was a harlot. Walid found it hard to believe that he was her first. He felt sorry for her. He said this with no malice. He was doing something wrong – but if the society in which they lived recognised their religious traditions, he could have taken her as a second wife; in this respect, his feelings were pure, he said, he wished that it were possible. He would have liked to give her children, to live as they now did, but without having to lie, and she would have supported Faïza, as she did already. His wife was too westernised to accept the idea of a second wife under her roof. He was committing a sin, that was true; but one that, in other circumstances, would not have been a sin. He was not stealing another man's wife. He was not involved with an infidel.

Aïcha, for her part, was utterly lost. She set her heart upon a man who was forbidden to her. She gave herself over to fornication and took pleasure in it. And, for the first time, she realised that expression, "I'm mad about him", could be taken literally. She was mad about this man. In his arms, she lost all inhibition. If she were truly honest, she would have realised that she was committing blasphemy: a part of her persisted in believing that their love was so pure that Allah must surely approve.

She avoided Faïza. The rupture had been made easier by the fact that the nurse had to work night shifts. Until the day when everything changed. One night, when Faïza was not on duty, she had knocked on Aïcha's door – I need to go out tonight, can you look after the boys? They were already in bed. Aïcha had settled herself in the living room so that she would hear if one of them woke up. She was watching television; by now she could understand German fairly well. When she heard Faïza pull into the garage, Aïcha had tidied the coffee table and steeled herself to say, I'm half asleep I think I'll go straight up to bed. But Faïza was sobbing. Aïcha had hesitated. She felt uncomfortable. She had been terrified of hearing Faïza say: I know everything, I'm going to kill you. Or perhaps she longed for it to happen.

Faïza was crying so hard she could barely speak, but between sobs she managed to say, "Could you make us both some mint verbena tea? Stay a while, please, I need to talk." Aïcha had foolishly asked, "Are you alright?" and Faïza had glared at her and said, "No, actually, I would have thought that was obvious . . ."

They went and sat at the kitchen table, each cradling a mug of steaming tea, and Faïza had said, "It's started again . . . I thought it was all over . . . I followed him. He's with her. I knew it. It's been going on for weeks. I followed him in the car. She lives just past

Arbeitslosenhaus. His car is parked outside the building. He's not even trying to hide it. When he started drinking again, I knew this would happen. But when he went to see a *hafiz* to break the spell – not that I believe in such things, but psychologically, you know . . . I thought he would be back to his old self. We've got three children. How could I cope on my own, with three children . . . and that French slut, always ready to spread her legs – she sleeps with everyone, I hope he's not going to end up giving me some disease . . . He doesn't treat French women the way he treats us. He knows that, where they're concerned, it's open season, so why wouldn't he . . . ?"

Bit by bit, Aïcha pieced the story together. Walid had had an affair with another woman. A French woman who worked at Amazon. He hadn't been made redundant. He had quit his job. He had been forced to choose between his wife and that whore. Because she was a whore, a woman who drinks and goes out and meets men and wears slutty clothes and rubs herself up against men and doesn't believe in anything. Walid had chosen his wife and children. He had walked away. But he had relapsed. He had seen her again. She lived on the riverbank. At the very spot where Aïcha had bumped into him the day of the rainstorm. Thinking back to his mood, to how he had behaved, she now sees the scene in a different light. He had been visiting his mistress and was worried that Aïcha might say something to his wife. Once again, Aïcha felt her whole world crumble. As though reality were no more than a paper screen, a falling curtain that did not correspond to anything. She had asked Allah to punish her. And He had done so more harshly than she could have imagined. She had said, I don't understand, Walid is a good Muslim, why would he do such a thing, and Faïza had laughed. "Just because you observe Ramadan doesn't mean you're a good

Muslim. He smokes, he drinks, he sleeps with whores . . . no, he is not a true believer. Besides, for as long as there are whores like her willing to spread their legs, there will be men to stick their cocks into them. They can't help themselves. The brain is much less powerful than the balls. Do you think I should kick him out?" And Aïcha had laid her hand on Faïza's. "He loves you. Anyone can see that. You are an amazing couple. He would be lost without you." "Then what should I do?" "Pray. You must pray for him to come back. Take care of your children. And book a wonderful holiday – the five of you should get away, you can arrange a holiday so amazing that, when he comes back, he will never think about her again."

She waits until the house is empty and sends Walid a text message, warning him that she will not be able to look after the children. Then she closes the door, and leaves the keys in the letterbox. Just at that moment, her phone rings. The Hyena, who has never called her on her mobile phone, says in a sad voice: "We've got a problem. Can you pack up your things and meet me outside the station? I'm on my way, I'm almost there, I'll pick you up. I've spoken to Faïza, I told her I've found a great job for you but that you have to leave today. I'll explain."

Three hours later, the Hyena pulls up beside her. The first thing she says is: "Do you know where Céleste is?" "No, you told us not to get in touch with each other." "Oh, yeah, shit, I forgot, you always do what you're supposed to. In one sense, that's a good thing, but right now, it's not terribly useful to me – I've no idea where she is. I have to warn her. I think Dopalet has managed to track you both down. I'll explain everything. Are you alright? No, you're obviously not alright, you've got a face like a slapped arse . . . Look, I'm really sorry, Aïcha, for rushing you like this."

The Hyena drives with broad, sweeping movements, masculine gestures. Aïcha leans her head against the passenger window. She looks at this woman who lives outside all the common norms of decency. And, for the first time, she realises that they are alike, that she has no right to judge her.

In the car, David Bowie sings "Blackstar" and the Hyena anxiously tugs at her hair. "He's dead, did you hear? You're too young to listen to this stuff." And Aïcha sees a tear form in the corner of her eye.

BOWIE HAS NOT EVEN BEEN DEAD THREE DAYS AND ALREADY Céleste is sick and tired of hearing "Let's Dance" and "Starman". Last night, they watched "Labyrinth" and she was the only one who didn't think it was genius. Hélène, the French girl who works with her in the kitchens and who suggested she rent a room here, cried every tear in her body over the sandwiches she was making when it happened. In the morning, when she arrives, she connects her phone via Bluetooth to the Bose speaker in the kitchen and that's it for the whole day. Céleste has never really listened to David Bowie. She's making up for it now.

Céleste is ironing the sheet they use as a screen for the video projector. They hang it from the top shelves, using weights to hold it down. It works brilliantly, but if the sheet falls down some day and brings a dumbbell down on somebody's head, it's likely to kill someone. The whole apartment stinks . . . The two Dutch girls who are squatting on the sofa are in an ongoing war with the shower. They're funny, they're cheerful, they're obliging. But they smell like jackals. Luckily, everyone in the place smokes, it goes some way to masking the acrid stench of sweat and mildew they trail after them.

Céleste has spent at least an hour ironing, she has already refilled the steam reservoir three times. She takes a toke on every spliff that goes around, and everyone is constantly skinning up.

Ironing when you're stoned is dank. She could spend all night doing it. Not that she's particularly good at it, the harder she tries to get rid of the creases, the more others appear. But since she's sick of watching movies starring actors with crumpled faces, she keeps at it.

Her hands hurt. She has burned herself, cut herself, banged herself. She would never have thought that preparing sandwiches, salads and croquettes could be such an ordeal. She remembers the bars she used to work in, how the kitchen staff were constantly bitching. She thought they were just whingers, that they did it to seem interesting. You'd think cutting up potatoes to make tortillas wouldn't be complicated, but it's hard fucking work.

In the first few days, she badly burned herself tossing frozen croquettes into boiling oil. She had been warned not to do it, but she was in a hurry. She blistered her whole forearm – the first thing she thought when she saw the wound was, phew, at least it didn't touch the tattoo. Hélène had asked if she was in pain and Céleste had pulled a face and said, no I'm fine actually it doesn't hurt at all – which means it's a deep burn. When it happened, she was immediately reminded of her opening scene in this drama: in her studio apartment, packing a bag, while downstairs the Hyena was waiting to take her who knew where in a 4×4 with tinted windows and she was only allowed out to piss in some field, since she couldn't go into a petrol station to use the bog in case they had C.C.T.V. At the time, she had thought, this is all a bit much, it's not like we robbed the Banque de France, but she hadn't argued.

She hadn't realised what was happening to her. Her mind was a blank. In the car, she sat in silence, mentally repeating, "I can do this. I'm a hard bitch, I don't cry, I take the punches." Deep down, she had not accepted that this was real, that tomorrow she would not be going home as though nothing had happened. When a burn is serious, you don't feel the pain immediately.

She had found herself in a tiny apartment, at the far end of a corridor, in the arse end of nowhere, a few kilometres outside Zaragoza in Spain. The Hyena left her with a friend, some guy who lived in the area and spoke French – the woman might not look like much but she's got a network of contacts to rival the Camorra. Actually, it looked like the sort of place E.T.A. might use as a bolthole, thought Céleste, using the logic of a policeman's daughter. It's a little neighbourhood a stone's throw from open fields and from the river, cosmopolitan enough that you're not worried if you run into a stranger but sufficiently off the beaten track that you never see a tourist. Her chances of running into someone from France who might recognise her were slim. The Hyena's friend regularly came by and restocked her fridge. Céleste was not used to spending so much time without talking to anyone. The death of her digital self was particularly painful. The Hyena had told her not to go online using any of her social media accounts. Céleste had said, "But people are going to be super-freaked if they don't see me post anything," and the Hyena had sighed. "The only people you need to reassure is your father, your friends will move on to something else, you'll see. It's not like there's a shortage of clickbait."

After two weeks, fucking hell, it dawned on her that people were a lot more creative before the internet was invented: with no access to the net she was bored out of her skull. She spent all day listening to Mary J. Blige and singing. She knew the whole back catalogue by heart. She spent the rest of her time sketching. Every time Esteban came by with supplies, she would say, "Get in touch with the Hyena, tell her I can't carry on like this – it's like I'm fucking dead, man." A little less distant than usual, he had said, "You'll have a job, it's just that the thing we had in mind fell through." "So who are you, exactly?" "The Hyena is an old friend. I had my own problems once upon a time and she really helped me out." She could get nothing else out of him, except a bunch of dumb promises – that this was just temporary, that they were working on making sure she had a social life. And the piss-poor advice: you should cut your hair, that way you won't be so recognisable. Although Céleste had been prepared to disappear for a few months, she thought it was a bit much to dump her in some godforsaken shithole and tell her not to see anybody. She had spent two more days holed up. Her only friend was Mary J. Blige – "Real Love", "Family Affair", "No More Drama" . . . Then one morning, in desperation, she had picked up the twenty-euro note Esteban had given her and had gone to the salon. It was here that she met Juanito. He's a stylist, but he's not gay. He's got a Mexican skull tattooed on his hand. She used her fingers to mime that she had come to have her hair cut short. She had shown him a photo so he would get the idea. Juanito had nodded. And then he had done something completely different. When she saw herself in the mirror – shaved temples and a little fringe – Céleste wasn't exactly Yaaas! but she liked this guy too much to rip him a new one. Goth girl gone. Juanito spoke a few words of French, just enough to understand that she did not have a mobile phone, "kaput, kaput" – maybe kaput is universal. He arranged to meet her that night in the bar next to the salon. And after ten minutes, he took her back to her place. Not speaking the same language, they had to find other ways to communicate.

He got into the habit of dropping by to see her after work. He would make gin and tonic. He would rock up with huge balloon glasses, ice, cinnamon stick and he would pour the tonic quickly so the bubbles burst. From the start, she was really into him – she was completely gone. With him, it was different, he had his life.

When he told her that he'd been offered a couple of weeks working as a stylist on a shoot in Catalonia and he was leaving the following day, Céleste hadn't thought twice. "Take me with you." Awkward moment: he had a girlfriend waiting for him there. A regular bae he had never mentioned. But Céleste had got it into her head that she could not stand another day buried in this hell-hole, so she said, "Take me." She'd had a bellyful of the Hyena's plans.

This is how she came to cross Spain from west to east with a guy she was so hopelessly in love with she had to hold back tears when she looked at his face, because she knew that when they came to the end of the journey he would disappear. And there were no second thoughts: he dropped her off, as arranged, on Plaza de Cataluña. She never saw him again.

People often make good decisions for bad reasons. She was convinced that Juanito was too into her, that it had to be reciprocal, that all she had to do was wait, that love would prevail and all that drivel.

On the day she arrived, she met up with Nora, a girl she'd known when she was studying at the Beaux-Arts who had moved to Barcelona ten years earlier. To work in graphic design, though in the end she became a waitress. Céleste decided she was done with the Hyena's paranoid fantasies. She didn't use her existing Facebook account, but she went online using a different identity. How else could she get in touch with her friends?

Nora had said, you can stay at ours, there's five of us. You can crash on the sofa, no problem. After that, Hélène, who's also French, had said, the restaurant I'm working in is looking for a prep chef, and bingo. That was how it had all started. This house – it's the G.O.A.T. For the first few days, she had cried over Juanito. But she didn't suffer for long. All the people living in the apartment are amazing. They're fam. Not one of them gets on her tits. Sure, she's got more in common with some than with others. She slipped into the group with no problems. Diego likes to think he's swank, he's not from around here, he slicks his hair back like an Italian stallion and he likes motorbikes and surfing. They speak English to each other and he treats her like his kid sister. Hélène is older than the others, but mentally she's, like, fourteen – she gets home from work, pours boiling water over some instant noodles and slumps on the sofa watching reality T.V. shows on her phone with headphones on. She follows every version of "The Voice" – American, Australian, British . . . She shares the biggest bedroom with Myriam, a trilingual, super-educated undocumented Turkish girl who left her country because she says it's shit there. She works as a cleaner, but Céleste has noticed she always seems to have wads of cash. She wouldn't be at all surprised if "cleaning" is actually the horizontal mambo. Karim is the youngest, he has the scuzziest room, and has painted it completely red, he wants to be a painter – artist, not housepainter. Although he's enrolled at the Bellas Artes, he rarely shows up to class and spends most of his time getting shitfaced on rum, sometimes he'll collapse in mid-sentence and it takes four of them to put him to bed, fully dressed.

He's really sweet to Céleste, he stole a "Sons of Anarchy" sweatshirt . from some shop in the city for her. He steals all the time. He never gets caught, he's agile as an acrobat. Angela is a poet and a foot-baller, her feet are destroyed and she works for some posh clothes shop for tourists and at night, when she hasn't got training, she rolls spliffs, and lays out her notebooks all around. When the muse visits, she's capable of writing a dozen poems in a single session. The following morning, she rereads them and rips up half of them. Céleste can't tell the difference between a good poem and a shit one. Which is probably why she's not a poet. Angela has a thing with Pablo, the only rich kid in the gang, but he's from Venezuela, so even though, back in his country, his family are loaded, once his monthly allowance has been converted into euros, it's not exactly guap. He's studying to be a webmaster, but he spends most of his time strung out on Molly, he'll gently open the fridge door and wave everyone over to look at the beautiful glow – and when he's not off his tits, he's watching Venezuelan T.V. programmes that leave him so bummed that someone has to go out and score some speed just to perk him up.

They have parties all the time, the downstairs neighbours are a Russian couple who spend all their time beating the shit out of each other, screaming and screwing (still screaming) – you need a keen ear to tell the difference between fights and fucks . . . Basically, they never complain about the noise since they're making too much themselves to hear it. And next door is a sublet for tour-ists, so even if they complain, no-one gives a shit. They're hardly going to call the police, since they've no right to be there.

Céleste was destined to land here – she hadn't even spent a week crashing on the sofa when Virginia, who had the room at the back, announced that she'd found a job in Vienna, and Hélène had said, do you want the room? It's about two hundred euros a month, all in . . .

The place is always crawling with friends of someone or other, Céleste gets a lot of work doing small tattoos – she charges so little that it barely covers the cost of the needles and the gloves, but she wants to keep her hand in. She does a lot of infinity symbols: in the world of tattoos, ∞ is the new dolphin. And then there are the flowers and the butterflies, because she's a girl, and everyone assumes she'll be good at them. She hates doing butterflies, but she doesn't give people a hard time. Thirty euros here, fifty euros there . . . plus her shifts in the kitchen – she regularly gets called in, the head chef is a lipstick lesbian with a thing for French girls.

She loves her new life. She has considered going back to Paris – she doesn't give a shit about Dopalet. He didn't grass them up to the feds. Her father would know if he had. He still claims she's living at his place, for tax purposes. The cops would have been banging on his door, pronto. Céleste thinks that the Hyena is paranoid. The needle-dick fucking producer wouldn't have the cojones to pay someone to break her legs. The guy got what he deserved. The more time passes, the less she feels she is in danger. But she's happier in Barcelona than she was in Paris. For someone her age, there's a lot more work. And a lot less hassle. Hélène wants to move to Berlin, and Céleste thinks maybe she'll go with her.

She has not yet told her father where she really is. But she's not planning on lying to him long-term. She told him she's doing an internship with a tattoo artist in Australia. He huffed and puffed because she didn't even take the time to say goodbye. But given that his current girlfriend is pregnant, and he thinks that bothers

Céleste, he probably assumed she was salty. And, as it goes, it probably suits him for her to be on the other side of the world. At his age, with a new baby, life's complicated enough. Céleste doesn't care one way or another about having a little sister. But her father is convinced that she's devastated.

In the early days, she and Aïcha would chat using the comments section of Justin Bieber's Insta page. They assumed no-one was going to wade through all that shit for two girls talking about nothing much. Because everything they say had to be coded, they couldn't really tell each other very much. So Céleste gave up. Besides, Aïcha wouldn't approve of her doing a runner. She's too serious. If someone says "hide", she hides. Céleste is more of a free spirit. She's not hung up on religion.

Céleste smooths out the sheet in front of her. It is more creased than ever. Sprawled on a cushion on the floor, Pablo has been on his phone for hours, playing some game where you have to smash glass panels in some weird zero-gravity world. She tried watching over his shoulder and it made her feel seasick. Hélène is on her phone, swiping through photos of David Bowie's ex-wife, who's like sixty but has pigtails and she's on some kind of Big Brother show, and they tell her that David is dead and ask her not to tell anyone else but she goes right out and tells some kid that David's dead and the girl thinks she's talking about some guy called David who's on the show with them and the ex-wife thinks she's crying because she loved Bowie, but the girl's too young to know who the fuck he was or give a shit, and then all hell breaks loose. Fuck's sake, Céleste can't wait for people in this house to get over Bowie's death.

*

She checks the time. The night before, some guy got in touch about a tattoo. She's made a new Facebook page, creating a pseudo from her paternal grandmother's first name, Blanche, and her mother's maiden name, Klint. The guy wants a realistic wolf tattoo. She doesn't really do animals, and realism isn't her thing, but she sent him a sketch and he wrote back saying, "O.K. But not too big." That's the deal here – "not too big". Partly, it's about the price, but mostly it's that people assume you can tattoo the Sistine chapel on their little finger – what's the big deal? A wolf needs a whole shoulder at the very least, otherwise what's the point? They're pussies – they want a tattoo, but they're afraid people will see it. That said, given her wolf sketch, maybe it's best if it's not too big. Looks more like Snoopy tripping balls. She was surprised he went for it. She asked the size of his arm, so she could prepare the stencil, and he replied, "Two iPhone 6s."

He asked her if she had a studio. Normally, she works in her bedroom, drawing the curtains so the neighbours opposite don't grass her up. She doesn't have a licence to tattoo at home. And she's not registered. The client is French. She has no idea how he stumbled on her Facebook page. He wants her to do the tattoo at his place, because he's a snowflake and needs to have a nana nap afterwards. The only reason she didn't tell him to go fuck himself is because when she said it would cost about a hundred euros, he didn't quibble. And she needs that money. She has arranged to meet him in a bar, so she can get a good look at him before going back to his place. You never know. She hopes he's not some pickup artist. She hasn't posted a photo of herself online. She's not that stupid. Since she shaved her head, guys have been less grabby with her. But even so. The French are always the worst. Everyone here thinks so. All the girls who work in bars, restaurants and museums say the same thing – French guys are the worst. You can spot them at five hundred metres. They're always the ones yelling and killing everyone else's buzz. They're always the ones putting the moves on girls. Even Italians aren't that bad. And that's saying something.

THREE EUROS FOR A BOTTLE OF WATER AT A BRANCH OF PAUL at the Gare de Lyon, these people are taking the piss. Max refused to pay. He pushed away the paper bag with the ham and cheese baguette, the bottle of water and the canelé – ten euros for this, are they fucking kidding?

The cashier pulled a face, like it was a big deal for her to cancel the transaction. She can go fuck herself. He saw a video on the net: the whole train station is full of rats scurrying between the croissants. Another good reason to throw the sandwich back in her face. Paris is overrun with rats. Apparently, if you leave a sandwich lying around in one of the squares in the Marais, pigeons and rats fight over it. Not a pretty thought.

Max hates making a fuss in a shop, getting wound up like this. But he's pretty strung out right now.

Little Céleste took a savage beat-down. He's never seen anyone take a beating like it. It's not like she's dead or anything. But, even so . . . Max can be very brutal verbally. He knows that when he shouts, he's the man. It scares the shit out of people. He's always like that. But he rarely uses his fists. He's never even raised a hand to his son. He's seen his fair share of street brawls, he went on demos when he was young, he saw the cops batter his friends with truncheons and he didn't bat an eye. He's not some piss-weak little faggot. But he's not violent.

His plan was to put Céleste out of action, lock her up as arranged and leave her to scream and shout until Dopalet showed up. He felt pretty sure that giving it a little of the Lord Kossity growl would be enough to get her to play along. He planned to give her the fright of her life. Hence the idea of roping in a couple of Hell's Angels buddies who have the sort of faces you don't argue with. They would be waiting at the house, Max would bring her back and *boo!* They'd jump out and that would be that. The girl would be primed, psychologically. She'd see all these guys standing around, she'd be terrified they might rape her, she'd keep a low profile. A simple, pragmatic, intelligent plan. Once they had her tied up, a couple of slaps and she'd spill everything she knew. Then Dopalet could decide what he wanted to do to her.

His part of the job went off smoothly. Though he'd been shitting bricks before meeting up with Céleste who was waiting for him in a bar in El Raval. From the moment he recognised her, he hated her. Hated her for showing up. How many times do girls have to be told that you don't meet up with some stranger, even in a public place? Now, if she'd had a guy with her – or even just a couple of girlfriends – he would have had to backtrack. He would have had to come up with a different plan. Or even give up. But she rocked up on her own, not even suspicious – the girl is an XXS model, she can't weigh more than fifty kilos. But sexy as fuck. Full of shit, but pretty. Not much more than a kid. Max didn't know that things were going to go pear-shaped, so he was professional. Part of him thought it would teach her a lesson. Dopalet had told him about the attack, it was vicious. You can't just allow kids to go round breaking into other people's apartments and brutally torturing them for no reason. So, although he wasn't exactly comfortable with it, he was thinking, I need to knock some sense into her. She was asking for it. And anyway, he doesn't like girls who crop their hair short. Is it really too much to ask for them to have a little fucking thought for their femininity? You really think you can pass for a guy with a body like that?

How often do you hear about women being killed by mentally disturbed loners? All the time. Before the recent fashion for mass murderers, new serial killers seemed to turn up every other day. How many times has she heard the story of the jogger, the hitch-hiker, the waitress, the girl coming out of the métro, the girl walking home, a girl minding her own business – raped mutilated tortured. You'd think she would have learned her lesson. Hell no. There she was, silly bitch, sitting waiting for him. They just don't listen. He chatted shit for fifteen minutes, explained why it would be easier to go to his place and do the tattoo there. And she followed him. He played the old guy who wants to be down with the kids. He's used to dealing with younger women, he knows how to reassure them. She followed him, and don't go telling him that, deep down, she didn't realise he wanted to hurt her. Women know. But they go along anyway. If they took precautions, guys wouldn't be able to abuse them. She came to the posh house on the outskirts of Barcelona. The isolated house where, even if she managed to escape from the cellar, she'd have to run five hundred metres before she could alert anyone. The house carefully chosen for the business at hand.

Max wasn't feeling it. But he'd cut a deal with Dopalet. He couldn't turn back now. At the end of the day, he had to make the call: "Mission accomplished, we're waiting for you." Aside from the shekels – always welcome – Max was thinking about the bond that this would create. This shared secret would be the basis of great things together. Max is not lacking in ideas. He's lacking in funds.

He couldn't have known that the situation would get out of hand. Nor how quickly or how violently. He had argued that he wanted the tattoo done at his place because he was scared that, afterwards, he'd be in no fit state to get home. It was Dopalet who had briefed him that nausea was a common side effect of getting a tattoo. Céleste had gently mocked him. She thought this was his first time, that he was worrying about nothing. She reassured him: "You're not going to feel so bad you can't get into a taxi." But she had let herself be persuaded. And she must have needed the money. When he said, "I'd rather pay double and have a decent tattoo than a wolf that looks like shit but only cost a hundred euros," he realised he had touched a nerve.

When he locked the door behind them, she had whipped round, startled, but he had laughed. "I freak out easily, I'm always scared someone will break in while I'm at home." She smiled, completely missing the irony: this was what she had done to Dopalet. She had burst into his apartment without warning and fucked up his whole life. All this because of a misunderstanding. Or that, at least, was Dopalet's story. Max thinks it might have been a bit more complicated. But that's none of his business. Max had said, "I'll keep an eye on her, you come talk to her when you want." And Dopalet had put up a decent budget to get the job done. Honestly, Max's part in the plan went off perfectly. The problems started with the Hell's Angels.

All Franck and Thierry had to do was jump out of the kitchen and scare the shit out of her. Max had brought along some handcuffs because, psychologically, he thought it might break her. But basically, just a couple of slaps and then lock her up. Before she did a runner... As plans go, his really wasn't complicated. He intended to get her to confess where her accomplice, Aïcha, was hiding out before Dopalet showed up. That way, Max would have something on the producer that he could later use to blackmail him.

The problem was that, once Franck and Thierry kicked off, Max had not been able to calm them down. These guys must have taken a hell of a lot of shit from women in their lives to be so vicious now. They beat her to a bloody pulp. Max intervened: "Easy, guys, we need her to be able to talk, and besides, we have to leave something for our sponsor." But Franck shot him a threatening look. "I don't need you telling me how to do my fucking job!" After that, everything went to shit. What Max witnessed that night was something he wishes he had never seen. Teach her a little lesson, that was the agreement, not launch into a remake of "Deliverance". But just try stopping them... Try explaining to two unhinged monsters that this wasn't part of the deal. Technically, this means that if they're caught, Max will be considered an accessory. To everything. As will Dopalet, come to that.

While the whole thing was playing out, Max had time to reproach himself for a number of things. First off, it had been foolish to think he could control Franck. The guy grew up as a Hell's Angel in Grenoble. He says he resigned from the charter when he got into smack; as he puts it, the chances of getting into hard drugs after the age of thirty are infinitesimal and I'm part of that percentage – until I turned thirty, I drank, I took a little coke, but I never got into the dark side of drugs. Then I discovered smack, I started taking it to ease the comedown from the coke. And that was that.

That's his official version. But, as events around him are taking a decidedly unpleasant turn, Max remembers a different version of the story. Apparently, Franck had a thing for kids. We're not talking sassy little sluts here, we're talking little girls. Although Max isn't even sure they were girls. When you're into ten-year-olds, maybe you don't care whether they're girls or boys. Besides, given he's thick as a bucket of shit, who knows whether he can tell the difference.

Max hadn't immediately thought of Franck. He doesn't usually work with guys like that. He's old enough to realise that some characters are best avoided.

But he had to move fast and Franck was the only person he knew who had contacts in Barcelona. It had only taken Max a few days to track down Céleste. If getting Xavier, Sylvie, Lydia and Vernon to talk had been a nightmare . . . finding Céleste had been a piece of cake. In less than forty-eight hours, Max was on Daniel's Facebook page, and the dumb fuck had clicked Like on all the kid's new tattoos. Kids and the internet – they never expect it to come back and bite them in the arse – they still don't realise that everything they do is visible, all it takes is someone determined to find you.

So, when he realised that this was going down in Barcelona, Franck was the first name that sprang to mind. And the biker said, "A house with a soundproofed room? I know just the place." Because Dopalet has one great advantage: being a producer, he knows that the best way to solve a problem is to throw money at it. So, the house with the little soundproofed cellar that used to be a rehearsal room – no problem. And the henchmen Max needed to help him out – no sweat, whatever it takes. It was at this point that Max misjudged the situation. He assumed that, having had his fair share of run-ins with the cops, Franck would have more finesse in getting someone to talk. This was a mistake. Franck and Thierry – it was total carnage. They fucked him over and he never even saw it coming.

The other thing that occurred to him when he saw that things were getting out of hand and there was nothing he could do was that it's not easy being a guy. If he'd been a girl, he could have waved his little hands in the air and squealed hysterically: "Stop it, stop it, you brutes, you've gone too far," and everyone would have thought that was completely normal. They might even have been moved to pity and listened. But when you're a guy, you can't do that shit. Either he could physically overpower them and re-establish himself as the alpha male, or he could do what he actually did – play the bored, jaded man-of-the-world: "Easy, guys, easy – we still need her to talk when you're done." But if he found what was happening physically sickening, he still sided with them. So, when Franck opened his flies, Max stepped out of the room and waited for it to be over. Céleste wasn't making any noise by this stage. She offered no resistance. They'd beaten her so badly she might even have been unconscious. Max had spared himself the spectacle.

This was what he had been afraid of. Sure, kidnapping is serious. But if you handle things properly, the kid's not likely to go to the cops. After all, she's got a lot to answer for. It's borderline, but doable. But this – he listened to the sounds coming from the other room and realised that there was no way they could let her go. The thing he really feared was how the boss would react when he saw the state of the kid. But Max didn't have the guts to go back and see what the two guys were doing. He was terrified of them. Anyone would have been.

When they finally calmed down, it was Max who had gone in to check on her and give her some sleeping pills. His hands were shaking. He could never have worked in an abattoir. He's too sensitive. She was whimpering, one of her eyes was swollen shut. He wiped her down with a cloth, to get rid of the blood and the sperm. The two bikers had cracked open a bottle of whisky. Max couldn't comfort her as he would have liked. He felt pity for her. And a little disgust. But mostly compassion. He wrapped her up in a blanket he had bought especially for her and he didn't ask for help to carry her up to the bedroom. He tied her to the bed – just one hand. He couldn't take the risk of her escaping. What had happened was too serious.

Thrilled with their little performance, the two meatheads poured him a glass of whisky. Choking back his rage, Max said, "You went a little hard on her," and Franck puffed out his cheeks, "She's had worse. You get skanks like that everywhere. Won't be the first prick she's had, don't you worry," and Max thought, Jesus fucking Christ, this guy is the bastard son of Goebbels, I can't believe anyone could be so vicious. Adopting a sententious tone, he said only, "I hope the producer will give us the money as arranged, this wasn't exactly what he asked for," and from the tone of Franck's response – "He'd better fuckin' pay up if he knows what's good for him" – Max was once again reminded he had made a serious cock-up. He should never work with gangsters. When they see a guy like Max, they know he's not in the same league. They don't take him seriously. In his defence, it's not as though he usually gets his hands dirty.

He has had precious little experience when it comes to kidnapping. So he had no choice but to take whoever was available . . .

As planned, Dopalet had jumped on the first flight. Max had steeled himself for the inevitable dressing-down. He had spent half the day on the bog, clutching his stomach and literally shitting himself. He hadn't been so terrified since school when some hulking thug was waiting outside the gates after class to give him a beating for some dumb remark.

The bikers, for their part, were in fine form. Some people are made for this kind of shit. Stick them in the French Foreign Legion and they'd collapse under the weight of their medals.

Max was trying to come up with some explanation that would appease Dopalet. He gets along well with the producer. The first time they met, he thought, "The guy's a complete arsehole." But later he realised Dopalet was sensitive, curious, well travelled. Someone worth getting to know. In conversation, he has lots of funny stories and some quite interesting theories about cinema . . . but the only thing he's really interested in is boxed fucking sets.

Max hates T.V. series – not that he has shared this opinion with his new friend. Back in the day, people used to laugh at soap operas or "Dallas", but now they're all the rage, everyone thinks they're genius. How to kill off brain cells by bombarding them with obnoxious, ideologically dubious garbage in thirteen hour-long episodes. It's about as healthy as eating at McDo morning, noon and night. It's the times we live in: people ridicule intelligence. The world belongs to guys like Franck and Thierry, cretinous thugs who think the pinnacle of personal development is a beat-down.

On this point, Max has been honest with Dopalet: "How can a guy like you, with a background in cinema and an appreciation for

Truffaut, Pasolini and Bergman, spend the day watching zombies attacking a bunch of idiots . . . ?" Dopalet laughs, he likes to be challenged a little. But he doesn't react. He's like everyone else, he has admitted defeat. He's stopped fighting.

Dopalet told him about Bleach's tapes. He's not just looking for the two girls, he also wants to get his hands on those recordings. Max plays the life coach: "Stop trying to get them back by force, trying to get revenge and whatever . . . you'll lose everything you've got. No, if you want them to hand over the tapes Bleach made and never mention them to anyone, it's simple: hire them. You produce the convergences. Get them used to having money sloshing around. Once you've done that, you can ask them whatever you like, you know how this works better than I do. Nothing can resist gentrification. Of the people in the group, I can think of at least three who would be eating out of your hand if you bankrolled them, though they'd swear otherwise. Buy a screenplay from Xavier and the guy will bring you the tapes on a silver platter. Hire Sylvia to be a toilet attendant and she'll do anything you ask. Pamela might put on airs, but tell her you've got a part in a movie for her and she'll betray the lot of them. And if one of them causes trouble, you get the others to keep him quiet."

Max may have clusterfucked the kidnapping of Céleste, his skill set doesn't extend to this kind of operation. But he knows he's not wrong about the internal working of the group. The more he learns about these convergences, the more he is convinced there is a shit-ton of money to be made. People want to be taken out of themselves. People want magic. They want to believe. They need to dance. He instinctively knows that he could sell them this dream.

But now, with the bruised and battered girl lying on the mattress in the cellar . . . his dreams of being a super-producer have taken a serious hit.

Dopalet showed up. "Did something go wrong?" he said to Max. "You're white as a sheet." Franck laughed. Dopalet stared at him, concerned. Max led Dopalet down the steps into the cellar. He watched the producer's expression as he looked at the blanket, the naked body, the handcuffs, the shattered face. Thierry had made a couple of return visits while they were waiting, and the girl's body is covered with dried cum. It was horrifying. Max was mortified, he had no tears left to cry, nothing left to throw up – he was beyond hopeless. Trapped. And then – surprise, surprise: Dopalet looked pleased. He stood in the doorway, a satisfied smile playing on his face, jerked his chin at the girl and whispered, "It's her, alright." Franck said, "Just as well," and Dopalet brought a hand up to his mouth to stifle a giggle. He didn't hang about for long, he didn't want her to come round and recognise him.

Max had thought, I don't believe it, he's bound to kick off. He'll say this wasn't what we agreed and all that shit. But no. Dopalet had gone back upstairs and all he wanted to know was where Aïcha was. "In Germany," Thierry said. "But she doesn't know where. If she did, she'd have talked. I'm sure she'd have blabbed – she's not what you might call reliable." Arms folded, staring at his shoes, Max had stood in silence, thinking: maybe I'm the one who's insane, I must be the last snowflake in the fucking country. Because Dopalet had not been shocked. Relieved, maybe.

Dopalet had not raised an eyebrow as he listened to Franck's plan: shoot a gram of smack into her arm, as if she misjudged the hit, wait for her to OD, then dump the body somewhere in Santa

Coloma – this would be the delicate part of the operation, according to the biker, since it meant unloading her while ensuring there were no witnesses or C.C.T.V. cameras. But he could sort it, he said. When they found her with a needle in her arm, the police were hardly likely to launch a detailed investigation: young girl gets into hard drugs and doesn't realise she needs to start out slow. The only time Dopalet balked was when Franck said: "I want five Gs right now, and five more after the body has been found and the coroner rules it an accidental death. If I'm caught dumping the body, I want five grand to go to my wife." There was some argument over this particular detail, but as for the overall plan – that after beating and raping the girl, the best solution was for them to murder her – Max got the impression he was the only one who had any qualms. Dopalet really needed to stop watching those box sets.

THE HYENA IS PERCHED ON THE EDGE OF A CONCRETE PLANTER in which a lone shrub survives, surrounded by cigarette butts. She's waiting for the dope dealers. In Aubervilliers, they don't come out until late afternoon. On Saturdays, they don't show before 6.00 p.m. The square is deserted. She hates this area. Like every area where you only ever run into guys. A girlfriend gave her the keys to her workshop, a huge loft space rented from the city council, she's been crashing there while working out what to do next.

She's not planning to stay in Paris. She's spent too long at the camp, she's grown soft. Every day, she crosses the périphérique and every day, at the porte de Pantin, traffic is slowed to a crawl by the convoys of refugees who eke out a living there. Though crushed by fate, subjected to the same privations, the expressions on their faces are different. Now timid, now furious, now wild, now dangerous, now pensive . . . It's impossible to imagine what their lives were like a few months ago – did he go to school that little boy who's managed to absorb some words of French and now taps on the windows of passing cars? Did he have parents who worried about keeping him safe, did he grow up in a lonely house or was he running around barefoot in some shanty town? Now, he begs the drivers of cars stopped in traffic for food or money. The Hyena has seen him several times, he reminds her of the kid in "War of the Buttons". She finds the city suffocating. Poverty has spread, as though someone tipped a sackful of misery into the streets and the corridors of the métro. Paris has become a dystopian piece of concept art, a gallery of atrocities, a daily display of all the things man can deny his neighbour. She used to know how to deal with it, how to get to where she was going, thinking this is terrible and instantly moving on to something else, some other thought. Suffering has always been a part of the landscape and, to some extent, you just had to get used to the idea. But the extent has changed. She feels that to get used to this would be toxic.

At the camp, the Hyena had retreated from communal reality. She would never have imagined that she could spend so much time totally immersed in the group. Still less that she would feel that sense of belonging. It was a collective conscious uncoupling. She has rarely felt so happy, for so long, in any given place. To the point where, when Céleste disappeared, she didn't immediately hop on a train to go and find out what had happened. Dopalet's son, Antoine, sent news whenever he visited his father. He said the producer was getting back on his feet, that he was busy with various projects, that he'd stopped talking about revenge. She had believed him. She had wanted it to be true. She had thought, everything's going to be fine. She had lost the sense of urgency. It had felt good to trust.

Vernon's departure took her by surprise. Upsettingly brutal, it had been completely at odds with the atmosphere that defined their adventure. Like the others, the Hyena felt as though she was being punished. And yet, almost immediately, she had approved of his decision. She too felt a dark cloud, some as yet unspecified danger, lowering over them. It was time.

She left. She made a few phone calls, found this apartment

where she could stay for a while. Lydia had moved in with her. She's working on her biography of Bleach. She says she's nearly finished; she's been saying this for several months. Olga showed up with her bags, because Sylvie's place is too cramped, whereas in Aubervilliers there's enough space for the dogs. The Hyena likes having Olga around. She radiates energy. With ineffable grace, she blends barbarian brutality with the gentleness of a little girl. And besides, the Hyena is used to dogs. To this life parallel to human existence, to this effusive tenderness. Later, Pamela asked if she could leave her bags there for a few days, and Jésus came with her.

When she pushes open the door to the loft, the Hyena has the strange impression of arriving at the camp, but indoors. It's the same experience, more stunted, perhaps. But something crucial – a sense of being together – survives.

From time to time, on the pretext of buying some weed for Lydia – who claims it helps her concentrate – she goes out and walks around the concourse of the building. The walls are inscribed with "Weed" and "Skunk", with arrows, so you don't go to the wrong courtyard.

As she waits for the dealers, she rolls a cigarette, carefully sprinkling the tobacco along the paper, leaning against a yellow pillar – a preposterously cheerful colour in this bleak landscape.

When Vernon called to tell her about his visit from Max, it brought her out of her torpor. She was back on autopilot. Unfortunately, her immediate reaction was not the correct one: she first went looking for Aïcha. At least she knew where to find her.

She left for three days, just enough time for the non-stop drive

Paris–Frankfurt–Amsterdam–Paris. Bowie pouring from the speakers all the way, like the phases of her life surfacing one by one. She had enjoyed the long drive, you can't cheat the kilometres, you have to get through them one by one. It leaves you time to think.

When she got back, the flurry of confessions began. First there was Daniel: "Céleste is in Barcelona. I found her online a while back. I didn't mention it to anyone because she seemed happy where she was." The Hyena can't help but wonder whether Daniel isn't a little bit slow on the uptake. Or maybe it's the testosterone. If it made people smarter, everyone would know. Then there was Xavier – at least he realised that he had fucked up, and lamely apologised, he had seen Céleste in Barcelona. When he was with Max. The Hyena had felt a faint urge to throttle him. If he had told her straight off, she wouldn't have gone looking for Aïcha first . . . Meanwhile, Sylvie was sobbing in the kitchen. She had answered every one of Max's questions. In fact, she had been cheerfully candid, never suspecting he was manipulating her.

And as she listened to them, one after the other, and the realisation dawned that the journey she had just made was the wrong one, the Hyena was thinking: this is why Vernon left. The conditions for entropy were all present. Discord is a plant that takes time to blossom, but the seeds had been there, just waiting to germinate. Their instincts were wrong. They should have talked to each other.

The kids from the estate show up, the junior dealers. "Are you looking for something, madame?" Every time she meets them, they are so friendly: not everything is fucked up. At least budding local dealers are trying to do their best.

As she pushes open the metal door to the loft, she recognises

Kiko's voice. Lydia turns to her, excitedly: "He's managed to access the bank accounts of Dopalet and Max, there are no direct transactions, but Max bought several tickets to Barcelona on his Carte Bleu, and Dopalet flew there a couple of days later. The dumb fuck flies Vueling – if I had that much money I wouldn't set foot on their planes . . . You know you should never piss on a budget airline? A stewardess told me that – they don't have time to clean between flights." Lydia's thought processes are not always linear. The Hyena often wonders what it will be like, this book she has spent so much time writing, and whether any human brain will be capable of following her labyrinthine thoughts. When Lydia thinks, she's like a rabbit on acid.

Kiko showed up with a tube of vitamin C tablets filled with cocaine. A big, fat, orange tube. With a flick of his thumb and a radiant smile, he pops the cap. He warns Daniel, "I'm only doing one line today. Just one. Care to join me?" and hardly has he snorted the first rail then he looks up at Daniel and says, "After the third one, tell me to stop, yeah?" Then he snorts like a bull and throws his head back and launches into the first bars of Buddy Holly's "Every Day", in a demented, disturbing falsetto. He keeps time by clicking his fingers and misses every beat.

Daniel watches with an amused grin. He sways to the rhythm, rolling his shoulders. Since he transitioned, his dancing has been a problem. He's sick of people thinking he's a gay guy when he's doing his best to dance like a man. He doesn't shake his hips, doesn't wave his hands. He just shuffles his feet from right to left, studiously avoiding anything that might pass for gracefulness. Head up, back stiff, he looks like an overheated Robocop. He takes out his phone and tries to regain his composure – he's not yet ready for dad dancing. He swipes through the photographs on his phone. "I'm always surprised by how fast I'm changing," he says. When he first started taking testosterone and checked out the forums he thought, fuck's sake, these guys have no lives, they spend hours discussing every fucking chest hair that sprouts. Now he understands. It is a constant fascination. His features are more angular, the hair on the crown of his head is thinning, the way he looks at people is different. Even a year ago, there was still a slight uncertainty in his gaze – his eyes seemed to be asking for permission. He was feminine. He worried whether people would let him be who he was. That's over. Now, he owns his look. A guy who's comfortable in his own skin. He's handsome. Girls treat him like a little pet. Strangers, passers-by, sales assistants, girls on his course, neighbours, the women who run the local shops – they all constantly fuss over him.

Sélim shows up with his bicycle under his arm. He is pouring sweat. Since the terrorist attacks, he can't bear to travel on the métro. The minute he hears a fire engine in the distance, his heart starts hammering. He no longer goes to restaurants. Or to the cinema. He is terrified when he's on the university campus. He's terrified when he sees a postman's trolley or a rucksack lying on the floor of a bus. A lot of Parisians feel like him, apparently. He is supposed to be meeting up with his daughter in Athens. He is traumatised at the thought of taking a plane. Sylvie gives him the number of a hypnotherapist she knows: "It really works. You'll see. It's amazing." And Kiko shakes his Vitamin C tube. "This works for everything. You want to give it a try? A quick toot when you get to the airport, and everything is easier."

Xavier is talking about Cologne. Hundreds of women assaulted in one night. He says he can't help thinking about his daughter, can't help imagining her in a train station being groped by the strange hands like some fucked-up funfair ride, and the worst of it is the thought of these anonymous hands, these men gathering in packs to molest women they don't respect – just thinking about it is enough to drive him crazy. This is the first time the Hyena has ever heard Xavier express concern about women's safety. He's angry that the others won't face up to what this means – that we can't avoid asking tough questions about the so-called melting pot if the people coming to live among us aren't prepared to live like us. Lydia puffs her cheeks as though about to blow some bubblegum: "You want to know the most shocking thing about your little New Year's story? It's that the women managed to go into a police station and complain that some guy groped their arse at night in the middle of a city and the cops didn't just laugh in their faces. Don't tell me you've never seen one of your mates hassling some girl in the street and thinking it was just a bit of fun." "Not groping them. Never."

The Hyena is sitting cross-legged on a corner of the sofa. Tracking down the apartment where Céleste had been living in Barcelona wasn't difficult. Once Daniel and Xavier admitted she was in the city, she simply tracked the Likes on the tattooist's new Facebook page, and found her roommates. They told her Céleste had disappeared. She had gone out to do a tattoo and never come back. No, they don't know anything else. They're worried. But helpless. They seem like nice kids.

The Hyena calls over to Kiko, "Hey, patron of the arts, can you pay for my flight to Barcelona?" And Kiko, who is used to such requests, brandishes the credit card he's been using to cut lines and says, "What the hell are you planning to do when you get there?"

And the Hyena retorts, "Not a fucking clue, man. When I get there, I'll wing it . . ."

She can hear the various conversations. The room is full, as it has been every night for the past few days. Words spill out, hissing and crackling like a forest fire, she hears snatches, tongues of flame lapping at her consciousness at regular intervals. A terrible feverishness is making it difficult to breathe. Nina Simone is singing "Mr Bojangles" and someone turns up the volume.

"I don't want her to leave her husband I don't want a relationship with her I like her a lot don't get me wrong she's an amazing woman but I'm not in love with her I mean I wouldn't rule out a threesome you know but the fact that I'm even thinking about that means I'm not in love."

"Who's got the skins? I bought two packs yesterday I don't know where the fuck they've gone."

"I was shocked by how much they charged when she said eight euros for a glass of wine I was stunned – I'm not used to drinking on café terraces in Paris anymore."

"I signed the petition against T.A.F.T.A. – we're up to a million signatures I think not that anyone will give a toss."

"I paid her a little attention and now she thinks I'm the love of her life but that's just because her husband neglects her."

"Can I have a look at your cigarette packet? I've never seen the one with the throat cancer photo. You should keep it, it's a stunning piece."

The room fills with a clamorous hubbub. Olga comes and sits next to her. "I want to go with you." "You don't have a passport. Besides, I don't know where I'm going to crash, I'm sorry, but it's easier if I go it alone." "Emilie said she'll lend me her passport."

"Is she completely nuts? You look nothing like her!" Olga sighs. "Then we can drive there. I want to go with you. I can be useful. If you need to scare the shit out of someone, I can help." "Honey, I don't want to sound hurtful, but I don't need anyone's help to terrify people."

Then Pamela Kant steps into the room and for a brief moment, there is silence. She is not dressed in her usual clothes – she's wearing Skin Two fetish gear: black leather thigh boots, shorts so minimalist they're practically panties. The Hyena had forgotten how well stacked she is. Although she has seen a lot of Pamela recently. But this outfit is sublime.

Aware of the effect she's created, Pamela does a little twirl, arms raised, radiant. "Hey kids! Guess who I got tarted up like this for? I've just been to see Max. Told him I'd had a word with Vernon. That we were interested in his plan for 'professional' convergences. He was suspicious, obviously. He seemed very uncomfortable. Almost as if he'd got a guilty conscience. But guess what?" – she arches her back, thrusts out her chest, makes a duckface pout, plants her hands on her hips and smiles – "I eventually got him to relax, he thought I was sincere – either that or he wasn't thinking at all . . . and when he had to go to the little boy's room, he forgot to take his phone. Thankfully he's the kind of dumb fuck who thinks 0000 is a safe passcode." Pamela takes out her phone, opens the Photos app and hands it to the Hyena. "So, I took a few screenshots of his G.P.S. while he was in Barcelona, and with a bit of luck . . . Céleste should be here," she says, pointing to a particular address. "I checked all the addresses he visited on Google Maps on the taxi ride here and I think this is the house we're interested in." Kiko throws up his hands to heaven. "Blessed be the sluts and their superpowers! Did he realise you checked his G.P.S. while he was off taking a piss?" Pamela does not smile as she says, "By the time I left his place, honey, checking the search history on his phone was the last thing on his mind." Olga stubbornly insists, "I want to go with you. Have you given back the rental car? Kiko, can you rent a car for us? I'm not staying here on my own, I want sun, sea and sadism. Xavier, can you look after the dogs, please?"

A *BUTANERO* WHEELS A HAND TRUCK ALONG THE STREETS OF Barceloneta, tapping the gas cylinders with a spanner. At every corner, he stops and listens for someone to call down and tell him to come up. Gusts of wind billow the laundry, swell drying beach wraps and set Catalan flags fluttering . . . Birds are singing in their tiny cages. Céleste gazes up at the balconies littered with a curious collection of hanging bicycles, water tanks, luxuriant plants and cleaning equipment . . .

The strangest thing, after everything that has happened, is how normal things are. The notion that, for other people, life has carried on. There is no logic to it. Reason, language, analysis – all these things are useless. We constantly delude ourselves when we pretend that things have an importance, a solidity, that life rests on a stable foundation.

It happened only a few days ago, yet already it seems to belong to a different era. Céleste heard them breaking the door down, the kick and the body slams, the deafening cacophony. She was accustomed to muffled sounds she could not quite identify, but this ruckus was too unbelievable to be just Franck, stoned, with Crazy Cavan cranked up to eleven, galumphing like a drunken elephant. She thought it might be the feds, she thought it might be her father. But what burst through the splintered door of her cell was Olga, the flame-haired giant. And Céleste's first thought was, thank God it's not my father. She could not have endured him seeing her in this state.

They found her. During the time she was held captive, she vacillated between the mercurial moments of hope that helped her to hold out – this couldn't carry on much longer, people would be searching for her everywhere, she was not going to die like a caged animal, something was bound to happen. Or she would find some way to escape. She would work herself into a frenzy, convinced that it was about to happen – believing that because the situation was unendurable, it was bound to stop. And less glorious moments, beyond grief and tears, when she tumbled into chasms of despair – there was no end to this pain. No-one could endure such black thoughts without losing some part of themselves.

Even when she saw Olga, she was still terrified. She thought they didn't realise that Franck was armed, that he was capable of anything. She had shrieked in horror because she immediately thought of failure and of the punishments that would follow. In that moment, she did not believe. She had lost all faith in a reality where her gaoler did not win every round of every imaginable game. Franck, who appears whenever he likes, does whatever he likes, while she obeys and cajoles – Céleste, meek, gentle, docile – prepared to do anything for the promise of an extra crust of bread, prepared to endure anything to avoid another beating. In a few short days, it had already become normal. She had quickly lost her humanity. What people call dignity, when they have not been exposed to torture on a daily basis. People get so worked up about it; but it is the first thing you lose.

Olga had wrapped her in a blanket that she found in one of the other rooms. The giant scooped her into her arms as though Céleste weighed no more than a child. She could not face climbing the cellar steps. She was raving – convinced that when they reached the top, they would find her torturers waiting. Olga had patience, she did not flag, her arms never faltered, she hugged the girl to her and Céleste felt a fierce anger emanating from her body, and, gradually, she realised that she was like an electrical appliance set back onto its base, she was recharging. She was not recovering her wits, that would not come until much later, but she felt an energy surging through her, a strength that, after long minutes, made it possible for her to say "I'm ready".

Upstairs, Franck was in no fit state to call the shots about anything. The image is burned onto Céleste's memory: the Hyena was kneeling on his chest, having to make no effort to keep him on the ground because he had stopped moving, Franck's face was turned towards the cellar door and, between punches, Céleste's eyes met his. He was streaming blood. At first, she felt pity. Then fear of the moment when he came round. Only as an afterthought did it occur to her that she could run – that it was finally possible to escape this hell. The daylight burned her eyes. And she wept. She is weak. It took only a few days for her to completely lose her mind. Mental well-being is a fragile thing, something we realise only when it implodes.

Olga did not let go of her. Céleste paid her no heed, but she could feel the massive body just behind her, within reach – her terror was palpable. Little by little, the words swirling around her became intelligible. The Hyena emerged from the house, shielding her eyes with her hand. Céleste noticed that she had washed them, that there was only a fine trace of blood around the fingernails. She had closed the door behind her and said to Olga, "What do we do now? Call the cops?" and Céleste had said, no not the police not now. The Hyena glanced over her shoulder and said, "I think they'll take care of the clean-up themselves," and the three of them got into the car, like three girls leaving a restaurant where they've just had afternoon tea. Except for one minor detail: Céleste was wearing nothing but the thick blanket given to her by Olga.

During the drive, they did not say a word. Céleste was shivering. Not with cold – the heat was oppressive. With fear. Fear dogged her like an old acquaintance. She did not want to talk. She did not think to say I'm relieved or thank you or how did you find me? Still less: sorry – you told me to lie low and I didn't listen. Something in her was not yet free. She stared out the window, saying to herself, all you could think about was this moment, your freedom. Well, here it is. See? But she was not here, she could not connect. She watched the scenery flash past, but she felt dissociated from it. Disconnected from events. The feeling persisted. She does not know how long it lasted, but by the time she was finally able to speak, they had been back at the hotel for some time. She had put on the clothes offered by the Hyena. She hadn't wanted to shower. Not yet. She felt she did not have the strength to stand, or to pull the curtain to cut herself off from the world. When she had recovered some strength and a little lucidity, her first words were: "Fuck, did you see the looks on their faces down at reception when we walked in?" Because, seeing Céleste struggling, Olga had once again swept her up in her arms, and this was how they had made their entrance, like the couple from "Corpse Bride", with the bride wrapped in a blanket. When she said this, the other two exchanged a distressed look, but the flame-haired giant played along, "Probably thought I'd given birth to the Little Mermaid," and this had made Céleste laugh. Since that moment, she has behaved as though nothing happened. When she went back to the apartment to pack up her things, she simply said, "I got into a spot of bother," and her roommates had looked at her bizarrely. But she didn't care. It was obvious that they were expecting something more from her. Something she couldn't give.

No, she didn't want to go to the police. She certainly didn't want to tell her father. She had no intention of going to see a doctor. She clung to words of no importance, to commonplace gestures, the mundane was all she could bear. So, when the women asked if she wanted to drive back to Paris with them, Céleste had said, "About fucking time, I've really missed Paris." She did not want to talk about it. She wasn't ready. She felt shamed by what had happened to her. She wanted to be left alone.

Everything was there, laid out in her memory, every hour she had spent in that hell. The beer bottles. Franck couldn't stay hard for long. So there were the bottles. And other objects, to use instead. The piss, in a corner of the room, the shit that she had to pick up in case he appeared and then wash her hands so she didn't smell too bad. All the tender words she had said to Franck to cajole him. That had been the worst thing, her tenderness. The brief period it took to break her. This is something she has sworn never to talk about to anyone. She owes her life to her complicity. Franck would stroke her cheek and say, "I'm taking a huge fucking risk by lying to them, you know. They think you're dead, but I can't bring myself to do it, because we get on so well, you and me."

There is a lump in her throat. Something she cannot spit out or something she cannot choke down. It's not difficult to understand what is wrong with her. The world had been shattered there –

against the four walls of that cellar. What happened down there will stay down there. He would leave her water in little plastic bottles. Never any food. She ate only when he appeared. There was no day, no night. She never knew how long he had been absent. It was the Hyena who told her he came every three days, because she checked his bank account and noticed he paid the motorway toll with his debit card. He made the return journey from Montpellier, where he lived, to Barcelona, where he was keeping her prisoner. It could have gone on for a long time, the house he was subletting had been standing empty, he could have renewed the lease for as long as he liked.

No, she doesn't want to take revenge on Dopalet, or on Max. When someone mentions revenge now, she thinks of punishment. She just wants to be left alone.

She sees the people around her smile. Their senseless happiness at having found her. This she knows: she will never again smile the way they do. She has lost her devil-may-care attitude. She managed to say thank you, on the drive back to Paris. Thank you for coming. Thank you for taking care of me. And Olga had made a vague gesture out the window and growled something. Arriving back in Aubervilliers, Paris was greyer and bleaker than her memory of it. There were lots of people. They were happy to see her. She recognised some of the faces, others were unfamiliar. Aïcha's father, Sélim, took her in his arms and cried. She pressed her body against his. It did something to her, feeling the racking sobs in his chest, the tears he shed. Then she had stepped away from him, the emotion was too intense, and she said, "Have you got anything to eat in this place? I'm fucking starving, we've been on the motorway all day and I hate motorway food," she said it to make things clear:

this is how people were to talk to her. About food, about the weather, about trivialities. Nothing else.

It is with the dogs that she feels most comfortable. She can't walk them by herself. She is terrified someone will steal one, kick it to death, or throw stones at it. And she won't know how to defend it. She is scared by the mute faces, the hidden intentions, by her own powerlessness. So she plays with the dogs in the safety of the loft. She doesn't talk much. Before, Céleste didn't give a damn about dogs, now they are all that matters.

Daniel came. He is the first person to talk to her normally. There was no concerned hug, no knowing look. He simply said, "Long time no see," with that smile she loves, that laid-back loutish smile. Céleste found him more handsome than she remembered. From his nonchalance, she assumed that terrible things must have happened to him, too. He had that delicate politeness of people who know that evil truly exists. And when it happens to you, it happens to you, no point banging on about it.

He said, "When are you going to start work on my back? Any ideas? I'm thinking maybe a boat. Old school. You did bring your tattooing gear, didn't you?"

The following morning, she sat down to draw and it was agonising. Every two minutes, she would jump to her feet, seized by an overpowering dread. She would make tea, toss the ball for the dogs, draw the curtains, go and ask Pamela for some rolling tobacco, find herself a piece of chocolate. She could not sit still. Her hands refused to do her bidding. Her mind even more so. She thought she had lost her touch, that this was something else that she had left back there, behind her, in that other time – a time separated from today by an impassable barrier.

It took a week before she finally managed to draw a boat. It took everything she had in her gut. Then Daniel had pulled off his sweater and, seeing the twin mastectomy scars, she traced them with her finger, as though drawn to them, not thinking that the gesture might be misplaced, "We'll have to cover these someday, don't you think?" and Daniel had straddled a chair, leaned his chin against the back and said, "Let's deal with my back first, darling." He was the first to play the game with her. The game of nothing ever happened. She laid the edge of her hand against his skin, pressed the pedal, and the sound of the needle swept her away. For the first time in weeks, she concentrated on something without being overcome by panic.

WHEN HE GETS TO PLACE DE LA RÉPUBLIQUE, PATRICE RUNS into Bébert – fifty-something, handsome, long blonde hair, grey at the roots. Skinny as a teenage girl and butch as a heavyweight boxer. Box-fresh gold creps. Black skin-tight trousers. He looks like he's heading to Ibiza. The disco starlet look has always been at odds with who Bébert is – a hardcore criminal who's spent most of his adult life banged up and would happily kill both his parents for a credit card and a P.I.N.

Patrice is surprised to see him here – "You're involved in the 'Nuit Debout' movement?" – and, surrounded by thousands of protestors, Bébert says, "I'm what?" He doesn't see the crowd. He probably thought there was a sale on. Or, more likely, he didn't give it a second thought. He doesn't give two fucks what's going on at place de la République, he's just passing through. Then he decodes the riddle at the heart of the question he has been asked: now you come to mention it, there are a lot of people . . . it reminds him of something. "This whole Occupy movement shit is for young people, isn't it? At my age . . . it's a bit late to go looking for legit work, don't you think?"

In fact, he gives zero fucks, since he's got two passes to see JoeyStarr at L'Olympia. The girl who was supposed to be coming with him – she works at Kenzo, and regularly gives him fucking divine duds, not his size, but who cares, right? – anyway, this girl has had a last-minute change of plan, so Bébert takes a step back and, with a triumphant air, as though laying an extravagant gift at Patrice's feet, he says, "You want to come?" Patrice says, "You might be able to sell the tickets," and Bébert shakes his head, "I'm on the guest list, I go in via the stage door – if the guys found out I'd sold All Access to a couple of nobodies, I'd look like a complete fucking beta, I can't afford to lose face." But Patrice says, sorry, I'm waiting on some friends and Bébert throws up his hands, too bad, then hails a taxi. And it is Patrice's turn to notice that, around place de la République, the traffic is still flowing, with its taxis and its tail-backs, something he hadn't noticed even though he's been coming here every night after work for the past three weeks.

As usual, by late afternoon, the place is teeming. Patrice is happy as a pig in shit. For the past few years, he's felt like a nail being hit by a frenzied hammer day after day: the left-wing struggle was over. Any article by an economist suggesting that debt was a con trick, any criticism of the tendency to conflate refugees with potential terrorist rapists, any protest against the destruction of public pensions or the public service, has been greeted by howls from the media of regressive leftism, virtue signalling and failure to face reality while brandishing the spectre of Islamo-leftism. What is left is a socialist government pervaded by fascist ideologies, a government of opportunistic hard-right turncoats, of government ministers who see no problem in hanging out with members of the G.U.D. but wouldn't be seen dead with a trade-unionist, a socialism that doesn't want to talk about regulating the markets, and has only one idea: wooing far-right voters. It is a socialist government elected on a centre-left manifesto that immediately set about continuing the right-wing policies of its predecessors, embracing deregulation policies without protest. It is the left in power determined to put an end to the very idea of leftism. The newspaper headlines are all about the "rioters at place de la République", about the inability of Nuit Debout to "keep its troops on a tight leash". The journalists know what they're talking about when it comes to being kept on a tight leash. The totality of the press in France is owned by three billionaire industrialists, and anyone who writes for their papers defends their interests. Patrice has attended his fair share of demos. He has never seen such unwarranted, such outrageous police repression – not that the newspapers have reported on that.

By dint of hearing it repeated ad nauseam, the harassment has had its effect – there is only one possible reality, in which big bosses are unfettered, there is only one possible future, laissez-faire capitalism. There is only one valid interpretation of the facts, the free market cannot be subjected to constraint, nothing must stop the richest from taking ever more, nothing must stop the powerful for treating the powerless like slaves. The legacy of the Front populaire and the strikes of the 1970s must be crushed, equality is an outmoded concept. The freedom of the consumer is enough. In fact, it's more than enough – they can't understand what people are complaining about. What with the privatisation of profits and the socialisation of losses, the whole country is being dismantled and put into the service of the banks and the most disturbing thing is that it has been drummed into the heads of every man, woman and child that there is no alternative.

And here at place de la République, every Patrice in the greater Paris region can say: we do not accept this fiction. It is pathetic, and at the same time it is crucial. Those in power know it, which is why they turn a deaf ear. Rioters, they say, anti-Semitic, they say, unrealistic, they say. But there are still people, in France, in Spain, in Greece, in Portugal, in Ireland, even in Germany, though no-one ever talks about it – there are still people who do not believe that putting power in the hands of ignorant psychopaths from the "best" families is the only possible reality. People like him who believe that, if we are going to prioritise our problems, the aid given to the banks in the wake of the 2008 financial crash poses more serious issues than the arrival of a few thousand refugees.

It is a fairground atmosphere. There are pop-up stalls everywhere. France cannot help itself. Everything has to be structured. Press booths, Wi-Fi hotspots, book exchanges, forums. Endless stalls. People spread out, congregate in groups, sit on the ground or stroll around. It's bullshit to say that they're all hipster activists, the crowd here comes from all strata of society, a hodgepodge of individuals who have one thing in common: they are not about to allow themselves to be fleeced without putting up a fight.

Patrice spots Xavier outside Habitat, buying a sandwich from one of the stalls. He turns to Patrice, shocked, as though he were personally responsible for the on-site catering: "Five euros for a merguez and fries, that's exploitation! You call that anti-globalisation? I'm disappointed."

Skinhead crop, tight white T-shirt, pressed jeans, trainers – from his look, Xavier could be a socialist or a fascist. The two camps share the same masculine aesthetic. He blends into the background, and no-one would think to ask what the fuck he's doing here. Except Patrice, who knows him only too well. Xavier coolly says, "I'm down with everything that's being said here. I even listen in on nights when I don't come, I fire up Periscope, like it's the radio, and listen to the speeches. I broadly agree on the issues –

save the bees, the military junta in Benin, spiralling rents, the decline of national values, police brutality, massacres in the Congo, those who died for French Algeria, spoilt ballot papers, May '68, pension reform . . . overall, the issues don't seem too extreme. Where I might differ is on the solutions. But no-one here is offering any solutions . . . when you get to that point, I suspect I'll stop coming. Everyone wants to feed the refugees – I'm a Christian, man, I'm hardly going to be against that, I can see they're dying like dogs so even I'd be prepared to hand out soup and blankets. I know the classics: Jesus never told the poor to go get their immigration status sorted. I'd just like someone to explain to me – since you've got nothing against Islam – why Saudi Arabia isn't taking them in . . . ? I mean they wouldn't have far to schlep, would they? I understand that they want to remain Muslim. I'm just a little surprised that they don't settle in countries where they'd be more comfortable. Why come to our country? Don't tell me it's because there's lots of jobs – they know as well as you and me that there's no work here. On the other hand, there aren't as many executions, I'll grant you that."

They are joined by Vernon and Olga. Vernon came back. Just before they tracked down Céleste. He called Pamela and said, "Can someone give me a place to crash?" like it was an anodyne question, like they'd chatted the night before. In the same, offhand tone, Pamela said, "Aubervilliers isn't exactly verdant, Paris isn't very chill right now, but we're all here and there's room to spare." And the next day, there he was. Vernon is a man of few words. He said: "It feels good to be here," which, coming from him, was practically a soliloquy. On the night he arrived, he did what he does best: he played music. He'd prepared a playlist. And when he looked up from his laptop screen, Patrice could see that he was trembling with emotion. He had waited two days before asking, "What the fuck got into you, man? Weren't we good the way we were?" and Vernon, as though stating the obvious, said, "After the incident with Véro, things would never have been the same again. That's the way it is. You can't unring a bell."

Sylvie and Olga worked desperately to track Véro down in the bars of her former neighbourhood. She has moved out of the apartment. No-one knows what has become of her. She has disappeared without trace. The old bitch. For a long time, Patrice cursed the day that Véro decided to tell Vernon the truth, it would have been better if she'd said, Charles is dead, and refused to open the door to him, it would have spared them so much disappointment. Then, one fine morning, he faced the facts: it could never have lasted. In a sense, he agrees with Vernon. They needed to do a hard reset.

Olga is the only one in the group who spends her nights on place de la République. She's as much at home here as she is in her kitchen. Once, like everyone else, she even waited in line to speak into the microphone, but she prefers to hang out on her own, doing a free-style rap and bellowing like a calf. Patrice had been stupid enough to tease her, saying, "You should stand on a soapbox so everyone can see you." Olga had taken the quip literally and now she wanders around with a red plastic crate under her arm, which, someday or other, will collapse under her weight. The most amazing thing of all is that she invariably finds an audience. She was even seen, one night, leading about thirty people on a protest through the neighbouring streets. No-one knew what they were demanding, but they shouted slogans at the tops of their lungs. Olga is in fine form. As she says hello to Patrice and Xavier, she is already looking around for a pitch. Then she carefully sets down her red plastic crate, climbs onto it and launches into her diatribe. She has obviously been thinking about what she plans to say.

"Last night on T.V. I was listening to this woman, you know the kind of rich, educated woman who speaks the language of power, the sort of person who never questions anything, and certainly not their own intelligence, though they should, in fact it's getting to be an emergency, anyway, she was saying, 'Not all poor people are terrorists, fortunately.' She adds this 'fortunately' in that common-sense, no-nonsense, oh-my-dear tone: can you *imagine* if all the poor took up arms and refused to be downtrodden, we would be in the most terrible pickle, it would never end. 'Fortunately, not all poor people are terrorists!' Fortunately for who, exactly? Fortunately, she says – that decent poor people meekly allow themselves to be led to the slaughterhouse, otherwise can you imagine the trouble there would be at every savage cut . . . Even as she is praising the poor for their meekness in that genteel French of courtesans welcomed at the Elysée Palace this woman knows that the likes of Goodyear, Air France, the post office workers and ArcelorMittal are being trampled and imprisoned. She knows about the endless lines of refugees being held in camps so they can be shipped off to Turkey. She knows that, only a stone's throw from her opulent dining room, poverty has soared. They all know. They celebrate submissiveness. They are thrilled that we're so naive, so stupid. 'Fortunately,' they say, 'fortunately the poor allow the rich to climb on their backs.' Another time, on T.V., there was this bourgeois bitch talking in the same posh Palace accent, and she says, 'I'm

Islamophobic.' She's not ashamed to admit it. When you're a bourgeois bitch, everything smells of roses, even your own shit, but if it comes out of your arse, why put it on the table? She's Islamophobic. She felt the need to say this. These are the same people who have no fucking problem with Islam when they're bidding for a contract with Saudi Arabia, or rubbing shoulders with the Sheikh-of-the-day. When she says she's Islamophobic, she's not thinking about the Arab woman in the queue behind her at Louis Vuitton in the eighth arrondissement. She's thinking about poor Arabs who are allowed to walk the same streets as she is, to work in the town hall, catch the bus, enrol their children in schools. These are the Arabs she doesn't want to put up with anymore. It's too much misery, we need to get rid of it: she is proudly Islamophobic in the name of liberty, equality and fraternity. She's not bothered by other religions. She's very clear: Islamophobic, but not racist. And when she throws open the doors to bigotry, she genuinely believes she's doing it for the good of the people. As though the people need pogroms, not funding for the public health service, or homeless shelters, as though the people need more homophobic murders, not more high school teachers. As though with a delicate aristocratic finger, she can point to the undeserving poor so that the 'people' can vent their frustrations, the way she might point to the macaroon she covets on the cake stand at Ladurée. As though wealth confers an inherent authority over the little people she hopes to divide, like Marie fucking Antoinette in her shepherdess outfit . . . But if you have the right to be Islamophobic, madame la Comtesse, how long do you think you can stop other people from being antisemitic and not be ashamed to admit it – since no-one's ashamed of anything anymore at the Palais – from being homophobic and not ashamed to admit it, from believing that queers should be wiped out, believing that a woman's place is in the home and those who dare to step outside should be disciplined, from believing that black people are monkeys and not be ashamed to admit it? What exactly are people at the Palace ashamed of? People are beginning to wonder . . . How about tax evasion, corruption, deportations, the destruction of the school system, the overstretched hospitals, contaminated food, arms sales, long-term unemployment? Let me tell you something, madame la Comtesse, we don't give a shit about that little Arab girl on the bus wearing a headscarf, what we care about is changing history so that little Arab girl isn't just a pawn used to serve your interest, to think about the greater good . . . We've realised that an Arab who gets out her hijab is an Arab who says fuck you. An Arab with a long memory. A communard, a communist, a Muslim, a picketer, a terrorist . . .

"What a pity the great and the good didn't think to join the Front National earlier. Now all the best jobs are taken, and they're trapped on the left wing. It's absurd. But that's no problem, they'll tell you – now that we all think the same thing, surely that must be proof that we're right, self-evidently right, since we see France from above?

"Stay tuned to the T.V., comrade, we're not done yet: two days later, monsieur le Comte shows up to tell us his life story. He's studied the labour laws. This man who's never worked for the minimum wage. And he has a message for the people: the new legislation proposed by labour minister Myriam El Khomri is brilliant, any honest worker should be delighted. The government has come up with a series of measures that have already been applied in dozens of other countries, measures that have never boosted the economy or helped anyone to put food on the table, measures that have served only to concentrate wealth in the hands of the rich and piss off everyone else, but here in France, they will work . . . They trot out hoary old clichés about the national debt, and they tell us, 'The time has come for you to make repayments. And to shut your mouth, like whores who have to spend their lives making repayments for the money spent by their pimp.' And do the people up at the Palace pay back money when they're caught with their hand in the cookie jar? Do they pay their taxes? They help themselves. You slog your guts out. And the kids you bring into the world are in debt. From the moment they're born, they owe money to their overlords. It's a clever move. You churn out little French citizens who belong to them body and soul before they've even learned to walk. But this isn't a war. This isn't a class war. This isn't the rich bleeding dry the poor. Our culture, French culture isn't about violence. French culture is not arms sales and colonisation and war it's not indiscriminate bombing and genocide and supporting vicious dictators. No, no, no – don't you get it? French culture is the Enlightenment. That just proves that we're not ragheads, that we're nothing like them. Because Arabs . . . well, they've got a culture of violence . . . but rich people aren't violent. Never. Private greed before public need. But apart from that – no violence."

Patrice gives Xavier a sidelong glance. He has long since given up arguing with Olga. She runs rings around him. It is a torrent of words she mastered during the convergences, when people showed up and she joined in their conversations. She won't stop until she has shouted herself hoarse.

*

They are joined by Daniel and Kiko. The trader has just come back from a spa in Brittany. Patrice wonders how he manages to lie still for all those massages and still take all that coke. Kiko is hyper. "Since we're planning to restart the convergences, we need our own currency." Around him, people glance at each other, wondering whether this time he has finally flipped out, or whether this is just another crisis. He brandishes a book, a history of Brittany he bought at the station before boarding the train. "There's no such thing as a society that doesn't print money. That's the only way for us to set ourselves up as a state within a state." He probably read three sentences at random during the journey, then spent two hours in the buffet car getting himself all worked up. He looks good. He must have spent time on the tanning beds at the spa. Olga folds her arms and sighs. "And people say I'm batshit crazy . . . I swear, if you didn't have so much money, you'd have been locked up in an asylum years ago. What exactly are we supposed to do with this money? Sell each other peanuts?" "Try to think long-term for once, Olga. We don't have an army, we don't have a currency, we've got a guru who packs his bags and fucks off at the slightest comment . . . we're a joke." "Exactly," Olga says. "That's what I'm saying. That's the whole concept: we're a joke."

Kiko has various nervous tics. He gestures to the crowd. "Instead of screaming into the void, Olga, go up and take the mic, tell them we need to demolish the stock exchange. They won't listen to me. But I've got a vision. The Bourse is ten minutes from here. It's symbolic, and right now it's pretty much empty. We need to pull it down, stone by stone. We need to stop burning cars and smashing shop windows, the Bourse is three métro stops from here, all we need is a few pickaxes and a little motivation."

*

Vernon has his hands in his pockets. As is his wont, he doesn't get involved. He watches. Patrice is happy that he is back, though he cannot quite work out why. What the fuck is it about him that makes them so happy to have him around?

They have started dancing again, on certain nights. The artist's studio in Aubervilliers is vast and high-ceilinged – no-one is disturbed by them playing music until two o'clock in the morning. The last occasion was a week ago. Antoine Dopalet had come by to see them. Afraid that his father might find out he has been working as an informant for them, he came into the studio without taking off his motorcycle helmet. When Céleste disappeared, he was in Libya, having been invited to one of the contemporary art symposiums that take him to the four corners of the earth. When contacted on Skype, he had been categorical: his father wasn't involved. He wouldn't have someone kidnapped, he wasn't that crazy. "What about eliminating her," the Hyena asked, "do you think he's capable?" and Antoine shrugged. "He could press charges, obviously, in fact he'd have every right. A beating, I don't know, maybe . . . he's in a blind rage. But it wouldn't go any further. Vernon must have misunderstood what Max said. If Céleste didn't come home, it's probably because she owes someone money and decided to disappear. It's not like it would be the first time she took off . . ."

He refused to budge. Even after Kiko got access to the bank accounts of Max and Dopalet, and had proof they were in Barcelona on the same dates . . . This was just a coincidence – surprising, certainly, but Antoine could see nothing suspicious about two Parisians being in Barcelona on the same weekend. It's a favourite holiday spot for French people.

*

When Céleste was found, Antoine had been shocked but emphatic: his father had not been involved in this barbaric act. All the same, he arranged to spend a weekend in Paris so he could reassure everyone. But nothing about his visit to his father had been reassuring. Especially not the state in which he found Dopalet: pale and haggard from too much coke and too little sleep, barely coherent, opening the door to him wearing a silk dressing gown, claiming he had been very ill, that he hadn't been into the office in some time, but that he'd watched the "Godfather" trilogy several times and had decided he wanted to make a gangster movie. To Antoine he had seemed rambling and confused. He had enquired about his father's health: "You really don't look well, you know." "It's the full moon. I've always been sensitive to the full moon." "Are you sure it's not the cocaine, Papa?" "The coke? No, that's never stopped me sleeping . . ." But he had agreed to take the Ambien offered by his son, who always had some on him to deal with jetlag. In fact, he had taken two, gone into his room, and within seconds he was out like a light.

Alone in the apartment, Antoine had undertaken a cursory investigation. He found the e-mail from Max which left little doubt about the nature of their partnership . . . And the son had been forced to recant: his father had ordered Céleste's kidnapping. Going back through his old man's e-mails, he found the address where Céleste had been held prisoner. Before setting off, Dopalet had Googled the neighbourhood where she would be. On his own computer. Finally, after rummaging around a little, Antoine stumbled on a cheap, shitty little mobile phone on which the text messages had been deleted, but not the call history. The Hyena had confirmed: one of the two most frequently called numbers belonged to Max.

Antoine was appalled – the thought that his father was capable of ordering a kidnapping, a rape, and of leaving the young woman so that her abductor could kill her and dispose of the body was beyond his comprehension. The fact that he had been dumb enough to call his accomplices using a burner phone – something he had probably seen in third-rate thrillers – only to keep the phone in a drawer in his apartment, simply added to his distress. Not only was his father a vicious bastard, he was a clueless vicious bastard.

He had left the apartment, but, two days later, he had managed to find a one-hour window in his hectic schedule as a rising star in the art world who is required to be permanently available, to drop by and see his father "on the off-chance". He had called ahead – "I'm just round the corner, I bought some spirulina and I got some for you too, you looked completely shattered the other day" – and his father, who had spent a lifetime keeping him at arm's length, since he invariably had something more important to do than spend time with his son, had said in a tone that Antoine had never heard before, "Sure, drop by, son, I'm just having a little drink with a few friends." Jesus fuck, when he saw the friends. This was no movie-star machismo. It's not hard to tell the difference between some candy-ass actor telling a make-up artist to piss off and a hardened criminal who's already done his fifteen years. These guys were friendly, polite, clean-cut. They looked like hardened killers. With them was a little dark-haired girl, no more than twenty, pretty but forlorn, almost autistic, whose presence at this meeting was difficult to understand. His father had given him some bullshit excuse – they were working on a project for a T.V. series with some guys who were "in the life". He was off his face. One of the other guys had snickered, "Yeah, I'm pretty good at choreographing fight scenes."

This was the day that Antoine cancelled all his appointments and turned up, wearing his motorbike helmet, at the studio in Aubervilliers.

"You can't hide Céleste here. I don't know what they're planning, but you won't be able to protect her. You need to call the police. If only to stop my father from the serious fuck-up he's about to commit. Hyena, are you sure that Aïcha is safe where she is?" and the Hyena stared at him quizzically, as though she was thinking about something else. Céleste was in a corner of the loft, working on Daniel's tattoo, and between the whirr of the needle and Missy Elliott cranked up to eleven, she could not hear their whispered exchange. "We can make sure there are always two people with her," Patrice suggested. Pamela said, "I know an empty house in the Landes, the woman who owns it offered to lend it to us for two or three months. If the offer still stands, we say nothing to anyone and hide out there." Still Antoine was insistent: "We can't keep the police out of this. It might sound weird coming from me, but the best way to protect my father from himself is to have him banged up . . . I don't know what the fuck he was planning with those guys. But it wasn't good. He has to be stopped," and Pamela said, "Céleste doesn't even want to talk about going to the police. It's up to her whether to press charges, we're not going to do it for her."

That evening, to ward off the fear they could feel crawling in their bellies, they had danced. Vernon had hooked up a couple of speakers playing Bleach's soundwaves and now dropped the needle on "She's a Lady". The stentorian voice of Tom Jones filled the room. There were no more than ten people. Patrice just had time to think, it can't possibly work as well as it did at the convergences, I mean, sure, I'll dance, but it won't be like the other times, before everything clicked into place. Fuck. Just thinking about it now gives him goose bumps. They threw themselves into it with an energy born of despair, a sadness at losing the camp, a fury that they had arrived too late to protect Céleste, the shame that they could do nothing to ease her pain, their joy at being reunited, and it had taken off.

At first, Céleste had stayed on the sidelines, then she had come closer, her movements slow and sensual, and Patrice had a flash – Valérie Kaprisky in that '80s film, that movie directed by Żuławski . . . She pounded her feet on the floor and flailed her arms, it was tribal, she was in a trance. The others formed a circle around her as though they were Sioux warriors and had rehearsed this choreography – they danced around her, spinning wildly, a frenzied, whirling waltz.

And as day was breaking, Céleste said, "I'd love to see what they're like, the convergences." And that's how it began. No-one else would have dared make the suggestion. All eyes turned to Vernon, who threw his hands into the air. "I'm up for it whenever you like, Céleste. It's a bit more complicated for Pamela . . . she's the one who gets lumbered with all the difficult work of finding a site that's free and . . ." Pamela grabbed him around the waist. "I just wanted to say I'm sorry about what happened. We never talked about it. I was a complete bitch. It was horrible. And I forgive you for being dumb enough to storm off like that. I'll call Jésus and we'll head down to see what state the house is in."

Céleste had already gone to bed without waiting to hear the end of the discussion. She does that strange thing – she constantly behaves as though nothing has happened. The other women all have an opinion about this, the same opinion: it's completely normal. It would be months before she could face up to such a thing. And Patrice listens, not daring to ask the question at the back of his mind: how many of you have been raped? Because there is something implicit in their silence, something he finds unsettling. The impression that all of them have been through this, one way or another. All except Pamela, who is the only one to say "I've never been raped" before going on to tell a harrowing story about a guy who promised the XXX girls a series of film shoots in Hungary only to confiscate their passports as soon as they arrived and force them to do a striptease tour around the country that was unplanned and unpaid. And Patrice was not quite sure what Pamela meant by "striptease tour" because Pamela told the story with undisguised terror. They had had no mobile phones, no money, no passports, they didn't dare run away for fear of what would happen to the others and, besides, in the arse end of Hungary, you're not keen to find out how friendly the locals are when you're dressed like a slut and haven't got any other clothes to wear. The more he listens, the more Patrice wonders why there are no stories about a woman taking to the streets with a knife and killing thirty guys in a night. Not one.

The camp has changed him. Until now, it had never occurred to him to storm out, slam the door and simply go for a walk before a quarrel with Pénélope got out of hand. He is convinced it's because of the convergences. They change something, at a chemical level.

He is calmer now. It feels as though these days he is driving a high-end car with perfectly calibrated brakes, whereas before he was hurtling downhill on a skateboard. Obviously, it makes for smoother handling. He doesn't find himself veering off the road anymore, and ending up, wheels spinning, in a ditch.

He asked the Hyena on the one night she came down to place de la République to say hello to Olga. She said, I've always hated gatherings like this, I'm constantly worried someone will come up to me and start mansplaining something, but she hung around long enough to have a beer with him. He asked point-blank: "Have you ever been raped?" He was expecting some sickening story. The Hyena had looked horrified, "I've never touched a cock. Not once in my whole fucking life. I don't even want to think about it," and Patrice had wanted to hug her. Finally. He had finally found a woman without a harrowing story to tell, it made a change.

Even at the Nuit Debout protests, women have every reason to complain. If they spend the night on place de la République, they are constantly hassled by drunk guys groping their arses and even physically attacking them. Things have got to such a point that Patrice can't help but wonder why we don't hear stories about armies of women with hunting knives disembowelling guys just to restore calm.

If women cannot feel safe at night on place de la République because the men have been drinking and feel entitled to touch them up, whether they like it or not . . . how the fuck can men be protesting about the violence done by economic liberalism when they're happy to exert their power over women at the first opportunity? Guys who are incapable of accepting that if they make half the population uncomfortable when they're drunk they should maybe stop drinking and find something better to do aren't genuinely trying to rethink the balance of power. They're just guys who are frustrated that they don't get to wield the power. That said, Olga is a force of law and order unto herself – after dark, she hunts down the drunk lechers and metes out her own brand of punishment, and suffice it to say that, after an encounter with her, they won't be thinking about groping someone's arse again for a while. It'll take at least ten days before they can even get it up. And Patrice has yet to see a guy willing to take on Olga, even when he's blind drunk. She's someone else who has changed since she came to the camp. Before, she was a big brute, now she's one hundred per cent Godzilla. She's really blossomed in the group.

Whichever way you look at it, these gatherings are merely a beginning. But given that, for once, people seemed determined to come up with something other than a new swastika, Patrice wants to be involved.

THE HOUSE IS SO DRAB THAT IT WOULD ALMOST BE UGLY but for the fact that it is surrounded by century-old elms that mask the unprepossessing building. The path that leads to the front door is flanked with oak trees whose tops converge into a lush vault, it feels like entering a palace.

Between fierce downpours, it is warm enough to go outside. Although it is May, the weather has been dreadful. Olga stubbornly insisted on staying in Paris as long as possible, she spent several nights sleeping on place de la République saying, "It doesn't bother me, I'm used to it," and then she gave up. The Seine burst its banks and, ever since, the city has been inundated. Olga draws her own conclusions: "If we want to start a revolution in France, we'll have to do it indoors. We don't have the weather for an outdoor revolution. It's not like I'm used to creature comforts, but ten days up to my knees in water and even I'm forced to give up." At the camp she wanders around, one hand clutching a bag of crisps and the other holding a tincture of essential oils that supposedly cures the common cold, sipping straight from the bottle – and none of them dare point out that this is not how essential oils are usually applied.

She follows Xavier's poodle, step by step, to make sure it doesn't run off. Left to her own devices, the dog sets off through the thickets, across the fields that lead to the nearby farms and stops in the middle of a herd of cows. Then, she grazes. Engrossed in doing something she loves, the poodle doesn't hear her name being called, so getting her to come home is almost a military operation, creeping between the cattle, trying not to start a stampede.

Vernon has made the most of a sunny spell to bring the chaise longue outside. It's not warm enough for sunbathing, but at least he is getting some fresh air. They have been holed up inside 24/7 ever since they arrived. He feels a joy that he can't put into words. The outside world is collapsing. It is elegantly crumbling, breaking down, its forms disintegrating, not with a bang but a whimper. A gentle collective euphoria pervades every particle of the house. The reality beyond these walls seems remote. He already finds it difficult to remember that there was a hiatus.

Daniel arrived with a new friend, Rodrigue. He strums an acoustic guitar. His forehead is slashed by a long dark fringe. On his neck, he has a tattoo of a raven. He is intensely shy. When he sings, his voice loses its timidity, it is more magnetic than his speaking voice. His voice quivers with emotion as he sings "Under the Bridge". Last night he told Vernon he spent twenty years playing in a hard-core punk band, and has only just quit. He told his bandmates after the soundcheck, before a gig in the suburbs of Paris. I'm quitting at the end of this tour. None of them asked why. He finished the tour dates and never saw them again. Twenty years of his life, over, just like that. He says they were relieved. I was the one who had trouble making time to tour. I'm the only one who's got a nine-to-five. I read meters for a water company, I can sort out time off with my supervisor to play gigs, but even so. I slowed them down.

Emilie appears with an orange towel under one arm and announces that there's no hot water and she doesn't have the energy for a cold shower. Then she stands next to the guitarist and her voice joins his. She is wearing a black dress that buttons up the front and makes her look like the heroine of some old Italian movie. She has the breasts of a different era, heavy, ponderous, Rubenesque.

Rodrigue segues into the opening chords of "Purple Rain". Sitting a few metres away on white plastic chairs whose legs are sinking into the wet grass, Sylvie and Pénélope loudly comment:

"Damn, all the times we've danced to Prince."

"Remember Vanity 6? 'Nasty Girl'."

"2016, Jesus, what a fucking shitty year."

"Did you know that Jesus appeared to Vanity when she OD'd? He told her that if she promised to abandon her Vanity persona, He'd save her."

"The real Jesus Christ would never say something like that. I'm absolutely sure. God is pure love; He'd never tell Vanity to put her clothes back on."

Xavier comes and stands next to Rodrigue, his hands on his hips. Addressing the company at large, he announces, "Greetings alter-globalists, I'm so fucking happy to be here. I don't know why. But I'm happy." His hulking frame seems all the more colossal next to the puny guitarist. He waits for Rodrigue to finish playing then reaches for the guitar, "May I?", he pulls up a stool. He launches into a punk riff, playing bar chords with his index finger across the fretboard. Idly he sings, "*Ils marchent dans la rue comme des soldats perdus / Une croix sur le front comme seule décoration. / Ils n'ont rien prévu pour leur promotion / Même pas de se servir de la révolution.*"

And Patrice takes his head in his hands and whimpers, "Oh shit, not French punk!" but like all the guys his age who dabble in the music scene, he knows all the words and ends up singing: "*Tous mes camarades sont des soldats perdus / Pensent qu'à la musique et aux filles presque nues. / On les accuse d'avoir des idées reçues / Peu importent leurs idées puisqu'il y a l'amitié.*"

Vernon grabs his pouch of tobacco pouch, gets to his feet and goes to join the girls. His hips ache a little. It is not the first time he feels pain as he stretches. He is worried that these twinges may be related to changes in the weather, which would mean rheumatism. He's ready for a lot of things, but certainly not rheumatism.

Lydia has her notebook on her lap; she summarises:

"So, I've got: Lemmy, Bowie and Roger. Now we've just got to decide where to go from here. Where do we start?"

"You mean if we include everyone, it's not a list, it's a telephone directory."

"How about Joe Strummer? What do you think? We've got to start somewhere."

"Joe Strummer – that makes no sense, that means leaving out Janis Joplin, Jimi Hendrix, it means leaving out Elvis! I can't imagine founding a church without Elvis."

"Not to mention Nina Simone. And James Brown."

"James Brown came after Joe Strummer."

"But why Joe Strummer? Do you have a particular reason in mind, or is this some random shit?"

"It's just a cut-off date. We have to have one."

"What we need is common sense, not a cut-off date. So, here's my list: Joe Strummer Janis Joplin Elvis Presley Prince David Bowie Lemmy . . ."

"Amy Winehouse, Michael Jackson, Joey Ramone, Dee Dee Ramone."

"Kurt Cobain. Whitney Houston."

"Whitney Houston? Really?"

"Absofuckinglutely! Can you imagine a church without Saint Rita?"

"We've already got Amy."

"The lost women, we can have two saints, it seems the minimum, given who we're dealing with."

They're planning to redecorate a church. They're already talking about the next convergence and they've asked Pamela if she can find an abandoned church. One they can decorate with icons of the gods of rock, a few drawings, a whole concept. They're investing a lot of energy in this project. Vernon is sceptical: "But what are you planning to do in this church of yours?" "Take drugs and listen to music."

Behind him, Vernon hears Xavier and Patrick singing, "*Dis, Papa, comment qu'tu faisais / Pour monter à l'assaut / Quand ta jeunesse fondait / Brûlée par des salauds? / Eux, ils faisaient la guerre / Sur cartes d'états major / Toi, tu buvais d'la bière / Pour supporter la mort . . .*" Lydia frowns, turns from them to Vernon and says, "What the hell's got into them?" "I know it's hard to believe, but they were young once."

Jésus is coasting down the tarmacked driveway on an electric longboard – a bit like an electric scooter with no handlebar that you have to steer without using your hands. Effortlessly gliding along, he makes it look easy, but Vernon has already tried riding this thing, and it turns out it's an extreme sport. He watches as the young man flashes past and wonders what it must be like to go through life being so astonishingly beautiful. It's almost a handicap – when talking to Jésus it's difficult to think of anything else, to get past the magnetic pull he exerts, wittingly or unwittingly, on all those who come within his orbit.

A few raindrops splash against their foreheads, they glance up to see whether it's another downpour. They all scrabble to their feet, collect the ashtrays glasses cups lighters the little amplifier and everyone heads back to the living room. They barely have time to shut the doors before a torrential cloudburst drenches the lawn.

Everyone finds a place to perch in the vast living room that is almost empty except for a sofa and numerous scatter cushions. Lydia plugs in her rose-gold iPod, which looks prehistoric, though it's not even ten years old, and uses her finger to scroll through her library, deciding what to play. As she scrolls through the tracks, the iPod makes the soft clicking sound characteristic of that distant era. When she comes to "Where Did Our Love Go", she presses PLAY and Vernon gives her a thumbs up.

Lying on her back, surrounded by notebooks, Olga reads aloud in a low voice the texts she has prepared for the next convergence. Her nights at place de la République were rewarding, she has enough material to keep her going.

"How do we hope when hope is dead? Our mission is not to offer a welcome to the wretched of the earth. Our mission is to live cut off from the world by walls. Our mission is to live surrounded by barbed wire, armed guards and customs posts. Our mission is to eat sugar by the ton, to cut down vast forests, to produce billions of rolls of toilet paper, to stroll idly between overladen supermarket shelves, to prize manufactured goods. Our mission is to sink migrant ships before they affect tourism. Our mission is to be inflexible to reject accident to slather ourselves in sunscreen to gorge on ice cream to entangle ourselves in the interweb to swallow the same bullshit theories, our mission is to count the number of extinct species, to plunder those most in need, to swill gallons of soda. Our mission is contempt – contempt for everything that is free, everything that is given, contempt for beauty, for the sacred, for other people's work, other people's consent, other people's lives . . ."

Xavier raises his arms, grabs a wrist with the opposite hand and stretches himself. "It's too long and it's not particularly witty, this speech of yours," he says. "Just listening made me want to top myself . . . You should think about doing poetry slams, Olga. I think you've got a future as a poet for primary school kids." Olga gives him a sidelong glance, but does not rise to the bait. She says, "You're lucky I'm so magnanimous." Xavier is depressed. Marie-Ange has gone, leaving their daughter with him. Her company proposed that she manage the launch of an e-consultancy platform in Macedonia. She accepted. Maybe it's better if I go alone, she said to Xavier. He didn't try to dissuade her. Actually, I was pretty surprised myself, he says. We're fond of each other. Financially, we know we wouldn't be able to survive independently. If I had to pay rent, I'd have to live with you guys and if I was here all the time, I'd go insane, I'd probably kill someone. Besides, this is no place to bring up a child. She'd have to change schools every five minutes, it's ridiculous.

Marie-Ange will be spending a year over in Macedonia. He says, "The most difficult thing is to watch a dream die." He says, "When I think about my love for Marie-Ange, I'm reminded of my dog, the one that had cancer, when the vet came to put her down. That's love – the lifespan of a dog. And it's always the same: one day you realise it's over, and there's nothing you can do. You'll find yourself with a box full of ashes, you can always put it on the mantelpiece. There's no going back. You can't bring a dead love back to life."

He gets to his feet, goes over and carefully cuts thin slices from a huge, round wheel of Edam cheese. Sélim pushes open the door, he is drenched. He says, I parked just outside the gate, Jesus, it's bucketing down, and Emilie hands him a towel. He takes off his jacket and hangs it over a radiator. He is just back from seeing his daughter in Athens. He is bubbling with energy. Before he even sits down, he has launched into a detailed description of the refugees who have settled there, the solidarity of the Greek citizens in spite of the terrible poverty afflicting all of them. "How's Aïcha?" the Hyena asks. Sélim stops in his tracks, he considers. "She's changing so fast. Sometimes I feel like the Aïcha who starts a sentence isn't quite the same as the one who ends it. She's pregnant. She wouldn't talk to me about the father, but I'm guessing it's not an immaculate conception . . ."

The Hyena turns to him. "She's keeping it?" Sélim rolls his eyes to heaven. "I didn't even dare mention the word abortion." "Is she happy?" Xavier asks and Sélim says, "She's learning Greek, and, weirdly, I think she's pretty alright." All eyes turn towards the stairs, where Céleste has just appeared. She repeats, "She's having a baby?" Then, with a joy so feverish it is unsettling, she races down the steps and throws her arms around Sélim's neck. "I'm so happy. You've no idea."

Sélim pours himself a glass of wine. He says, "I feel too young to be a grandfather, but I feel ready. On the other hand, I'd like to persuade her to come back to France. It's hard bringing up a kid on your own, I should know. I wish I could help." Olga says, "Why don't we just kill Dopalet? He doesn't know me, he's never seen me, I'll just wait outside his building, cut his throat, and go straight home . . . Who's going to work out what happened? Huh? Who?"

Then Céleste opens the door and walks out into the rain. She walks straight ahead. Without a word, the Hyena follows, allowing her a few metres' advantage. Vernon watches the scene from a distance – the shadowy figure of Céleste, screaming. Her arms stiffly pressed against her body, fists probably clenched, head thrown back, she screams like a woman possessed, then raises her arms, shadowboxing, she stumbles, recovers, starts throwing punches at the empty air. A panic attack, like a storm suddenly breaking, but when the Hyena comes closer and touches her arm, Céleste turns towards them and Vernon sees she has an absurd fit of the giggles. He goes to join them. His boots sinking into the long grass make for difficult going. He is not sure that he's doing the right thing, he has no right to get involved – Céleste has not asked anything of him, or even shown him any particular affection. A voice says "try" and he steps closer. Céleste turns around, and her smile has transformed into a mask of hatred, she stares into his eyes and says, this is your fault, all of it, from the very beginning, you were the one who started it. It's you. Then she pummels his face, his chest, kicks at his shins in a wild fury, she howls, but Vernon does not step away. He can feel the blows. He can smell the earth, that distinctive, reassuring scent. Then Céleste slows, her screams give way to a choking cough, she bends, her body gives way. Very slowly, Vernon lays a hand on her back. She is sobbing. He opens his arms, she hesitates, then she presses herself against him and collapses. Her whole body is wracked with tears. Hands in his pockets, Xavier comments: "Fuck's sake, you alter-globalist snowflakes are such drama queens." Standing next to him, glass in hand, Sylvie bites her lower lip, and says, "She's doing what she needs to. There's not much you can do in this kind of situation except scream. Scream, and wait . . ."

Back inside, someone cranks up the volume, and through the curtain of rain, unfurling in the darkness, comes the smoky drawl of Leonard Cohen singing "You want it darker".

"PAPA, DO YOU KNOW WHERE THE LIGHTER FUEL FOR MY ZIPPO is? I found the gas in the sideboard, but not the lighter fuel."

In the bathroom, Solange doesn't hear his reply. Her nose is pressed to the mirror. She has torn a Kleenex in half and is carefully popping blackheads. There are a lot of spots that she hadn't noticed. Disgusting, repulsive. She splashes her face with cold water and looks again – she is finding it hard to breathe. Tomorrow is the big day. It's weird how normal everything feels.

Her father cuts the bread on the same red plastic plate he has always used. The kitchen table has never changed, either. She grew up in this house, just as her mother and her grandmother did before her. The kitchen is huge. The chimney breast was taken out when she was a little girl and replaced with a big freezer.

It has been raining all month. The paths are still sodden, it will take time for them to dry out. Once upon a time, the weather was the most important topic of conversation in the family. Would there be enough rain this year? Would it freeze in spring? Would there be enough sunshine? Since her father sold off the land, it no longer matters.

From their house to the village is a twenty-minute walk. If you want to buy bread or a pouch of tobacco, you have to cycle. She spent her childhood on a bicycle. She's glad she's not a little girl anymore. She never got along with her sister. Mostly, she remembers being alone. She didn't hang out with other children. Her father didn't like her bringing them back to the house. They were ill-mannered, they didn't take off their muddy boots before going up to her room to play, they never washed their hands before lunch. He called them disgusting little pigs.

Besides, her family was not well thought of. Parents didn't like the idea of their children playing at her house. In a village, everyone knows everything. They knew her mother was a drunk. As a child, Solange genuinely believed her mother was just taking a nap. It was the other kids who said, don't be silly, your *maman* is a wino. It was not the truth that shocked Solange but the fact that it had been kept from her. But it occurred to her that, even for a postwoman who had to get up early, it wasn't normal to take a nap every day, to be so tired that she didn't come down to dinner. Her father never said a word. He must have been disappointed that his wife was not up to scratch, and the children she had borne him seemed defective too. Solange didn't like helping out around the farm. Except picking plums, which was something she loved doing. Everything else stinks, she used to say, the animals the dung the fertilisers all smelled so strong they made her feel sick. The only real skill she acquired was thanks to her uncle, who took her hunting, his sons hated to go, they said it was boring. Solange is good with a gun. It's in their blood. It's in the family. Her father would smile sardonically as he watched her at the shooting range at the fair and say, "That's not going to help us marry her off." But all the same, it made him happy, his little girl coming home with the biggest cuddly toy.

*

Her sister, Orphée, was not built for farm life either. But at least she got good grades in school. The two girls hated each other. They pulled each other's hair, spat at each other. They never played together. Her sister always wanted to be in charge, but if Solange did what she was told, she called her a copycat. Orphée was good at gym, she loved Barbie dolls, she did her homework, she was neat, she had beautiful hair. By the time she was six, Solange was convinced that when her sister grew up she would meet a guy have children have a nice house finish her studies get an interesting job and be successful at everything. Orphée seemed destined to do everything better than anyone else. But then she went completely off the rails. Batshit cray cray, a complete whack job. No-one ever knew what happened: she turned twenty and *bang*. These days Solange finds it hard to believe that she used to be jealous of her sister because her life was perfect. Now she lies in a puddle on the floor. She's always talking about killing herself. She's not just crazy, she's boring AF. But maybe all crazy people are boring. Orphée says she's not depressed. But she never stops crying. The meds have left her puffy and bloated. She looks like a crumpled sea lion. She has moved back into her old room, next to Solange's. She lives with her father and never sees anyone else. Total loser.

Her father has changed since Orphée came back home. Always a man of few words, he has now retreated into almost total silence. He spends his days on the internet. He has huge hands, the fingers misshapen by years of farm work, it's funny, seeing his paws on the keyboard, Solange wonders how he manages to press the right keys. He has sold off his land. He has no pension – he didn't pay enough in contributions. At the slightest movement, he grimaces and touches his back. This man who never had a pain in his life, whom Solange cannot even remember taking to his bed with flu, is suddenly crippled by back pain. He always loved watching movies. Now that's all he does. They got a letter from their I.S.P. warning them to stop torrenting and he just crumpled it up and threw it in the bin without a word. He is going deaf, but refuses to wear a hearing aid. Her father always cut an elegant figure when he went into the village. People said, it's a pity such a handsome, dapper, hardworking man didn't land himself a decent wife. At home he wears his threadbare trousers and a shapeless beige sweater riddled with holes, but when he needs to run an errand he puts on his suit and his hat as he used to do. These days he rarely goes down to the village. He doesn't suffer arseholes gladly. He always was too clever for his own good; he sees what is coming before other people. It drives him crazy. Those who stare, wide-eyed, into the darkness are cursed with a terrible loneliness. Solange knows how it feels.

The atmosphere at home is bleak. Not that it was ever particularly joyous, but these days it's worse. Her mother has swapped booze for prescription pills – not the same ones as Solange's sister. She is even more befuddled than when her best friend was a bottle. The kitchen sideboard is littered with boxes of medication. When her mother was forty-two the post office said, we no longer need post-women, we'll train you to work at the counter. But for her, doing her rounds kept her on an even keel – five hours on her feet, cycling twenty kilometres every day, then home, first little glass of white wine, and so on until she lapsed into a coma. She never managed to adjust to working at the counter. To make matters worse, they started hassling her to sell mobile phones to customers, she argued that the post office has clients, not customers, and her boss laughed in her face. Solange's mother drifted into depression. Suddenly, she was drinking less. With the pills she's taking, she doesn't need to drink as much, she needs less, she's in a fog from the moment she wakes up. These days, she's like a ghost. Her body is there but there is no-one home.

From a large plastic Carrefour bag, Solange takes a pain au lait and lets it melt in her mouth, the dough immediately crumbles and sticks to her teeth. It is something she has always loved. She says:

"I saw Richard's mother yesterday."

"Did she recognise you?"

"Of course."

"With your hair cropped short like that, you're barely recognisable."

It upset her father, her short hair. She cut it last month. Because of some pathetic Brazilian woman on T.V. who gives women make-overs the way you might pimp up a car. On the show, there was a girl who looked a bit like Solange – the presenter took her out into the street and people were saying she wasn't ugly, but she needed to make the most of herself. Then they cropped her hair short and she really did look a lot better. So, Solange had gone to the Dessange salon, in Epinal. The stylist looked at her dolefully, "We'll need to use conditioner, long hair needs a lot of care and attention," and Solange watched locks of her hair fall and, before it was over, she realised she'd made a terrible mistake. She felt like crying. She had always worn her hair long with a fringe. Until this was cut away, she never realised that she had the face of a halfwit. She's uglier now than she was before. When her father saw her come home with her hair cropped short, she could tell how upset he was. But what could she do? The damage was done. It pains her to think that this is how he will remember her. Because although he doesn't know it, he will remember this morning. She hadn't wanted to hurt her father. He's had more than his fair share. The problem is that if no-one is prepared to rock the boat, nothing will ever change. She loathes bohemian culture and its fetishisation of home comforts. You can't make an omelette without breaking eggs. She's always found that expression funny. Solange says:

"She showed me the pictures of Richard's little boy. He's a beautiful child."

"When it comes to churning out kids, that family are champions. But not one of them in the house actually has a job. How is he planning to raise the boy?"

Solange and Richard had been friends in primary school. There are numerous photos of them, side by side. They looked like two peas in a pod. The same blue eyes, the same white-blonde hair. There are lots of stories about her and Richard, who would wander round hand in hand when they were knee high to a grasshopper, slipping out of school to hunt leeches. They would catch them in water bottles. Leeches or tadpoles. Theirs was a childhood of nettle stings, snakes slithering through the grass, wellington boots and dandelions. She has no bad memories of childhood, full-time sadness was something that came later. Richard started playing with other boys, who didn't want a girl in their gang. Round about the time she learned to read, school became boring, while home life was oppressive. Fortunately, there was the internet. This was what saved her.

Her father would yell that it was nothing but online gaming, and she was wasting her life. But she was glad of the online games, and the forums she discovered while searching for cheats for Grand Theft Auto. She shrugs.

"So, Richard hasn't got a job? His wife is a teacher, or at least that's what Richard's mother said."

"God, but that woman can talk! Do you think that's reasonable, for a man to depend on his wife to put food on the table? It may be the modern way, but that doesn't make it right."

"It's a beautiful baby. We need babies. Besides, they'll do what everyone else does – they'll find work elsewhere."

Her father gives her a black look. A look that says: so, what are you waiting for? It's not that he wants her to leave, but she's twenty-two years old, it's high time that she found a job. That she settled down, as they say. It's bad enough that his other daughter has moved home as mad as a box of frogs. Solange suddenly feels like laughing – she can't say anything, but he doesn't need to worry. By tomorrow, she won't be a burden anymore. He doesn't know it yet, but he won't have to worry about money anymore, he'll even have enough to put her mother in a nursing home and get her back on her feet. She'll have enough to keep them.

His father drinks his coffee from a bowl. He could never get used to using a mug. He couldn't see the point. Solange loves him for that. This morning, she loves his every gesture. We only truly appreciate what we are about to lose. She adds sugar to hers, and a lot of milk, because she likes her coffee cold. She leans back against the sink and a sudden urge to cry forces her to be silent. She smiles. He groans and shakes his head, muttering something she can't quite hear, then puts his empty bowl in the sink. The T.V. in the kitchen is constantly tuned to B.F.M. They have a television in every room, and all of them are blaring whenever he is at home. Solange has never heard anyone in the village nostalgically reminisce about the days before television. Missing the silence and the dinners by the fire is all very well for crusty hipsters who know nothing about rural life and imagine that people used to converse over their meals. But what is there to talk about around here? The rain. But you can't spend half an hour talking about rain. Either there's enough rain or there isn't. You're not going to spend all night talking about it.

The cemetery is at the far end of the village, on a small hill. Her grandmother's grave is in disarray. The family rarely visits. Except on All Saints' Day, when her parents gather up the plastic plant pot and the leaves brought in on the breeze. They leave a new pot. Same time next year. Solange doesn't often visit either. Except on important occasions. She sits on the shiny, grey, marble slab. Her grandmother's name was Odette. She adored her grandchildren. And she loved dancing, driving her car and musicals. She used to make stylish outfits for herself with her sewing machine. She would draw and cut out intricate patterns and then *tac tac tac* with the pedal, pins clenched between her teeth, she made elegant jackets, evening dresses. She recreated the clothes she saw in catalogues. She could make anything. She was the one who used to take Solange shopping for school supplies in late summer. She used to take Orphée, too, but never on the same day. She always said that it was normal for girls to want to be unique. Even today, Solange still loves to wander through the stationery department of a department store. It reminds her of days that were focused on her, when the trolley was full, they would leave it outside a branch of Flunch and go in for lunch. Hamburger and fries. "You understand, Odette. I know you understand. It's for the country. We can't just sit idly by with our arms folded. I know you understand. We have to make things happen, stir up the anthill. Because other people – sorry, but they're like cattle. Sometimes you need to give history a good kick in the arse if you want things to change. And afterwards, I'll write, Odette, I'll write down everything I've got inside my head, I'll write it down and that way people will know who I am, they'll read what I've written. I'll be an example. I know you understand. I am so scared I've got tummy ache. Ever since yesterday, when I knew it was happening. I've got the shits, Mamy. I've got the shits. But I won't back down. Anything rather than this tepid apathy. Anything."

She is one of the chosen. She is responding to a calling. To an inner voice that tells her "Go . . . go . . . go!" and Max is the first person who has ever understood this. It was strange, how they met. She's always hanging out in online forums, she has been for years; in theory, it's a video games forum, but to her it's like home. Her username is "coyote666". It's also her Twitter handle. She didn't want to use a girl's name – a girl in a gaming forum has no cred, the only guys not insulting you are trying to fuck you. She struck up a conversation with this super funny guy, "2Kool4Skool", they've been throwing shade on a bunch of immigrationist cucks who are completely out of their depth. They hit it off straight away. Max says he realised that the first night – he says she's intense, she's edgy, anyone can tell she's got a calling. After a couple of days, he suggests they meet up IRL, says there's stuff he wants to talk to her about, but Solange says not possible, bruh, I'm overbooked.

Because it's tough for her to admit that she's not who she claims to be, she's not a boy. So this is the funny part: Max insists, says it's important, says he feels a connection. And he's the first one to confess: he's not twenty-three, maybe, like, double that. He was afraid she would take it badly, but she replied, "Well, my name is Solange," and at first she wondered if maybe he was queer, because he went cold on her. But later he realised that she hadn't lied about anything else – she's a true-blue patriot, she can whip any guy's arse at any game . . . and he was hooked.

Luckily, Max didn't dump her. He gave meaning to everything that quivered inside her, lacerating her soul, yet still inchoate, everything she could sense without knowing how to marshal it. She is defending a memory. She serves it, according to her strengths. She will strike out at random, under cover of darkness. She is filled with hope. Violent acts of violence that create order. Desperate, courageous acts can stir the embers and rekindle the flame. Others will follow. The time has come to act. Max realised this as soon as he saw her. He is like her. They love the same things and hate the same things – moribund democracy, the hypocritical brain-warping rhetoric, the lie factories, the fake news hacks, the liberal media scum, the fool's game, a France mortally wounded by interracial breeding and dwindling morality. The lack of faith. Of honesty. An obsessive fetishisation of human life that forgets that sometimes great ideas must be presented dripping with blood.

Max can finish Solange's sentences. They complement each other. He is the one who helped her prepare everything. He's the one who will publish what she has written when she surrenders herself. Because she is not going to run. She will face the people of France with her head held high. And it is Max who will make sure that her family never wants for anything. Because he knows people who will never give up, and who are ready to help a lone soldier.

She will call for revolution. She knows that there are others, like her, wandering in the dark, lost and filled with rage. Powerless, they will realise that the time has come. You must strike at the soft underbelly of these sordid times. You must strike at those who dance when times are serious. The hedonists and the degenerates.

Everything is in place. She is ready.

ON THE OPPOSITE PLATFORM OF THE MÉTRO STATION, A young man in a black leather jacket is scrawling on a blue advertising poster with a red marker, "The crimes of the state are greater than the crimes of those they incarcerate." He hesitates over the second "c" of "incarcerate": should it be "c" or "s"? Léonard shouts over and gestures with his hand – "c". It's not a great slogan, but he may as well get the spelling right.

On his headphones, he is listening to "Lemonade". He is thinking about Antoine. A chill runs down his spine. When the record was first released, Antoine would hold forth for hours at a time about how it had revolutionised pop history, how it was as important as "Thriller" or "Nevermind". Antoine loved to expound his – sometimes absurd – theories, often defending them to the point of dishonesty. If someone pointed out that he had argued precisely the opposite a week earlier, he would immediately calm down, give a broad grin and say, "Yeah, well, I guess they're both true, aren't they?" Antoine was witty, he liked to be the centre of attention. He loved to make people laugh. He was a fortunate young man. The failure of his marriage meant he had enough rough edges not to become just one more preachy know-it-all. Life smiled on him because he smiled at life. Until his senseless death. On the night of the massacre.

This is the world we live in now. This is what it has come to. The minute we hear a fire engine, we click on a news feed to make sure it's nothing serious. When he opens Twitter, Léonard is relieved to find that no-one is tweeting about some terrible atrocity. We live with the notion that something terrible can happen. We all take public transport, we sit on café terraces to smoke a cigarette, we go to gigs. We go out clubbing. And now we realise that some of us will never make it home.

Léonard went back on the meds three weeks ago. He did his calculations as he took a quarter of a tablet this morning. He hides them at the bottom of his sponge bag. He doesn't want to talk about it. He's ashamed that he needs to take them. He no longer sees the shrink who gave him the prescription. He could put up with the constant gnawing at his solar plexus as anxiety begins to bite. He could put up with the obsessive thoughts that wake him up in the night. But he didn't have the strength to come to terms with Antoine's death without a crutch.

It was a wise decision: ten days later, the Orlando nightclub shooting happened. In a statement, the murderer's father said, "This has nothing to do with religion . . . We were in Downtown Miami, Bayside, people were playing music. And he saw two men kissing each other in front of his wife and kid and he got very angry." This has nothing to do with religion – the problem is that queers refuse to hide anymore. People like him are disgusting. This is something he learned as a little boy. Something he learned in his own home. Today, his parents have come to terms with the situation. But before they admitted defeat, they fought with all their might. They refused to let Léonard come home. They didn't want the neighbours to see. He's not the kind of faggot that mothers say would make a fine son-in-law. He's a queen. People only have to see the way he walks to realise. His mother would say, "Don't come home for Christmas, please. Whenever you come, I can't go to the hairdresser's for months, I'm the laughing stock of the neighbourhood." After Orlando, there were the headlines. Newspapers avoided the word "gay". No-one mentioned the identity of the victims, because they knew that if they did, their readers would feel no sympathy for them. Faggots. After the Bataclan massacre, the fundamentalist Catholics who dared to say that the attackers and the victims were equally sinful were excoriated by the press. But Orlando is different. After Orlando, they had the right to say "*bravo*". No-one contradicted them.

On the night of the Bataclan massacre, Léonard had been in the thirteenth arrondissement, at a party on a houseboat. The taxi that brought him home had not charged him, even though he hadn't been in the area affected. It was a night of humanity – everyone felt red raw and people were not ashamed to reassure each other. After Orlando, there was nothing of that. He has not encountered a single taxi driver who feels sorry.

With the massacre at Rennes-le-Château, the newspapers started out liking the victims. Even online trolls waited a few days before criticising them. Then, gradually, it became more acrimonious. People who didn't have their mobile phones with them, people who used Linux on their home computers – who uses Linux if they've got nothing to hide? People with no fixed address. There were rumours that the group included a large number of political radicals. In fact, tracts containing extremist propaganda had been found at the site. There was talk of a Muslim. There was a lesbian, and a former prostitute, and others who, during the post-mortem, turned out to have different genitals from those expected. There was a former stock market trader turned drug dealer. There was even talk of a guru, because people did not know what to make up to sully the memory of the dead. Gradually, public opinion decided it was a settling of scores between political radicals, unless it had something to do with sordid sexual practices, some depraved ritual?

The pills help. He sleeps for seven hours straight. His thoughts are no longer obsessive. They glide. Physically, he is not as strong. He can feel it in his legs when he walks, a weakness. Minor irritations no longer cling to him. He thinks about Antoine, and tears well in his eyes. He rides on the métro and is surprised to find himself thinking about something else. He needed to start taking the pills again.

Léonard would like someone to explain how somebody like him, who has taken so much coke, champagne and Ecstasy, who smokes weed at every opportunity and never passes up a line of smack if it's offered, is so reluctant to swallow a quarter of a tablet every morning. It's not a question of legality – he enjoys a shot of vodka in a bar as much as he does swallowing a tab of Molly. He doesn't enjoy the company of dealers, and would prefer to know what his coke has been cut with. The distinction is between recreational drugs and therapeutic drugs. One says you're going to have fun, go on a psychedelic journey, modify reality, enhance your perception, experiment – the other says that you're sick, you're weak, you need to be cured.

Recently Léonard has been getting on his boyfriend's nerves. Jean-Michel talks to him in an irritable tone he hasn't heard before. He gets annoyed when he sees Léonard coming out of a hotel room with a coffee in one hand, checking his phone while trying to push his suitcase with his feet. He says tersely, "Fuck's sake, can't you concentrate on what you're doing sometimes?" There is something about him that people, eventually, cannot bear. They withdraw the love they have invested. The way a stockholder might sell off his portfolio when he realises he has backed the wrong horse. Leonardo is not a good horse. No matter how much effort he makes, Jean-Michel will leave him. Like the others.

Léonard went back on the pills two days after the shooting. Nobody knows what Antoine was doing at this rave. He was curious about street culture. He had made a name for himself in the art world by ripping it a new arsehole – in other words, through graffiti, back in the day when it seemed unlikely that hip-hop would end up in galleries. He'd become a curator with a bright future, all the galleries fought over him. But he still spent time in the hood, it was important to him not to lose contact with the streets.

There were a hundred or so people at this rave, some wild private party. Not one of them survived. The girl who carried out the attack was well trained. And armed to the teeth. The newspapers talked about someone with mental health issues. A lone wolf. But it wasn't out in the sticks that she managed to acquire the arsenal she used to massacre so many people.

Léonard would take any drug in the world if it meant he did not have to imagine the terror that Antoine must have felt when the first grenade exploded. Didn't have to try to imagine his last thoughts. What do you think, when you're utterly terrified?

The girl had stood around waiting for the wounded and the survivors to move so she could shoot them, one by one, using an assault rifle. She had stationed herself above the dancers, she had taken a high-power flashlight to light up the scene. Afterwards, she had killed herself – a bullet to the head in the middle of the woods, only a few metres from the scene of the crime. It was not a terrorist attack. It was not political. According to the media. Léonard is all too aware that any drug that makes it possible not to imagine the scene is useful.

After every terrorist attack since *Charlie Hebdo*, just the thought of the conversations he will have to have makes him feel physically sick. He has walked away from people he considered friends. He has lived in France for more than thirty years. There have always been conversations that he has had to avoid. He cannot bear the litany of excuses for Islam anymore. A lot of people feel the need to be wary when it comes to condemning massacres that have been committed by others. He grew up in Israel. The constant fear returned, intact, in January 2015. Fear is like riding a bicycle; you never forget. He was twelve when his parents moved to France. They came one summer, he assumed it was just a holiday, but he never saw Bat Yam again. Back then, no-one talked to their children. They simply took them. The first thing he found surprising, in Nice, where they settled, was the way people boarded a bus without troubling to keep an eye out, the way that, when they saw an unattended bag lying on a seat, they didn't panic. They weren't afraid. Back in Bat Yam, children were free, they did as they pleased. But being vigilant was part of everyday life. At every bomb scare, people went down into the shelters. At first, it was France that seemed strange. The only things he liked here were baguettes and Palmitos. It took him a long time to settle in.

*

Antoine's father is inconsolable. Léonard waited a few days before calling to offer his condolences. Laurent Dopalet was incoherent. He was devastated by grief. Léonard said, if you need anything at all, please, don't hesitate and Antoine's father said: come and see me, please, I'd like to talk to you about him.

Since then, Léonard has had lunch with Dopalet every Thursday. Instead of going to the stand-up paddle course he loved. But Antoine's father needs support. He's mixing whisky and sleeping pills, he's often unintelligible. In his lucid moments, he wants to talk about Antoine, or listen to Léonard evoke old memories. Forgotten images of childhood and adolescence resurface.

When social media began to suspect that the victims of the massacre were not as innocent as they first assumed, Leonardo thought that Dopalet would go mad. Obviously, the campaign of harassment and insults was not the main tragedy. It was the straw that breaks the camel's back – something so unfair, so repulsive, that you throw in the towel, you sink back into madness. As the producer himself says, "In the end, what is most horrifying is not the tragedy itself, it's the reaction of the survivors."

One Thursday, as they were having lunch in a Japanese restaurant in the thirteenth arrondissement, Dopalet, who had been half-comatose, suddenly recovered his self-control, and the look in his eyes was heart-wrenching, filled with boundless grief. He was a ruined man. In a flash of energy that was not quite lucid he said: "You'd make a good screenwriter. A great screenwriter." Léonard is a graphic designer. He doesn't even know how to start a new paragraph in Word. As he usually did with Dopalet's non sequiturs, he said, "I don't think so." But the producer swayed in his seat, refusing to drop the subject. He had had an idea. The first in a long time. "I'll teach you. You'll be a brilliant writer. We'll tell their story. You and me. A true story. I won't allow them to sully the memory of my son. It'll be a series. The story of these people, their tragic story . . . You're the one I want to write it with, Léo." And then he had smiled for the first time in months. A poor smile that chilled the heart. Léo made no attempt to contradict him. Antoine's father had ordered wine, he was finally waking up, with difficulty, he had found something to cling to. This ludicrous idea made him sit up. Then he added, "Besides, you're Jewish. That's good. That will be useful. Always have a Jew on your team." Léonard did not hold it against him. The man was drowning, he didn't know what he was saying anymore.

The preposterous project refuses to die. Every Thursday, when Léonard has lunch with Antoine's father, he brings the U.S.B. thumb drive with the screenplay they are co-writing. Often, he has doubts: what good is he doing by supporting Dopalet in this insane project? But there is no graceful way to recover from the most unbearable of all griefs – the death of a beloved son.

WHEN HE SEES HIMSELF IN A MIRROR, HE IS DISFIGURED. He can see non-existent scars. The face of a burns victim, the face of a casualty of war. He remembers his real face, it did not look like this. It has been obliterated by his screams.

Marcia is sitting at the white, circular, living-room table drinking jasmine tea. On her lap is the flea-ridden kitten she rescued the night before from the garbage room. It is tiny, she is sure it is only a baby. Its white fur is crawling with parasites. Its eyes are a deep blue, and it is not wild. The vet diagnosed severe dehydration, and then examined its teeth and declared the cat was about three years old. Once it had been fed and dewormed, it would probably be healthy.

Marcia called it Roger. She wanted to keep it. She was sure that having a cat for company would do Vernon good. She had not realised that the dogs, too, are dead. That he watched them crawl, wounded, and take a bullet. But Vernon did not say anything. There is no way she could know. Having checked online, Marcia found the cat's owner. A woman who could precisely describe the dark patch on his belly, and the fact that he has one black paw when all the others are white. There is no doubt that it's her cat. She will come by and pick him up after work. She says: I'll bring champagne. She says: I'd almost given up hope, I'm so happy. Marcia is disappointed. She had wanted to adopt Roger. She says, even if you didn't like him, you could have fed him when I wasn't in Paris. Vernon forces himself to say: "It's O.K. You've still got me." And Marcia turns, startled to hear his voice.

She makes the most of her last moments with the cat, which allows itself to be stroked. She checks out Brazilian blogs, glasses perched on her forehead, as always when she is reading intently. She feels sad. She experiences the things that have been happening in her country in recent months with a particular intensity. Expatriates experience events after the fact, but this does not make them any less tragic, quite the reverse. Distance is like a sounding board. Not many people here can understand. She says, I need to make some new friends, people from back home, people like me.

Vernon washes the dishes in cold water. The boiler is broken, there is no hot water in the kitchen. But since Marcia is subletting, she doesn't want to contact the landlord and risk getting into trouble. He rinses the dishes, his hands are red with cold. Feeling something – anything – is fascinating.

After the shooting, Vernon walked straight ahead. He collapsed in a village square where a woman called Stéphanie took him in. She translated books from Italian and lived alone with her dog. She looked after him. She lived on the top floor of a block of flats perched on a hill. She collected turtles – stuffed turtles, plastic turtles, postcards of turtles. There were turtles everywhere. And a Himalayan salt lamp that gave off electrical waves. Vernon doesn't know how long he stayed there. He did not speak to her, she spent her days ignoring him, puffing on an e-cigarette, tapping on her keyboard. She probably guessed where he had come from. It was all anyone talked about in the days that followed. He had been the only one to get out alive. Stéphanie was black, with close-cropped hair. She listened constantly to C.D.s of rainstorms and forest murmurs. It was hideous. Vernon spent several days shivering with fever. He wanted to leave but could not summon the strength to cross the threshold and step out into the street. Every morning she performed funny stretches on a blue yoga mat. Vernon slept on the sofa and, from the first day, she covered him with a red wool blanket that never left his side all the time he was there.

One afternoon, while she was out shopping, he summoned the courage to walk out the door. He walked down nine floors. He could not bear the thought of taking the lift. He stole the red wool blanket. He ran away like a cat, like a thankless animal. Each step was agony, the descent was endless. He had to think about where to place his foot to bear his weight, he clung to the banister like a worn-out old man.

He startled a young couple, appearing soundlessly behind them, and they startled him, too, as they flinched, as though caught in flagrante delicto. The girl would have been about fifteen, Vernon was struck by her huge blue eyes, the paleness of her skin and her hair, which seemed dyed, being a blue-black too deep to seem natural. She was pretty, the boy was tall, he had strong legs, the thighs of a footballer. The boy got up to allow Vernon to pass, avoiding his gaze. The boy was beautiful too. Vernon found it disturbing to think that in the outside world people continued to live, to be beautiful, to hide, to kiss. They were luminous and gentle. They seemed very far away. On the far side of the curtain of his consciousness.

*

Vernon walked for a long time. He was hungry, cold, his feet blistered, his hip ached. When he encountered people, he reached out his hand. He carried on walking. In Toulouse, without knowing why, he boarded a train for Paris. The ticket collector, an elderly cantankerous man, was furious that Vernon had boarded with no ticket and no papers. He railed at him, demanding to see proof of his identity, his address, demanding some official document. Vernon had stared out the window at the landscape flashing past, he could not even feign interest. Eventually, the man sat down on the seat next to him and wrote out the fine. Like Vernon, he was tired, he no longer had the energy to be rude. He stared at Vernon before walking away. "Good luck, what do you want me to say . . . Next time try and find something, I don't know, a bill, anything . . . That way at least you can pretend. You can't do this anymore, you understand? With everything that's happening . . . you can't just wander around with no papers."

Pain overwhelmed him, without warning, as though he were waking from a dream – a lacerating knife wound. It was all over. There was nothing left. The rest of the time he forgot, he forgot to think.

Vernon was sprawled in one of the walkways at Châtelet station, a few metres from a guitarist of about his own age. He had not tried to go any further. He had lain down, his face to the wall, he felt as though he had arrived. Every night, a métro worker came by and said, "We're closing," always the same worker, polite and decisive. Vernon would find a heating vent and lie down. Sometimes he had to walk some distance. At dawn, he would always go back to Châtelet métro station. As though he knew; as though he had an appointment. And yet he was not expecting anything. Everyone was dead now. All the people he had known were dead. Mariana had shown up, unannounced, the night before the convergence. He had been happy to see her. He remembered her mouth when she had an orgasm, her parted lips, her teeth. He could still remember; that was the worst of it. His throat was hard as stone, every breath was an effort.

It was at Châtelet that Marcia walked past him one day. Vernon did not see her. He was lying on his side, as usual. She says she did not recognise him straight away. "I don't usually look at beggars in the métro, I'm too busy slipping past, trying to move as quickly as possible, dodging people. But I recognised you, and I thought it was someone who looked like you. I felt a chill. I went on my way, carried on to Line 4, I didn't know what I was doing. Your name had been on the list of victims. I wonder whose body they identified as yours. They printed your picture with the others – Marc Campadre – I never knew your name . . . I cried so much. You, Kiko, Gaëlle . . . all the others. I'd fallen out with Kiko . . . he acted like a shit, you know what he could be like, and all the coke he took made him more of an arsehole. I regretted it. I felt sorry I'd never picked up my phone, and said, c'mon, it's O.K., why don't we meet up? I bumped into Gaëlle one night at a Saint-Laurent soirée, she told me a little about the convergences, she said I should come along, but I never did. We always manage to convince ourselves we're too busy. I didn't know whether I should see you again. I knew I had hurt you. I wasn't toying with you, I was always honest – but I had other things going on, I didn't have the headspace for being in love. But it meant a lot to me that you were . . . When I saw your name among the victims, I suddenly realised that I cared about you more than I'd realised. You know how it is, there's no arguing with the smallest violin in the world . . . When I saw you in the métro, I thought I was hallucinating, I kept on walking . . . but just as I was about to board the train, I came to my senses, I turned back. I wanted to be sure. And there you were. You were in such a state, *chéri* . . . It wasn't the sight of you that scared me, it was the fucking awful smell . . . I must truly love you like a brother to have bent over you because – and I know I shouldn't really say this – you stank like rat's piss . . . Your lips formed words, but there was no sound, you were silently delirious. If I'm honest, I hesitated. I knew that if I stayed, I'd take care of you, help you up, move you into my place, and that would completely change my life when I'd only been in my new apartment for two months and I was happy being on my own . . . I knew I'd look after you and it was pretty obvious that it wouldn't be an easy ride . . . I could have talked to a cop, said, you know that guy everyone thinks is dead, I've just seen him, look! But I couldn't do that to you. I didn't want to do that to you. When I saw you pressed against that wall, stinking of piss and muttering to yourself, I thought, for fuck's sake, I would have been better off staying with you the first time we met . . . I'm sorry to say that, but it's true. So I talked to you. Passers-by slowed and stared at us, wondering what the hell I was doing there, shaking some guy who wasn't moving . . . they thought you were dead. People say that Parisians would step over a corpse in the métro without breaking their stride. That day, I found out it was just an urban myth: everyone wanted to do something – is there anything I can do to help, do you think it's serious? Parisians come in all shapes and sizes, there are arseholes, sure, but there are good Samaritans too, and let me tell you, if you want them to leave you in peace, you'll have a hell of a job . . ."

Vernon immediately remembered Marcia's voice. He thought he was dreaming. He did not often dream. Then he recognised her perfume. And he realised that Marcia was actually there, kneeling beside him, and it did not make him happy. Her presence unsettled him. She was wearing a skin-tight denim outfit straight out of the 1980s, and her hair was different from how he remembered it – pulled back and ironed smooth. It was Marcia, but it didn't look like her. She had helped him to his feet, got him onto the métro, she stood bolt upright, arrogantly staring people down since everyone in the carriage was looking around to find the source of the stench. They moved away, pressing handkerchiefs to their noses, they shifted seats. And Marcia puffed out her chest and held her head high, defying anyone to complain. Vernon had said nothing. But a flicker of consciousness began to unfurl. He thought about "The Adventures of Pinocchio", a T.V. series by Luigi Comencini he used to watch as a little boy. It had terrified him. The creepy lady with the purple hair and hat with the veil. Marcia wasn't wearing a hat with a veil, but in his memory she is. She had become that lady.

She is here, and he misses her. She does not fill his need for her. It is Marcia. These are her gestures, her clothes, her voice. But her presence does not snuff out her absence. Vernon no longer feels things. He is capable only of missing them. It is not even an absence. Simply an emptiness. What has been ripped away. That is all there is.

He can speak. A little. He can say, you make coffee exactly the way I like it. And he sees the smile. He feels bored for her. It is enough for her to make him happy, she is happy every time he says something. For the first few days, he simply lay there, unmoving. But now, he folds away the sofa bed he sleeps on, puts back the cushions, folds the sheets and puts them in the dresser in the hall. He wants to be as little trouble as possible. Marcia says he is making great progress. But what is he progressing towards? She says he needs to let time takes its course. But what time? What is she expecting?

When Marcia leaves the apartment, he sweeps the small living room, the kitchen, the balcony. He keeps an eye on the time, and throws open the windows just before she gets back because he knows she likes the place to smell fresh, she talks about the flow of chi. So, he does his best to help the chi to flow, he is afraid that he stinks. His smell has changed. Marcia says no, you're imagining things, you smell like a guy, all guys smell like that . . . even when they're clean . . . His sweat is not the same: it reeks of mingled fear and morbid sadness. His smell bothers him. He has become a block of misery. That's another reason he airs the apartment. He needs to do things. His thoughts have resumed their usual course, there are gaps, but things are coming back. A series of words, of conclusions, of lists.

He does not feel anything. He does not make any effort. He does not want to get over it. Though he feels sorry, given everything that Marcia has done for him. And she still worries when he can't manage to eat. He cannot get it down. Just eating half an apple takes superhuman effort. He finds it reassuring, feeling his body waste away. He doesn't like her to worry, this is the most intense emotion that he feels. He doesn't want to eat. He enjoys being like a bird. Weightless. Almost absent.

He has learned to keep out complex thoughts. They inexorably lead him to an excruciating furnace. He never utters the name of the attacker. Never mentions the tragedy. Or the date. He does not want to know. This is a vast area into which he dares not venture.

His nights are restless. He does not want to wake Marcia, but if he falls asleep, he can't control his screams. Marcia gets up, takes him in her arms and rocks him. She never complains. Sometimes, at night, she manages to give him a brief sense of security. The moment he pulls away from her, he is afraid to sleep. He feels it is dangerous to let go. When he has nightmares, she wraps her legs and arms around him and falls asleep next to him. He says nothing, but he wonders what it is all in aid of. Where are they headed? Why go to so much trouble? He has no intention of getting better. It would be inappropriate.

He complicates her life with all manner of injunctions. He can't bear to watch television. Marcia doesn't turn it on anymore. The only show they can watch, on the computer, without him risking a panic attack is "RuPaul's Drag Race". Marcia knows every season by heart, the names of all the contestants, the backstage scandals. Vernon pays no attention to what's happening. But it doesn't bother him. And she likes to sit next to him, nibbling roasted sunflower seeds and commenting on the action. She sometimes even manages to elicit a smile from him.

But when it comes to television or the internet, he simply can't.

Several times, he has unthinkingly switched on the T.V. To have something to pit against the silence. Every time he stumbles on scenes of terrible violence. Every time. Gallons of blood, torture, screaming, death, fire. Fictional footage, images from Aleppo – it doesn't matter to him whether it is real or not. He doesn't want to know. They want it to start all over again. It drives him insane. He has paranoid delusions – this is the only thing they're interested in: mass graves, corpses, mountains of bodies, misery and the tears of the survivors.

Marcia patiently mops his brow. "Who are 'they'?"

He doesn't want to think about it. Every time he has tried to watch something on T.V. or something online, he has seen a head being severed a grenade being thrown a house exploding an eye being ripped out a passer-by eviscerated a blood-smeared woman pleading for her child to be spared. He can no longer turn on the television without seeing death. He knows that he will finally be better when the day comes that he can enjoy it, like everyone else. Gorge on it. So, Marcia sets the laptop down on the coffee table and she says, "You can trust RuPaul, there's never any blood. You'll get to meet Alaska Thunderfuck, I just *adore* Alaska." There is something contagious about her excitement at sharing the show with him. But when he forgets his grief, he feels uncomfortable. He does not want to move on. Like a child who refuses to get out of the swimming pool.

Music bothers him. Now. He makes an effort. He doesn't complain. He has made Marcia's life difficult enough – she can never invite people round, never turn on the radio, has to hide in her room to use the internet, she never brings home a newspaper – he doesn't want her to feel that she cannot put on a record. All he hears is a series of notes. He cannot hear the connection. He prefers the nothingness of time passing. The nothingness of hours.

She blocked the rear exit doors. Vernon was looking elsewhere. Nobody saw her, there were no screams before it happened, because no-one saw it coming. She lobbed three grenades. When the first one exploded, everyone knew what was happening. There had already been so many terrorist attacks, so many stories of mass killers – instantly, the people standing around looked at each other in horror, at the second explosion, they threw themselves on the ground, no-one could see where the shots were coming from, the room filled with smoke, people were coughing, running, stumbling – stumbling over corpses. Vernon could just make out her silhouette. She was wearing a gas mask to protect her from the smoke. She aimed for the head, then the heart, two bullets per body. She raked a high-powered flashlight over the scene, to see if anything moved in the smoke. Like a video game. The following morning, the police counted more than three hundred spent cartridges.

If Vernon allows a thought to unfurl – he sees things. The grenades the AK-47 the bullets. Manufactured objects. Which were not deflected from their proper purpose. They are churned out in factories for precisely this purpose. To kill dismember slash burn. There are no accidents. There are high-performance objects. We know what they will be used for. What purpose they serve. There is no uncertainty. People are shocked. Despite the fact that it is hardly likely that a grenade will be used as a paperweight. A grenade does exactly what it is supposed to do. Like an AK-47. Like the gun. The only variant in the equation is: did you know the people before they became corpses?

He blocks out these thoughts. They serve no purpose. He is not used to them. He will make no effort to get used to them. He will not recover.

Céleste was pirouetting, eyes closed, palms slowly raised, delicately placing her high heels on the floor, she seemed at peace.

Her body traced a backward curve. A perfect curve. At the first explosion.

She was the first that Vernon saw fall.

He did not see everyone. He tripped on someone's shoulder, Xavier collapsed on top of him – then someone he didn't know. He didn't play dead in order to protect himself. Olga screamed and stepped backwards, then fell on top of them. Vernon couldn't move. He could see. He should have screamed. Told her not to forget him. He did not see Mariana fall; but her name was on the list. Every name was on that list.

Marcia looks after him. Unhesitating, uncomplaining, expecting nothing in return. For months, she has been running towels under the cold tap, leaving them in the freezer for a few minutes, then pressing them against his temples. She says he's burning up.

Vernon does jigsaw puzzles. He is not trying to keep himself busy, but he feels it is less awkward for her if she sees him doing something. Someone had given her a thousand-piece jigsaw of birds of the world. An old-fashioned drawing, brightly coloured, realistic. She had left it in its box, thinking, what fucking idiot gives someone a shitty present like this? Vernon set to work with extraordinary precision. When he had finished, Marcia ordered another puzzle, just to see. Five hundred pieces this time, a picture of a tiger in the snow. That's a lot of shades of white. Vernon can spend hours sorting the pieces, staring at the cover, looking for some movement, some shadow that allows him to get his bearings.

Vernon is the only survivor. For a long time, he hoped he might hear that someone else had survived. Not anymore. Long after she had left, long after the gunfire outside stopped, he struggled to crawl out from beneath the bodies. Around him, everyone looked like they were asleep. The bodies were connected by a pool of blood that slowly spread. It was the only movement in the room.

This is what weapons are made for. They had served their purpose.

In the darkness, Vernon witnessed a distant scene framed by the open factory doors – the figure of a man firing a bullet into the back of the girl's head. He recognised Max. He saw him walk away. He knew now what had happened. It seemed completely insane. But he knew. Dopalet had had his revenge. He doesn't mention this to Marcia. It is meaningless now.

It was perhaps the most extraordinary convergence they had held. The reverberation was exceptional, the girls from Bordeaux excelled themselves, the sound seemed to pour from the walls and envelop the dancers.

He told none of this to Marcia. Telling things is futile. What's done is done. What happened next doesn't interest him. The newspaper articles the social networks the comments left by people the tributes and the conspiracy theories. His lips feel as though they weigh a ton. His tongue is heavy. It feels huge inside his mouth. It disgusts him.

He is aware that Marcia has become unusually attentive. At first he thought that she was frustrated by the pity she felt for him, so was being more solicitous than usual. But one night she sat down next to him. She didn't suggest that they watch RuPaul.

"Look. I'm not sure if I should mention this. I don't even know if you'd be interested . . . but I can't bear to see you every day and not know what you would think about it . . . and I'm afraid you'll hate me if you find out from somewhere else. It's a series. A T.V. producer came up with the idea of turning your story into a series. It's the father of Antoine, one of the guys who was there that night. The poor man . . . losing his son like that . . . Anyway, to try and get through the ordeal, he's written a treatment for a television series, at first he was just trying to make sense of it, to survive. But it's become a huge success. The music is amazing, and the production is brilliant – nothing like those meathead action series, it's a completely different vibe, it's totally addictive . . . I've been watching it – I didn't say anything, but I've been watching it – the whole world is watching it. I don't think it's particularly realistic, it's pretty much based on the story of Christ . . . so, your character, I'm sorry to have to tell you, you're Jesus, and Alex Bleach is sort of John the Baptist . . . and then there are all the disciples . . . So, since it's been a mega hit, they haven't wasted any time – there's a manga version now. Your character is amazing. He looks exactly like you. And, I don't know where they dug it out, but they've found some book written by Lydia Bazooka, they've published speeches by Olga . . . It's crazy, anything and everything about Subutex is big business. I never talked to you about it, but actually, after the tragedy . . . the stuff people were saying online was pretty grim – you remember what it's like, when it's not trolls it's your friendly local neo-Nazis, so a lot of what was being said was really ugly. But now . . . Vernon, because of the manga, everyone knows your face. And it's been a hit everywhere from Poland to Sydney via Berlin, Tokyo and New York. Dopalet and Max, the two guys who came up with it, are amazing, the business double act of the year . . . I couldn't keep it to myself any longer, Vernon. Do you understand? Do you want to see what it's like?"

No. Vernon didn't want to see. Marcia had to broach the subject several times before she managed to elicit a little interest. Dopalet, clearly, was perfectly adapted to the world in which he lived. He ordered a massacre. Then he turned it into a T.V. series. Vernon feels no anger at this. It is of no interest. Factories churn out grenades, Dopalet churns out history.

On the table, Marcia's mobile vibrates. She checks the screen and sighs.

"Roger's owner is downstairs. I'll go and gather up the stuff the vet gave me, the prescription, the flea powder, so she can take it with her . . ."

"Aren't you going to ask her to come up?"

"What if she sees you? What if she recognises you?"

"I can put on a hoodie. I can stay in the bathroom."

"Everyone thinks you're dead, Vernon."

"You say that all the time. It doesn't bother me if people believe that."

VERNON SUBUTEX DIED AT THE AGE OF SEVENTY-TWO, OF pneumonia. He was never again homeless. He spent his last days with Aïcha and her daughter Sabra, on the island of Hydra. The circumstances in which they met up again are unclear. Subutex never showed the slightest interest in the convergences that began to occur all over Europe in the years that followed the massacre.

Shortly before his death, Sabra published a series of blog posts recounting her teenage years with Subutex. There were accusations that the texts were fictional, but numerous holidaymakers who visited the island confirmed that there was a man whose physical resemblance to the hero of the Vernon Subutex manga was unsettling. It was sometime around 2077 that people first began to talk about the resurrection of the prophet. The legend did much to promote the convergences.

In 2085, music was banned from all civilisations administering the Great Territories. The three monotheistic megalopolises, the post-Marxist continent and the indigenous continent of America censored all forms of music in compliance with laws that, though contradictory, agreed on one point: music was a symptom of moral decline, and was seen as a danger to social cohesion. To some, it inflamed profane sexual desires, to others, it posed an obstacle to the rigorous worship of God, while, to others still, it represented the paradigmatic prop of ultra-liberal pleasure.

By 2100, groups gathering for clandestine convergences were persecuted and executed. Any individual aiding or abetting them was severely punished. At the time, the movement was confined to Europe, large swathes of which were still inhabited despite the nuclear catastrophes. Repression was savage, but adepts of the Subutex sect were, by nature, difficult to apprehend. They moved in small groups, lived off-grid, and were experts at subterfuge. They tended to settle in the deep forests, but were also able to live for weeks at a time in city centres, usually in cellars and basements, without being detected. They had developed the sense of the hunted. They were alert to the slightest sound, quick to disappear, nimble, able to go without food for long periods. Furthermore, a kind of inanity and idiocy that characterised their religion made their actions difficult to predict. It proved impossible to completely eradicate this nomadic people.

Necessary energy-saving measures led the governments of the great civilisations to ban all energy consumption in Europe. Local peoples were herded into a series of camps where they were tasked with producing energy, but were not permitted to use that energy. Such actions further threatened peoples who had already been weakened by protracted wars, pollution and the displacement of populations. Unable to adapt and technologically backward, Europeans were dependent on the internet – a rudimentary global intelligence that connected them. Disciples of the convergences thrived during the chaos that followed the banning of electric energy, they were used to living in the dark, to migrating to avoid the harsh winters, to navigating by the stars and communicating using primitive means. They had also developed a means of communicating using paper as a medium – they exchanged information by means of letters and texts using a keyboardless writing technique that had disappeared decades earlier, but which they continued to pass down to each other. The sounds that characterised their religion were transmitted using another ancient technique – known as vinyl – which they learned to operate by producing their own energy. It was precisely their archaism that made it possible for them to survive. They were few in number. They caused little harm – even their thefts were small-scale, a crate of protein powder, a solar panel, nothing that would justify a large-scale hunt.

By dint of ignoring them, in time people forgot them.

It was then that Europe was divided into three administrative areas: energy production camps, camps for organ donation and human experimentation, and holiday resorts. Certain European cities were completely decontaminated, enshrined under glass and devoted to tourism. It is believed that this was when the disciples of the convergences were forced to flee Europe to move to the Great Territories. They had become as pliant as water, well versed in map-making and smuggling contraband, capable of identifying and exploiting the slightest chink in the armour intended to prevent contaminated European bodies from crossing their borders.

The first evidence of the disciples of the convergence in the Great Territories dates from the end of the second century of the third millennium. In the East, in North Antarctica, in southern Africa, even in the Caribbean. The great civilisations had emerged from their obscurantism. Music was no longer forbidden. It had fallen into disuse.

The peoples of the convergence found unexpected support among the developed populations. Scholars, researchers and enlightened souls were curious about this white subculture, some going so far as to consider this primitive art form to be an entirely different culture. It was they who archived onto permanent media thousands of hours of music, together with the founding texts of the faith.

When they became aware of this new fad, the authorities of the Great Territories published a number of official statements – Subutex had not been a prophet, any more than Alex Bleach had been, and the three apostles – known by the names Olga Isladovic, Lydia Bazooka and Laurent Dopalet – were usurpers. But the cult of the convergence continued to grow. They were characterised by a series of mass dances, performed using two sonic media mixed in parallel – something that left scholars puzzled: none of them could understand why integrated individuals would wish to sense-lessly cavort to crude harmonies.

It was not until the development of kinesics and time travel that the phenomenon could be truly understood. Just as, before the domestication of fire, bipeds had struck stones together to ignite dry grass without realising what they were doing, so this group of primitive Europeans had "cobbled together" a system for opening "the great doors".

Prior to the Subutex sect, there are two examples of civilisations that opened the "great doors" – the Egyptians and the Mayans. But unlike the great masters of alchemy and resonant magic, the Subutex sect had no understanding of kinesis. Only by the purest chance were they able to correctly combine a genotypic communion of synchronous energies, corresponding waves and cardiac rhythm progressions . . . This hypothesis requires so many coincidences that it may seem fanciful – nonetheless these are the facts.

The great doors were opened at various locations in the late twentieth century throughout European territories that had not yet been contaminated – today, they are commonly used. Entities – animal, alien, divine, post-mortem, ultra-frequency – are familiar with the gateway. We call this crossroads: *Lost Paradise*. It entails travelling through a land before the great catastrophes of the early twenty-first century. In doing so, we can communicate with living animals, the daylight is not artificial, the air is breathable, some practitioners even swim without protection in the waters.

The most surprising practice – in the sense that it has no practical or academic purpose – remains the dancing. Numerous invisible entities mingle with the dancing throng.

Proponents of the convergence do not proselytise. The saints revered by devotees are numerous, and the liturgy that has developed around the gods of rock is completely unintelligible to the neophyte. We must emphasise the utter gratuitousness of these practices, which entail no prohibitions.

In 2186, Chahida, a descendant of Aïcha, belonging to the family of Sélim, the diplomat, known as a disciple of the first circle, applied to the world governing body for official recognition for the Subutex sect. Such recognition was denied. But the laws inciting persecution were repealed, as a result of the great interest aroused by the opening of the great doors by the original disciples. This is why, against all odds, people continue to dance in the dark, to a primitive music whose creed still shows no sign of waning in the twilight of the third millennium.

THE END

A New Library from MacLehose Press

This book is part of a new international library for literature in translation. MacLehose Press has become known for its wide-ranging list of best-selling European crime writers, eclectic non-fiction and winners of the Nobel and Independent Foreign Fiction prizes, and for the many awards given to our translators. In their own countries, our writers are celebrated as the very best.

Join us on our journey to **READ THE WORLD**.

www.maclehosepress.com